W9-AXK-772

Out

Natsuo Kirino, born in 1951, quickly established a reputation in Japan as one of a rare breed of crime writer whose work goes well beyond the conventional crime novel. This fact has been demonstrated by her winning not only Japan's top mystery award, for *Out*, but one of its major literary awards, the Naoki Prize for *Soft Cheeks*. Several of her books have also been turned into movies. *Out* is the first of her novels to appear in English.

Stephen Snyder, a professor at the University of Colorado at Boulder, is known for his excellent translations of contemporary Japanese fiction, among them Ryu Murakami's *Coin Locker Babies* and Miri Yu's *Gold Rush*.

Natsuo Kirino

OUT

TRANSLATED FROM THE JAPANESE BY
Stephen Snyder

VINTAGE

Published by Vintage 2004

2 4 6 8 10 9 7 5 3 1

First published in Japanese in 1997 by Kodansha Ltd

First published in Great Britain in 2004 by Vintage

Vintage
Random House, 20 Vauxhall Bridge Road,
London SW1V 2SA

Random House Australia (Pty) Limited
20 Alfred Street, Milsons Point, Sydney,
New South Wales 2061, Australia

Random House New Zealand Limited
18 Poland Road, Glenfield,
Auckland 10, New Zealand

Random House (Pty) Limited
Endulini, 5A Jubilee Road, Parktown 2193,
South Africa

The Random House Group Limited Reg. No. 954009
www.randomhouse.co.uk

A CIP catalogue record for this book
is available from the British Library

ISBN 0 099 47228 7

Papers used by Random House are natural, recyclable products made from wood grown in sustainable forests. The manufacturing processes conform to the environmental regulations of the country of origin

Typeset by SX Composing DTP, Rayleigh, Essex
Printed and bound in Great Britain by
Biddles Ltd, King's Lynn

'The way to despair is to refuse
to have any kind of experience . . .'

Flannery O'Connor

A Note on the Currency

Calculated at a rate of 200 yen to the pound, the monetary figures in this book would convert as follows:

¥1,000 = £5
¥5,000 = £25
¥10,000 = £50
¥50,000 = £250
¥100,000 =£500
¥1,000,000 = £5,000
¥10,000,000 = £50,000

Night Shift

1

She got to the parking lot earlier than usual. The thick, damp July darkness engulfed her as she stepped out of the car. Perhaps it was the heat and humidity, but the night seemed especially black and heavy. Feeling a bit short of breath, Masako Katori looked up at the starless night sky. Her skin, which had been cool and dry in the air-conditioned car, began to feel sticky. Mixed in with the exhaust fumes from the Shin-Oume Expressway, she could smell the faint odour of deep-fried food, the odour of the boxed-lunch factory where she was going to work.

'I want to go home.' The moment the smell hit her, the words came into her head. She didn't know exactly what home it was she wanted to go to, certainly not the one she'd just left. But why didn't she want to go back there? And where did she want to go? She felt lost.

From midnight until five-thirty without a break, she had to stand at the conveyor belt making boxed lunches. For a part-time job, the pay was good, but the work was back-breaking. More than once, when she was feeling unwell, she'd been stopped here in the parking lot by the thought of the hard shift ahead. But this was different, this feeling of aimlessness. As she always did at this moment, she lit a cigarette, but tonight she realised for the first time that she did it to cover the smell of the factory.

The boxed-lunch factory was in the middle of the Musashi-Murayama district, facing a road that was abutting the grey wall of a large automobile plant. Otherwise, the area was given over to dusty fields and a cluster of small auto repair shops. The land was flat and the sky stretched in every direction. The parking lot was a three-minute walk from Masako's workplace, beyond another factory, now abandoned. It was no more than a vacant lot that had been roughly graded. The parking spaces had once been marked off with strips of tape, but dust had long since made them almost invisible. The employees' cars were parked at random angles across the lot. It was a place where no one would be likely to notice someone hiding in the grass or behind a car. The whole effect was somehow sinister, and Masako glanced around nervously as she locked the car.

She heard the sound of tyres, and for an instant the overgrown summer grass that bordered the lot shone in the yellow headlights. A green Volkswagen Golf cabriolet, top down, drove into the lot, and her plump co-worker, Kuniko Jonouchi, nodded from the driver's seat.

'Sorry I'm late,' she said, pulling the car into the space next to Masako's faded red Corolla. Her driving seemed careless, and she made more noise than necessary putting on the hand brake and closing the car door. Everything about her was shrill and gaudy. Masako stubbed out her cigarette with the toe of her sneaker.

'Nice car,' she said. The subject of Kuniko's car had come up a number of times at the factory.

'You really think so?' Kuniko said, sticking out her tongue in pleasure at the compliment. 'But it's got me up to my eyes in debt.' Masako gave a non-committal laugh. The car didn't seem to be the only source of Kuniko's debts. She had nothing but designer accessories, and her clothes were obviously expensive.

'Let's go,' Masako said. Sometime after the New Year, she'd begun to hear talk of a strange man hanging around the road that led from the parking lot to the factory. And then several of the part-timers had reported being pulled into the shadows and assaulted before barely escaping; so the company had just issued a warning that the women should walk in groups. They set off through the summer darkness along the unpaved, ill-lit road. On the right was a ragged line of apartment blocks and farmhouses with large gardens – not particularly appealing but at least a sign of life in the area. On the left, beyond an overgrown ditch, was a lonely row of abandoned buildings: an older boxed-lunch factory, a derelict bowling alley. The victims said that their attacker had dragged them between the deserted buildings, and so Masako kept careful watch as she and Kuniko hurried along.

From one of the apartment houses on the right, they could hear a man and woman arguing in Portuguese; more than likely they worked at the factory. In addition to the housewives who worked part-time, the factory employed a large number of Brazilians, both ethnic and of Japanese descent, many of them married couples.

'Everybody's saying that the pervert is probably a Brazilian,' said Kuniko, frowning into the darkness. Masako walked on without answering. It didn't make much difference where the man was from, she thought, there was no cure for the kind of depression that came from working in that factory. The women would just have to protect themselves as best they could. 'They say he's a big, strong man, that he grabs the women and holds them without saying a word.' Something in Kuniko's tone betrayed a hint of longing. Masako felt that Kuniko was somehow blocked, closed off, like a thick cloud cover obscuring the stars at night. From behind them came the sound of squeaking bicycle brakes, and when they turned nervously to look, they found an older woman straddling her bike.

'So it's you two,' she said. 'Hi.' It was Yoshie Azuma. She was a widow in her late fifties, with nimble fingers that made her the fastest worker on the line. The other women had taken to calling her 'Skipper' out of grudging respect.

'Ah, the Skipper. Good morning,' Masako said, sounding relieved. Kuniko said nothing but dropped back a step.

'Don't you start calling me that, too,' said Yoshie, but she seemed secretly pleased with the name. Climbing off her bike, she fell in step with the other two. She was small but solidly built in a low-slung way that seemed ideally suited to physical labour. Yet her face was fine featured and pale, floating up now almost seductively out of the darkness. It was perhaps this contradiction that made her seem unhappy, somehow unfortunate. 'I suppose you're walking together because of the fuss they've been making about that pervert,' she said.

'That's right,' said Masako. 'Kuniko's still young enough to be in danger.' Kuniko giggled. She was twenty-nine. Yoshie skirted a puddle that was glimmering in the dim light and turned to look at Masako.

'You're still in the running yourself,' she said. 'You're what, forty-three?'

'Don't be silly,' Masako said, suppressing a laugh. The compliment made her feel self-conscious in a way she rarely did anymore.

'Then you're all dried up, are you? Cold and dry?' Yoshie's tone was teasing, but it seemed to Masako that she'd hit the nail on the head. She did feel cold and dry, almost reptilian, as she slithered along now.

'But aren't you a bit later than usual today?' she said, to change the subject.

'Oh, Granny's been a little difficult.' Yoshie frowned and fell silent. She was caring for her bedridden mother-in-law at home. Masako stared straight ahead, deciding to avoid any more questions. As they cleared the row of deserted buildings on the left, they came upon several of the white trucks that delivered the boxed lunches to convenience stores across the city, and beyond the trucks loomed the factory itself, shining dimly in the fluorescent light like a nightless city.

They waited while Yoshie went to park her bike in the racks

next to the factory, and then climbed the green, Astroturf-covered stairs that led up the side of the building. The entrance was on the second floor. To the right was the office, and down the corridor was the workers' rest area and the locker rooms. The factory itself was on the ground floor, so once they'd changed, they would make their way downstairs. Shoes had to be removed on the red synthetic carpet at the factory entrance. The flourescent light washed out the colour of the carpet, so that the hallway looked rather gloomy. The complexions of the women around her also seemed darkened, and as she looked at her weary companions, Masako wondered if she looked as bad herself. Komada, the tight-lipped company health inspector, was stationed in front of the cubbyholes where they stored their shoes, and as each woman walked by, she rubbed her back with a spool of sticky tape to remove any dust or dirt she might be bringing in.

They entered the large tatami-mat room that served as the employees' lounge. Small groups of people were chatting here and there, having already changed into their white uniforms. They sipped tea or munched snacks as they waited for work to begin, while a few had found spots in the corner to lie down for a quick nap. Of the nearly one hundred workers on the night shift, about a third were Brazilian, and of these roughly half were men. And since it was the middle of the summer holidays, the number of student workers had increased somewhat; still, the great majority of the employees were part-timers, housewives in their forties or fifties.

The three women exchanged nods with friends as they made their way toward the changing room, but then they noticed Yayoi Yamamoto sitting alone in a corner. She looked up at them as they approached, but no smile came to her face and she remained slumped on the tatami.

'Morning,' Masako said to her, and at last she smiled faintly for a moment. 'You look exhausted.' Yayoi nodded weakly and gave them a despondent look but still didn't answer. Yayoi was the best-looking of the four women – in fact, she was the most attractive woman on the night shift. Her face was almost flawless, with a broad forehead and a nice balance between the eyes and the brow, an upturned nose and full lips. Her body, too, though petite, was perfect. Her looks were so conspicuous at the factory that a number of women had taken to bullying her, though others were nice to her. Masako had adopted the role of her protector, perhaps because the two of them were so different. While Masako herself did her best to live her life according to reason and common sense, Yayoi seemed to be dragging a great deal of emotional baggage through the world. Almost unconsciously, she held on to old sorrows, playing the role of a pretty woman at the mercy of cluttered and volatile feelings.

'What's up?' asked Yoshie, thumping her on the shoulder with a rough, red hand. 'You look bad.' Yayoi gave a violent start and Yoshie turned toward Masako, who signalled the other two to go on without her and sat down in front of Yayoi.

'Are you sick?' she asked.

'No, it's nothing.'

'Did you have another fight with your husband?'

'I'd be happier if he were still even willing to fight with me,' she said glumly, her bleary eyes staring off at some point beyond Masako. Realising they would have to start work soon, Masako began gathering her hair into a bun.

'What happened?' she said.

'I'll tell you later,' said Yayoi.

'Why not now?' Masako urged, glancing at the clock on the wall.

'No, later. It's a long story.' A look of rage appeared on Yayoi's face for an instant, then vanished. Giving up the effort, Masako rose to go.

'Okay,' she said. She hurried into the changing room to find her uniform. It was only nominally a room, with no more than a curtain separating it from the lounge. On the wall were crowded rows of sturdy hangers, like those at a department store sale. In the section for the daytime employees, the soiled white uniforms hung in tight clusters, while the space reserved for the night shift was bright with multicoloured street clothes.

'We'll see you down there,' said Yoshie as she and Kuniko left the lounge. It was time to punch in. According to the rules, they had to punch the time clock between 11.45 and midnight and then wait downstairs at the entrance to the factory floor.

Masako pulled her hanger from the bar. It held a white gown with a zipper down the front and a pair of work pants with elastic at the waist. She quickly slipped the gown over her shoulders and, noting the position of the men in the room, pulled off her jeans, then stepped into the work pants. There was no separate changing room for the men, and though she'd been working here nearly two years she still couldn't get used to the arrangement.

After slipping a black net over the hair she'd already gathered with a barrette, she covered her head with the paper hat they all wore, more like a shower cap than a real hat. Someone had nicknamed them 'locusts' for their bug-like shape. She picked up a clear plastic apron and left the changing room, only to find Yayoi still sitting where she'd left her, as if she had nothing better to do.

'Hey! Better get a move on,' she said, but when she saw how slow she was to get up, she was more worried than bothered. Almost all the other employees had already left the lounge; only a few Brazilian men still lingered on the tatami. They were leaning against the wall smoking, their thick legs thrown out in front of them.

'Morning,' said one of them, raising a hand that was still wrapped around a cigarette butt. Masako nodded, giving him a thin smile. The name tag on his chest said 'Kazuo Miyamori,' but Masako couldn't help thinking how foreign he looked, with his darkish skin, caved-in face and protruding forehead. She imagined he did one of the more physical jobs, such as shuttling rice to the automated feeder. 'Good morning,' he said, this time to Yayoi, though she was too distracted to look at him. He seemed disappointed, but then this kind of thing happened often enough in this cold, unfriendly workplace.

They went into the toilet for a moment before donning their masks and aprons. Hands were rubbed raw with scrubbing brushes and then disinfected. They punched their time cards, stepped into the white work shoes, and were checked once more by the health inspector, who had taken up a new station by the stairs that led down to the plant. Once again Komada rubbed their backs with the tape roller while carefully inspecting their fingernails and hands.

'No cuts?' Even the smallest scratch on a finger meant you were ineligible for any job that involved touching food. Masako and Yayoi held up their hands for inspection. Yayoi seemed about to collapse as she stood waiting for the test to end.

'Are you all right?' Masako asked.

'Yes, I guess,' said Yayoi.

'Your kids okay?'

'Unh. . . ,' she answered vaguely. Masako looked over at her again, but the hat and mask concealed everything but her listless eyes. Yayoi seemed oblivious to Masako's stare.

The sharp blast of cold air mixed with the odours of various foods made the descent into the factory seem like stepping into a huge refrigerator. A dull chill came creeping up through their shoes from the concrete floor. Even in summer, the factory was icy.

At the bottom of the stairs they joined the other workers waiting to enter. Yoshie and Kuniko, who were further up in the line, turned to signal to them. The four women always worked together and tried to help each other out, otherwise the job would have been even tougher.

The door opened and the workers filed in. They washed again up to the elbows, and their ankle-length aprons were disinfected. By the time Yayoi and Masako finished washing and moved on to the factory floor, the other women had already begun preparations at the conveyor belt.

'Hurry up!' Yoshie scolded Masako. 'Nakayama's coming.' Nakayama was the foreman on the night shift. He was young, just over thirty, with a foul mouth and an obsession with quotas that earned him the hatred of the part-timers.

'Sorry!' said Masako, picking up her disposable gloves and sterile towel and bringing a set for Yayoi as well. As she stuffed them into her hands, Yayoi looked down at them as if just realising she was at work.

'Pull yourself together,' Masako told her.

'Thanks,' Yayoi murmured. As they took their places toward the front of the line, Yoshie showed them the instructions for the day.

'We're starting with curry lunches. Twelve hundred of them. I'll take rice, and you work boxes, okay?' 'Rice' meant being at the head of the line as the linchpin of the whole process, the one who determined the speed of the line. Yoshie, who was particularly good at it, always volunteered for rice duty, while Masako took the job of handing her the containers. As she began arranging the plastic boxes, she turned to look at Yayoi. She had moved too slowly to get the easiest job of spooning on the curry. Kuniko, who had managed to get one of these positions, looked back at her and shrugged. They could try to look out for her, she seemed to say, but if she couldn't manage this much for herself, what could they do?

'What's up with her?' Yoshie asked, frowning toward Yayoi. 'Is she sick?' Masako shook her head but said nothing. Yayoi did seem unusually distracted. Masako watched as she wandered away from the line, where there were no places left, and headed around toward the position for smoothing the rice, a particularly hard job. Suppressing the urge to speak more sharply, she whispered to Yayoi as she approached: 'That's hard work.'

'I know.'

'Hurry up and get started,' the foreman barked, striding toward them. 'What the hell are you doing?' His expression was obscured by the brim of his work cap, but his small eyes were bright with menace behind his glasses.

'Guess who's here,' Yoshie muttered.

'The asshole,' Masako hissed, furious at Nakayama's tone of voice. She detested this overbearing foreman.

'I was told to smooth the rice,' a woman who appeared to be new said timidly. 'What do I do?'

'You stand here and level it off after I put it in,' Yoshie said, in a tone that by her standards was pleasant. 'Then push it along for the curry. She'll be doing exactly the same thing, so just watch her,' she added, pointing at Yayoi on the other side of the line.

'I see,' said the newcomer, who apparently still didn't understand and continued to stare about her in bewilderment. But Yoshie, who didn't beat about the bush, flipped the switch on the conveyor belt. As it groaned to life, Masako noted that she had set the speed a bit faster than normal. Perhaps because everyone seemed a bit slow today, she was determined to speed things up.

Masako began passing the containers to Yoshie with a practised hand. A perfect square of rice emerged from the mouth of the rice dispenser and flopped into the container that Yoshie held beneath it. She then quickly weighed each portion on the scale next to her and sent it on down the line with a flourish.

Beyond Yoshie was a long line of workers: one to even out the rice, one to add the curry sauce, one to slice the deep-fried chicken, another to lay it on top of the curry. Then someone to measure out the pickles into their cup, someone to add the plastic lid, someone to tape on a spoon, and finally someone to place the seal on the box. Each meal made its way down the line, assembled in so many small increments, until at last a curry lunch was complete.

This was the way the shift always began. Masako glanced around at the clock on the wall. Barely five after twelve. Still five and a half hours of standing on the cold concrete floor. They had to take turns going to the bathroom, one at a time, with a replacement filling in on the line. You had to announce that you wanted to go and then wait your turn, which sometimes took as long as two hours in coming. They'd discovered long ago that to make the job as bearable as possible meant not only looking out for themselves but also working together as a team. This was the secret to lasting at a place like this without ruining your health.

About an hour into the shift, they began to hear sounds of distress from the new woman. Almost immediately, efficiency began dropping on the line and they had to cut the pace. Masako noticed that Yayoi, trying to help out, had begun reaching across to take some of the newcomer's boxes, though today she'd seemed hardly able to handle her own. The veterans on the line all knew that smoothing the rice was a particularly tough job since it had cooled into a hard lump by the time it left the machine. It took a good deal of strength in the wrists and fingers to flatten the little squares of cold, compact rice in the few seconds the box was in front of you, and the half-stooping position made it hard on the back. After about an hour of this, pain would be shooting from your spine through your shoulders, and it became difficult to lift your arms. Which was precisely why the work was often left to unsuspecting beginners – though at the moment, Yayoi, who was anything but a beginner, was hard at work at the station, with a sullen but resigned look on her face.

At last they were finished with the twelve hundred curry lunches. The women on the line cleaned the conveyor and quickly moved to another station for their next assignment: two thousand special 'Lunch of Champions' boxes. The 'Lunch of Champions' had more components than the curry lunches, so the line was longer, filled out by a number of Brazilians.

Yoshie and Masako, as usual, took the rice spots. Kuniko, who was always quick to size up the situation, was saving the easiest job of saucing the fried pork for Yayoi. You took two pieces of pork, one in each hand, dipped them in the sauce, and then placed them in the box, sauced sides together. It was a good station, a bit shielded from the frenzy of the line, something even Yayoi could manage. Masako relaxed a bit and focused on her work.

But just as they had finished with this assignment and were starting to clean up the line, there was an enormous crash as something heavy was knocked over, and everyone turned to look. Yayoi had stumbled against the cauldron full of sauce and fallen flat on her back. The heavy metal lid clattered away, rolling off toward the next conveyor belt, while a sea of viscous brown sauce spread out around them. The floor of the factory was always slick with spattered grease and food, but the workers were all used to the slippery conditions and this sort of accident almost never happened.

'What the hell are you doing?!' Nakayama yelled, descending on them, his face pale with anger. 'How could you have spilt all this?!'

'I'm sorry,' said Yayoi as some men with mops came running up, 'I slipped.' She made no move to get up, seeming almost stunned as she sat in the pool of sauce.

'Come on,' said Masako, bending over her. 'You're getting soaked.' As she helped her to her feet, she caught a glimpse of a large, dark bruise on Yayoi's stomach where the shirt of her uniform was pushed up. Was this the reason she seemed so distracted? The contusion was unmistakable on her white stomach, like a mark of Cain. Masako clicked her tongue disapprovingly, but hurried to straighten Yayoi's uniform to hide the bruise from view. There were no spare uniforms to be had, so after a few moments to collect herself, Yayoi was forced to continue work with her back and sleeves covered in sauce. The thick liquid quickly congealed to a brown crust that didn't soak through the cloth, though the smell was overwhelming.

Five-thirty a.m. No overtime today, so the workers made their way back to the second floor. After they had changed into their street clothes, the four women usually bought drinks from the vending machines in the lounge and sat chatting for twenty minutes or so before they headed home.

'You weren't yourself today,' said Yoshie, turning to Yayoi. 'You okay?' Age and fatigue showed on Yoshie's face, made plain by the hard night's work. Yayoi took a sip of coffee from her paper cup and thought a moment before answering.

'I had a fight with my husband yesterday,' she said.

'Nothing special about that, is there?' laughed Yoshie, glancing over at Kuniko with a conspiratorial look. Kuniko's eyes narrowed as she slipped a thin menthol cigarette into her mouth.

'You and Kenji get along, don't you?' she asked in a non-committal tone. 'He takes the kids out all the time, I thought you said.'

'Not recently,' Yayoi muttered. Masako said nothing but studied Yayoi's face. Once you sat down and held still for a few minutes, the fatigue seemed to work its way through your whole body.

'Life's long, and there are going to be times like this, highs and lows.' Yoshie, who was herself a widow, seemed anxious to dismiss the whole discussion with a platitude, but Yayoi's tone turned harsh.

'But he's used up all our savings,' she spat out. The others fell silent, startled by this sudden admission.

Masako had lit a cigarette, and as she took a drag she broke the silence. 'What did he use it on?'

'Gambling,' said Yayoi. 'I think he plays baccarat or something.'

'But I thought your husband was a pretty reliable guy. Why would he get mixed up in gambling?' Yoshie seemed amazed.

'Don't ask me,' Yayoi sighed, shaking her head. 'I think there's some place he goes to play, but I don't know much about it.'

'How much did you have?' Kuniko asked, unable to conceal her curiosity.

'About five million,' Yayoi said, her voice fading to a whisper. Kuniko gulped and for a moment looked almost jealous.

'That's terrible,' she muttered.

'And last night he hit me.' Showing the anger Masako had seen earlier, Yayoi lifted her T-shirt and displayed the bruise. Yoshie and Kuniko exchanged glances.

'But I bet he's feeling sorry now,' said Yoshie in a conciliatory tone. 'My husband and I used to fight all the time, and he was a brute. But yours isn't like that, is he?'

'I don't know any more,' Yayoi said, rubbing her stomach.

It was already light outside. The day seemed to be shaping up like the one before it, hot and humid. Yoshie and Yayoi, who commuted on bicycle, said goodbye in front of the factory as Masako and Kuniko headed for the parking lot.

'Not much of a rainy season this year,' Masako said as they walked.

'We'll probably have a water shortage,' said Kuniko, looking up at the leaden sky. Her face was covered with grease from the night's work.

'If things keep up like this,' said Masako.

'What do you think Yayoi's going to do?' Kuniko asked, breaking into a yawn. Masako shrugged. 'If it were me, I'd divorce him. Nobody would ask any questions, not after he used up all the savings.'

'I suppose so,' Masako murmured, but it occurred to her that Yayoi's children were still small, so it wasn't as simple as Kuniko made it sound. They were all heading home, but maybe it wasn't just Masako who wasn't sure where home was. They walked on to the parking lot in silence.

'Goodnight,' Kuniko said as she opened the door of her car.

'Night,' Masako answered, never quite sure it sounded right in the morning. Fatigue overtook her as she flopped down into the car, shielding her eyes from the morning glare.

2

Kuniko turned the key of her Golf and the roar of the engine echoed comfortingly through the parking lot. Nice to have a reliable car in a place like this, though last year she had spent more than two hundred thousand on repairs.

'See you then,' Masako said, waving quickly as she put her own car in gear and pulled out of the lot. Though she had more experience than the rest of them and they tended to rely on her, she struck Kuniko as a bit cold. Kuniko bowed slightly and watched her go. The two of them were very different, and she found herself feeling relieved when Masako was out of sight. In general, when she said goodbye to her friends at the factory, it was as if a heavy veil fell away, letting the real Kuniko show through.

Masako had stopped at the light just outside the parking lot. As Kuniko stared across the lot at the back of her scratched and dented Corolla, she wondered how she could put up with such an old car. The dilapidated state of the red paintwork suggested the car had already been driven well over a hundred thousand kilometres – and the bumper stickers promoting safe driving were really too tacky. She drove a second-hand car herself, but precisely because it was secondhand, she made sure it was nice-looking. If not, then why not go get a loan and buy a new one? Masako wasn't bad-looking for her age and she had a certain style, but she should think a bit more about the impression she made.

Kuniko popped one of her husband's cassettes into the stereo and a shrill female voice filled the car with a cloying pop tune. Beginning to feel the heat, she ejected the tape. At the best of times, she wasn't really interested in music anyway. She had only put it in to mark her liberation from the night's work and to test the gadgets in her car. Adjusting the vents on the air-conditioner in her direction, she put down the top of the convertible, watching as it slowly withdrew like a snake shedding its skin. She loved this kind of moment when something ordinary could be made to seem dramatic and exciting. If only her whole life could be that way.

Still, she thought, going back to Masako, why do you suppose she always wears jeans and her son's old shirts? Come winter, she added a sweatshirt or some ratty sweater, over which – worse yet – she'd throw on an old down jacket with patches of tape to keep the feathers from spewing out. That was really too much. It made her look like one of those scrawny trees at Christmas: her skinny shape, the slightly dark skin, the piercing eyes, the thin lips and narrow nose – no excess anywhere. If she would only use a little make-up and wear something expensive, more like Kuniko's own clothes, she'd look five years younger and quite attractive. It really was a shame. Kuniko's feelings toward the woman were complicated, part envy and part antipathy.

But the real point, she thought, is that I'm ugly. Ugly and fat. Peering into the rear-view mirror, she felt that wave of hopelessness which always swept over her. Her face was broad and jowly, but the eyes that peered back at her were tiny. Her nose was wide and sloping, but her mouth was small and pouty.

Everything's mismatched, she thought, and it all looks hideous after a long night shift. She pulled a sheet of facial paper from her Prada make-up pouch and patted around the shiny areas.

She knew how things worked. A woman who wasn't attractive could not expect to get a high-paying job. Why else would she be working the night shift in a factory like this? But the stress of the job made her eat more. And the more she ate, the fatter she got. Suddenly feeling furious with everyone and everything, she jammed the car in gear, released the brake, and stomped on the gas. She checked the mirror as the Golf shot out of the parking lot, delighted at the little cloud of dust she left behind.

She turned on to the Shin-Oume Expressway and drove toward the city for a few minutes before turning right in the direction of Kunitachi. Beyond the pear orchards on the left, a tight cluster of old apartment blocks came into view. The place Kuniko called home.

She hated living there, truly hated it. But at the end of the day, given what she and Tetsuya, her live-in partner, earned, it was all they could afford. She wished suddenly that she were a different woman, living a different life, in a different place, with a different man. 'Different', of course, meant several rungs up the ladder. These rungs on the ladder were everything to Kuniko, and only occasionally did she wonder if there was something wrong with her incessant daydreams about this 'different' life.

She pulled the Golf into her designated space in the parking lot. The other cars were all sub-compacts, all domestic. Feeling particularly pleased with her own imported model, she closed the door with a loud slam. Serves them right if it wakes somebody. Still, if one of the neighbours started shouting, she knew she'd be forced to offer an apology. For the time being, she had to make do here as best she could. She rode up to the fifth floor in the graffiti-covered elevator and then picked her way down the passage strewn with tricycles and Styrofoam boxes to her own apartment.

As she unlocked the door and let herself into the darkened room, she could hear a harsh snore, like the sound of an animal sleeping in there; but she was so used to the sound, she barely noticed it. She pulled the morning paper from the mailbox and put it on the dining-room table they'd bought on credit. Other than the TV listings, she never read the paper. It seemed a waste and she'd often thought of cancelling the subscription, but she did need the classifieds. She extracted the 'Help Wanted, Female' pages from the reams of real estate ads and set them aside, intending to look through them carefully later on.

The room was warm and humid. She turned on the air-conditioner and opened the refrigerator. She could never get to sleep, as hungry as she was, but there was nothing to eat. She'd bought potato salad and rice balls at the supermarket last night, but they were nowhere to be seen. No doubt Tetsuya had eaten them without giving it a second thought. Angry now, Kuniko yanked at the tab on a can of beer. Opening a bag of snack cakes, she turned on the television, changed the channel to a morning talk show, and sat back to listen to the celebrity gossip while she waited for the beer to take effect.

'Turn it down!' Tetsuya yelled almost instantly from the bedroom.

'Why?' Kuniko answered. 'It's time for you to get up anyway.'

'I've still got ten minutes!' he yelled again, and Kuniko felt something hit her arm. Looking down, she saw a disposable lighter that Tetsuya must have thrown. The skin on her arm was turning red. She picked up the lighter and went to stand over the bed where Tetsuya was sprawled.

'Shithead. Do you know how tired I am?'

'What?' he said, a look of foreboding on his face. 'I'm the one who's tired.'

'So you think that gives you the right to throw this shit at me?' She flicked the lighter and held it near his face.

'Cut it out!' he wailed, knocking her hand away. The lighter shot across the room, rolling along the tatami, as Kuniko gave a stinging slap to Tetsuya's hand.

'Listen, you asshole! I've about had it. . . . You look at me when I'm talking to you!'

'Fuck off,' he said. 'It's too early.'

'Shut up, you. And I suppose you ate my salad, too.'

'Keep it down, okay?' said Tetsuya, scowling. He was a size smaller than Kuniko and much more delicate. The year before last, when he'd finally found a regular job at a hospital, he had been forced to cut his shoulder-length hair, but it made him look even seedier. Kuniko hadn't liked it at all. The Tetsuya who had wandered the streets of Shibuya hadn't been any brighter, but at least he'd been cute. She'd worked in a video-game arcade in those days, also in Shibuya. She'd been much thinner then and able to attract a man like Tetsuya easily enough, though the credit line she'd run up decking herself out in clothes and accessories meant that she was still scrambling today.

'You ate it,' she said. 'Admit it and apologise.' Without warning, she jumped on top of him, using her weight to hold him down.

'I told you to stop it!' he shrieked.

'Admit it and I'll let you go.'

'Okay, I ate it. I'm sorry. But there wasn't anything else when I got home.'

'So why didn't you get something yourself?'

'I know, I know,' he pleaded. He twisted his head away as Kuniko slipped her hand between his legs, but he was still soft.

'So, not even a morning hard-on now?' she taunted.

'Get off me! Get *off*! You're heavy – do you know how much you weigh?'

'How dare you!' Kuniko shrieked, wrapping her thighs around his thin neck. Tetsuya tried to cry out, to apologise, but no sound emerged. She grunted and at last rolled off him. Their sex life of late had been nothing but disappointments. Though he was younger than she was, he was all but useless. As she stalked back to the other room, she could see him slowly sitting up.

'Now I'm going to be late,' he moaned. She ignored him and lit a cigarette as he emerged from the bedroom in a T-shirt and gaudy boxers, rubbing his throat. He took a cigarette from her pack of menthols on the kitchen table.

'Those are mine,' she said. 'Leave them alone.'

'I only want one,' he muttered.

'Fine, that'll be twenty yen,' she said, sticking out her hand. Tetsuya let out a sigh, knowing from her tone that she wasn't joking. Keeping one eye on him, Kuniko went back to watching TV. Fifteen minutes later, he left for work without a word, and Kuniko lay down on the bed, fitting her larger form into the narrow depression he had left.

It was nearly two o'clock when she woke up. Turning on the television, she had a cigarette and watched the talk shows as she waited for her body to come to life. The afternoon shows were almost indistinguishable from the morning ones she'd watched before going to bed, but she didn't care. She was hungry, so she went out to buy something without even washing her face. Near the entrance to the apartment complex was a convenience store that happened to sell her factory's boxed lunches. She picked up a 'Lunch of Champions' and checked the label: 'Miyoshi Foods, Higashi Yamato Factory, shipped at 7.00 a.m.' No doubt about it, it had come off their line. She'd had one of the easiest jobs, putting in the scrambled egg, and still Nakayama had yelled at her to cut down on the portion. He really was an asshole. She'd like to scramble him one of these days. But last night's shift had been an unusually easy one. As long as she stuck close to Yoshie and Masako, she could have her pick of the cushy jobs. She chuckled softly.

Back in her apartment, she watched TV while she ate her lunch and drank some oolong tea. As she bit into a piece of pork soaked in brown sauce, she remembered how Yayoi had kicked over the pot. The woman had been a mess this morning, she thought, so absent-minded that she was no help at all. In fact, she was a real drag on the team. So what if her husband was beating her up; if it were Kuniko, she'd just hit him back. Polishing off the pork cutlet, she poured some soy sauce over a pack of frozen dumplings and slathered them with mustard. As she was digging into them, she found herself thinking about Yayoi again. If she were that pretty, she wouldn't be caught dead working the night shift in a factory; she'd get a job at a bar or a pub, or even someplace slightly disreputable – it wouldn't matter as long as the pay was good. The only problem was that she wasn't pretty like Yayoi, and she had no confidence in her own looks or style.

A special feature on high-school girls came on, and Kuniko found herself setting aside her chopsticks and focusing on the programme. A girl with long, straight, dyed-brown hair was talking. Her face had been disguised with digital blurring and her voice was distorted, but Kuniko could tell that she was pretty and stylish.

'Men are wallets, just wallets,' she was saying. 'Me? What did I get out of them? A suit, a ¥450,000 suit.'

'Shit!' Kuniko shouted at the TV. 'Stupid little creep.' A suit costing that much must be Chanel or Armani. *I* want a Chanel suit, but if a little slut like that can get one for nothing, what's the point? 'Damn, damn, damn,' she kept muttering.

The only good that had come out of working at the factory was meeting Masako, she thought, chewing on a lump of cold rice. She'd heard that Masako used to have a job at a good company, but she'd been forced out when they'd been restructured. She sensed that she wasn't the kind of woman who would go on slaving on the night shift at the factory for ever. She might be promoted to a regular employee, or even to management. And when she was, good things were bound to happen to anyone who stuck close to her. The one hitch in the plan was that Masako didn't seem to trust her.

When she had eaten every last scrap in the lunch container and practically licked it clean, she tossed it in the garbage can next to the sink. Then she studied the Help Wanted section she'd saved from the newspaper. On her current salary at the factory, she could never hope to pay back the mountain of debt she'd run up; in fact, it was all she could do to manage the interest. But the pay for daytime work was even worse than what she was getting now. She'd have to work eight hours to make what she made now in five and a half, so there was no point in giving up the night shift. But then she had to sleep all day. It was a vicious circle. The bottom line was that Kuniko didn't want to admit she was bone idle. But at the same time, she was unable to bring herself to acknowledge how huge her debts had become. The interest alone was now so crushing that she had no idea whether she was even paying off the principal any more, no idea what the principal was.

In the evening, she put on her make-up and her imitation Chanel suit and went out. She needed to find herself some sort of part-time job that she could do before going to the factory at eleven thirty. A housewife who lived next door was just pulling up to the racks as Kuniko went to get her bike. She was dressed in a cheap summer suit of the sort they sold at the supermarket, and carrying shopping bags. She looked tired. They must work hard at those company jobs, Kuniko told herself, bowing slightly at her, and the woman smiled back, sniffing the air as she passed. She can probably smell my perfume, Kuniko thought, it's 'Coco' today – though I doubt she has any idea about expensive scents. They were forbidden to wear perfume at the factory, but she'd be taking a bath before setting out for work.

She straddled the bike and set off clumsily down the busy,

narrow street. The pub was near the next station, Higashi Yamato. There was probably no parking lot, so she'd have to go by bike, which was a drawback. What would she do on rainy days? Still, it was better than walking all the way to the station. If things went well and she got the job, she would think about moving.

Twenty minutes later she was standing in front of the pub. 'Bel Fiore', the sign read. She'd thought that her chances for getting the job were poor, but seeing how remote and seedy the place was, she changed her mind. She could feel her spirits rising, her heart racing for the first time in a long while.

'Hostess. 18–30 yrs old. ¥3600/hr. Uniform rental. 5.00 p.m.–1.00 a.m. nightly. No drinking necessary.'

Recalling the details of the advertisement, Kuniko thought she might even quit the factory if she got the job. It took her a whole night of hard work making boxed lunches to earn what she'd earn in two hours here. Though she had just made a resolution to stick close to Masako no matter what, she could already feel herself moving in another direction.

A group of young men in flashy suits stood by the door with a girl in a miniskirt who seemed to be advertising the place. 'I phoned earlier about the job,' Kuniko said to one of the men.

'You want to go around back,' he said, staring at her with a surprised look.

'Thanks,' she said. As she walked away, she could sense that they were watching her and she thought she heard someone laugh. When she reached the spot where the man had pointed, she turned into an alley where she found a metal door with a small sign for 'Bel Fiore'. 'Excuse me,' she said as she pushed it open and peered in. 'I phoned earlier.' A middle-aged man dressed in black was just hanging up the phone. Rubbing the deep wrinkles on his forehead, he studied Kuniko for a moment.

'Ah, yes. Come in,' he said eventually. His look was a bit unnerving but his voice was low and gentle. 'Have a seat,' he said, waving toward a sofa set in front of the desk. Trying to look confident, Kuniko sat down, keeping her back straight. The man held out a name card that identified him as the manager. He bowed slightly, but as he raised his head it was clear that he'd quickly sized her up. She was miserably uncomfortable now, but she plunged ahead.

'I'd like to apply for the hostess job you advertised.'

'I see. Then maybe we should have a little chat,' the man said pleasantly, sitting down in a chair opposite the couch. 'So tell me, how old are you?'

'Twenty-nine.'

'I see,' he said again. 'And do you have some proof of your age?'

'Oh, I didn't bring any with me today.' Almost as soon as the words were out, the man's tone changed.

'Okay. You ever done this kind of work before?' he asked bluntly.

'No, never.' She wasn't sure what she would do if he said they weren't hiring housewives, but the man had no more questions.

'The fact is,' he said, getting up from the chair, 'the minute the ad came out we had six girls, all about nineteen, show up. We like them fresh like that; seems to be what the customers want.'

'I see,' said Kuniko. But it's not just age, she thought, her spirits falling like an elevator. If she were pretty and stylish, her age probably wouldn't matter. Age wasn't really the problem at all, she thought, her insecurities now in the ascendant.

'Sorry you had to go to all this trouble,' said the manager, 'but I'm afraid at the present time . . .'

'I understand,' Kuniko blurted out, nodding hastily.

'If you don't mind my asking, what d'you do now?'

'I work part-time in the neighbourhood.'

'That's probably best anyway,' he said. 'This is hard work. The customers are spending ten or twenty thousand an hour, so they don't like to go home empty-handed. You're a big girl; you get my drift. They want "relief". That's not the kind of work you're looking for, is it?' The man gave a coarse laugh. 'Sorry you came all this way,' he said, slipping a thin envelope into her hand. 'This is for cab fare.' Probably a thousand yen, she guessed. 'But just for the record,' he added, '– you're really over thirty, aren't you?'

'No, I'm not.'

'Whatever you say,' he sniffed, no longer bothering to hide his scorn.

Feeling thoroughly depressed, Kuniko went out the back door of the pub, as she couldn't face the touts at the front again. A side street took her back to the restaurant where she'd left her bicycle, and since she was hungry and in a foul mood, she decided to go inside and use the money for a meal.

'Rice bowl with beef,' she ordered, then glanced around and found herself staring into a large mirror. There, staring back at her, was her own blank, homely face, perched on her own thick neck. She turned quickly away, recognising that the mirror probably reflected her true age, thirty-three. She had lied about her age to her friends at the factory, too.

Sighing, she opened the envelope. Two thousand. Not bad! Well, who cares anyway? She lit a cigarette and tucked it in the corner of her mouth. There was still some time before she had to head to the factory.

3

As Yoshie opened the door, she detected the faint smell of urine mixed with disinfectant. No matter how often she aired the house, no matter how hard she scrubbed the floor, she could never get rid of this odour. She rubbed her fingers over her eyes to stop the twitching, the result of too little sleep. Her precious few hours of rest were still hours away.

Behind the narrow, dirt-floored entrance was a three-mat tatami room crowded with an old low table, a chest of drawers, the TV, and other furnishings. It was in this small room that Yoshie and her daughter, Miki, ate their meals and watched TV. Since the room opened right on to the entrance, they were immediately exposed to any visitor who came to the door, and in the winter the room was so cold and drafty it was almost unbearable. Miki said the place was a disgrace, but in such a small house there was little Yoshie could do.

Yoshie had brought home her factory uniform to wash. As she put the laundry bag in the corner, she glanced into the six-mat tatami room through the open sliding doors. The curtains were drawn so the room was dim, but she sensed a slight movement on the futon that lay on the floor. Her mother-in-law, who had been bedridden for more than six years, must be awake; but Yoshie said nothing, standing stock-still in the middle of the room. She worked as hard as anyone at the factory, and when she came home, she felt like a worn-out rag. What she wouldn't give to lie down and sleep, even for just an hour. Massaging her own stiff, fleshy shoulders, she looked around at the dark, shabby house.

The sliding doors to the small room on her right were shut tight, as if to exclude everyone and everything. This was Miki's room. Until she was in middle school, Miki had slept with her grandmother in the six-mat room, but as she got older, it became impossible to force the girl to accept this arrangement. After that, Yoshie herself had moved in with the old woman, but she found she couldn't sleep well next to her and lately the whole situation was becoming unbearable. Perhaps she, too, was getting old. Only a small area of bare tatami was exposed in the crowded front room, but she sat down there now.

She lifted the top off the teapot on the low table and found that the tea leaves from the pot she'd drunk before setting out for work were still there. She considered how much work it would be to throw them out and wash the pot, and decided it wasn't worth the effort. She was willing to put herself out for others, but when it was just for her, it hardly mattered. She filled the pot with lukewarm water from the kettle, and then sat for a while sipping the tasteless tea and staring off into space. She had something on her mind, something bigger than the usual problems.

The landlord had told her that he wanted to tear down their old wooden house and build a nice apartment building that would be more comfortable to live in; but Yoshie was worried that it was just a pretext to force them out. If that happened, they had nowhere else to go. And even if they could come back to the new building, the rent was bound to be higher. If they had to go elsewhere, it would take an enormous sum to get them into another apartment, but they were barely getting by as it was, with nothing left over for this kind of emergency.

'I need money.' The thought had become something of an obsession. She had used up the modest insurance settlement from her husband's death taking care of her mother-in-law, and now their savings were all but gone, too. She had only graduated from middle school herself and was determined to send Miki at least to a junior college, but she couldn't see how she'd manage. Saving for retirement – that was completely out of the question. Though the night shift at the factory was hard, quitting was never an option. In fact, she had just about decided to look for a second job during the day, but that left the problem of finding someone to take care of the old woman. She was usually good at coming up with a solution, but the more she thought about it the more stymied she became.

All this made her let out an audible sigh, which drew a quick response from the sickroom.

'Yoshie, is that you?' came a faint voice.

'Yes, I'm back.'

'My diaper's wet,' said the voice. There was a polite hesitation in the tone, but it was still clearly an order.

'All right,' said Yoshie. After a final sip of the weak, tepid tea, she hoisted herself to her feet. She had long since forgotten how mean her mother-in-law had been to her in the first years of her marriage. She was just a pitiful old woman now, who couldn't get along without her.

None of them could get along without her – when you thought about it, that was her reason for living. It was that way too at the factory. They called her Skipper, and she did, in fact, run the line. The role kept her going, helped her survive the dreary work; it was her one source of pride. But the painful truth was that there was no one to help *her*. Instead, all she had was her pride, goading her to keep working no matter how hard it was. Yoshie had wrapped up everything personal that mattered in a tight package and stored it away somewhere far out of sight, and in its place she had developed a single obsession: diligence. This was her trick for getting by.

Without a word she went into the six-mat room, only to be confronted by a strong faecal smell. Overcoming her revulsion, she went quietly to slide back the curtains and open the window, allowing the stench to escape. Outside, less than a metre away, was the kitchen window of an identical ageing wooden cottage. As if she knew what was coming, the housewife in the kitchen instantly slammed the window with an irritated gesture. Yoshie was furious, but at the same time she could sympathise with the woman, who must have been able to smell the invalid's excrement since dawn.

'Hurry up, dear,' the old woman murmured as she shifted uneasily on the futon, apparently unaware of her situation.

'Hold still,' said Yoshie. 'You'll make a mess.'

'But it's uncomfortable.'

'I'm sure it is.' As she pulled back the light summer blanket and started to untie her mother-in-law's nightgown, she thought how much better it would be if she were changing a baby's diaper. She could remember getting her hands dirty while changing a baby or having the diaper leak on her clothes, but it had never bothered her. So why should this seem so filthy?

Suddenly, Yayoi Yamamoto came to mind. She still had small children; and hadn't she just been celebrating the fact that the younger one was finally out of diapers? Yoshie could remember what a happy moment that had been. Nevertheless, Yayoi had seemed strange of late. Her husband had thumped her in the stomach, but Yoshie could imagine that Yayoi had somehow got on his nerves. She knew from experience that while it was convenient for a man to have a hardworking wife, a lazy one could also find it a nuisance. Her own husband had been like that. She thought about the man who had died of cirrhosis five years earlier. No matter how much she'd slaved for her mother-in-law or taken odd jobs to supplement the household budget, her husband had just grown more depressed.

Yayoi's husband was probably sick of her exactly because she tried so hard. The odds were he was a selfish slob, just like her own husband had been. That was just how it worked out: the laziest men always seemed to end up with the most energetic women. Still, there was nothing to do but keep your head down and put up with it. She decided that Yayoi and she had this much in common.

She changed the diaper with a practised hand. After rinsing it out in the toilet, she would pop it in the washing machine in the bathroom. She knew she could be using disposable diapers, but they seemed far too expensive.

'I'm all sweaty,' the old woman said as Yoshie was leaving the room. It was her way of asking Yoshie to change her nightgown, but that would have to wait.

'I know,' she said.

'But it's uncomfortable,' the woman moaned. 'I'll catch a cold.'

'I'll do it when I finish with this.'

'I think you make me wait on purpose.'

'You know I don't.' Her answer was civil enough, but for a brief moment she felt an urge to strangle the old bitch. I wish you *would* catch a cold, she thought, I wish you'd catch pneumonia and die. What a relief it would be. But she quickly suppressed the idea. What was she thinking? How could she wish away somebody who needed her? That was inviting disaster.

The alarm clock in the next room went off. Almost seven already; time for Miki to get up and on the move. She went to a nearby city high school.

'Miki. Wake up,' she called, opening the sliding doors. The girl, in a T-shirt and shorts, looked up sullenly, then turned away in disgust.

'I hear you,' she muttered. 'But don't open the door with that in your hands.'

Yoshie apologised, before heading for the small bathroom which was next to the kitchen, but Miki's lack of understanding had upset her. She used to be such a nice girl and had even helped with her grandmother's care. Yoshie knew, however, that as she grew older Miki was naturally comparing her situation with that of her friends, and she must feel embarrassed. She also knew that she could never bring herself to scold her daughter for feeling this way; in truth, she herself was ashamed of the way they lived.

Still, what could she do? Who was going to save them from all this? They had to go on living. And even if she felt like a slave, even if it seemed as though she would always be doing the dirty work, who else was there? She had to keep trying. If she didn't, it would be all over. She needed to think of a plan, a way out . . . but before she did, she had to get back to work.

Miki had come into the bathroom and was washing with a new brand of cleansing foam: Yoshie could tell at once from the fragrance. She had bought it, along with her contacts and her hair mousse, with the money from her part-time job. In the morning light, the girl's hair had a dyed-brown sheen.

When she'd finished washing the diaper and disinfecting her hands, she looked up at Miki, who was brushing her hair and studying herself intently in the mirror.

'Did you dye your hair?' she asked.

'A little,' the girl answered, continuing to brush.

'It makes you look like a juvenile delinquent.'

'No one says "juvenile delinquent" any more,' said Miki, doubling up with laughter. 'No one's said that in years except you. And besides, everybody's doing their hair.'

'I suppose so,' her mother murmured. Miki had become loud and her taste had turned garish recently, and it was worrying. 'What are you going to do about a summer job?' she asked, to change the subject.

'I've found something,' said Miki as she sprayed something on her long hair.

'Where?'

'A fast-food place across from the station.'

'How much do they pay?'

'High-school students get ¥800 an hour.' Her mother was silent for a moment, absorbing the shock: that was ¥70 more per hour than they made on the day shift at the factory. Was it just being young that made them worth so much? 'Something wrong?' Miki asked, studying her mother's face.

'No, nothing. Did everything go okay with Grandma last night?' she went on, to change the subject again.

'She had nightmares. Calling out Grandpa's name and making lots of noise.' Yoshie remembered that the old woman had seemed particularly fretful before she'd left for work, whining like a baby and refusing to let her go. She'd complained about being left in the house, about being so helpless. Ever since a stroke had paralysed her right side, she'd been much meeker and quieter, but just recently the selfish, infantile tendency in her had come to the fore again.

'That's strange,' said Yoshie. 'You don't suppose she's getting senile?'

'Ugh. I hope not. I really don't want to have to look after her.'

'Don't say that. I need you to take care of her and make sure she's comfortable.'

'No way,' Miki barked. 'I get too tired.' Pulling a drink carton from the refrigerator, she plunged a straw into it and began sucking. It took Yoshie a moment to recognise it as a breakfast substitute she'd bought at the convenience store, one all her friends seemed to be drinking. She could have had a perfectly good breakfast with the rice and miso soup I went to the trouble of making the night before, thought Yoshie. Her heart sank at the thought of the needless extravagance. And Miki seemed to be repeating the sin at lunch. She used to eat the lunch Yoshie put together from whatever she had in the house, but now she was going to fast-food restaurants with her friends. Where was she getting the money? Unconsciously, she'd begun to stare at her daughter inquisitively.

'What are you looking at?' Miki asked, turning her head and scowling.

'Nothing,' said Yoshie.

'Did you remember the money for the school trip I told you is due tomorrow?' Miki said. Yoshie, who had completely forgotten about the trip, looked taken aback.

'How much was it?' she asked.

'Eighty-three thousand.'

Yoshie gulped. 'Was it that much?'

'I told you!' Miki shouted, suddenly furious. Yoshie fell silent, wondering where she would come up with that kind of money, while Miki quickly got dressed and left for school. No doubt about it, she thought, feeling all the more depressed, I need more money.

'Yoshie,' her mother-in-law called, sounding impatient. Yoshie gathered up the diaper she'd just washed and went into the back room. After struggling to take off her soiled nightgown and put on a clean one, she fed her breakfast and changed her diaper again. It was nearly 9.00 a.m. by the time she'd finished the mountain of laundry and finally crawled into the futon stretched out next to her mother-in-law's. They could both sleep until around noon, but then the old woman would wake up and make a fuss until Yoshie fixed her lunch.

Yoshie slept only a few hours each day. In the afternoon, she was barely able to doze between nursing chores, and then in the evening she would sleep a bit more before leaving for the factory. At best, she managed only about six fragmented hours of sleep, barely enough to get by on. This was her daily routine, but she worried that she would soon reach the breaking point.

Though pay day wasn't until the end of the month, she decided to call the payroll office at the factory to see if she could borrow against her wages.

'Sorry, we don't make exceptions.' The accounting manager's tone was frosty.

'I know,' said Yoshie, 'but I've been here quite a while.'

'Yes, but rules are rules,' he said, turning her down cold. 'And by the way, Mrs Azuma, you've got to start taking at least one day off a week or we'll have trouble with the labour bureau.'

'I understand,' said Yoshie. She'd recently been working seven days a week for the overtime pay.

'You get welfare payments, don't you? If you go over the allowable income, they'll cut you off.' Unexpectedly, Yoshie found herself apologising and bowing as she hung up. Now she had only her last resort: Masako. How many times had she already asked her for help in an emergency?

'Hello,' her husky voice said. It sounded as though she'd just woken up.

'It's me,' said Yoshie. 'Did I wake you?'

'Ah, the Skipper. No, I was just getting up,' said Masako.

'I've got a favour to ask, but you've got to tell me if you can't manage it.'

'I'll tell you,' said Masako. 'What is it?' Yoshie hesitated, wondering whether her friend would really be frank with her. But this was Masako. More than once at the factory she'd been amazed at her openness, her lack of pretence.

'I'm wondering if you could lend me some money,' she said at last.

'How much?'

'Eighty-three thousand. It's for Miki's class trip, and I'm completely strapped.'

'No problem,' said Masako. Though she was sure that Masako herself couldn't easily spare the money, she was delighted that she'd agreed so easily.

'Thanks,' she said. 'You don't know how much I appreciate this.'

'I'll stop at the bank and bring it this evening,' said Masako. Yoshie went limp with relief. It was humiliating to have to borrow money, but she was glad to know she had a friend like her.

She had just dozed off with her head resting on the low table when the doorbell rang. Masako stood in the entrance, her face dark against the sunset.

'Hi,' Masako said. 'I got to thinking about it and realised that you wouldn't want to leave the cash sitting around the factory, so I brought it over.' She handed her the bank envelope. No doubt the thought had occurred to her as she was making the withdrawal and she'd come all this way to deliver the money. It was so like Masako, so sensible. But beyond that, Yoshie realised, it was also quite kind, for she had understood that Yoshie wouldn't want to be seen borrowing money at the factory.

'Thank you. I'll pay you back at the end of the month.'

'Take your time.'

'No, I know you've got loans yourself.'

'Don't worry about it,' Masako said, smiling slightly. Yoshie stared at her in something approaching wonder, having so rarely seen her smile at work.

'But . . .' she stammered.

'Don't worry about it, Skipper,' Masako repeated, closing the subject. Her expression suddenly turned serious, and a small vertical line, a scar perhaps, appeared next to her right eyebrow. Yoshie knew that the mark was a sign that Masako, too, had worries, but the thought made her uncomfortable. She had no idea what might be on her friend's mind, and she feared that even if she did find out, it might be something an ordinary woman like her would have trouble understanding.

'Why does someone like you work at a place like that?' she asked suddenly.

'Don't be silly,' Masako said. 'So, I'll see you later,' she added. Giving a quick wave, she turned and headed back toward the red Corolla she'd left parked on the main street.

Almost before she was out of sight, Miki appeared, coming home from school. Yoshie handed her the envelope as she walked in the door.

'Here's the money,' she said.

'How much?' Miki asked, taking it as if she'd been expecting nothing less and peering quickly inside.

'Eighty-three thousand.'

'Thanks.' Miki carelessly tucked the envelope into a pocket in her black backpack. Catching a glimpse of the satisfied look on her daughter's face, Yoshie suddenly had the feeling that she'd been taken for a ride, that the real price of the trip was somewhat less than the sum in the envelope. But as always, her instinct was to avoid facing facts. Miki had no reason to lie to her, not when she knew how hard up she was. How could she?

4

Mitsuyoshi Satake's eyes were fixed on the little silver balls in motion. Word had gone out that new machines were arriving, so he'd got up early to line up for one. He'd been playing now for three hours, so he was about due for a pay-off. All he had to do was be patient. Perhaps because he'd had too little sleep, his eyes burned as he stared at the bright-coloured machine. He fished a bottle of eye drops out of the Italian leather pouch that lay on the railing in front of him and, resting his shooting hand for a moment, placed a drop in each eye. As the medicine soaked into his dry eyes, tears began to flow, and Satake, who had hardly ever cried since he was a small boy, took a certain pleasure from the warm liquid trickling down his cheeks. He let the tears flow, resisting the urge to wipe them away.

At the next machine was a woman wearing a backpack. She glanced over at his tear-streaked face, and Satake could see in her expression both a certain curiosity and a frank disinclination to get involved with a man dressed as flashily as he was. He stared back through his tears at her smooth cheeks and decided that she was barely twenty years old. He was in the habit of sizing up a woman like this without necessarily making contact.

Satake himself was forty-three. His close-cropped head was set on a thick neck atop a powerful body – a generally thuggish appearance – but his eyes had an intelligent look, slanting up at the corners, his nose was well formed, and his hands were rather beautiful. The contradiction between the powerful body and the sensitive face and hands was odd to say the least.

With one beautiful hand, Satake pulled a designer handkerchief from the pocket of his sharply tailored black pants and dabbed at his eyes. Noticing the small tear stains on the black silk of his made-to-order shirt, he carefully dabbed at these as well. The flashy clothes and the Gucci loafers he wore without socks were just his work outfit, the equivalent for him of the business suit that the young woman at the next machine would have felt more comfortable sitting beside.

He glanced at the solid gold Rolex on his wrist. It was almost two o'clock and time to go. But just as he was looking down at the balls left in his tray and beginning to gather up his things, his luck came in: a flood of pachinko balls instantly filled the pocket and began flowing over into the tray.

'Shit,' he blurted out, disgusted at the timing. He nudged the woman next to him, who looked back in slight alarm. 'I've got to go,' he said. 'They're yours if you want them.'

'Thanks,' the woman muttered, looking pleased but wary. It was obvious she wouldn't make a move to take the balls until she was sure he was leaving. Smiling ruefully, he took his bag and stood up. As he walked down the aisle between the deafening pachinko machines underscored by the heavy bass line of the rap music pouring from the speakers, he thought about how he must look to young women these days.

Out on the street beyond the automatic doors, he was met by a new wall of noise: speakers announcing the next show at a movie theatre, men hawking cheap goods on the corner, a popular tune blaring from a karaoke studio. While it was somehow comforting to immerse himself in the familiar air of Kabuki-cho, he had a vague sense that he didn't have to be here. Looking up at the sliver of overcast sky visible through the grimy buildings, he wondered how much longer the humid, threatening heat would continue.

He tucked his bag under his arm and set off at a quick pace, but as he was passing the Koma Theatre, he realised there was a piece of chewing gum stuck to the leather sole of his loafer. He stopped for a moment to try to scrape it on the kerb, but the gum was sticky from the heat and hard to get off. By this point, Satake was thoroughly irritated. The sidewalk itself was sticky with dark stains, reminders of the food and drink consumed and then left behind by the young people who gathered in this neighbourhood at night. As Satake picked his way through the mess, he nearly bumped into a line of old ladies waiting for a concert at the theater. Raising his hand, he tried to cut through them, but the women were lost in their chatter and didn't notice. He stood for a moment in disbelief but then smiled and walked around them. No point in getting pissed off with people you didn't know. No, the gum was the bigger problem right now.

A man handing out fliers, another advertising some kind of girlie show, and a gaggle of sluttish high-school girls – they all gave Satake a wide berth. They knew the streets well enough to read the danger signals he was giving out. Plunging his hands in his pockets, he turned into a back street with a scowl on his face.

The club Satake owned, 'Mika', was in a building that faced an alley off the street that led to the ward office. Springing up the stairs, he pushed open the black door at the end of the passage on the second floor. With all the lights on, the room was unnaturally brighter than the pale shimmer of daylight that came through the frosted glass of the windows. The glass was etched with designs that seemed vaguely Grecian. A woman was sitting at a table near the door, waiting for Satake. She knew how much he hated to be kept waiting and so had come early.

'Thanks for meeting me here,' he said.

'That's fine,' she replied. Reika Cho was Taiwanese. Though her intonation was sometimes a bit odd, she spoke perfect Japanese, which was one reason Satake had agreed to make her the manager of his club. She was already in her late thirties, but she was proud of her smooth white skin and tended to favour low-cut blouses. Her make-up was limited to a gash of bright red lipstick. Around her long white neck she wore an intricate jade pendant and a large gold coin. She had apparently just lit a cigarette as he walked in, and now let out a long stream of smoke as she bowed slightly in his direction.

'Sorry to bother you. I know how busy you are,' he said.

'Not at all,' she said. 'What could be more important than a meeting with Satake-san?' There was something flirtatious in her tone, but Satake decided to ignore it and sat down across from her. He looked around at his club with an air of satisfaction. The colour scheme was based on a dark shade of pink, with rococo-style furniture. There was a karaoke machine near the entrance and a white piano surrounded by four tables. On a lower level toward the back were twelve more tables – a sizeable place, all in all, with a hint of old Shanghai about it.

Reika folded her pale, slender fingers in front of her and looked at him. One hand was adorned with a large jade ring. As if to throw her off guard, instead of taking up the matter they had met to discuss, Satake pointed at the vases of flowers placed around the room.

'Reika-san, you should know better than to forget to change the water in the flowers.' The vases were filled with extravagant bunches of lilies, roses and orchids, but the water had gone cloudy and the flowers were wilting.

'Oh? Yes, I'm sorry,' Reika said, her eyes following his around the room.

'You should at least be able to handle that,' he added, making a joke of it, though privately the complaint was real enough. Still, she was otherwise efficient at running the club.

'But what was it you wanted to discuss?' she asked, smiling brightly and apparently intent on changing the subject. 'Is it about the receipts?'

'No, it's about a customer. Have you been having any problems lately?'

'What sort of problems?' Reika asked. He could see the cogs turning in her head.

'It was something I heard from Anna,' said Satake, leaning forward as he noticed her tensing slightly. Anna Ri, from Shanghai, was the top hostess at Mika and its principal draw. Reika knew that Satake took special care of her and listened to what she said.

'And what did you hear?' she asked.

'Is there a customer by the name of Yamamoto?'

'We get several of them with that name. . . . Oh wait, I know who you mean,' Reika nodded, as if suddenly remembering. 'He's quite a fan of Anna's, I believe.'

'So she says. And that's okay, if he pays his bill; but seems he's been waiting for her outside the club and following her around.'

'Is that so?' said Reika, leaning back to emphasise how surprised she was.

'And yesterday I had a call from her saying that the guy had somehow found out where she lives and had shown up at her apartment,' Satake added.

'Now that you mention it, he has been a bit slow with his bill,' Reika said, with growing consternation.

'I've warned you about these jerks with eyes too big for their expense accounts. Next time he shows up, figure out a way to send him packing. I don't want Anna hooking up with a creep like that.'

'I understand,' she said. 'But what can I tell him?'

'That's up to you. It comes with the job,' Satake said. The rebuff seemed to put her on her mettle, and her expression changed, her lips narrowing to a fine crease.

'I understand,' she said again. 'I'll give strict orders to the floor manager.' The floor manager was a young Taiwanese who'd been off the last two days with a cold.

'And when she hasn't any customers, send Anna home by taxi.'

'I'll do just that,' said Reika, her head bobbing. The conversation at an end, Satake grunted and stood to go. She followed him to the door, as if her were a customer.

'And Cho-san,' he said, 'don't forget about the flowers.' As he watched her smile uncertainly in reply, he realised he would soon have to start looking for a better manager. The hostesses were a different story; they'd all been selected for their looks and youth and a certain class they gave the place. To Satake, they were so much living merchandise. But the manager was the one who had to make the sales.

Leaving Mika, Satake climbed the stairs to another club on the floor above and stood at the door. This one was called 'Playground' and featured baccarat tables. Here, too, he employed a full-time manager, and Satake, as owner, put in an appearance only a few times a week. About a year before, the mahjong parlour above Mika had gone under. Satake rented the space and opened an after-hours baccarat club for the customers at Mika. Since he didn't have a gaming licence, he couldn't advertise, and he had never intended it to be more than a sideline. But somehow word had got around and the place had been a hit. He had started in a low-key way with two mini-baccarat tables, but when the crowds grew, he hired several professional dealers, added a full-sized table, and kept it open every night from nine until dawn. Now the money was rolling in.

Satake carefully wound up the loose cord on the white sign and polished the brass doorknob with his handkerchief, but he resisted the urge to go in for a full-scale inspection the way he did at Mika. This was, after all, a gambling club, one of his pet projects, and it was also a gold mine. The cell phone in the bag under his arm began to ring.

'Where are you, honey? I have to go get my hair done.' Anna's

Japanese wasn't always perfect, but cute nonetheless. No one had taught her to talk like that – it just came naturally – but it was clearly a wonderful tool for getting men to do her bidding.

'Sorry,' he said. 'Sit tight and I'll be right there.' He had almost thirty Chinese hostesses working for him, but Anna's looks and brains set her apart from the rest. And he was just on the verge of getting her the right kind of patron. All her previous customers had been hand-picked, and he wasn't going to let some pushy asshole with an empty wallet step in and mess up his plans.

Satake made his way out of Kabuki-cho and back to the white Mercedes he had parked nearby. It was a ten-minute drive to Anna's apartment in Okubo. Though it was a new building, there was no security in the lobby. If this guy was really stalking her, she would probably have to move elsewhere. He rang the doorbell on the sixth floor.

'It's me,' he said into the intercom.

'It's open,' said a low, sweet voice. As he opened the door, a fragile-looking toy poodle came yipping around his legs. It had apparently heard him coming and was waiting for him. He disliked the dog, but Anna adored it, so he had to at least pretend to indulge it. He pushed it back with the toe of his shoe.

'Don't you think you're being a bit too laid-back about locking the door?' he called.

'What does that mean, "laid-back"?' Anna shouted from the bedroom. Satake decided against answering the question. The little dog was writhing with pleasure at his feet, so he teased it with his shoe while he waited for her. The hall of the apartment was filled with rows of shoes in various colours and styles. It had been Satake who had put them in some semblance of order so that she could find the pair she wanted when it was time to go out.

Anna appeared at last, looking as flamboyant as usual. Her long, wavy black hair was pulled back in a pony-tail, her eyes concealed behind Chanel sunglasses. She wore a large T-shirt with lamé embroidery over leopard-skin tights. Even behind the large sunglasses it was immediately apparent that her flawless skin needed no make-up. Satake studied her face, noting again the thick, slightly curled lips that were so enticing to most men.

'Same place as usual?' he asked.

'Uh-uh.' She worked her bare feet into a pair of enamelled mules, the red polish on her toenails showing through the open toes. At this point, the dog, realising it was about to be left behind, stood on its back legs and began barking frantically.

'Now, Jewel,' she said, as if scolding a child, 'you mustn't be naughty.'

They left the apartment and waited at the elevator. Anna generally rose sometime after noon and went out shopping or for a beauty treatment. After that she would go to get her hair done, have something light to eat, and set out for Mika. Whenever he was free, Satake would chauffeur her on her rounds, just in case someone else came along and grabbed her when he wasn't looking. As they stepped into the elevator, his cell phone rang again.

'Satake-san?'

'Kunimatsu? Is that you?' Kunimatsu was the manager at Playground. Satake glanced over at Anna, and for a second she returned the look before glancing away in apparent disinterest and busying herself with a bottle of nail polish, the same shade she wore on her toenails. 'What's up?' Satake said into the phone.

'There's something I'd like to get your advice about. Do you have any time later today?' Kunimatsu's shrill voice echoed in the tight space of the elevator, and Satake held the phone away from his ear as he answered.

'Sure,' he said. 'I'm taking Anna to the beauty parlour now, so I'll have time while she's there.'

'Where will you be?' Kunimatsu asked.

'Nakano. Why don't we meet there?' After deciding on the

time and place, Satake hung up. The elevator had reached the ground floor, and Anna, getting off first, turned to look at him coyly.

'Sweetie, did you talk to Cho-san 'bout that little problem?' she asked.

'I told her not to let him into the club any more. You just do your job and don't worry about it.'

'Okay,' she said, looking up at him over the top of the sunglasses. 'But even if he doesn't come to the club, he could still come here,' she added.

'Don't you worry about it,' he repeated. 'I'll keep an eye out.'

'But I think I'd still like to move,' she said.

'Okay. If it keeps up, I'll think about it.'

'Good,' she said.

'What's he like anyway?' Satake asked. He rarely showed his face at Mika.

'He gets so angry if they try to give him any of the other girls.' Anna grimaced. 'He's always making trouble, and then just recently he stopped paying his bills and asked for credit. I hate that! Everyone knows there are rules about that kind of thing, even in a place like ours.' She finished her little speech as she lowered herself into the Mercedes. Anna may have looked like a beautiful doll, but inside she was a sturdy young woman from Shanghai. She had come to Japan four years earlier to study Japanese, and even now her visa status suggested she should still be attending language classes.

After dropping Anna at the hairdresser, Satake headed for the café where they had agreed to meet. Kunimatsu, who had arrived first, waved discreetly from a table at the back.

'Thanks for coming,' he said, smiling amiably as Satake settled into the deep sofa. In his polo shirt and golf pants, Kunimatsu, who wasn't yet forty, looked more like an instructor at a sports club than a casino manager. In fact, though, he had been in the business quite a while. Satake had recruited him from a mahjong place in the Ginza where he'd been an assistant manager for some years.

'So what's up?' he asked, lighting a cigarette.

'It's probably not that important,' Kunimatsu began, 'but I'm a bit worried about one of the customers.'

'Worried how?' said Satake. 'You think he's a cop?' The old saying that 'the nail that sticks up gets hammered down' went double for this business. If word got out that Playground was making money, the police were likely to make it a scapegoat for all the other gambling clubs.

'No, no, not that,' said Kunimatsu, fluttering his long fingers. 'It's a man who's been coming almost every night lately, and losing heavily.'

'Nobody who plays baccarat every night wins,' Satake laughed. Kunimatsu, too, gave a laugh as he stirred the straw in his orange juice. Neither he nor Satake could drink. Satake took a sip of the iced café au lait sitting in front of him. 'So how much has he lost?' he asked.

'About four or five million in the last two months. Not all that much, really, but once they get started they usually don't stop.'

'But it's small-stakes stuff, right? So what's worrying you?' said Satake.

'Well, the other night he suddenly started asking to borrow from the house.' In general, Satake's club operated strictly on a cash-stakes basis, but on rare occasions a regular customer was sometimes advanced a few hundred thousand yen, though no more. He must have seen someone else taking advantage of this service.

'Then don't mess around with him,' Satake said. 'Throw him out.'

'Which is exactly what I did. I was polite enough about it, but I made it clear he wasn't welcome. He made a helluva fuss before leaving.'

'A loser,' said Satake. 'What does he do, anyway?'

'Works for some little company somewhere. Actually, I wouldn't have bothered you about it at all except that I had an idea he was stopping in at Mika, too, so I called Cho-san. She tells me he's blacklisted there as well.'

'It's Yamamoto. Women and money.' Satake sighed and stubbed out his cigarette. There were plenty of men falling all over themselves for his beautiful young Chinese hostesses, but when the money ran out, they usually came to their senses and gave up on the women. But this character seemed to be trying to win at baccarat in order to keep seeing Anna. Or maybe he had suddenly realised how much he'd spent on her and was trying to win some of it back. Whichever it was, Yamamoto had come unglued, and Satake had seen enough people like him to know that neither the woman nor the gambling was any fun for him any more. He probably hadn't even meant to cause so much trouble, but Satake could sense the danger to both Anna and his business.

'If he shows up again, could I tell him that the owner wants to have a word with him?' Kunimatsu asked.

'Okay. Call me if he comes, but I'm not sure he's going to get it, even coming from me.'

'No, I guarantee that when he sees that the owner looks like a yakuza, that'll be the last of him.' Satake laughed quietly at the little joke, but his dark eyes didn't change. 'You know, you really can be pretty scary,' Kunimatsu went on, seemingly oblivious.

'You think so?' said Satake.

'Those clothes, that look – you'll send him running.'

'What's so scary?'

'Well, you look nice enough, but there's something a bit . . . disturbing. . . .' Just then, the cell phone in Satake's bag rang, as if to put a damper on Kunimatsu's laughter. It was Anna.

'Honey, I'm finished,' she said. The words – the exact same words – sent a jolt of recognition through him.

The woman had gasped beneath his heavy body. He rubbed against her, lubricated by the warm, sticky liquid, but as her body gradually grew cold, he felt as though they'd been glued together. She seemed to be seesawing between agony and ecstasy, but finally Satake pressed his lips over hers to quiet the groans – of pain or pleasure – that were leaking from her mouth. He found the hole that he had made in her side and worked his finger deep into the opening. Blood was pumping from the wound, staining their sex a gruesome crimson. He wanted to get further inside, to melt into her. As he was about to come, he pulled his lips from hers and she whispered in his ear: 'I'm finished . . . finished.'

'I know,' he'd said, and he could still hear the exact sound of his own voice.

Satake had once killed a woman.

During high school he'd had a fight with his father and left home for good. For a while, he made it as a mahjong hustler, until a gang member from a yakuza family took him under his wing. His patron was getting rich in the prostitution and drug rackets in Shinjuku, and Satake took on the job of making sure that none of the girls decided to jump ship. One day, however, something bad happened. The gang had learned that a certain woman was recruiting their girls for another gang, and had sent Satake to work her over; but he had killed her instead. He was twenty-six at the time, and he spent seven years in jail for the crime, a fact that not even Anna knew, let alone Kunimatsu or Cho-san. It was his prison record, though, that had convinced him to keep a low profile in his businesses, hiring Cho and the Taiwanese floor manager for Mika and Kunimatsu for the casino.

Now, almost twenty years later, he could still recall the whole incident in vivid detail – the sound of her voice, the expression on her face at the moment she died, the sensation of her fingers scraping across his back, the chill running down his spine. The fact was, you never really knew your own limits until you'd killed someone – there was nothing else quite like it. To be sure, there was a deep sense of guilt, but Satake had also discovered in himself a tendency to enjoy inflicting pain, as well as a powerful charge from the proximity to death itself.

'That's kind of overdoing it.' The other guys in the gang had looked at him in disgust when they saw what he'd done, though they were used to violence themselves. He would never forget the look of revulsion on their faces, but in the end he told himself that no one else could understand what had passed between the two of them.

While he was inside, he'd been haunted by the memory of torturing her to death – but what troubled him wasn't guilt so much as the desire to do it all over again. Ironically, though, when he finally got out, he was completely impotent. It wasn't until some years later that he realised that the intensity of the moment when he'd killed her had somehow shut him off from the more mundane experience. When you discovered your limits, it seemed, you sealed the knowledge away, and ever since, Satake had been very careful not to break the seal. No one else could really know the self-control this required or the loneliness it entailed. Still, since they could never see this hidden self, women came to him, defences down, and became his pets. And since they lacked the power to disturb his well-guarded dream, they remained nothing more than lovely pets.

Satake knew that the only woman who could ever really understand him, the only one who could tempt him – to heaven or to hell – was the woman he'd killed. So it was only in his dreams that he could be with a woman, only in his dreams that he could find that intensity again. But that was enough. And because he lived only in his dreams, there was no pimp more considerate than he was. He kept the face of the woman he'd killed locked away inside him, a face he had never seen before the day they met. But in the end, this arrangement had made him a bitter man. And though he had no desire ever to open the lid he had closed on his personal hell, now, with just a few words from Anna, the lid had been knocked loose. Satake quickly wiped the sweat off his forehead, hoping that Kunimatsu hadn't noticed.

When he got to the beauty salon, Anna was waiting outside. He opened the door and waited for her to get in. Seeing the way Anna's hair had been set, piled up on her head 1970s style, Satake laughed out loud.

'That takes me back,' he said. 'That's how all the women wore their hair when I was young.'

'That's ancient history,' Anna said.

'More than twenty years ago, before you were born,' he said. He studied her for a moment. It was somehow miraculous that a woman could be so beautiful and have a good head on her shoulders, and plenty of nerve, too. Lately, she had also started to show signs of the pride that went with being his number one girl, a kind of unapproachable self-possession. Privately, he even felt a certain sympathy for the men who'd fallen for her. As he steered the Mercedes away from the kerb, he found himself gazing at the seam of her tights where it dug into her thigh; the flesh was soft yet elastic, the effect one of luxuriance.

'Always stay this beautiful,' he said eventually. 'I'll take care of the rest.' He knew how short-lived beauty was and that when she got older, he would have to look for a new Anna. The remark had been meant to acknowledge this.

'Then you'll have to sleep with me, at least once,' said Anna, her tone both seductive and almost serious. Satake knew that the people in the clubs, ignorant as they were of his past, thought he was a cold fish.

'I don't think so,' he said. 'As products go, you're much too valuable.'

'Am I a product?' she asked.

'Yes,' he said. 'A beautiful, dreamy toy.' For some reason, the word 'toy' reminded him of the other woman, but he was temporarily distracted by the tail lights of the car ahead and the thought passed. 'A very expensive toy, one that only rich men can play with.'

'But what if I fall in love, then someone else might get me.'

'You won't,' said Satake, looking over at this new, more assertive Anna.

'I will,' she replied, reaching over and folding her hand around Satake's as it rested on the steering wheel. He immediately returned the hand to the soft surface of her thigh. Satake lived his life in the secret embrace of a dark memory, and the only woman he needed wasn't alive. His main source of satisfaction now was to make a series of pretty toys available to the men who wanted them. Hence his concern over the success of his two clubs, and hence the need to see to the matter at hand: getting rid of this man named Yamamoto.

That evening, as Satake was getting ready to leave his own apartment in West Shinjuku, a call came from Kunimatsu.

'Yamamoto's here,' he said. 'He wants to play, for about twenty or thirty thousand. What should I do? Kick him out?'

'No, let him play. I'll be right there.' Satake put on a collarless shirt and a grey sharkskin suit he'd just had made and left the apartment. After parking the car at a batting cage in Shinjuku, he first looked in at Mika. Anna glanced up from her table at the back and waved. She had on her work face: sexy yet somehow utterly innocent. As if not to be outdone by Anna, the other girls looked stunning as well. Satisfied that they passed muster, he summoned Cho-san. She made her way through the club, discreetly greeting the customers, and stood next to him.

'Thanks for making time,' he said, 'and thanks for putting Kunimatsu wise to that guy.'

'Sure. I hadn't realised he was going upstairs as well.'

'And having no more luck up there,' said Satake. Cho giggled. In her pale green Chinese-style dress, she looked younger yet somehow more reliable than usual. But when he glanced around at the vases, he noticed that the water was still cloudy and the flowers even more wilted. Without saying anything, though, he took his leave, anxious now to get a look at this Yamamoto who was after Anna.

Going up to the third floor, he stood at the door to Playground. He had told Kunimatsu to keep the sign unlit so as not to attract the cops' attention, but once you opened the door, there was no hiding the noise and excitement of a casino that came pouring out. Satake slipped inside and surveyed his club. In about seventy square metres, he had managed to arrange two small baccarat tables that could accommodate seven customers and one full-sized table where fourteen could play for higher stakes. At the moment, there were crowds around all three. In attendance were three black-suited men, Kunimatsu among them, and three girls in bunny costumes to serve drinks and snacks, all circulating briskly through the room.

The dealer at one of the smaller tables noticed him come in and nodded, though his hands never stopped stacking the chips that lay in front of him. Satake nodded back. He was familiar with this type of disciplined, skilled young man from his mahjong days. All in all, he found the whole club exactly to his liking.

Baccarat was a simple game. The customers bet on either the player or the banker to win the hand, and the dealer took a five-percent commission from the banker's winnings as the house cut.

That was all there was to it. The mark of a good dealer was his ability to get the customers to compete against each other, but the game was such that most people got caught up in it without much coaxing.

The player and the banker were each dealt two cards, as in blackjack, but the object in baccarat was to get cards adding up to, or as close as possible to, nine. The player or banker was allowed to draw a third card depending on the total of the original hand. If the player was dealt cards totalling eight or nine, that was considered a 'natural', and he either won or tied, and the banker wasn't allowed to take another card. If the player was dealt a six or seven, he would 'stand' and wait to see the banker's cards. Below five, he took a third card. Besides that, there were just a few simple rules relating to particular card totals.

The secret of the game's popularity was that anyone could learn to play almost immediately; and because of this, the place always seemed to be full of respectable-looking young businessmen or office girls on their way home from work. But Satake knew the truth about his customers. Though the atmosphere of the place was trendier than a traditional casino, Playground attracted a crowd of losers and scumbags. Still, he was more than happy to watch them throw their money away.

'There he is,' Kunimatsu whispered in his ear, pointing at a man seated next to one of the tables, sipping a drink and watching the other customers play. 'And he's already down about a hundred thousand for the night.' Satake moved to a corner of the room where he could observe Yamamoto without being noticed.

He seemed to be in his mid-thirties. Short-sleeved white shirt, nondescript tie, grey pants. A forgettable man with a forgettable face. You would never notice him in the endless crowds of other office workers. So then what was this nobody doing falling for Anna? She was still just twenty-three, the prettiest girl in Mika, which was full of pretty girls. But more than that, she was his number one – Yamamoto was way out of his league by any standards. Anna was right: just as there were rules in gambling, there were rules in this game as well; and it made Satake, who was himself so scrupulous, furious to see someone like Yamamoto ignoring them.

The game at Yamamoto's table was coming to an end. The cards in the tray would give out in another round or two. Trying to look decisive, Yamamoto took the few chips he had left and bet them all on the player's hand. Almost everyone else around the table immediately bet on the banker, anxious to avoid following Yamamoto's lead. The dealer, pretending not to notice the stampede to the banker's side, quickly dealt the cards. The player drew two face cards, or zero. Loser, Satake thought to himself. The banker's cards totalled three, so both sides had to take a third card. The player took the card dealt him and, in the customary fashion, curled up both edges before looking at it. Then he threw it down in disgust. Another face card. The banker flashed a smile of relief and showed a four. Zero to seven, bank wins, and the game was over.

'The card shark gets bitten,' Satake muttered, and Kunimatsu, who was standing close by, chuckled softly. A young woman dealer took over at the table, and several of the customers changed places as well, but Yamamoto, though he was now out of chips, sat where he was and sulked. A young woman dressed like a bar hostess who was waiting for the place at the table glanced over at Kunimatsu by way of protest. Satake signalled that he was ready to step in and walked up behind Yamamoto.

'Excuse me,' he said.

'Yeah?' A shock must have gone through Yamamoto as he turned to look: the hard body, the soft face, and the outfit that could only suggest one profession. He managed to keep it from showing on his face, but inside everything was probably numb.

'If you aren't going to play, would you mind letting this customer have your seat?' Satake said.

'Why should I?'

'Because people are waiting.' Satake's tone was still polite.

'Who says I can't sit here and watch?' He had apparently had a few too many free drinks, and was flicking the ash from his cigarette on to the table. Satake called an assistant manager and asked him to clean up the mess.

'I'm sorry, but I'd like to have a word with you. Please come this way.'

'You can tell me here,' Yamamoto muttered. The other customers at the table eyed him with distaste, and several of them, noticing Satake standing behind him, seemed scared and looked away.

'No, I think you'd better follow me.' Yamamoto made a show of being offended, but Satake managed to lead him to the door. When they reached the dimly lit corridor outside, he turned to face him. 'I've been told that you've asked to borrow money from the house, and I wanted to inform you that making loans to customers is against our policy. If you need funds to play with, please make arrangements elsewhere.'

'This is a business, isn't it?' Yamamoto said, beginning to look like a pouting child. 'People ask to borrow money all the time.'

'That's exactly why we don't do it,' said Satake. 'And another thing, I have to ask you to stop following Anna around. She's still young, and you've been frightening her.'

'Hold on. Who says you can tell me what to do when it comes to her?' Yamamoto looked indignant. 'I'm still a customer, aren't I? I've spent enough money on her, that's for sure.'

'And we appreciate it. But you should stop following her. It's not allowed to see the girls outside the club.'

'Who says?' he snorted. 'She's a hooker, isn't she?'

'She's way too good for the likes of you.' Satake was losing his temper. 'We asked you nicely to stay away, now fuck off!'

'Who the fuck d'you think you are?!' Yamamoto shouted, suddenly throwing a punch. Satake blocked it with his right arm and grabbed him by the collar. Planting a knee in his groin, he pinned him against the wall and held him immobile and gasping for air.

'Go home now, before you get hurt,' he hissed. Just then, a group of business types came up the stairs and, seeing the two of them at it, hurried inside Playground. This was exactly the kind of thing that started rumours that the mob was running the show, which was never good for business. He loosened his grip. Given an opening, Yamamoto threw a wild punch that caught him on the jaw. Satake swore, then jabbed his elbow into the man's stomach and, when he doubled over, kicked him down the stairs. As he watched him roll down and come to rest sitting on the landing, for a moment he felt the rush of adrenalin that fighting had once given him. But only for an instant, before his carefully cultivated self-control kicked in again. 'If you come back, I'll kill you, asshole,' he called down at him.

Yamamoto sat in a daze, wiping the blood from his mouth. Maybe he hadn't even heard the threat. A bunch of young women heading upstairs stopped short, screamed, and ran back down. Shit, thought Satake, not wanting women to get scared away as well.

It never occurred to him to wonder what else might happen to Yamamoto that night as he straightened his suit and went back inside.

5

Hate: that's what you call this feeling. The thought occurred to Yayoi Yamamoto as she looked at her naked, thirty-four-year-old body in the full-length mirror. Right near her solar plexus was a conspicuous dark-blue bruise. Her husband had punched her there last night, and with the blow a new feeling had risen inside her. No, that wasn't exactly true. The feeling had been there from before. She shook her head and the naked woman in the mirror shook hers as well. It had definitely been there before; it was just that she'd never been able to put a name to it. As soon as she'd realised that it was 'hatred', it had spread like a dark cloud and taken possession of her, so that now there was nothing else inside.

'He can't do that,' she said aloud, and as she did so, she burst out crying. The tears dribbled down her face, falling in the space between her small but well-formed breasts. When they reached the bruise, another surge of pain ran through her and she crouched down on the tatami. It was so sensitive that even liquid or a draft made it hurt, and no one, she felt, could ever make it better.

Perhaps sensing her movements, the children sleeping nearby in their tiny futons began to stir. Yayoi jumped up, wiped away the tears, and wrapped herself in a towel. She didn't want the kids to see the bruise, or the tears. But, realising that she had to bear this treatment alone, she felt so isolated that her tears started flowing again; and the worst thing of all was that the source of her pain was the one person she was closest to. She had no idea how she could get out of this hell, but at the moment she was fighting just to keep from crying like a baby.

The older child, a five-year-old boy, frowned in his sleep and turned over on his stomach, and then his three-year-old brother flipped over on his back. If she woke them up, she wouldn't be able to go to the factory, so she crept away from the mirror and out of the bedroom. Closing the sliding doors as quietly as she could, she turned out the light, hoping with all her heart that they would sleep until morning.

She quietly made her way to the living room and the tiny

adjoining kitchen and hunted through the pile of laundry on the dining table for her underwear – panties and a plain, cheap bra they sold at the supermarket. She remembered how she'd had nothing but beautiful lace lingerie before she was married, because Kenji had liked it so much. She could never have imagined then that this was the future that was waiting for them: a loser obsessed with a woman he could never have, a wife who detested him, and an unbridgeable gulf separating them. They would never again be on the same side of the gulf, because she could never bring herself to forgive him.

He probably wouldn't be back again this evening by the time she had to go to work; and even when he did come home, she was nervous about leaving the children with someone so unreliable. The older boy in particular was unusually sensitive and easily hurt. Then, on top of everything else, three months ago Kenji had stopped bringing home his paycheck, and she had been forced to try to feed herself and the children on the little bit she earned at the factory. It was all too much, this sneaky husband who would slink home late at night and go to bed while she was at work, only to argue endlessly with her when she arrived back exhausted in the morning. All they ever did otherwise was exchange cutting, ice-cold looks. She was sick to death of the whole thing. Breathing a sigh, she crouched over to put on her panties, which made her double up with pain again from the bruise. As she cried out involuntarily and curled into a ball on the couch, the cat, Milk, perked up its ears and looked at her. It had spent last night under the couch, letting out long, plaintive howls.

The memory of that night made her skin crawl. Never before had she had cause to hate anyone, but the dirty cloud of emotions that engulfed her now contained not just anger, but real hatred. She'd been raised in a quiet provincial city as the only child of dull but well-meaning parents. After graduating from a junior college in Yamanashi Prefecture, she had gone to Tokyo to work as a sales assistant for a well-known tile company. As an attractive young woman, she had received a good deal of attention from the men at the company, and in retrospect that had probably been the best period in her life. She could have had her pick of the lot of them, but she'd fallen in love with Kenji, who came to the office quite often in the course of his duties at a second-rate construction supplies company.

She had chosen him because he pursued her more aggressively than anyone else, and up until their wedding day everything had seemed like a lovely dream that would go on for ever. But almost as soon as they were married, Yayoi's illusions began to fade. Kenji left her behind to go out drinking and gambling, and soon she spent most of her time home alone. It wasn't, of course, until fairly recently that she'd realised that he was fundamentally the type of man who only wanted what belonged to others. He had wanted her because she had been the spoilt pet of the company, but once he had her, he lost interest. In the final analysis, he was an unhappy man, one who was forever chasing illusions.

Last night, for God knows what reason, Kenji had actually come home before ten o'clock. The children had finally gone to sleep, and Yayoi had been in the kitchen doing the dishes as quietly as she could when she sensed something and turned around. He was standing directly behind her, looking at her back as though the sight of it filled him with loathing. Startled, Yayoi dropped the soapy sponge into the sink.

'You frightened me,' she said.

'Why? Did you think it was another man?' For once he wasn't drunk, but he was clearly in a bad mood. Still, Yayoi was used to that.

'And why not?' she said, picking up the sponge. 'When was the last time you were home at this hour?' she added, unable to resist the jab. To be honest, she would have preferred it if he hadn't come home. 'Why so early?'

'No money,' he said.

'How could that be? You haven't given us anything in months.' Though she had her back to him again, she knew he was smirking.

'Nope, I'm flat broke. And I've used up all the savings.'

'You what?' she said, her voice breaking. The two of them had put aside more than five million yen – almost enough for the down payment on a condominium. Why else had she been breaking her back at the factory? 'How could you? You've been keeping your whole salary; how could you spend our savings as well?'

'Gambling,' he said. 'A game called baccarat.'

'Tell me you're kidding.' She was too shocked to think of anything else to say.

'I'm not,' he said.

'But it didn't all belong to you.'

'Or to you.' So often he had nothing to say to her, but tonight he had a smart answer for everything. 'So, maybe it'd be better if I just left. What do you think?' Why was he trying to needle her? What was bugging him? Usually he made no effort to draw his family into his little dramas, so why was tonight different?

'That wouldn't solve the problem,' she said, her tone icy.

'Then what would? You tell me.' His face took on a crafty look, as if he'd got her trapped.

'Well, for one thing, it would help if that slut would dump you,' she said, furious now. 'She's the cause of all this.' Almost instantly, she felt something hard and heavy thump her in the stomach and she toppled over, on the verge of losing consciousness from the pain. She had no idea what had happened to her, but she knew that she couldn't breathe, that her chest was convulsing. She groaned and curled up in a ball, and then felt another blow to her back. She screamed.

'Dumb fuck!' Kenji yelled. Out of the corner of her eye she

could see him rubbing his fist as he went into the bathroom. She lay groaning on the floor for a while, listening to the sound of water running in the bathroom.

When she finally began to recover a bit, she realised she was still clutching the sponge in her soapy hand. She pulled up her T-shirt and found a blue-black bruise just below her chest. The sight of it seemed like the final sign that she and Kenji were finished. She let out a long sigh. As she did so, the doors to the bedroom slid open and Takashi, the older boy, looked out at her with fear in his eyes.

'Mama, what's wrong?' he asked.

'Nothing, honey,' she managed to get out. 'Mama fell down, but she's fine now. Go back to sleep.' Seeming to understand, the boy slid the door shut. Yayoi knew he was worried about his brother, sleeping in the next futon. If even a small child could be considerate like that, what had gone wrong with Kenji? Obviously, people changed. Or maybe he'd always been that way.

Pressing on her stomach, she made her way over to the table and sat down. She took slow, even breaths to control the pain. There was the crash of a plastic bucket in the bathroom. She laughed quietly and buried her face in her hands. It was miserable to be living with such a man.

Suddenly realising that she was still in her underwear, she pulled on a polo shirt and a pair of jeans. She had lost so much weight recently that the jeans slipped down to her hips, so she went to look for a belt. It would soon be time to leave for the factory. She didn't want to go, but if she didn't show up, Masako and the others would worry about her. Masako in particular wasn't one to overlook any sign of trouble. There was something a bit unnerving about it, but at the same time she felt a strong urge to open up to the woman. Maybe it was because she somehow knew that Masako could be relied upon. If something happened, she was probably the only one Yayoi had to cling to. It was only a glimmer of hope but the thought sent her shuffling more quickly around the house.

Hearing a sound in the entrance hall, Yayoi tensed. Had Kenji come home early again tonight? But when no one came into the living room, she wondered if it could be somebody else and hurried out to the door. There she found Kenji, sitting on the edge of the floor with his back to her. His shoulders were slumped as he stared in front of him, and the back of his shirt was dirty. Apparently, he didn't realise she was there. As she thought about the night before, a tide of loathing welled up inside her. It would be better if a man like this never came home, if she never had to see his face again.

'Oh,' Kenji said, turning around at last. 'You haven't left yet?' He had apparently been in a fight, and there was blood oozing from a cut on his lip. Yayoi said nothing but stood rooted to the spot, trying to control the anger that was coursing through her. 'What's the matter?' Kenji muttered, apparently oblivious to her rage. 'Can't you be nice once in a while?'

At that moment, her patience snapped. With lightning speed she slipped off her belt and wrapped it around his neck.

Kenji made choking sounds, trying to look around at her, but Yayoi pulled up and back, tightening the belt in one motion. Gasping, he tried to get his fingers around the belt, but it had already dug into his neck. Yayoi watched intently as he scratched at the leather, and then yanked even harder. His neck bent back at an odd angle, and his fingers twitched meaninglessly in the air. *He needs to suffer more,* she thought. *He's got no right to go on living like this!* She planted her left foot on the floor, and with the right one she pushed against his back. A sound like a frog's croak escaped from somewhere in his throat. It feels so good, she told herself. Strange that she'd never known she had such cruelty inside. Still, she found this thrilling.

Kenji had gone limp by now. He sat awkwardly on the step, shoes still on his feet. His torso bent over his knees while his neck arched back.

'Not yet,' Yayoi murmured, continuing to pull on the belt. 'I still don't forgive you.' It wasn't so much that she wanted him to die like this, just that she wanted to be sure she would never have to see his face again, never have to hear his voice.

How long had she stayed like that? He lay on his back now, completely still, so she reached down and felt for a pulse in his neck. Nothing. There was a small wet patch on the front of his pants. Realising that he must have pissed himself in the final seconds made her want to laugh.

'Couldn't you have been nice once in a while?' she said aloud.

She had no idea how much longer she stood there, but at last she came to her senses, realising that Milk was crying.

'What are we going to do now, Milk?' she muttered. 'I've killed him.' The cat made a sound like a little shriek, and Yayoi gave the same in reply. She had done something that was irreversible, but she felt absolutely no regret. So be it, she whispered to herself. She'd had no other choice.

Going back to the living room, she calmly looked at the clock on the wall. Just eleven. Almost time to leave for the factory. She phoned Masako's house.

'Hello?' Fortunately, it was Masako who answered. Yayoi took a deep breath.

'It's me, Yayoi,' she said.

'Hi,' said Masako. 'What's up? Are you taking the night off?'

'No, I just don't know what to do.'

'About what?' She sounded genuinely concerned. 'Has something happened?'

'It has.' She might as well get it over with. 'I've killed him.' There was a brief silence, and then Masako spoke again, her voice still calm.

'Are you serious?'

'Dead serious,' Yayoi said. 'I've strangled him.' There was another pause, this one perhaps half a minute long; but Yayoi knew somehow that it wasn't because Masako was shocked but rather because she was thinking over the situation. When she spoke again, Yayoi knew she'd been right.

'But what do you want to do?' Masako said. Yayoi was quiet for a moment, not fully understanding what she was asking. 'I mean, tell me what you want to do about this. I'm willing to help.'

'Me? I'd like things to go on just as they have been. My kids are still small, and . . .' As she spoke, tears welled up in her eyes and the horror of the situation finally hit her.

'I understand,' Masako said. 'I'll be right over. Did anyone else see what happened?'

'I don't know,' Yayoi said, looking around. Her eyes fell on Milk, who was cowering under the sofa. 'Just the cat,' she told her.

'Okay,' Masako said, a hint of gentle laughter in her voice. 'Wait right there.'

'Thank you,' Yayoi said, hanging up. As she crouched down to wait, her kneecap rubbed up against her stomach, but she no longer felt any pain.

6

When she hung up the phone, Masako noticed that the words on the calendar hanging right in front of her looked blurry. It was the first time she could remember being dizzy from shock. She had known something was wrong with Yayoi last night, but she didn't like to intrude in other people's lives. Still, here she was, getting involved. Was she just asking for trouble? She steadied herself against the wall and waited for her vision to return to normal, then suddenly remembered that her son, Nobuki, had been stretched out on the couch watching television. She spun around, but he was nowhere to be seen. He must have gone up to his room while she was talking to Yayoi. Her husband, Yoshiki, had had a drink after dinner and gone to bed early, so it seemed that no one in the house had heard what she'd said on the phone. Feeling slightly relieved, she began to think about what to do next. But she realised there was no time to think; she had to act. She would come up with some sort of plan in the car.

Grabbing her keys, she yelled up the stairs, 'I'm leaving for work. Make sure you turn off the gas.' There was no answer. She knew that Nobuki had begun smoking and drinking recently while she was out of the house, but she also knew there was little she could do about it. He was heading into the summer of his seventeenth year, apparently without any idea what he wanted to do or be, without any hopes or passions.

As a freshman at a public high school, the boy had been caught with some tickets to a rave that someone had forced on him. He was accused of trying to sell them and expelled from school. The harshness of the punishment was clearly meant as a warning to the other students, but, whatever the reason, the shock seemed to affect his nerves and he suddenly stopped talking. For a time, Masako searched desperately for a way to reach her son, but no one seemed to have the answer; and she suspected that Nobuki himself had become resigned to this state of affairs. At any rate, the time for searching for solutions had passed. It was enough, perhaps, that he went each day to his part-time job as a plasterer. When you had children, Masako believed, you couldn't just cut them off if things didn't go as planned.

She stood in front of the small room off the entrance hall, listening to the faint sound of her husband snoring through the thin door. The room had originally been intended for storage, but at some point he had begun sleeping here. She lingered by the door for a moment, thinking. In actual fact, they had begun sleeping in separate rooms before they'd moved to this house, while Masako was still working in an office. She was used to it now, the three of them in different rooms, and she no longer thought of it as lonely or abnormal.

Yoshiki worked for a construction company that was affiliated with one of the big real estate conglomerates. The name of the company sounded impressive enough, but he'd once said that when things got tough financially the parent company didn't treat them very well. Beyond that, though, he had never had much to say about work, and he disliked it when she brought up the subject. She had no idea what sort of businessman he was, what he was like at the office.

He had been two years ahead of her in the high school where they'd met. She had been attracted to what seemed to be a personal integrity that kept him aloof from the world, but she had to admit that this same integrity, this unwillingness to deceive or embellish, made him uniquely unsuited to a competitive business like construction. And the proof was he had already strayed far off a successful career track. More than likely Yoshiki had his own path to follow, one that had very little to do with other people. It was his alone; no one else had made him follow it. Masako knew that there was more than a little resemblance between her husband, who hated the business world and spent his free time shut away in this little room like some mountain hermit, and her son who had given up communicating with the world altogether. For her part, she had decided that there was very little she could do or say to either of them.

They were quite a trio: a son who had given up both education and conversation, a husband in the grips of a depression, and Masako who had opted for the night shift after being downsized from her own company. Just as they had decided to sleep in separate bedrooms, they seemed to have chosen to shoulder their own separate burdens and inhabit their own isolated reality.

Yoshiki had said nothing to her when she was unable to find another job and ended up on the night shift at the boxed-lunch factory. Masako had sensed, however, that his silence wasn't so much a sign of apathy as an indication that he had abandoned the futile struggle and had begun building his own cocoon, a cocoon that she couldn't penetrate. Her husband's hands, which no longer reached out to touch her, were busy at work now constructing a shell. Both she and their son were somehow tainted by the outside world and so they had to be rejected along with everything else, no matter how much it hurt them.

So if she couldn't even manage to get things right in her own family, why was she getting mixed up in Yayoi's affairs? At a loss for an answer, Masako opened the flimsy front door and stepped outside. The air felt much cooler than it had last night. She looked up, catching sight of a dim, reddish moon floating above the rooftops. An evil omen, she thought, looking away. Yayoi had just killed her husband. What could be more ill-omened than that?

Her Corolla was squeezed into the small parking space in front of the house. The driver's side door could only be opened a crack, but Masako managed to slip in. Starting the car, she pulled out into the street and set off. The noise of the engine seemed to echo through the quiet residential streets and surrounding fields. The neighbourhood was a remote and peaceful one, but no one had ever complained about the late-night noise. Instead, when she had started at the factory her neighbours had grilled her about where she was going so late at night.

Yayoi's house was quite close to the factory in Musashi Murayama. She would go there before heading to work, but she was already conscious that she would have to avoid being seen. She suddenly remembered her standing agreement to meet Kuniko at the parking lot at 11.30 to walk together to the factory. She might not be in time for that. Kuniko was always suspicious when it came to things like this, so she would have to find a way to throw her off the scent.

Still, the whole errand would probably be useless. More than likely, someone in the neighbourhood had already guessed that something had happened at the Yamamoto house. Or maybe Yayoi herself had already gone to the police. It was even possible that the whole thing was some fantasy that Yayoi had made up. Suddenly impatient, Masako stepped on the accelerator. As she did so, the scent of gardenias growing in the hedge that lined the road came pouring in through the open window. It filled the car for a moment and then disappeared again into the darkness. In much the same way, the sympathy she'd felt for Yayoi seemed to be dissipating. What does she want from me? What a nuisance this all was! She decided to wait until she saw Yayoi face to face, and then decide whether she would help her.

A white figure was standing at the corner of the cinderblock wall that ran along the alley where Yayoi lived. Masako stepped on the brake.

'Masako!' Yayoi seemed bewildered. She was wearing a white polo shirt and loose jeans. As she looked at her, Masako swallowed hard, moved by the defencelessness of this pale shadow floating in the darkness.

'What are you doing?' she asked her.

'The cat's run away,' Yayoi said, beginning to cry as she stood by the car. 'The kids love it, but it saw what I did and it was terrified.'

Masako put her finger to her lips to signal for silence. It took a moment, but finally Yayoi seemed to understand what she meant and glanced around nervously. Her fingers were braced against the glass of the car window, and the instant Masako noticed they were trembling ever so slightly, she decided that she would do what she could to help.

As she drove on slowly down the alley, Masako looked up at the windows of the neighbouring houses. At eleven o'clock on a weekday night, the only lights left on were shining dimly in what appeared to be bedroom windows. Everything else was quiet and dark. Since it was cooler now, air-conditioners had been turned off and windows were open. They would have to be careful about noise. She was suddenly conscious of the clatter of Yayoi's sandals.

The Yamamotos rented a place at the very end of the alley, one of a cluster of prefabricated houses put up about fifteen years ago. Despite the relatively high rent for places like this, the house was small and inconvenient, and the family would have been saving up to get out of here. But that was all over now. People were always being driven to do stupid things. What could have driven Yayoi to do this? Or rather, what was it her husband had been driven to do that made Yayoi so angry? Turning these questions over in her mind, Masako climbed out of the car as quietly as she could. Yayoi was running down the alley toward her.

'Now don't be shocked,' she said, seeming to hesitate slightly before opening the door to the house. Masako realised immediately that Yayoi had been referring not to what she'd done but to the sight that greeted her as the door swung open: there was Kenji, right in front of her, laid out limp on the floor. He was very clearly dead, the brown leather belt still wrapped around his neck. His eyes were half open and the tip of his tongue protruded between his lips. His complexion was pale and bloodless rather than red and congested.

Masako had been prepared for a shock, but now that she was actually staring at the body, she found that she was surprisingly calm. Perhaps because she didn't know Kenji at all, the corpse seemed to be nothing more than a person who was lying absolutely still and whose face looked ridiculously relaxed. Still, the idea that Yayoi, who had always seemed like the image of the perfect wife and mother, was in reality a murderer – that would take some getting used to.

'He's still warm,' Yayoi said. She had rolled up the leg of his pants and was feeling his shin. Her hand played over his skin, as if needing to confirm that he was dead.

'So it actually happened,' Masako said quietly in a grim voice.

'Did you think I was making it up?' Yayoi asked. 'You know I would never do something like that.' She almost seemed to be smiling, in spite of the dark look Masako gave her, though it could have been just a twitch.

'So what are you going to do? You're not going to the police?'

'I'm not,' Yayoi said with a firm shake of the head. 'You may think I'm crazy, but I don't feel like I've done anything wrong. He deserved to die, so I've decided to pretend that he just went off somewhere instead of coming home tonight.'

Masako glanced at her watch, the wheels beginning to turn in her brain. Already 11.20. They needed to be at the factory by 11.45 at the latest.

'Well, I guess there *are* a lot of people who just wander off and are never heard from again. But do you think anyone saw him coming from the station?'

'You don't usually pass anybody at this time of night. I really doubt it.'

'If he phoned anyone along the way, it's all over,' Masako told her.

'I could still say that he never made it home.' Yayoi was warming to her role.

'I suppose. But if the police question you, could you really play dumb?'

'I'm sure I could. I'm sure. . . .' Yayoi nodded, her eyes wide. She looked so sweet, and much younger than thirty-four. With a face like that, no one was likely to suspect her. Still, the whole thing was risky.

'Then what do you want to do?' Masako's tone was cautious.

'Put him in your trunk, and then . . .'

'And then?'

'Go somewhere tomorrow and get rid of him,' she concluded. Masako knew that was probably their only option, and all too quickly she found herself agreeing to it.

'All right, but we've got to hurry. Let's get him out to the car.'

'I don't know how to thank you, but I'll find a way. I can pay you,' Yayoi said.

'I don't want your money.'

'Why not? Why would you be willing to do all this?' she went on as she lifted Kenji by the arms.

'I'm not sure,' said Masako, grabbing the limp legs of the man who had once been Yayoi's husband. 'But I'll figure that out later.' Kenji had been about 168 centimetres tall, roughly the same height as Masako. But men were heavier, bigger boned, and the two of them were barely able to lift him and carry him out the door. If someone had seen them, it would probably just have looked like two women carrying a man who was dead drunk. Except for the belt . . . which was still wrapped around his neck and was now scraping along the ground. Masako watched in silence as Yayoi yanked it off and wrapped it around her own waist.

'You haven't left anything he had with him?' she asked.

'No, he wasn't carrying anything.' They bent his arms and legs and stuffed him into the trunk.

'We can't miss work tonight,' Masako said when they'd finished. 'For one thing, we've got to start building your alibi. So we'll have to leave him in the parking lot overnight. We can think about what to do with him while we're at the factory.'

'I suppose I'd better take my bike like always.'

'Right. And act as though nothing's happened.'

'OK then. Masako-san, I'm grateful to you for taking care of him like this.' Now that the body was out of the house, Yayoi suddenly seemed almost businesslike. There was even a hint of relief on her face, as if she'd just finished a particularly difficult chore. Or had she already convinced herself that Kenji really had simply vanished off the face of the earth? Feeling a bit rattled by the change that had come over her, Masako walked around and got in the car.

'You'll give yourself away if you're too cheerful,' she murmured as she fastened her seat belt.

Yayoi's eyes grew wide and she pressed her hand over her mouth, as though trying to control her excitement. 'Is that how I look?' she asked.

'A bit,' said Masako.

'Okay,' she said. 'But what should we do about the cat? It might be a problem if the kids make a fuss.'

'It'll come back,' said Masako, but Yayoi shook her head as if she knew better.

'It might be a problem,' she repeated. 'What'll we do?'

Masako started the car and pulled out of the alley. As she drove, the body in the trunk began weighing on her mind. What if she were stopped and searched for some reason? Or rear-ended? But thoughts that would make most people more cautious sent Masako speeding through the darkened streets as if someone were chasing her; and in fact someone was – the body in her trunk. Careful now, she told herself.

When she finally reached the parking lot, Kuniko's Golf was already in its usual spot. She was probably worried about being late and had gone on ahead. Masako climbed out of the car, lit a cigarette, and glanced around the lot. Tonight, for the first time, there was no trace of the usual stench of fried food and exhaust fumes, though maybe she was just too nervous to smell it. Walking around behind the car, she stared at the trunk. There was a body in there, and tomorrow she would be figuring out how to get rid of it; and here she was, doing things she wouldn't have even been able to imagine a few hours ago. The thought made her realise that she could perhaps understand Yayoi's sense of liberation.

After checking once more to make sure that the trunk was locked, she set out along the dark road, cigarette still in hand. She didn't have much time left, and tonight of all nights she wanted to avoid doing anything out of the ordinary that would attract attention. But just as she was coming to the abandoned factory that lined one side of her route, a man in a cap jumped out of the shadows on the left and grabbed her arm. Shocked, but trying not to lose control, she realised that she'd completely forgotten about the reports of a pervert of some kind lurking in the area. Before she could even cry out, the man began dragging her toward the empty building.

'Stop!' she screamed at last, her voice piercing the darkness. At the sudden sound, the man panicked. He cupped his hand over her mouth and tried to pull her down into the tall, thick grass that grew at the edge of the road. Fortunately, though, Masako's height allowed her to turn her shoulder and catch his arm, dislodging his hand slightly from her mouth. While he was struggling to regain his grip, she swung her bag and managed to get her mouth free. Still, the other hand held her arm and was dragging her to the ground. Just as Kuniko had said, the man wasn't big, but he was solidly built, with a distinct smell of cologne coming from him.

'What do you want with me?' she yelled. 'There are plenty of younger women around.' This time she could feel his grip loosen slightly at the sound of her voice. Now she was all but certain that it must be one of the men from the factory who would have known her at least by sight, and she made a desperate effort to shake free and get back to the road. The man was quicker, however, and he slipped around her and tried to push her back toward the ruined factory. She remembered that there was a drainage ditch that ran along the road here, and there were holes in the cement slabs that covered it. Stepping gingerly to avoid them, she backed away from the man, keeping her eyes on his face. She couldn't see him clearly, but in the reddish light of the moon she caught a sudden glimpse of the black eyes staring out from beneath the cap.

'You're Miyamori, aren't you?' she said, throwing out the first name that came into her head. From his reaction she could see that she'd been right. 'Kazuo Miyamori, that's who you are,' she said, pressing her advantage. 'If you let me go, I won't tell anyone. I don't want to be late tonight, but I'll meet you some other time, I promise.' The man gulped but said nothing to her unexpected proposal. 'Let me go now, and we can meet again another time, just the two of us.' This time the man answered, and from the sound of his heavily accented voice, she was sure that it was Miyamori.

'Really?' he said. 'When?'

'Tomorrow night. Right here.'

'What time?'

'Nine.' Instead of answering, he suddenly embraced her and pressed his lips to hers. Held tight against his hard chest, she felt the breath being crushed out of her. As she struggled, her legs became tangled in his and they fell with a loud clatter against the rusty metal shutter of the delivery bay in the old factory. Startled, the man froze and looked around nervously; and while he was doing this, Masako pushed him away, grabbed her bag, and got to her feet. In her haste, however, she tripped over a stack of empty cans.

'Find someone younger for your fun!' she screamed at him, suddenly furious. The man's arms fell limp at his side and he looked at her in a daze. Rubbing his spit from her lips with the back of her hand, she pushed through the thick grass.

'I'll be waiting for you tomorrow,' he called, his voice low and pleading. Without looking back, Masako picked her way over the concrete culvert and sprinted down the road. How could this have happened today, when she thought she was being so careful? For the first time in quite a while, she felt a surge of dark rage, tinged with irritation at her own blundering. But who'd have thought that the pervert could be someone like Kazuo Miyamori? She even remembered saying hello to him before the last shift. The thought made her blood boil.

As she ran up the stairs to the factory door, combing her fingers through her dishevelled hair, she found Komada, the health inspector, just getting up to go.

'Good morning,' Masako called. At the sound of her breathless voice, Komada turned.

'Hurry up,' she said. 'You're the last.' While the sticky tape was being rolled across her back, Masako heard her laugh for the first time in ages. 'What have you been up to?' she asked. 'You've got dirt and grass all over you.'

'I was in a hurry and I fell down.'

'On your back? You didn't hurt your hands, did you?' If there was the tiniest scratch, you weren't allowed to touch the food. Masako hurriedly inspected her fingers: dirt under the fingernails but otherwise no damage. Relieved, she shook her head.

Pleased that she had managed to avoid any suspicion about the attack, she gave a non-committal laugh and headed for the changing room. It was already empty, so she threw on her work clothes, grabbed her plastic apron and cap, and ran to the bathroom. Checking her face in the mirror, she found a small smear of blood oozing from her lip. 'Shit,' she muttered, rinsing it off. There was also a bruise on her left forearm, probably from being dragged through the grass. She wanted no trace of that man anywhere on her body. She wanted to strip down on the spot and examine herself; but that would make her late, and the evidence would be recorded on her time card. She held her anger in check as best she could, but when she remembered Miyamori telling her that he would 'wait for her tomorrow', the thought that she couldn't have him arrested, that she couldn't even file a complaint, nearly made her lose control.

She carefully washed her hands before running downstairs to the factory floor. The time clock read 11.59. She'd made it just in time, but it was later than she usually punched in – and she'd had better evenings.

The women were just filing into the plant and beginning the sterilisation procedure. She noticed Yoshie and Kuniko waving to her from the front of the line and then realised that Yayoi was standing right next to her, her face covered by her mask and cap.

'You're late,' Yayoi said, her voice barely audible. 'I was worried.'

'Sorry,' Masako muttered.

She peered at her. 'Did something happen?'

'No, nothing. How about you – you didn't have cuts on your hand, did you? They write it down if you do.'

'No problem,' said Yayoi, staring off into the gaping, frigid factory. 'I somehow feel as though I've gotten stronger,' she added, but the slight tremor in her voice didn't escape Masako.

'You're going to need that strength,' she said. 'But at least it's a choice you've made yourself.'

'That's right,' said Yayoi. They lined up behind the last of the workers waiting for the disinfectant wash. Yoshie, who had already taken her place at the head of the conveyor belt, glanced around again, urging them to hurry.

'So how do you plan to do it?' Masako whispered, as she scrubbed her hands and arms under the powerful jets.

'I don't know,' Yayoi muttered, her weariness suddenly visible in her sunken eyes.

'It's your problem, so you'll have to figure it out,' Masako told her before heading off toward the head of the line where Yoshie was waiting. As she made her way through the room, she looked for Kazuo Miyamori among the Brazilian employees in their blue caps, but there was no sign of him. She was certain now that it had been him.

'Thanks again,' Yoshie said to her as she approached. Masako was confused for a moment.

'For what?' she said.

'You've got to be kidding. For the money, of course, and for delivering it. You really saved my skin. I'll pay you back as soon as we get paid.' Yoshie gave her a nudge with her elbow as she passed along the work order for eight hundred and fifty grilled beef lunches. Masako grimaced, amazed that something that happened only this evening already seemed like the distant past. It had been a long day.

'You didn't show,' said Kuniko, who had brazenly taken over the job of passing Yoshie the containers since Masako was late.

'Sorry. Something came up and I got a late start.'

'Really?' Kuniko said. 'I called you just before I left to be sure you'd be there.'

'And no one answered? I guess it must have been after I left.'

'I guess so. But if you left that early, why were you so late getting here?'

'I had some shopping to do and got delayed,' Masako said, her tone discouraging any further questions. Kuniko fell silent, but Masako could tell that she wasn't satisfied. She'd been right: they would have to be careful of Kuniko and her intuition.

Masako noticed that as Yoshie was preparing to start the rice machine, she kept glancing down the line. Following her gaze, she spotted Yayoi standing off to the side, as if lost in a fog. She looked rather conspicuous, with her back covered by the large brown stain of dried sauce from last night.

'Did something happen to you two?' Yoshie said.

'Why do you ask?' said Masako.

'Well, she's looking dazed and you were late.'

'She looked dazed last night, too,' Masako reminded her. 'Forget about us, Skipper, and start worrying about Nakayama. He'll be around any second; better get the line rolling.' The only stations left were for the difficult job of laying out the meat. Masako took one of them, and Yoshie, giving up her probing with a slight nod, threw the switch. The work order itself was sent down the line first for the workers to read. Then the automated rice-delivery system started with a thud, and the first square lump of rice dropped into the container that Kuniko had handed to Yoshie. Another long, hard night had begun.

While she was separating the curled, cold pieces of meat, Masako felt someone watching her and looked up. Yayoi had taken the spot directly opposite her.

'What?' Masako whispered.

'If he ended up like this,' Yayoi whispered back, her frantic-looking eyes wandering to the chopped meat on the line, 'they'd never figure out who it was.'

'Shut up,' Masako hissed, glancing at the women on either side. Fortunately, they didn't seem to be paying any attention. She shot a reproachful look across the line, and Yayoi lowered her eyes. First she seems too cheerful and then she melts into tears. Masako suddenly had serious doubts about whether Yayoi would be able to cope with what lay ahead. But now that she was an accomplice, Yayoi's problem was hers as well.

7

In the factory, sealed as it was like a stainless-steel box, there was no way of knowing what the weather was like outside. As they dragged themselves back upstairs at 5.30, the first person in line let out a groan.

'Oh no! It's raining!' Instantly Masako thought of the trunk of her

Corolla being pelted with rain. They would have to decide soon what they were going to do.

'You in a hurry today?' Yoshie asked as she pulled off her mask. Bending over, she used it to wipe the grease off her shoes.

'Why?' Masako said, using her own mask to clean the sides of the sneakers she wore on the factory floor.

'Why? Because you look like you've seen a ghost and I want to know what's wrong.' Yoshie, who was shorter and rounder, glanced up at her tall, thin friend; but Masako had already stored her shoes in the cupboard and was staring out the window at the grey morning sky. She'd imagined a heavy rain, but it was a soft drizzle she saw falling on the test track of the car factory across the way.

'You'll put wrinkles on that face of yours with all that worrying,' Yoshie said, refusing to let the matter drop.

'Something important has come up,' Masako said, still lost in thought. She had begun to worry that Yayoi was planning to spend the day getting rid of Kenji's body, when what she really ought to do was go home and play the part of the worried wife. If she did, though, that left Masako to deal with the body, and it had just dawned on her that she would never be able to get it out of the trunk by herself. She studied Yoshie's attractive face for a moment and then made her decision. 'Skipper, I've got a favour to ask.'

'You know I'd do anything you want,' said Yoshie, who was always ready to help. 'I owe you a lot.' Masako, however, was still wondering just how to explain the situation as she got in line to punch out. Suddenly remembering that she should be keeping track of Yayoi, she looked around and saw her straggling up the stairs at the very end of the line. Kuniko, on the other hand, had hurried ahead and was waiting for them. She had obviously sensed that something was going on with Masako and Yayoi and would be sulking at being left out. Yoshie joined Masako in line.

'Can you keep a secret?' Masako asked, her tone quite serious.

'And who would I tell?' said Yoshie, sounding almost indignant. 'What is it?!' Still finding it difficult to actually say what Yayoi had done, Masako punched her time card and stood in silence for a moment, her arms folded across her chest.

'I'll tell you later,' she said eventually. 'When we're alone.'

'Okay,' Yoshie murmured, turning to look at the sky outside the window. Since she commuted on her bicycle, she was probably worried about the rain, Masako thought.

'But you can't even tell Kuniko,' she said.

'I promise.' From her friend's voice Yoshie had guessed that it was something important and let the matter drop for the moment. They were about to turn the corner into the lounge when they heard Komada, the health inspector, telling Yayoi off.

'Yamamoto-san, make sure you wash your uniform today. We don't want to be treated to a third night of smelling that sauce.'

Yayoi, after apologising, pulled off her cap and wandered over to where Masako was standing. Her hair stuck out at odd angles from her hairnet and there were dark circles under her eyes, but if anything she looked even better than usual. A part-time student worker with dyed blond hair who had taken off his own mask and cap stood staring at her, openly impressed.

Masako pulled her aside. 'You need to get home quickly and stay there.'

'But . . . ,' Yayoi murmured.

'The Skipper and I will handle it.'

'The Skipper?' she said doubtfully, glancing toward the changing room. 'Have you told her?'

'Not yet, but I won't be able to move it alone. If she won't do it, you'll have to. But you're going to be the first one they suspect, so if possible you should be at home pretending that nothing's happened.'

Yayoi sighed, seeming finally to understand what her role was. 'You're right,' she agreed.

'Go home, and do just what you always do,' Masako told her. 'Then, around noon, call your husband's office and ask if he's there. When they tell you he's not, say that he didn't come home last night and that you're very worried. If they tell you to file a missing persons report, do it. You need to do everything you can to avoid suspicion.'

'I will,' said Yayoi.

'And don't call me today. If something happens, I'll call you.'

'Masako,' she asked, 'what are you planning to do?'

'Just what you said we should,' she told her, smiling bitterly. 'That's the plan.'

Yayoi gasped, the colour draining from her cheeks. 'You really mean it?' Masako stared for a moment at her pale face before answering.

'Yes. At least I'm going to try.'

'I don't know how to thank you,' Yayoi said, her eyes swimming. 'I can't believe you'd do this for me.'

'Don't thank me yet,' said Masako. 'I don't know if I'll be able to manage it or not. But I think it's better than burying it in the mountains. It's got to vanish without a trace. We don't want any evidence at all.'

When her turn had come, Masako had gone to use the bathroom, and it was there she decided that Yayoi's suggestion had been the right one. As she stared at the large blue plastic pails by the bathroom door, she knew it was the only workable plan.

'But it's a crime,' Yayoi murmured, as if suddenly thinking better of it. 'I don't want to drag you into this.'

'I know,' said Masako. 'But I'm going to try to look at it as just one more unpleasant job. And getting it picked up with the trash is the best way, afterward. That is, if it doesn't bother you. It's your husband we're going to chop up and toss out. Are you sure you can handle that?'

'Yes,' said Yayoi, a faint smile playing across her lips again.

'Actually, it serves him right.'

'You're scary,' said Masako, watching her intently.

'So are you,' said Yayoi.

'No, it's not quite the same for me.'

'Why not?'

'Because I'm treating this as just a job.' Yayoi looked slightly puzzled.

'Masako-san,' she said, 'what did you do before you came to work here?'

'The same as you. I had a husband, and a child, and a job. But I was alone.' Yayoi looked down, perhaps to hide her tears, and her shoulders drooped. 'No crying, now,' Masako said, patting her gently on the back. 'It's all over, and you're the one who ended it.' Yayoi nodded as her friend shepherded her into the lounge. Yoshie and Kuniko had already changed and were sitting together drinking coffee. Kuniko was watching them suspiciously, a thin cigarette dangling from the corner of her mouth.

'Kuniko, would you mind going on ahead today? There's something I've got to talk over with the Skipper,' Masako told her. Kuniko shot a questioning look at Yoshie.

'What could it be that doesn't include me?' she wondered aloud.

'A loan,' said Yoshie. 'You know, money . . . that you borrow. As in, I'm borrowing money from Masako.' At this, Kuniko nodded a bit reluctantly, shouldered her fake Chanel bag, and stood up. Masako waved quickly and went into the changing room, while Yoshie, satisfied with her ruse to get rid of Kuniko, sipped at her paper cup of sugary coffee.

Masako changed quickly and then casually picked up two plastic aprons that belonged to women who had apparently moved on to other jobs. She slipped them into her bag. She had also stuffed several pairs of latex gloves in her pocket. Going back to the lounge, she sat down next to Yoshie. The tatami mat was still warm where Kuniko had been sitting. As she was pulling out her cigarettes, Yayoi, who had also changed, came up and began to sit down with them, but Masako warned her off with a nod.

'Well, I'll be going then,' Yayoi said, obviously reluctant to do so; and she wandered off towards the door, turning several times to look back anxiously at Masako.

As she disappeared around the corner, Yoshie whispered urgently: 'What's this all about? I won't be able to stand it if you don't tell me.'

'Just listen and try not to act shocked,' Masako said, looking her straight in the eye. 'Yayoi's killed her husband.' Yoshie's mouth hung open for a moment, her chapped lips trembling.

'Not act shocked. . . ?' she whispered at last.

'I know,' said Masako. 'But it's true, and there's no way to undo it. I've decided to try to help her, and I want to know if you'll help, too.'

'Are you out of your mind?!' Yoshie shrieked, but then, realising there were people around, lowered her voice. 'She should go turn herself in – right now.'

'But she's got little kids, and he was beating her. She did it in self-defence. You can see the relief on her face.'

'But she *killed* him,' Yoshie gulped.

'How many times have you thought you'd like to kill your mother-in-law?' Masako watched her face stiffen.

'Lots,' she said, draining her coffee cup. 'But thinking about it and actually doing it are two different things.'

'They are. But something made Yayoi cross that line. And it does happen, doesn't it, Skipper? That's why I'm going to do what I can to help.'

'Do *what*?!' Yoshie's voice rang out across the room this time and nearly everyone turned to look. The group of Brazilian men, camped out in their usual spot against the wall, peered curiously at her. 'There's nothing you *can* do,' she continued, seeming to shrink into herself. 'Nothing.'

'Still, I'm going to try,' said Masako.

'But why should you? Why should I? The whole thing gives me the creeps – becoming accomplices to a murder.'

'Not accomplices,' Masako insisted. 'We didn't kill him.'

'But I'm sure they send people to jail too for dumping dead bodies.'

'Yes, maybe,' said Masako. 'Dumping them . . . or dismantling them a bit, either one.'

'What do you mean?' said Yoshie, her tongue running back and forth over her lips as she tried to cope with this new puzzle. 'What are you planning to do?'

'I'm going to cut him up and throw away the pieces. Then Yayoi can go on just as before, as though nothing's happened. They'll register her husband as missing, and that'll be the end of it.'

'Forget it,' said Yoshie, shaking her head stubbornly. 'I couldn't. Not that.'

'Fine,' said Masako, reaching across the table with her hand open. 'Then pay back the money I lent you last night. Now.'

Yoshie sat quietly for a time, a pained expression on her face, while Masako stubbed out her cigarette in the empty coffee cup. A repellent smell of sugar, instant coffee and ashes briefly filled their nostrils; but Masako ignored it and lit another cigarette.

'All right then,' said Yoshie finally, having apparently made up her mind. 'I can't give you back the money, so I guess I'll have to help.'

'Thank you. I knew I could count on you, Skipper.'

'But there's one thing you've got to tell me,' said Yoshie, looking up at her. 'I'm doing this because you helped me out, but why would you be willing to do something like this for Yayoi?'

'I'm not sure I know myself,' said Masako. 'But I can tell you this: if you'd been the one in this fix, I'd have done the same for you.' There seemed nothing left to say, and Yoshie fell silent.

*

Nearly everyone else had left the factory when Masako and Yoshie walked down the stairs at the main entrance. A gentle, early-morning rain was falling, and Yoshie went to get the umbrella she'd left in the rack next to the door. Masako hadn't brought one and was facing a wet walk to the parking lot.

'I'll see you at my house at nine, then,' she said.

'I'll be there,' said Yoshie, straddling her bicycle and pedalling wearily off into the rain. Masako watched her go and then started for the parking lot at a brisk pace; but before she'd gone more than a few steps she noticed a man standing in the shadow of the sycamore trees that lined the road. It was Kazuo Miyamori, dressed now in a white T-shirt, jeans and a black cap. He was staring at his feet and holding out a clear plastic umbrella, without making any effort to keep his own head covered, which was soaking wet.

'How do you say "Go to hell" in Brazilian?' Masako said as she walked past him. He looked up, apparently confused, and started after her.

'Umbrella,' he said, waving it at her.

'I don't want it,' she said, brushing it away. 'Not from you.' The umbrella fell on the cracked sidewalk and lay there. The road was deserted and the clatter it made echoed in the silence. Masako could sense that Kazuo was taken aback. She remembered the hurt look on his face two nights ago when Yayoi had ignored his greeting. He's just a baby, she thought. She realised that he was following her, and as she turned to look at him it occurred to her that his lost expression made things more complicated. But the dark eyes under the brim of the cap were the same ones she'd seen in the reddish moonlight the night before.

'Leave me alone!' she shouted at him.

'I'm sorry,' he said, coming quickly around in front of her and placing his hands on his solid chest. She knew this meant he was apologising 'with all his heart', but she still ignored him and turned right, down the street that led by the abandoned factory, the street where he had attacked her. She could tell that he was still following her, but she felt only a vague apprehension and the desire to drive the memories of the attack out of her head.

'Will you come tonight?' he asked.

'You're dreaming,' she said.

'But . . .' he murmured as she broke into a run. The delivery bay of the old factory came quickly into view. The brown metal shutters where he had pinned her showed no sign of any dents as they went on rusting in the rain. The grass she had trampled in her attempt to get away bore no trace of the struggle. Suddenly, she was filled with rage that everything could go on as before, as if nothing had happened. The humiliation and self-loathing of last night came rushing back and she stopped, waiting for him to reach her. She was so furious she didn't know what she might do; but Kazuo, unsuspecting, approached, with the umbrella now in his hand again, and stood looking at her.

'Now get this straight,' she hissed. 'If you ever try this again I'm going to the police . . . and to management and you'll be out of a job.'

'I understand,' he said, nodding as if in relief. Then his dark face looked up at her. She finally realised that he'd been terrified that she would tell someone.

'Don't get all excited. I haven't forgiven you for anything.' She turned on her heel and walked away, and this time she knew he wasn't following her. She didn't turn around until she reached the entrance to the parking lot, but when she did, she could see him still standing where she'd left him.

'Idiot!' she wanted to call out, but she suppressed the urge, unsure exactly who to take it out on. She looked around for her Corolla and found it parked in the same spot. She tried to imagine the object in the trunk, and it suddenly seemed strange beyond belief that dawn had come as usual, that it should be raining so normally, when that utterly lifeless thing was still in there. And then she realised that everything, even that pig of a young man who'd just been apologising to her so desperately, only reminded her of the body in the trunk; and it wasn't really the Miyamori boy she wanted to punish so much as the lifeless Kenji – and herself for getting caught up in all this.

She unlocked the trunk and opened it a bit. Peeking in, she could see grey pants and a few inches of hairy leg sticking out below the cuff – exactly the place Yayoi had touched the night before to see if the body was still warm. The skin was pale, and the hair seemed slightly dirty somehow, like a fraying rag. 'A thing. It's just a thing,' she muttered, closing the trunk.

Bathroom

1

Masako stood in the bathroom doorway, listening to the sound of the rain through the window. Nobuki, who had apparently been the last one to use the bath, had drained the water and replaced the plastic cover. Though the walls and tiles were dry now, the room was still filled with the clean smell of bath water, the smell of a quiet, peaceful home. Masako felt the urge to throw open the window and let in the damp air from outside.

The little house seemed to be demanding all sorts of things of her: to be swept from top to bottom, to have its overgrown yard weeded, the smell of cigarettes purged, to have the sizeable loans owed on it repaid. Still, despite all its urgent demands, Masako could never bring herself to feel that this was really her home. Why was it that she always felt unsettled here, like a temporary lodger?

When she had pulled out of the parking lot with Kenji's body in the trunk, she had already come to a decision. Once she got home, she went straight to the bathroom to begin thinking about how to lay out the corpse and get the job done. Though she knew the feeling was possibly the sign of a sick mind, there was a part of her that was exhilarated by the challenge. She stepped barefoot into the tiled washing area and lay down on her back. She and Kenji were roughly the same height, so he should easily fit if they laid him out at an angle like this. It was ironic but fortunate that Yoshiki had insisted on the architect making this part of the house larger than usual.

Masako could feel the cool of the tiles on her back as she lay looking out the window. The sky was grey and without depth. Remembering the sight of Kazuo Miyamori standing in the rain, she rolled up the sleeve of her shirt. The bruise on her arm had clearly been left by his large thumb, and it occurred to her that it had been a long time since she'd felt such strength from a man's hands.

'What are you doing?' said a voice from the dark doorway. Sitting up, Masako could see Yoshiki, still in his pyjamas, staring in at her from the dressing area. 'What are you doing in there?' he asked again. Masako jumped up and stared back at him as she rolled down her sleeve. He was barely awake and hadn't yet combed his wispy hair or put on his glasses, but there he was, watching her with a sour look on his face. The way he scowled when he was trying to focus on something reminded her of Nobuki.

'Nothing,' she said. 'I was just thinking of taking a shower.' Yoshiki listened to her awkward lie and then looked past her, out the window.

'It's raining,' he said. 'Won't be hot today.'

'I know, but I got all sweaty at the factory.'

'Suit yourself. But for a second there I thought you'd gone crazy.'

'Why would you think that?'

'What would you think if you saw somebody staring off into space and then suddenly flopping down on the bathroom floor?' It made Masako uncomfortable to realise that he'd been watching her through the open door for some time. But then it seemed that recently Yoshiki had been watching both Nobuki and her from a distance, as if maintaining the space between them were part of his defence.

'You might have told me you were standing there,' she said. He merely shrugged without answering, and Masako squeezed past him out of the room. 'Do you want some breakfast?' she called back, heading for the kitchen without hearing his reply. Dumping some beans into the noisy coffee grinder, she set about making their usual meal of toast and scrambled eggs. It had been some time now since the house had been filled in the morning with the smell of rice cooking in the automatic steamer. When their son had suddenly stopped needing a lunch for school, there was no more call for a large pot of rice.

'Pretty gloomy,' Yoshiki muttered, looking out the window as he sat down at the table after washing his face. It struck Masako that the comment could apply to their household as easily as to the weather. It seemed suffocating, somehow, to face her husband across the breakfast table on such a rainy morning, without even the cheerful patter of the television or the radio. She rubbed her temples, which were throbbing from exhaustion. Yoshiki took a sip of coffee. As he opened the newspaper, a heavy bundle of advertisements slipped out on to the table. Masako gathered them up and began skimming the supermarket inserts.

'What happened to your arm?' he asked abruptly. Masako looked up with a puzzled expression. 'Your arm,' he repeated, pointing at the spot. 'You've got a bruise.'

'I bumped it at the factory,' she said, frowning slightly. Whether he believed her or not, he dropped the subject, but Masako remembered that she'd been thinking about Kazuo Miyamori's thumb while she was staring at the bruise. Yoshiki was sensitive about this kind of thing and was no doubt suspicious. Still, he wasn't asking any more questions – probably because he didn't really want to know anything about her. Resigning herself to his lack of interest, she lit a cigarette. Yoshiki, who didn't smoke, turned irritably toward the window.

Suddenly, they heard the sound of someone charging down the stairs. Yoshiki tensed visibly as Nobuki appeared in the doorway dressed in an oversized T-shirt and sloppy, knee-length pants. As he entered the room, Masako could see him switch off the noisy, youthful energy he'd had a moment before and shroud his face behind a blank stare. Still, the mask couldn't hide the eyes which seemed dissatisfied with everything they saw, or the large mouth clenched in hostility. In some ways, he was the image of Yoshiki as a young man. Nobuki went straight to the refrigerator and began drinking from the bottle of mineral water.

'Use a glass,' Masako said, but he ignored her and went on drinking. As she watched his recently developed Adam's apple bob up and down, she felt herself losing control. 'You may not want to say anything,' she said, getting up from the table, 'but I know you can hear me.' She tried to wrench the bottle out of his hand, but he elbowed her aside. The blow was painful – the boy had suddenly grown so tall and solid – and Masako slumped heavily against the sink. Nobuki, looking as though nothing had happened, slowly replaced the cap on the bottle and put it back in the refrigerator.

'I don't care if you don't talk,' she said, 'but you can't act like that.' Nobuki mugged astonishment and looked down at her dully; and as he did so, she thought again how like a total stranger her own son seemed – a stranger she didn't like much at that. On an impulse, she reached out and slapped him. The skin on his cheek, which she had touched for only an instant, was taut and smooth, with no trace of the baby fat he'd had so recently. Her palm stung where she'd hit him. He stood for a moment, startled, and then pushed past her and disappeared into the bathroom without a word.

She didn't know what she was hoping for; it seemed as though everything she said or did was as useless as sprinkling water on a scorching desert. She stared at her bright red palm for a moment and then looked over at Yoshiki; but he sat motionless, eyes glued to the newspaper, as if he had no son, as if there had never been a boy named Nobuki in his life.

'I give up,' she said. 'It's hopeless.' To the extent he seemed to notice him at all, Yoshiki had apparently given up on the boy as well. All in pursuit of some sort of spiritual goal. Yoshiki seemed to find less evolved beings irritating. For his part, Nobuki still bore a grudge against his father for having failed to support him during his crisis at school. In the end the three of them were so completely estranged that it was hard to understand why they even lived together.

If I were to tell them that there was a dead body in the trunk of my car, how would they react, Masako wondered. Would Nobuki be so shocked that he'd finally say something? Would Yoshiki be so furious that he'd hit her? No, they probably wouldn't even believe her. Masako was beginning to suspect that she was the one who'd grown away from her little family, but that didn't make her feel especially lonely.

A short time later both her husband and her son had made their hurried departures for work and the house was quiet again. Masako finished her coffee and lay down on the sofa in the living room for a nap, but she found it hard to get to sleep.

The bell on the intercom rang.

'It's me.' Yoshie's voice sounded timid. Masako had half expected her not to come at all, but Yoshie was too loyal for that. When she opened the door, she found her friend dressed in the same shabby clothes she'd had on that morning at the factory, a faded pink T-shirt and sweat pants that were worn at the knees. She peered into the house, apparently terrified.

'It's not here,' said Masako, pointing at the car parked next to the door. 'It's in the trunk.' Yoshie seemed to shrink away from it.

'I'm sorry,' she said, 'but I just can't do this. You've got to let me back out.' She had barely spoken when she pushed her way into the entrance hall and threw herself down prostrate on the floor. Masako stood watching her grovel like a frog, wondering idly when Yoshie had started perming her hair. She had expected something like this to happen and was hardly surprised.

'If I say "no", will you go running to the police?' she asked finally. When Yoshie looked up, her face was pale.

'No,' she said, shaking her head. 'Never.'

'But you still can't pay back the money. In other words, you'll send your daughter on her school trip, but when it comes to a once-in-a-lifetime favour, you can't be bothered.'

'But Masako, this isn't any normal favour. You're talking about helping out with a murder.'

'I said it was "once-in-a-lifetime".'

'But it's *murder*,' Yoshie repeated.

'So you'd do it if it were something else? If it were robbery or burglary? Is it really all that different?' said Masako, as if turning the question over in her own mind. Her friend's eyes widened in shock and Masako laughed quietly.

'It is different,' Yoshie murmured.

'Who says so?'

'It's not a matter of anybody saying so. It just is – any civilised person knows that.' Masako watched quietly as Yoshie ran her hands over her tangled hair, still staring at the floor. It was a habit she had when she was upset about something.

'Fine,' Masako said at last. 'Then at least help me carry it in from the car. I can't get it all the way to the bathroom by myself.'

'I've got to get home. My mother-in-law will be waking up soon.'

'It won't take long,' said Masako, slipping into Yoshiki's sandals and going out the door. It was still raining, but that meant there was no one in the street. It was also fortunate that Masako's house was across the street from a vacant lot where the red clay was turned up in preparation for construction. The houses along the street were built close together, but since she was at the end, her entrance was shielded from view.

She felt for the keys in her pocket as she glanced around. No one in sight – now was her chance. But Yoshie still hadn't come out of the house.

'Are you going to help me or not?' she called out irritably.

'Just to carry it,' Yoshie muttered, appearing in the doorway. Masako picked up the blue plastic tarp that she'd left by the entrance. Yoshie still seemed to be hesitating, but Masako went around to the back of the car and opened the trunk.

'Oh!' Yoshie blurted out as she peered over her shoulder. Kenji's face was staring up at them. His eyes were half open, and he looked utterly relaxed, with a thin line of dried saliva running across his cheek. His legs had gone rigid, with the knees slightly bent, and his arms were frozen over his head. His fingers seemed to be grasping for something. A raw red burn mark was visible around his neck, which was stretched to an unnatural length. Masako remembered how Yayoi had removed the belt last night and wrapped it around her own waist. Then she realised that Yoshie had been saying something.

'What did you say?' she asked. Yoshie was standing behind her with her palms together, and as Masako turned, she raised her voice slightly so that the prayer she was chanting was now audible.

'Namu Amida Butsu,' she was repeating over and over.

'Don't you think that's a bit of a giveaway?' Masako said, gently tapping Yoshie's hands. 'Cut that out and help me get him inside.' Ignoring the sour look this provoked, she wrapped the tarp around the body. Then, signalling Yoshie to take one end, she worked her hands under the armpits. Reluctantly, Yoshie grasped the ankles and they lifted Kenji out of the trunk. The fact that the body had stiffened helped a bit, but it was heavy and awkward to hold and they staggered under the weight. Still, the door was only a few steps away, and they soon had him in the house. 'Can we get him back to the bath, Skipper?' Masako panted.

'All right,' said Yoshie, slipping out of her canvas shoes and stepping up into the house. 'Where is it?'

'All the way at the back,' said Masako. Though they had to put him down to rest several times, they finally managed to carry him as far as the changing room. Once there, Masako removed the plastic tarp and spread it on the tiles next to the tub in the washing area. She'd realised it might cause problems if bits of flesh got stuck between the tiles. 'Help me get him in here,' she said. Yoshie nodded, her resistance apparently weakening, and the two of them laid out the body diagonally in the rectangular room, just as Masako had planned earlier that morning.

'Miserable,' Yoshie murmured, '– to end up like this. I bet he never expected his own wife would do him in. I hope he goes straight to heaven.'

'I wouldn't bet on it,' said Masako.

'You're a cold fish,' Yoshie said. The tone was reproachful, but Masako could tell Yoshie was beginning to regain her composure, so she quickly moved on to her next request.

'I'll get some scissors,' she said. 'Would you at least help me cut the clothes off?'

'What are you going to do with them?' Yoshie asked.

'Cut them up and throw them away.'

Yoshie sighed loudly, but she had clearly given in. 'Have you emptied his pockets?' she asked.

'No, he must still have his wallet and his train pass. Will you check?' said Masako, going to get the scissors from the bedroom. When she got back, Yoshie had lined up the contents of Kenji's pockets in the doorway: a worn black leather wallet, a key holder, a train pass, and some change. Masako looked through the wallet and found a few credit cards and almost ¥30,000 in cash. The key in the holder was apparently to Yayoi's house. 'We've got to get rid of all this,' she said at last.

'What will you do with the money?' Yoshie asked.

'You can have it.'

'But it's Yayoi's. Still,' she added as if arguing with herself, 'it does seem strange to give his money back to the wife who killed him.'

'Exactly. Why don't you keep it for your trouble,' said Masako. She noticed a relieved look pass across Yoshie's face. There were plenty of vacant lots and fields in the area, she thought, stuffing the empty wallet into a small plastic bag along with the key holder, credit cards, and train pass. If she could manage to bury the bag somewhere, it would probably never be found.

Yoshie tucked the money into her pants pocket with an apologetic look. 'There's something funny about a necktie on a man who's been strangled to death,' she said, beginning to work at the knot on the tie. The knot, however, was pulled tight and Masako grew frustrated as she watched her struggle with it.

'We don't have time for that,' she told her. 'Someone might come home soon. Just cut it off and be done with it.'

'Wait a minute,' Yoshie said angrily. 'Don't you have any respect for the dead? You ought to be ashamed of yourself!'

'Respect for the dead,' Masako repeated as she pulled off Kenji's shoes and stuffed them into another bag. 'I'm trying to think of this as an inanimate object.'

'An object? What are you talking about? It's a human being.'

'It was a human being, but now it's an object. That's how I've decided to see it.'

'Then you've decided wrong,' said Yoshie, her voice shaking with uncharacteristic indignation. 'If this is an object, then what is that old woman I'm looking after?'

'A living human being, of course,' said Masako.

'I don't agree. If this fellow here's an object, then so is my mother-in-law. And then we're all objects – the living and the dead. There's no difference.' She's probably right, thought Masako, struck by the force of her remarks. She remembered opening the trunk in the parking lot that morning. The dawn had come, the rain was falling, and she'd felt alive, animated. But the dead were inanimate, immobile, and she'd decided to think of Kenji as a thing rather than a person. At the time, it had seemed like a good way to cope with her fear. 'But that's not right,' Yoshie went on. 'Living people are people, but dead bodies aren't just things. It's plain arrogance to think so.'

'I suppose you're right,' said Masako. 'But it would be easier if they were objects.'

'Why?'

'Because it would be less frightening. I won't be able to do it if I don't think of him that way.'

'Do what?'

'Cut him up,' said Masako.

'But why do we have to do that, anyway? That's what I don't understand.' Yoshie was almost shouting. 'It'll come back to haunt us. Heaven will punish us both for this.'

'I don't care,' said Masako.

'Why? Why don't you care?' She didn't care, Masako realised, because she was almost anxious for whatever punishment that might come, but she knew that would be hard to explain to her. Instead of answering, she began peeling off Kenji's black socks.

As her hands touched the bare skin for the first time, a shock ran through her. The body felt cold and foreign, and she wondered whether she would actually be able to cut it up as she'd planned. There would probably be lots of blood, and the organs would flop out. The sense of facing a challenge that she'd felt earlier in the morning faded. Her heart began racing and she felt faint. Suddenly, she felt sure that it was against all human instincts to touch, or even look at, a dead body.

'I can't stand touching him,' Yoshie blurted out, as if reading her mind. 'D'you have any gloves?' Remembering that she'd taken some from the factory, Masako went to get them, along with the two aprons. Meanwhile, Yoshie had neatly folded the tie she had finally managed to remove, and had began unbuttoning the shirt. Handing her the gloves, Masako slipped on another pair, found the scissors, and started cutting off the pants, beginning from the cuff. A few minutes later, Kenji lay naked on the floor. The blood had apparently collected on the side of the body that had faced down in the trunk, and purplish marks were visible under the skin.

'We did this when my husband died,' Yoshie muttered, glancing at the shrunken penis. 'We got him undressed and washed the body. Don't you think Yayoi should see him? We shouldn't really be doing this.' She stood holding the apron and staring at the body.

'You worry too much,' said Masako, getting tired of the display of emotion. 'She's already agreed to everything. If she has regrets later, that's her problem.' Yoshie sighed, looking at Masako with a hint of fear in her eyes. Still irritated, Masako continued with the subject she knew would bother Yoshie the most. 'So let's start by cutting off the head,' she said. 'It gives me the creeps to have him staring at us like that.'

'So now you've got the creeps?' Yoshie said.

'But you're the one talking about hauntings,' Masako shot back.

'No, I'm over that,' Yoshie said.

'Then you do it.'

'No!' she said, sounding terrified. 'I told you I couldn't.' But Masako already knew that she wouldn't be able to dismember the body by herself, and she was determined now to get some help. She made a proposal.

'Yayoi said she wanted to pay us back. Would you do it if money were involved?' Yoshie looked up, as if jerked by a string. Her sunken eyes had a perplexed look. 'I told her she didn't need to pay me, but now that I think about it I'll probably take something. It's more businesslike that way.'

'How much?' Yoshie whispered, glancing queasily at Kenji's lifeless eyes.

'How much do you want? I'll negotiate for you.'

'A hundred thousand?' Yoshie suggested.

'Too little. How about five?'

'With that kind of money, I could find a new place to live,' she murmured. 'So you're planning to buy me in, knowing I can't resist.' Precisely, thought Masako, though she pretended not to hear.

'Please,' she said. 'I need your help, Skipper.'

'Okay, okay. You've got it,' said Yoshie, the prospect of money having finally broken down her resistance. Tying on the apron, she slipped out of her white socks and began rolling up the legs of her sweat pants. 'You'd better get out of those,' she said, pointing at Masako's jeans. 'They'll get covered with blood.' Masako obediently went into the changing room, stripped off her jeans, and fished a pair of shorts out of the laundry basket. As she was climbing into them, she caught sight of herself in the mirror. There, staring back at her, was her own face, but with an expression that was grimmer than any she'd ever seen before. Turning, she found Yoshie standing behind her, looking more bewildered than dangerous.

Stepping back into the bath area, Masako bent down and began feeling Kenji's neck for the best place to begin sawing. She glanced at the large Adam's apple, and remembered how Nobuki's throat had bobbed up and down that morning. It wasn't a helpful train of thought, so she forced herself to concentrate on the task at hand.

'Do you suppose we can just saw right through the neck?' she asked Yoshie.

'It might tear up the skin, so we should probably start with a knife. If that doesn't work, we can figure out something else.' Now that it had become a job, Yoshie was once again in charge, as if she were directing operations from her place at the head of the assembly line. Masako hurried off to the kitchen and brought back her sharpest sashimi knives and the toolbox where they kept the saw. It had also occurred to her that they would need plastic bags later to dispose of the pieces, so they might as well have them handy to fill as they went along. She counted all the bags she had: nearly a hundred. She'd bought them at the local supermarket – the standard kind recommended by the city government and thus particularly hard to trace.

'I think we should double-bag everything, and if we do that I've got enough for about fifty packages. How does that sound?' Masako asked.

'Then we should probably start with the big joints and chop it small later,' said Yoshie, testing the blade of her knife. There was a slight tremor in her hand. Bending over, Masako poked her finger under Kenji's Adam's apple in search of the vertebrae and then quickly inserted her own knife. It struck bone almost immediately, so she twisted the blade to avoid the obstacle, and as she did this a stream of darkish blood oozed from the wound. Surprised by the sheer amount of it, she stopped for a moment.

'I must have hit an artery.'

'You must have,' Yoshie agreed. In no time at all, the plastic tarp was a sea of red, and Masako was fumbling to pull the plug for the drain in the floor. The thick blood swirled into a dense foam as it flowed down the drain, and it gave Masako a strange feeling to imagine it mixing in the sewer with the water from last night's bath. As she worked, her gloves became so sticky that it became difficult to move her fingers. Locating the shower hose, Yoshie attached it to the faucet and rinsed her hands, but the room was still choked with the stench of blood.

Once she could use the saw, she got through the neck with relative ease, and when his head fell away with a dull thud, Kenji's body was suddenly transformed into nothing more than a strangely shaped object. Masako pushed one of the bags inside another, wrapped up the head, and put it on the lid that covered the bath tub.

'I suppose we ought to drain the rest of the blood,' Yoshie said, raising the headless body by the legs. Raw flesh was visible around the gaping hole of the trachea, and blood flowed in a continuous stream from the severed arteries. As she watched, Masako's whole body broke out in gooseflesh. But though the sight was utterly ghoulish, somehow she felt calmer than she would have imagined. Most of all, she wanted the whole thing to be over as quickly as possible. She found that concentrating on the process helped to deaden her jangling nerves.

Next she used her knife to cut around the hip joints. Watching the blade slip through the layers of yellow fat, she heard Yoshie mutter that it looked 'exactly like a broiler'. When she reached bone, she braced her foot on top of Kenji's leg and began sawing the femur in just the same way as one would cut through a log. Though it took a bit of time, in the end the legs came away easily as well. The shoulders, however, were more difficult, and she had trouble deciding where to make the incisions. The fact that rigor mortis had set in didn't make things any easier in this case. Beads of sweat formed on her forehead, and Yoshie was beginning to grow impatient.

'My mother-in-law will be waking up soon. We've got to get finished.'

'I know,' said Masako. 'Why don't you help more with the cutting?'

'But we've only got one saw.'

'I should have asked you to bring one with you.'

'But if you had, I would never have come,' Yoshie said, sounding shocked.

'Good point,' said Masako, suddenly wanting to laugh. There was something so absurd about the whole situation, about the two of them having such an inane conversation while they cut up a total stranger by the name of Kenji. They stood for a moment over the body, eyeing each other as their bloody hands dangled limp at their sides. 'When do you put out the garbage at your house, Skipper?' she asked finally.

'Tomorrow, Thursday. . . .'

'Same as here, so it all has to go tomorrow morning. We'll have to divide it up.'

'But I could never carry that many bags,' Yoshie pointed out.

'I'll drive you.'

'Don't you think a red car coming around to drop off garbage might be a little noticeable?' Yoshie said. 'You know how people watch the drop-off spots.'

'I suppose so.' Masako was just beginning to realise that getting rid of the body was going to be harder than she'd imagined. And Yoshie was still impatient.

'Just get it over with. We'll worry about the garbage later.'

'Okay,' said Masako, picking up the saw and beginning to work on the shoulder. When the arms were off, they decided to deal with the organs. Masako took a knife and made a deep cut from the base of the throat down to the groin. As she sliced through the intestines, the room was choked with the smell of the rotting contents of Kenji's stomach mixed with the alcohol he'd drunk the night before. The two women clutched their hands over their noses.

'Wash it down the drain,' Masako gasped, signalling to Yoshie. But then she changed her mind, realising it could cause trouble if it clogged the pipes. She decided to bag the contents of the intestines as well. Just as she was getting started, though, the bell on the intercom rang and they froze. It was already after 10.30.

'Your husband or your son?' Yoshie whispered nervously. Masako shook her head.

'They shouldn't be home yet,' she said.

'Okay, then let's not answer.' After ringing a few more times, the intercom fell silent.

'Who could it have been?' Yoshie hissed.

'Probably just a salesman,' said Masako. 'If someone asks later, I'll say I was sleeping.' She picked up the saw, which was now greasy with fat. There was still a bit more work to be done, but there was no turning back now.

2

As Masako and Yoshie had been starting to work on the body, Kuniko Jonouchi was driving aimlessly around the Higashi Yamato suburb of Tokyo. She had nowhere to go and nothing to do and was feeling a bit desperate, which for her was unusual. She stopped the car next to a brand-new fountain in the circle in front of the station. The pointlessness of the fountain on this rainy morning suited her mood exactly, thought Kuniko, in a rare moment of self-consciousness, and even then they tended to make her feel uncomfortable.

She glanced nervously a number of times at a telephone booth next to a fence built around a construction site. She had all but decided that she should call Masako and ask to borrow the money. It was true that she found Masako a bit scary, and she was never quite sure what she was thinking, but at this point she had no other choice. She needed cash and she needed it today.

Kuniko climbed out of her car and put up her umbrella; but as she was doing this, a bus parked behind her blasted its air brakes at her. The driver slid open the window.

'You can't park here!' he shouted.

Shut up, asshole, she thought to herself, yet even the unspoken swearword sounded lame this morning. Shuffling back to her damp, forlorn Golf, she started the engine and pulled back into the stream of traffic. She had no idea where she was headed and no clue where to find a pay phone. Still, it hardly mattered since the traffic was nearly at a standstill.

What to do? She sighed, peering out through the fogged-up windshield. The broken defroster bothered her, but not nearly as much as her lack of a plan.

When she'd come home this morning from the factory, there had been no sign of Tetsuya who should have been asleep in the bedroom. Obviously, he was still mad after the fight they'd had last night and had decided to stay somewhere else. Well, what did she care? She'd be better off if a bum like that never came home. She had gone straight to bed and was just dozing off when the phone rang. It was still barely 7.00 a.m. and she sounded a bit grumpy when she answered.

'I'm very sorry to disturb you so early,' the voice on the other end said with exaggerated politeness, 'but is that Kuniko Jonouchi?'

'What do you want?' Kuniko muttered.

'I'm calling from the Million Consumers Centre,' the man said. Kuniko was suddenly wide awake. How could she have forgotten something so important? The man continued his well-rehearsed patter. 'I thought it might have slipped your mind, so I'm calling to remind you that your payment was due yesterday. I believe we still haven't received your deposit. I'm sure you're aware of the payment schedule: your fourth payment of ¥55,200 was due on the twentieth. If we do not receive payment today, you will incur a penalty fee and we will be sending around a collection agent. We would appreciate your immediate attention to this matter.'

The call was from a local loan shark. Kuniko had been hounded by creditors for several years, having run up large car loans and credit-card bills. Sometime last year she had realised that she wasn't even thinking of paying back the principal any longer but was just trying to keep up with the interest. Then even that began to prove difficult, and she started going to loan sharks to borrow against her pay-cheque. And now the loan sharks were after her and she had nowhere else to turn. Her debts had doubled in almost no time, and both the regular creditors and the loan sharks were threatening to blacklist her.

Things had got worse when she'd been stupid enough to believe the advertisements from a local 'credit agency'. 'Monthly payments got you down? Need cash in a hurry?' they had asked, and she had answered with an emphatic 'Yes' – the first step toward the current mess. A pleasant enough older woman had come to see her and, with nothing more than her driver's licence and the name of her husband's company, had handed over ¥300,000, a sum that had allowed her make the interest payments on her credit cards and pay-cheque loans. Kuniko had been too focused on just getting by for the moment to realise that this new debt carried a forty-per-cent interest rate. So when she'd scrounged the money from Tetsuya to repay it, the woman told her that the amount had already swollen to ¥500,000.

This meant she *had* to dig up some cash today. The can where they kept the money for household expenses had nothing in it but small change – when had that been spent? Beginning to feel a bit shaky, she took her fake Gucci wallet from her bag, but with pay day still a few days off, she only had a few thousand yen left. Her only hope was to try to find Tetsuya and get the money from him again. 'Where could he have gone?' she said aloud, flipping through her address book for his office number. She dialled the number, but no one answered – still too early. Even if she did get through, though, he probably wouldn't take the call. She was getting rattled now. If she didn't make the payment today, someone, a yakuza-type most likely, would pay her a visit. Despite her brassy looks, Kuniko was really quite timid, and the thing that scared her most at the moment was the thought of this man.

She shuffled into the bedroom and opened the bottom drawer of the dresser, looking for an old nest egg that just might still be hiding among the underwear and socks; but though she pawed through the bras and nylons, she came up empty-handed. Then, seized by a nasty suspicion, she began opening other drawers, only to discover that all of Tetsuya's clothing was gone. After last night's fight, he must have pocketed every last yen in the house and left home.

With sleep now out of the question, Kuniko jumped in her car and drove to the cash machine by the station. When she checked the balance on their joint account, it came up zero. More of his handiwork. At this rate, she wouldn't even be able to make the rent. She was almost pulling her hair out in fury as she headed back to the car.

Finally escaping the traffic, she turned left at a light and came to a row of older, one-storey municipal housing units. A brand-new telephone booth stood out against the dingy background. Pulling over, she jumped out of the car without bothering to take her umbrella and ran to the booth.

'Hello, is that Max Pharmaceuticals? I'd like to speak to Jonouchi in the sales department.'

The reply came as a shock. 'Jonouchi quit last month,' said the voice on the other end of the line. Kuniko had always thought of Tetsuya as a fool, an incompetent, but he had put one over on her. In a rage, she threw down the tattered telephone book and began stamping on it with her damp shoes, sending shreds of paper swirling around. Still not appeased, she slammed down the receiver with all her might. *Shit! Shit!* What should I do? They're coming today, and I've got nowhere to hide. She would *have* to ask Masako, she decided. Hadn't Yoshie just this morning been saying she was going to borrow money from her? So why couldn't she ask, too? If Masako refused, it would just prove what a cold fish she was. Since she was completely self-centred, Kuniko thought it natural that Masako would be willing to lend to her if she were willing to lend to anyone.

She slid her phone card back into the slot and tried dialling Masako's number, but the phone seemed to be broken now. No matter how many times she inserted the card, it came sliding back out. Clucking with annoyance, she gave up on it and decided to pay Masako a visit. Her house wasn't far away. Kuniko had been there once and thought she could manage to find it again. Climbing back into her car, she unfolded a large map and held it up with one hand as she pulled back on to the main road.

Masako's house was small, but it was in a neighbourhood of newer, made-to-order homes, which in itself made Kuniko jealous. Still, she thought, remembering how careless Masako was about her clothes, it couldn't be all that fancy. She took some comfort in this analysis, despite the fact that she was here to borrow money. Across the street, land that had recently been a field was being readied for construction. Kuniko parked in front of a mound of clay and walked toward Masako's house. A familiar bike was parked out front – the Skipper's. Immediately assuming that Yoshie had beaten her there for the loan, Kuniko was worried. Maybe Yoshie didn't have a payment due today, though, so she wouldn't mind letting her go first. That's how she'd put it.

She rang the bell on the intercom, but there was no answer. She rang again, but the house was quiet. Perhaps they've gone out somewhere, she thought, but Masako's Corolla was parked in front, and so was Yoshie's bike. Strange. Maybe they're both sleeping – the thought occurred naturally to Kuniko, who was herself short of sleep. But then she remembered that Yoshie was taking care of her invalid mother-in-law, and she would never allow herself to fall asleep at someone else's house.

Suddenly suspicious, she walked around to the back of the house, umbrella still in hand. Once she'd reached the garden, she could peek through the lace curtains into what appeared to be the living room, but it was dark and silent. There was a light on, however, at the far end of the corridor. Perhaps they couldn't hear the intercom that far back in the house.

Heading back toward the front, she circled the house again, this time in the opposite direction, and came to a window that seemed to be the bathroom. The light was on, and she could hear Masako and Yoshie talking quietly. What could they be doing back here? She reached through the metal bars and tapped on the window.

'Hey, it's Kuniko,' she called. The voices inside fell silent. 'I'm sorry, but I stopped by because I've got a favour to ask. Is the Skipper in there, too?' There was another short silence, before the window shot open and Masako peered out with an angry look on her face.

'What do you want?' she said.

'I want to ask a favour,' said Kuniko in her sweetest tone of voice, intent on winning over a hostile Masako and getting at least ¥55,200 out of her, plus a little extra to live on, hopefully.

'What sort of favour?'

'I'd rather not say right here,' said Kuniko, looking back over her shoulder at the neighbour's house just a few steps away. She was standing right in front of a small, half-open window that was probably also a bathroom.

'I'm a bit busy at the moment,' said Masako, not bothering to hide her irritation. 'Just spit it out.'

'Well,' she began, but then stopped, suddenly curious about what Masako and Yoshie could be doing in the bathroom. Catching a whiff of something faintly putrid, she sniffed noisily. As Masako slammed the window shut, she cried out 'Wait,' pressing desperately on the window frame, determined to make her case. 'I'm in trouble,' she called.

'Okay,' Masako said quietly, perhaps afraid of causing a scene in the neighbourhood. 'Go round to the front. I'll be right there.'

Kuniko was relieved that Masako had given in, but her interest had been piqued by something rather strange she'd seen in the instant before the window had been closed: it was almost certainly a piece of meat – and the thought made her heart jump. Whatever it was, it was huge; but if they were cutting up a side of beef or pork, why were they doing it in the bathroom? Masako's behaviour had been odd, and though Kuniko was sure she was in there, Yoshie hadn't shown her face.

She waited at the front door, but Masako didn't come for several minutes. Growing impatient, she walked back to the bathroom. Now she could hear the sound of running water; they seemed to be washing something, and they were talking again in low voices. By now, Kuniko was determined to find out what they were up to, all the more so because she thought it smelt of money.

She could hear Masako leaving the bathroom, so she hurried back to the front door and waited with an innocent look on her face. The door opened at last, though only a crack, and Masako peered out, dressed in a polo shirt and shorts. Her hair was pulled back in a messy bundle, and she seemed somehow even more intimidating than at the factory earlier. Kuniko felt cowed by her.

'So what's up?' Masako said.

'Could I come in for a moment?'

'What do you want?' she snapped.

'I'd prefer not to say out here,' Kuniko said, as sweetly as she could.

When Masako reluctantly agreed to let her in, Kuniko stepped inside and looked around. The entrance hall was small but neat. As might have been expected with Masako, there wasn't a single flower or picture or decoration of any kind to be seen. 'So what is it?' she demanded, planting herself directly in front of Kuniko so that she could go no further nor see into the house. Kuniko had always hated the way Masako behaved with her, so high and mighty, and was thinking right then that maybe she hated Masako herself just a bit.

'Well, I don't know how to say this but I need to borrow some money. I forgot about a payment that was due yesterday and I'm flat broke.'

'What about your husband?'

'He took all the money we had in the house and left me.'

'Left you?' Masako echoed. As Kuniko caught sight of the way that her expression relaxed just slightly at this news, she was sure she hated her. Still, she couldn't afford to let her feelings show at the moment, so she looked meekly at the floor.

'Yes,' she murmured, 'and I have no idea where he's gone. I don't know what to do.'

'I see,' said Masako. 'So how much do you need?'

'Fifty thousand – but I could make do with forty.'

'I don't have that kind of money here. I'd have to go to the bank'

'Would you mind?' said Kuniko. 'I'd really appreciate it.'

'I can't right now.'

'But you did it for the Skipper, didn't you?' she pressed, which made Masako frown uncomfortably.

'I need to know one thing – is there any chance you'll be able to pay me back?'

'Yes,' Kuniko insisted. 'I promise.' Masako fell silent for a moment, weighing the request, her hand wandering to her chin as she thought it over. Kuniko gave a start: there was something that looked like blood under her fingernails.

'At any rate, I can't do it today,' Masako said. 'I can probably help you out if you can wait till tomorrow.'

'Tomorrow's too late. If I don't make the payment today, they'll send their thugs to get it.'

'I'm afraid that's your problem.' Kuniko said nothing. She knew Masako was right, but she was always so cold-blooded about it.

Just then, Yoshie spoke up from behind them. 'I know it's none of my business, but I think you should give it to her,' she said. 'She's part of the group, isn't she?' Masako spun around to look at her, not bothering to hide her anger; but it didn't seem to be what Yoshie had said that upset her as much as the fact that she had shown herself at all. Yoshie was dressed just as she had been when they'd left the factory, but there were dark circles under her eyes and she looked even more exhausted. Certain now that the two of them were doing something they didn't want her to know about, Kuniko saw her chance to retaliate.

'What are you two up to, anyway?' she asked. Masako said nothing, but Yoshie looked away guiltily. 'What are you doing in the bathroom?'

'What do you think we're doing?' Masako said with a thin laugh. The look she gave her made Kuniko's skin crawl.

'I don't know. . . ,' she murmured.

'Did you see something?' Masako asked.

'Well, I thought I did – a piece of meat maybe.'

'I'll show you what it is,' said Masako abruptly. 'Come on.' Yoshie said something that sounded like an objection, but Masako grabbed Kuniko by the wrist. As the firm grip closed around her arm, a part of Kuniko – the timid part – was seized by an urge to run away as fast as she could. But another part of her wanted more than anything to see what was in the bathroom, especially if it might involve money; and it was this part that was gaining the upper hand.

'What are you doing?' Yoshie said, pulling on Masako's arm. 'Do you think this is a good idea?'

'Don't worry. She can help us.'

'I'm not so sure!' Her voice was at first hesitant, then shrill.

'Help with what, Skipper?' Kuniko asked, starting to panic, but

Yoshie didn't answer and just stared at the floor, arms folded, as Masako began dragging Kuniko down the passage toward the bathroom. When they reached the door, Kuniko caught sight of what appeared to be a human arm lying on the floor under the bright light, and she nearly fainted. 'What's that?' she gasped.

'Yayoi's husband,' Masako said, releasing her arm and lighting a cigarette. Remembering the dried blood under Masako's fingernails and the foul smell coming from the window, Kuniko clutched her hand to her mouth, fighting back the urge to vomit.

'Why? Why?' she muttered. Maybe what she was seeing wasn't real. Maybe they'd set up the whole thing to scare her, like a haunted house.

'Yayoi killed him,' Yoshie said, sighing.

'But what are you doing to him?' Kuniko asked.

'We're cutting him up. Getting on with the job,' Masako said, as if explaining something obvious to a child.

'That's not a job!'

'It certainly is!' Masako said flatly. 'And if you want money as badly as you seem to, you can help us.' At the mention of money, Kuniko's mind shifted gears.

'Help you how?'

'When we get him cut up and put in bags, you can help us get rid of them,' said Masako.

'Just get rid of them?'

'Yes.'

'And how much would I get?'

'How much do you want? I'll talk to Yayoi. But it means you'd be in on the whole thing, and you can't tell anyone.'

'I understand.' As soon as the words were out of her mouth, Kuniko realised with blank amazement that she'd been caught in the trap that Masako had laid to ensure her silence.

3

Yayoi Yamamoto opened her old red umbrella as she left the factory and got on her bicycle. As she pedalled away, she noticed that the light shining through the umbrella turned the bare skin of her arms a brilliant rose pink. It occurred to her that her cheeks probably had the same girlish glow. But in contrast to the rose-tinted world that followed along with her at the leisurely pace of her bicycle, the rest of the world was a grimmer shade – the wet asphalt of the street, the trees on either side in their newish foliage, the tightly shuttered houses. Though the umbrella created a pink cocoon, her surroundings became more sinister and depressing. Somehow, this seemed like a symbol of her own life now that she had killed Kenji.

Yayoi could recall almost every detail of the murder; after all, she had done it with her own hands. Yet at the same time, the fantasy that Kenji had simply disappeared somewhere was beginning to take root, without her recognising how self-serving this version of things might be. It had been so long since Kenji had been a real presence in the house that it was easier for her to embrace a fantasy in place of the reality that she had murdered him.

The nylon umbrella was heavy now, having absorbed a good deal of rain, and she lowered her arm for a moment. As she did so, she watched the rose-coloured world vanish and the rows of familiar little houses revert to their usual aspect. The rain fell gently, soaking her face and hair. Yayoi was overcome with the sensation that she had somehow been reborn, and she could feel a certain courage beginning to stir inside her.

As she approached the cinderblock wall that lined the road at the entrance to her alley, she remembered how she had waited there for Masako the night before. She would never forget how her friend had simply accepted what she'd done and agreed to help her. She would do anything now for Masako – all the more so since Masako had also taken on the grim task of disposing of the body.

Unlocking the door, Yayoi stepped into the dim house. Perhaps because the children were here, she was struck by the familiar smell of home, like the scent of a puppy sleeping in the sun. And now the house belonged to her and her kids and to no one else. Kenji wouldn't be coming back – but from now on she would have to be sure she didn't let on that she knew he wouldn't. She wondered a bit uneasily whether she'd be convincing in the role of the worried wife. After all, she still felt a tingle of excitement when she recalled the sight of his lifeless body slumped in the doorway. *Serves the bastard right!* She had never used that kind of language in her life before. Nor had she ever been hunting – so why had she felt the sort of thrill one got from chasing down an animal in the wild? Perhaps she'd always been that kind of person but had just never had a chance to find out.

Feeling a bit calmer, she looked around the entrance hall for traces of Kenji as she slipped out of her shoes. It occurred to her that she couldn't remember which shoes Kenji had been wearing. Checking the shoe cupboard, she saw to her relief that his new shoes were missing: at least Masako had not had to deal with his dirty old ones.

She peeked into the bedroom and noted happily that both children were still asleep. As she replaced the blanket that the younger boy had kicked off, she felt a momentary pang of regret for having robbed them of their father.

'But Papa wasn't the old Papa any more,' she muttered aloud, then realised to her horror that the older boy, five-year-old Takashi, was awake. He was looking around for her, his eyes blinking anxiously. Yayoi went to him and began gently patting his back. 'I'm home,' she said quietly. 'Everything's fine. Go back to sleep.'

'Is Papa home?' he asked.

'Not yet,' said Yayoi. He looked around nervously for a moment, but she went on patting him until he dropped off again. The thought of what she would be facing in the next few hours made her realise she should probably try to get some sleep herself. Under the circumstances, she doubted she'd be able to settle down; but as she rubbed the bruised spot on her stomach, she drifted off almost immediately.

'Mama, where's Milk?'

She woke abruptly when her younger boy, Yukihiro, jumped on her futon. It was difficult to pull herself away from her dreams and back to reality. Forcing her eyes open, she looked at the clock. It was already past 8.00 and she had to have the boys at their day-care centre by 9.00. She hopped out of bed still dressed, her clothes slightly damp with sweat.

'Mama, Milk's not here,' Yukihiro was still whining.

'He's around somewhere,' Yayoi said, folding up the futon as she replayed the events of the night before in her mind. She finally managed to remember that the cat had fled through the crack in the door after she'd killed Kenji. It seemed strange that some of the details were already becoming vague, as if they'd happened long ago.

'I said he isn't here!' the boy sobbed. He was the rougher, more boyish of her two sons, but he was unusually fond of the cat. She turned to look for the older boy with the idea of having him look after the little one.

'Takashi,' she called. 'Could you take your brother to look for Milk?' A moment later, Takashi appeared in his pyjamas, looking anxious and gloomy.

'Did Papa leave for work already?' he asked. For some time now, Kenji had been sleeping in the little room off the entrance hall when he got home late from work. Takashi had apparently gone to look for him there as soon as he woke up.

'No, he must have stayed somewhere else. He never came home last night.'

'That's not true,' Takashi said. 'He did come home.' Yayoi stared at him, horrified. When his pale, delicate face was strained with worry as it was now, he looked just like her.

'What time?' she asked. Hearing the quaver as her voice trailed off, she realised that this was the first round in what was going to be a long fight. She steeled herself for the task of deceiving her son.

'I don't know what time,' Takashi said, sounding very grown-up. 'But I heard him come in.' Yayoi felt a wave of relief.

'You heard him? You probably just heard Mama leaving for work. Now hurry up or we'll be late.' He started to protest, but she ignored him and turned to watch Yukihiro searching under the sofa and behind the kitchen cabinet. 'I'll look for the cat,' she said. 'You two get ready.'

Yayoi made breakfast with what she had in the kitchen and then dressed the boys in their rain ponchos. She put them on her bicycle, one in front and one behind, and rode them to the day-care centre; and when she had them safely delivered, she felt a certain peace of mind. She suddenly wanted to call Masako right away to find out how things had gone, or even to ride over to her house to see for herself. But Masako had said that she was to wait until she heard from her, so she gave up the idea of phoning and hurried home.

When she reached the alley, a middle-aged neighbour was shuffling about, umbrella in one hand, cleaning up the garbage collection area. As she worked, she grumbled to herself about the sloppy way the people in the nearby apartment building put out their trash. Yayoi greeted her reluctantly.

'Good morning,' she said. 'It's good of you to take care of this.' The woman's reply was unexpected.

'Oh, isn't that yours?' she asked, pointing toward a white cat that was hiding by a telephone pole. It was Milk.

'It is,' said Yayoi. 'Here, Milk! Here, Milk!' she called, holding out her hand. The cat arched its back and mewed. 'You'll get wet. Come inside,' she said, but Milk ran off in the opposite direction.

'That's odd,' said the woman. 'What do you suppose got into him?' Trying to control her impatience in front of her neighbour, Yayoi continued calling the cat's name. He'll probably never come back . . . just like Kenji. She stared blankly at the spot where he'd vanished.

Yayoi's daily schedule was an unusual one: after getting home in the early morning from the night shift, she would make breakfast for Kenji and the children, take the boys to the day-care centre, and only then would she get some sleep. She hadn't really wanted to work at night, but there weren't many places that would hire a mother with young children who had to take time off unexpectedly. Before starting at the boxed-lunch factory, she'd worked part-time as a checker at a supermarket; but between refusing to work Sundays and staying home frequently with sick children, she hadn't lasted long. The night shift was hard on her physically, but it did pay better than day work and she could put the children to bed before she had to leave for the factory. Also, she'd been fortunate to find co-workers like Masako and Yoshie.

She wondered how she was going to manage from now on without Kenji's salary. But they'd made do these past few months without it; this would be no different. They'd figure out something. It seemed to Yayoi that she'd somehow grown stronger since last night.

She wanted to make the call to Kenji's office as soon as possible, but it might seem strange if she called too early. Deciding to stick to her usual routine, she took half a sleeping pill and lay down. This time she had trouble falling asleep, and no sooner had she dozed off than she woke in a cold sweat from a vivid dream that she was lying next to Kenji. Shaking off its after-effects, she turned over and at last fell fast asleep.

Some time later, she woke to the distant sound of the telephone ringing. Thinking that it might be Masako, she hopped out of bed, only to find that she was still dizzy from the sleeping pill.

'My name is Hirosawa,' said the voice on the phone. 'Is your husband there?' The call was from the small construction-supplies company where Kenji worked. So it's starting, she thought, collecting herself.

'No,' she said. '. . . You mean he isn't there?'

'Not yet,' said Hirosawa. She had hesitated because she was unsure of the time. She turned to check the clock on the wall and saw that it was already past 1.00.

'Actually, my husband never came home last night. I don't know where he stayed, but I thought he'd be at the office by now. I know how angry he gets when I call there, so I was just wondering what I should do.'

'I see . . .' the man stammered, perhaps feeling he ought to keep up a show of male solidarity. 'You must have been worried.'

'Well, he's never done anything like this before, so I didn't know what to think. I was just about to phone you.' Yayoi had remembered that Hirosawa was the head of the sales section and Kenji's boss. Picturing his thin, unappealing face, she willed herself into the role of the worried yet slightly embarrassed wife.

'Now don't you worry,' said Hirosawa. 'He's probably just sleeping off a hangover somewhere. Oh, sorry – that probably doesn't make you feel much better. But your husband has never missed work for no reason, so I'm sure there's a simple explanation. Stress . . . yes, that's probably it. He's feeling under a strain and just went off somewhere. That happens a lot these days.'

'Without even phoning home?' Yayoi cut in.

'Well. . .' Hirosawa murmured, clearly at a loss.

'But what do you think I should do?'

'Well, why don't we do this. Let's wait until this evening, and if he still hasn't shown up by then, we could think about filing a missing persons report.'

'Where would I do that?' she asked. 'At the police station?'

'No, I don't think so. Why don't you let me check on that, and you sit tight and try not to worry. Men do stupid things sometimes, it's just the way we are. It's not as though he's really gone missing.'

After putting down the phone, Yayoi looked around the quiet room. She noticed that it had finally stopped raining, and then suddenly realised she was hungry. She hadn't eaten anything since last night. She thought about finishing off the leftovers from the breakfast she'd fed the boys, and perhaps there was some rice in the steamer; but at the sight of the food, she knew she couldn't eat it. As she poked at her plate with her chopsticks, the phone rang again.

'Hello. It's Hirosawa.'

'Oh, thank you for calling back. Did you find out anything?'

'Well, we talked it over here, and we're wondering how you'd feel about waiting until tomorrow morning before we call anyone.'

'Oh,' Yayoi sighed. 'Still, I see what you mean. It's embarrassing to make a fuss if it turns out to be nothing.'

'No, it's not that. It's just that we thought it might be best to wait a bit. And then if he's still not back tomorrow, we'd have to think something might have happened – an accident perhaps – and we'd want you to phone the police.'

'The police?' said Yayoi.

'Yes, if he wasn't back, you would just phone 911.' In other words, thought Yayoi, tomorrow morning I'll be phoning the police, because there's no way that Kenji is ever coming home again.

'But I'm too worried to wait,' she said. 'I think I'd rather phone this evening if he's still missing.'

'You mean contact the police?'

'Yes. I couldn't stand it if he's been in an accident and they've taken him somewhere. This is the first time anything like this has happened and I'm a little upset.'

'I understand,' he said. 'Then you should do whatever makes you feel comfortable. But I'm sure he'll be walking in the door any minute, looking pretty ashamed of himself.'

I seriously doubt it, she thought, deciding that she would go ahead and phone the police before the end of the day. That would be more natural, as though she were genuinely concerned. But when had she become so cold and calculating, she wondered, as she hung up the phone.

A little past 4.00, as she was getting ready to pick up the kids at the day-care centre, the phone rang again.

'It's me.' Masako's voice was low and clipped.

'Oh, I'm so glad,' said Yayoi, her voice trembling with a mixture of relief and anxiety. 'How did it go?'

'It's all over and you've got nothing to worry about. But the situation has changed slightly.'

'Changed how?'

'The Skipper and Kuniko helped out.' Yayoi had known that Yoshie was going to be asked, but nothing had been said about Kuniko. They all got along well enough at the factory, but still – was flashy Kuniko someone you could trust? She felt a sudden panic.

'Do you think Kuniko is okay?' she said. 'She won't talk, will she?'

'Well, we didn't have much choice. She showed up right in the middle of everything and saw what we were doing. But if you think about it, she already knew that your husband had hit you and that he'd gambled away all your savings. If she'd mentioned any of that to the police, they'd have suspected you.' True, thought Yayoi, feeling scared. It seemed that everything came out in the wash, every knot had a way of unravelling in the end. When she'd told her friends what had happened two nights ago, she had never in her wildest dreams imagined that she was going to murder Kenji. But there was nothing to be done about that now, and Masako was absolutely right. In fact, you could count on Masako generally to get things right. 'She agreed to help out, but there's a catch. She and Yoshie want to be paid. Do you think you can come up with about five hundred thousand?'

It had never occurred to her that she would be paying anybody, but she'd decided to do exactly as Masako instructed.

'Will that be enough for both of them?'

'Yes. Four hundred for the Skipper and one for Kuniko. She's just going to help us get rid of the bags. I think they'll settle for that. They seem to feel that since you killed him, you should pay to have the whole thing taken care of.'

'I understand. I'll ask my parents for the money right away.' Yayoi's parents, who lived in Yamanashi Prefecture, were far from wealthy. Her father had been in business but was on the verge of retirement. She hated asking them for money, but since Kenji had taken all the savings, she didn't even have enough to live on. She would have had to ask them at some point anyway, so it might as well be sooner than later.

'Good,' said Masako, her tone brisk and businesslike. 'But how did things go there?'

'His office called earlier to say he hadn't shown up. They wanted me to wait till tomorrow morning to report him missing, but I told them I was too worried and was going to call the police this evening.'

'That sounds good, like this isn't an everyday thing for you. Are you skipping work tonight?'

'I thought I should.'

'That's probably best. Good, then I'll call again tomorrow,' said Masako, sounding as though she was about to hang up now that they'd finished their business.

'Masako,' said Yayoi, stopping her.

'What?'

'What was it like?'

'Oh, that? It was a huge mess, but in the end we got it down to little pieces. The three of us divided up the bags and we'll dump them tomorrow morning. It's Thursday, and that's garbage day most places. We used extra-strong bags, so I don't think we'll have any leaks.'

'But where are you taking them?' Yayoi asked.

'We can't go too far. We'll have to do it in the neighbourhood, though it does seem a little risky. We'll try to be as discreet as possible.'

'Okay,' said Yayoi. 'And thanks.' Remembering the nosy neighbour she'd met that morning poking around in the garbage, she said a little prayer that it would all go as planned.

Almost as soon as she'd hung up, Yayoi picked up the phone again and, steeling herself, dialled a number she had never dialled before. A man's voice answered almost immediately.

'911,' he said. 'How can I help you?'

Yayoi hesitated. '. . . My husband didn't come home last night.' She wasn't sure what sort of reaction she was expecting, but his response seemed very businesslike. He asked her name and address and put her on hold. A moment later another man came on.

'Domestic Division,' the new man said. 'You say your husband didn't come home? How long has it been?'

'Since last night. And his office says he hasn't shown up there today.'

'Have you been having any trouble lately?' the man asked.

'No, nothing that I can think of.'

'Then I'd like you to wait until tomorrow, and if he still hasn't shown up, you should come in and file a report. This is the Musashi Yamato station; you know where that is?'

'But I don't think I can wait. I'm very worried.'

'Yes, but even if you come in now, we can only file the report. No one's going to go looking for him at this point.' The man's voice had grown gentler.

'Well, I don't know what to do,' Yayoi said. 'This hasn't ever happened before.'

'If it were a child or an old person, that would be a different story, but in this case we'd really like you to give it another day.'

'I understand,' Yayoi said. She'd done her duty for today. She let out a long sigh as she hung up.

'Mama, are you going to work tonight?' said Takashi while they were eating dinner.

'No, I'm staying here,' Yayoi told him.

'Why?'

'Your father hasn't come home yet and I'm worried.'

'Really?! You're worried, too?' Yayoi was startled at how relieved he seemed to know that she shared his concern. She began to realise that children have quite a shrewd idea of what goes on between people even when they appear so oblivious, and the thought worried her. Maybe Takashi *was* awake last night when Kenji came home and really did hear something. If that were the case, she thought anxiously, she would have to find a way to keep him quiet. As she sat thinking, Yukihiro spoke up.

'Mama! Milk's in the garden, but he won't come when I call him.'

'Who cares?' she shrieked, suddenly furious. 'I can't stand that cat!' The tone was so unusual for her that Yukihiro dropped his chopsticks and looked up at her in shock. Takashi looked away, as if not wanting to see anything. Noting his reaction, she decided she had better talk to Masako about Takashi and the cat as soon as possible. She had already decided it was best to leave everything to Masako. It never crossed her mind, though, that this was the same attitude she'd adopted years earlier when she had first fallen in love with Kenji.

4

Masako had spread a second plastic tarp on the lid covering the bath tub, and on it she had piled the forty-three bags. The lid had warped under the weight – which was approximately that of a grown man.

'Even without the blood, it's still pretty heavy,' she said, half to herself.

'I don't believe you,' Kuniko muttered.

'What did you say?' Masako asked.

'I said, "I don't believe you." I mean, this hasn't really bothered you at all, has it?' Kuniko was frowning in disgust.

'Who says it hasn't?' Masako shot back. 'But what bothers me more is someone who would run up a mountain of debt, drive around in an imported car, and then have the nerve to come to me for a loan.' Almost instantly, Kuniko's small eyes filled with tears. She usually wore elaborate make-up, but there'd been no time for that this morning. Oddly enough, her bare face looked younger and more innocent as a result.

'You think so?' she managed to say. 'But I'm still not as bad as you. You did this willingly, but I was tricked into it.'

'Really? Then you don't want the money?'

'No, I want it. I'm screwed without it.'

'You're screwed anyway,' said Masako, 'whether you make your payment or not. I know. I've seen lots of people like you.'

'Seen them where?'

'In my old job,' Masako said, looking calmly at her. A woman like this deserves what she gets, she was thinking.

'And just what was your old job?' Kuniko said, unable to hide her curiosity.

'None of your business,' Masako told her, shaking her head.

'Now she gets mysterious all of a sudden.'

'Just drop it. If you want the money, then take the bags.'

'I'll take them, but if you ask me, there are limits as to what a person can do.'

'I like that, coming from you,' Masako laughed. Kuniko seemed about to answer, but something – perhaps the thought of the yakuza who would be coming to see her – made her hold her tongue. Her tears had dried and, in their place, sweat was dripping down her nose. 'You helped us because you wanted the money. That makes you as guilty as the rest of us, so stop acting so priggish.'

Kuniko started to speak but the tears came welling up again and she fell silent.

'Sorry to butt in,' said Yoshie, her eyes puffy with exhaustion, 'but I've got to be getting home. My mother-in-law must be awake by now, and I've still got a lot to do.'

'Okay, Skipper,' said Masako, pointing at the bags of bones and flesh. 'I hate to ask, but could you take a few of these with you?' Yoshie grimaced.

'But I'm on a bike. I can't just load them in the basket. How am I going to hold my umbrella?' Masako glanced out the window. The rain had stopped, and there were patches of blue sky. It would get hot again in no time. They would have to get rid of the bags soon or they'd begin to smell. The intestines had already been half-rotten.

'It's stopped raining,' she said.

'But I just can't,' Yoshie protested.

'Then how are we going to offload them?' Masako asked, folding her arms and leaning against the tiled wall. She turned to look at Kuniko who was still standing in the changing room. 'You take some, too,' she said.

'You want me to put them in my trunk?!' Kuniko gasped.

'You bet I do. Are you telling me your car is too fancy?' Why did they seem so dense, she wondered. 'This isn't like the factory where you can punch out the minute the shift is over. You aren't finished here until you've found a place to get rid of these so they'll never be discovered. Then you'll get paid. And if somebody does find out about them, we have to be sure they can't be traced to us.'

'I wonder if we can trust Yayoi not to talk,' said Yoshie.

'If she does, we can say she was blackmailing us.'

'Fine, then I'll say that you were blackmailing me,' said Kuniko, determined to stir things up again.

'Go ahead. Then I won't have to pay you.'

'You really are horrible, you know that?' Kuniko said, stifling a sob, before thinking better of it and changing the subject. 'You know, I think it's so sad – about this poor man. And you don't seem to feel a thing. I can't believe it!'

'Will you shut up!' Masako bellowed. 'It has nothing to do with us! It's between Yayoi and him; and anyway, it's over.'

'But I can't help thinking,' Yoshie put in, her own voice growing emotional, 'that he might even be glad that we did this to him. I mean, when I used to read about these dismemberings, I thought it sounded terrible. But it's not really like that, is it? There's something about taking somebody apart so neatly, so completely, that feels almost respectful.' Here she goes again with her self-justifications, thought Masako. But even so, she had to admit that there *was* something proper and orderly, almost satisfying, about finishing filling the forty-three bags. She looked at them again, lined up neatly on the bath-tub cover.

After taking off the head, they had removed the arms and legs and then cut them up at the joints. Each foot had been divided into two parts, with the shins and thighs also being cut in half, making a total of six pieces and six bags per leg. The arms had been divided into five bits. As they were bagging them, it occurred to Masako that there was an outside chance that the hands would be found, so she'd had Yoshie slice off the fingerprints, as if she were shaving sashimi. In the end, they had twenty-two bags from just the arms and legs.

It was the torso that had presented the real problems and had taken the most time. First, they had cut it in half lengthwise and removed the organs. These alone had filled eight more bags. Then they'd sliced off the flesh and separated the ribcage, sawing it into neat rounds. Twenty bags, all told. When you counted the head, it came to a total of forty-three bags. Ideally, they would have made even smaller segments, but the work had been unfamiliar and had taken more than three hours. It was after 1.00, and they had reached the end of their time and energy.

Everything had gone into city-approved garbage bags, and these had been sealed and the tops folded down to double the thickness. Then they put each bag in a second one so that the contents were no longer visible through the opaque plastic. If nobody realised what was inside, the bags would simply be incinerated along with the rest of the garbage in Tokyo. The one drawback was the weight of the bags, which were a little over a kilogram each. To avoid attracting attention to the unusual contents, they took the precaution of mixing up different parts of the body: an organ with a piece of leg, a shoulder with the fingers. Kuniko had made a fuss about it, but Masako had insisted that she help with the bagging. Yoshie suggested that they wrap the parts in newspaper first, but then they realised that a particular edition of the paper could probably be traced to a specific neighbourhood or district, so they gave up on that idea. But even after the whole body was packed up, the problem remained: where were they going to dispose of the bags?

'Since you're on your bike, you take five,' Masako told Yoshie. 'Kuniko, you take fifteen, and I'll do the rest, along with the head. Wear gloves so you don't get fingerprints on them.'

'What are you going to do with the *head*?' Yoshie asked, looking uncomfortably at the largest bag. Even concealed by the plastic, it was still recognisable for what it was, sitting almost regally on the lid of the tub where they had left it when they first cut it from the body.

'The *head*?' Masako said, imitating Yoshie's reverent tone. 'I'll bury it somewhere later. I don't see any other way of getting rid of it. If they find that, we're in big trouble.'

'Once it's rotted, it won't matter,' said Yoshie.

'But they can identify it from dental records or something,' Kuniko put in, trying to sound knowledgeable. 'That's what they do in plane crashes.'

'Anyway, make sure you take the bags somewhere far from here, and don't leave them all in one spot. And be sure no one sees you,' said Masako.

'So it'd probably be best to do it tonight, on the way to the factory,' Yoshie said.

'But the cats and crows might get at them if they sit all night,' said Kuniko. 'Wouldn't it be better to do it early tomorrow morning?'

'As long as you find a place where nobody keeps track of the garbage, it doesn't really matter. But make sure you get as far from here as possible,' Masako repeated.

'Masako, there's just one more thing,' Kuniko added, almost timidly. 'I was wondering if we could get our money today – just fifty thousand, or even forty-five would do. So I can make my payment. And then if I could borrow just a bit more to live on for a few days . . .'

'Okay,' said Masako. 'I'll take it out of your share.'

'And how much is my share?' she asked. Her eyes were still wet with tears, but there was a glint in them now. Yoshie glanced at her and awkwardly patted her pocket. Only Masako knew that it contained the money from Kenji's wallet.

'Let's see,' said Masako. 'You filled the bags, but you didn't help with the dirty work, so I'd say ¥100,000 would be about right. And ¥400,000 for the Skipper. That is, if Yayoi can come up with that kind of money.' Yoshie and Kuniko glanced at one another with distinct disappointment in their eyes. But perhaps because Yoshie realised she was getting the bigger share, and perhaps because Kuniko decided she was glad she'd avoided the really nasty job – or maybe because both of them were more than a little afraid of Masako – neither of them said anything else.

'I'd better be going,' said Yoshie, before walking out the door without looking back.

'Masako, do you want to meet at the parking lot tonight?' Kuniko said.

'Oh. No, let's forget about that.' Kuniko eyed her suspiciously as Masako loaded the garbage bags into a larger plastic bag.

'Did something happen last night?' she asked. 'You were awfully late.'

'No, nothing.'

'Really?' she said, still looking dubiously at her.

When they were gone, Masako took her bags, along with Kenji's shredded clothes and other possessions, out to the trunk of her car. She would do a little reconnoitring on the way to work, then dump everything either tonight or tomorrow morning on the way home. Next, she found a stiff brush and scrubbed every inch of the bathroom. When she was done, however, she still had the feeling that there was blood sticking between the tiles. And even after she'd opened the windows and turned on the ventilation fan, she was sure she could smell the gore and decay.

No, it was just an illusion, a sign of weakness, she told herself. Yoshie had been convinced that her hands still smelt of blood even after she washed them, so she'd soaked them in cresol until they were almost ready to dissolve. And though she hadn't done anything but load the bags, the mere sight of the bits and pieces had sent Kuniko running to puke in the toilet. Ridiculously, while she was stuffing the bags, she'd sworn she would never eat meat again. Masako herself had managed to take the whole thing in her stride, relatively speaking. And if she was scrubbing the bathroom until it glistened, it was because she was worried that, in the unlikely event of a police search, they might turn up traces of blood. She made it a policy to take a rational approach to things, and it would be humiliating to find that she too was suffering from the same delusions.

She spotted a hair on the bathroom wall. Short and stiff, it was clearly a man's. Picking it up, she wondered whether it belonged to her husband or her son, or perhaps Kenji. But then she realised how silly it was to worry about it. Short of a DNA test, there was no way of telling whose head – either living or dead – it had come from. She washed it unceremoniously down the drain, and with it any fancies of her own.

After calling Yayoi about the money, she finally lay down in bed. It was already after four o'clock. Usually, she was in bed by nine in the morning and up again around four; so although her body was exhausted, her mind was unusually clear and she found it difficult to get to sleep. Getting out of bed again, she went to the refrigerator and drank a beer. She hadn't been this tense since she'd lost her previous job. Back in bed, she found herself still tossing and turning in the humid, late afternoon heat.

*

She had only meant to lie down for an hour or so, but when she opened her eyes she could feel the dank night air coming through the open window. Checking her wristwatch, which she'd left on, she found it was already past eight. She got out of bed. Despite the cool evening, her T-shirt was damp with sweat. She remembered that she'd had a number of bad dreams, but she couldn't recall what they were about. She could hear the sound of the front door opening. That would be Yoshiki or Nobuki, but she'd gone to bed without making dinner. She walked slowly toward the living room.

Her son was at the dining-room table eating a take-out meal that he'd apparently bought at the convenience store down the street. He'd probably come home earlier and, finding that there was nothing to eat, had gone out to get it. Masako stood next to the table. He said nothing to her, though his face looked slightly tense. It was possible he had sensed that something was different in the house, but, whatever the reason, he sat staring, ill at ease, somewhere beyond her. As she watched him, Masako reminded herself that he'd always been a sensitive child.

'Did you get anything for me?' she said.

Now that she had addressed him directly, he looked down at the food in front of him. He seemed defensive, almost as if he had something to protect. But what? Masako herself had long since discarded things that needed protecting.

'Is it good?' she asked. Still refusing to answer, Nobuki put down his chopsticks and stared at the table. Masako picked up the plastic lid and checked the date and place of manufacture: 'Miyoshi Foods, Higashi Yamato Factory, shipped at 3.00 p.m.' Perhaps it was a coincidence, or maybe Nobuki had done it on purpose, but it was one of the 'Lunch of Champions' meals, made at their own factory that afternoon. Finding the sight of the food painful, she looked around at the orderly living room. She thought about what she and the others had been doing here this afternoon, and it all seemed unreal. Nobuki picked up his chopsticks and quietly resumed his meal.

Masako sat down across from him and stared blankly as her mute son worked at his food. She remembered how she'd felt about Kuniko today, an almost savage sense that she wanted to be quit of any superficial, changeable human relations. But here before her was one relationship she couldn't change, and the thought made her feel utterly helpless.

Getting up from the table, she went into the darkened bathroom. She turned on the light and inspected the tiles she had scrubbed that afternoon. They had dried now and looked almost absurdly clean. She began filling the tub. Keeping one eye on the rising water level, she climbed out of her clothes and rinsed off with the shower hose in the washing area next to the tub. She remembered how anxious she had been to wash away any trace of Kazuo Miyamori last night at the factory. Since then she had stood ankle-deep in Kenji's blood and got bits of his flesh deep under her fingernails, yet somehow it was still the other man she wanted to wash away as she scrubbed her body. She thought over what Yoshie had said about the dead being no different from the living, and she nodded to herself as she stood under the shower. A dead body was revolting, but it couldn't move. Miyamori, on the other hand, could still make a grab for her, and that, she thought, made him worse.

Masako left the house two hours earlier than usual, with the various pieces of Kenji plus the head all safely stowed in her trunk. She noted with relief that her husband hadn't come home yet. Unlike her relationship with her son, her marriage was something she could change if she wanted to; maybe it was better not to dredge up her feelings about Kuniko.

She pulled on to the Shin-Oume Expressway, heading toward

the city. The inbound lanes were empty, and she drove slowly, looking about at the scenery. She was determined to forget the shift that lay ahead of her and the body behind her in the trunk and try to look at the familiar sights around her with fresh eyes. The road crossed a large viaduct at a place where a water purification plant stretched away to the left. From the top of the bridge, the lights of the Ferris wheel at the Seibu Amusement Park looked like an enormous coin sparkling in the distance. She had forgotten all about this spot. It had been ages ago, not since Nobuki was a small child, that they had last ridden the Ferris wheel. And now as he had turned into a stranger, she had crossed the border of a strange land.

The road followed the concrete wall of the Kodaira cemetery on the right for a time and then passed a huge driving range that looked at night like a giant birdcage. Masako turned right into Tanashi City. After heading on for a few minutes past private houses and the occasional field, she came to a large apartment complex. Since the company she'd worked for had been located in Tanashi, Masako knew her way around. She knew that these apartment blocks contained lots of units and that they were badly managed, and she remembered that the garbage collection area behind them was open and easily accessible. She parked next to the garbage shed and quickly took five bags from the trunk. There were several large blue garbage cans in the shed labeled 'Burnable' and 'Non-Burnable' in big letters, and stacked next to them were piles of plastic bags. Pushing some of them aside, she shoved the ones she'd brought deep into the pile. Kenji's body had become indistinguishable from the household trash it had joined.

She continued on her rounds. Each time she came across a large apartment building, she would check the layout, and if it seemed as though she could do so inconspicuously, she would drop off several bags. And as she drove through the neighbourhoods, if she found a lonely garbage collection spot, she would stealthily leave a few more. By the end of the day, not only had Kenji's body and clothes been cut to pieces, the pieces themselves had been scattered far and wide. All that remained was his head and the few things they had found in his pockets.

She would have to start for the factory now if she was to be on time for the shift. As the trunk had emptied, her spirits had lifted. She was a little worried about how Yoshie had managed without a car, but she hadn't taken many bags, so she had probably been able to offload them. At any rate, she knew she could rely on the Skipper. The real problem was Kuniko. It had been risky giving fifteen bags to a person like that, and it occurred to Masako that if they were still in her car when they got to the factory, she should probably take them herself.

Retracing her route in the other direction, she reached the factory parking lot in half an hour. Kuniko hadn't arrived yet, so she waited for a while in the Corolla. When there was still no sign of Kuniko's flashy car, she began to wonder if she'd decided to take the night off after the shock of the afternoon. Her first reaction was to be angry, but then she thought better of it, realising that there was nothing suspicious in Kuniko's missing work.

The air outside seemed drier and much cooler than it had earlier in the day, and Masako could distinctly smell the odour of fried food coming from the factory. She remembered the concrete cover over the culvert that followed the road by the abandoned factory, and the holes in the cover that she had noticed last night. If she dropped Kenji's key holder and wallet down one of them, they would probably never be found. And tomorrow she could find a spot to bury the head, somewhere near Lake Sayama.

She suddenly felt a strong desire to be rid of Kenji's possessions and free of the whole business. At the sight of the shutters and the thick stand of grass, she remembered that Kazuo had said he'd be waiting for her, but after their encounter this morning, she doubted he would keep his promise. Still, she looked around for a moment before she approached the edge of the drainage ditch. Straining her eyes in the darkness, she found several holes in the concrete. She took the key holder and the empty wallet from her bag and dropped them into one of them. Feeling a twinge of relief at the sound of the splash they made somewhere below her, she set off toward the twinkling lights of the factory. She never noticed Kazuo Miyamori, crouched next to the rusty shutter where he had pinned her the night before.

5

Kuniko took a deep breath the moment she had escaped Masako's house. The weather was showing signs of improvement, and there were even patches of blue sky here and there. The air was still damp, but it felt clean and fresh and it seemed to revive her a little. What spoilt it all, though, was this black bag she had with her, containing fifteen more bags full of the most horrifying stuff. At the thought, she gagged, her face twisting in a scowl. Even the air in her lungs which had seemed so clean a minute ago now felt warm and sickening.

She set the bag on the ground and fumbled with the lock of the trunk of the Golf. On opening it, she got a whiff of gasoline mixed with dust, and again thought she might vomit. But what she had to put in there was much worse, much more sickening. As she was scraping aside a layer of tools and umbrellas and shoes to make room for the bag, she realised she still couldn't fully believe what she'd just done. The unnerving feel of the pink lumps of flesh through her rubber gloves, the shards of white bone, the slabs of pale skin with tufts of hair – as the details came back to her, Kuniko again swore off meat for ever.

She had played along with Masako and promised to be careful

disposing of the bags, but now that she was standing here with them, she just wanted to unload them as soon as she could. In fact, she didn't even want to put this creepy stuff in her precious car for even a moment. It was probably already rotting and would start to stink up everything. The smell would get into her soft leather seats, and no amount of air freshener would cover it up. She'd be haunted by it for ever. By this point she had worked herself into a state and stood looking around Masako's neighbourhood for a place where she could simply dump the whole mess.

A short distance away, she could see a small cluster of houses that had just been built in the corner of one of the fields. Next to it, Kuniko noticed a concrete wall surrounding a trash collection site. Turning first to make sure that Masako wasn't watching, she headed in that direction, lugging the heavy black bag. She knew that if it were found here, it might be traced to Masako, but at this point she didn't care. They'd forced her into it, anyway, hadn't they? She tossed the bag into the neatly swept enclosure. The outer bag tore slightly as it landed, revealing one of the inner bags; but, telling herself she didn't care, Kuniko turned and ran.

'Wait!' a voice called out, and she stopped cold. An elderly man in work clothes stood in front of the place, an angry look on his tanned face. 'You don't live around here, do you?'

'No . . .' Kuniko stammered.

'You can't leave this here,' the man said, picking up the bag and shoving it at her. 'People like you are always coming around, so I keep an eye out from over there,' he said, nodding triumphantly toward the field.

'I'm very sorry,' said Kuniko, who tended to wilt under criticism. She took the bag and fled back to her car, where she tossed it in the trunk without a second thought and started the engine. Glancing in the rear-view mirror, she could see that the old man was still watching her. 'Stupid old coot,' she said, putting the car in gear. 'Drop dead!' She drove around aimlessly for a while, realising at last that it was going to be difficult to find a place to drop off the stuff without being noticed. She wondered gloomily why she had ever allowed herself to get mixed up in this. And why *fifteen* bags? They weighed so much she was likely to be noticed just lugging them around. But still, what she wanted most was just to be rid of them. Her eyes darted from side to side as she clutched the steering wheel, brooding. She was so distracted that several times she failed to notice when the red light had changed, and the car behind her gave a rude honk.

Passing again through a small city-run housing complex that she'd seen earlier in the day, she noticed a group of young mothers watching their children playing in a run-down park. She saw one of them toss the wrapper from a snack cake into a trash can next to a bench, and an idea suddenly popped into Kuniko's head: she would get rid of the bags in a park. There were always trash cans in parks, and not too many people around to notice. That was it! A park, preferably a big one with several unguarded entrances. Delighted with her idea, Kuniko felt almost cheerful. She drove along, humming to herself.

She had once come to Koganei Park with her friends from the factory to see the cherry blossom. Hadn't she heard somewhere that it was the largest park in Tokyo? Surely, if she left this God-awful garbage here, no one would find it. She drove around to the back of the park and stopped on the bank of the Shakujii River. No one was about on a weekday afternoon. Remembering the gloves Masako had given her, she put them on before taking the black bag out of the trunk. She entered the park through a back gate and carried the bag into a thick stand of tall trees that had been left to grow wild. The new foliage had a pungent smell. Leaving the path, she walked for a while though the dense, wet weeds. She soon noticed that her shoes were soaked and her hands were beginning to sweat inside the gloves. Panting from the weight of the bag, she looked around for a place to leave things without arousing suspicion, but as far as she could see, there were no trash cans here deep in the woods.

Unexpectedly, the trees thinned and she was standing on the edge of a large, open area. Since it had just stopped raining, there was almost no one in sight – a different place entirely from the crowded park she remembered from cherry blossom time. She took a quick inventory: two young men playing catch, a man taking a leisurely walk, a couple in bathing suits necking on a plastic tarp, a small cluster of housewives watching their children play, and an older man walking a big black dog. That was it. She wasn't likely to find a better spot, she thought, congratulating herself.

Walking from tree to tree as inconspicuously as she could, she made the rounds of the trash cans in the area. Her first stop was a large, basket-shaped one by the tennis courts. Leaving one bag there, she made her way to another can next to some playground equipment: two more bags. As she passed a group of old people out for a walk, she tried to look as nonchalant as possible, staring off into the woods. In all, she spent nearly an hour wandering the park in search of places where she could leave the bags without anyone noticing.

At last she was done, and along with feeling relieved Kuniko realised she was hungry, not having eaten anything since breakfast, so she went to look for a refreshment stand. When one came into view, she peeled off her gloves, stuffed them and the now empty black bag into her purse, and jogged up to the counter, where she bought herself a hotdog and a Coke. She then sat down on a long bench to enjoy them. Once she'd finished, she walked over to a garbage can to throw away the paper plate and cup; but, glancing inside it, she noticed a mass of flies gathered on a pile of noodles. If the bags ripped where she left them, she thought, the flies would come like this. The bits of flesh would rot, the flies would come, and then maggots. . . . Her mouth filled with a sour taste and, not for the first time that day, she felt like throwing up. She needed to get home and rest as soon as possible. Lighting a menthol cigarette, she set off across the wet grass.

A short time later, Kuniko staggered down the passageway in her building and stopped outside her door. As she stood there for a moment, dazed from lack of sleep, from the shock of what she'd seen at Masako's, and from her labours in the park, she realised that a young man who'd been standing in a corner was now walking slowly toward her. She gave him a quick once-over: dark suit, black attaché case – might be a salesman of some sort. She couldn't stand salesmen, so she quickly found her key and unlocked the door; but as she was about to slip inside, the man called out to her.

'Excuse me, but are you Jonouchi-san?' he said. The voice sounded somehow familiar. How did he know her name, though? She turned and gave him a suspicious look. Smiling broadly, the man came a few steps closer. She could see now that the dark suit was made of linen, with a small check pattern, and his tie was a nice shade of yellow. All in all, his clothes made a good impression, as did the man in them, with his slender build and dyed-brown hair. Noting that he looked a lot like the young celebrities you saw on TV, she found herself becoming curious. 'I'm sorry to ambush you like this,' he said. 'My name is Jumonji.'

Pulling a name card from his suit pocket, he handed it to her with a practiced motion. Kuniko glanced at the card and gasped in spite of herself when she read: 'Million Consumers Centre, Akira Jumonji, Managing Director'. She'd managed to borrow ¥50,000 from Masako, but in her rush to get rid of the bags, she'd completely forgotten to go to the bank to make the transfer. Why in the world had she gone to Masako in the first place? How stupid could she be? Normally, she hid her feelings pretty well, but her vexation showed plainly on her face.

'Look, I'm . . . I'm sorry, I've got the money, but I forgot to make the deposit. I've really got it, though.' As she pulled her wallet from her bag, the rubber gloves fell to the dirty concrete floor. Jumonji leaned over to pick them up and handed them back with a puzzled look. She felt more and more flustered; yet at the same time she was relieved that the visit was not from a yakuza type but a stylish and good-looking young man. This might just turn out okay, the optimist in her insisted. 'The payment was ¥55,200. Do you have any change?' she asked. She took the ¥50,000 she'd borrowed from Masako out of her wallet and, adding another ¥10,000 that she already had, held out the stack of bills.

'I'd rather not here,' he said, shaking his head.

'Fine,' said Kuniko, glancing at her watch. 'Shall we go and deposit it?' It was almost four o'clock, but they would still be able to make the transfer at an ATM.

'No, that won't be necessary. I can take it here, but I just thought you might prefer to do it someplace more private.'

'Oh, I understand,' said Kuniko, bowing shyly.

'I know how difficult this must be,' he said as he counted her change and wrote out a receipt. 'And I can tell you're acting in good faith. By the way,' he continued, his voice dropping to a whisper, 'I gather your husband has quit his job.'

'Ah, yes, he has.' Kuniko was surprised and a bit alarmed that he should know this much about her. 'You're very well informed,' she added.

'When something like this happens,' Jumonji said, the smile never leaving his face, 'we make it a policy to look into the situation. Where does your husband work now?' Looking at his pleasant face and listening to his soothing voice, Kuniko was lulled, and before she realised it she blurted out her secret.

'I don't really know.'

'I'm afraid I don't follow you.' His head was cocked to one side in just the way the cute young celebrities on TV quiz shows behaved when they didn't know the answer to some easy question. In her eagerness to help him out, she said too much again.

'You see, he never came home last night and I'm quite worried.'

'I hate to ask,' he continued, 'but were you legally married?'

'No, not exactly,' said Kuniko, lowering her voice. 'I guess you'd call it just living together.'

'Oh, I see,' he said with a sigh. The next door down the corridor opened and a young woman with a baby tied on her back emerged carrying a collapsible stroller. She bowed to Kuniko, making no effort to hide her curiosity about the man standing next to her. Jumonji said nothing more but merely nodded vaguely until the woman was out of sight. He seemed to be genuinely concerned about her welfare. 'If your husband has really left,' he went on when the woman was gone, 'what do you plan to do? I'm sorry to have to ask such a personal question, but will you be able to manage financially?'

Kuniko was stumped. That was exactly the trouble. Her monthly wages from the night shift at the factory came to ¥120,000, but almost all of that went on the interest payments on loans. She had been almost completely dependent on Tetsuya's measly salary for her living expenses. If he was really gone, then she could never make do with just a part-time salary. 'You're right,' she said. 'I'm going to have to look for a proper job.'

'Um,' said Jumonji, as if pondering the problem. His head was tilted at that charming angle again. 'If you found a job, I'm sure you could get by. It's the loans that might prove a bit difficult.'

'That's true,' said Kuniko, suddenly reluctant to say more.

'If you don't mind, I'd like to discuss your repayment schedule for a moment.' He seemed intent on following her into the apartment. Kuniko panicked: she'd never had time to clean up after her tantrum that morning and the place was a mess. She couldn't let such an attractive young man see it like this.

'But . . .' she murmured.

'Perhaps there's a restaurant or someplace nearby where we could chat?' he said. 'I've got my car.' Kuniko breathed a sigh of relief.

'Fine, give me just a second then. I'll be right back.'

'I'll wait for you downstairs. It's the navy blue Cima in the parking lot.' Smiling his friendly smile, he bowed once and disappeared down the passage.

A navy blue Cima! A chat at a restaurant about her payment schedule! Kuniko forgot all about what had happened at Masako's as she hurried into the apartment. Why had she gone out without any make-up, today of all days? Why had she let herself be seen in jeans and this T-shirt? She looked almost as bad as the Skipper! And why had she been so sure that they'd send a yakuza type to collect on her loan? She'd never imagined it would be someone so young, so good-looking. As she quickly spread foundation on her face, she pulled out his card. 'Million Consumers Centre, Akira Jumonji, Managing Director.' Managing Director. Wasn't that the boss? Captivated as she was by his looks, she never wondered why the boss should be checking on her loan in person, or why he should have a flashy stage name like Jumonji.

6

As he sipped his weak, tasteless coffee, Jumonji studied the face of the woman who sat across from him in the booth at the chain restaurant. While she had kept him waiting in the car, she had apparently applied a coat of make-up, and there was some improvement from what he'd seen in the half-light of the passageway at the apartment block. On the other hand, the layers of cheap foundation and eyeliner were like a slightly sinister mask, assumed to conceal her age and personality. To Jumonji, who as a matter of principle didn't care much for women over twenty, she looked repulsive at best – a living embodiment of his belief that all women as they grew older had something grimy about them.

Another bad credit risk, he thought to himself as he listened to her prattle on about the rigours of her factory job. His eyes had become fixed on her slightly protruding front teeth, one of which was tinged with a smear of rose-pink lipstick.

'So then, you're interested in finding a day job?' he asked.

'I am, but I haven't been able to find anything that suits me,' she said, sounding discouraged.

'Just what would you like to do?'

'I'd like to find something in an office, but nothing seems quite right.'

'If you keep looking, I'm sure you'll get something.' He was thinking that *he* would never hire her if she came to him. Her sloppy, self-indulgent nature was all too obvious, as though you could see through her like a jellyfish. In his thirty-one years, he had already met more people like this than he could count. If you didn't keep an eye on them, they would steal your pens and pencils, or make private calls on the company phone, or just not show up for work at all. Unless you caught them red-handed embezzling or up to some other scam, they came across as model employees. She was one of them, the type he'd never employ in his own office. 'For the moment then, you plan to get by on just the night job?' he asked.

'Night job?' Kuniko said, laughing flirtatiously. 'You make it sound as though I'm a hostess or something.' Laugh away, lady, thought Jumonji. I bet you wish you were a hostess, you and your lousy pile of debts. I'm starting to hate this woman, he thought, setting his heavy coffee cup down on the table with a thump.

'Mind if I speak frankly?' he said.

'No, go ahead,' said Kuniko, her face growing serious.

'To put it bluntly, do you think you'll be able to make next month's payment?' He was secretly quite proud of the expression he wore as he said this, with his well-shaped eyebrows arched at the corners and sincerity sparkling in his eyes. Few women could resist this look, and sure enough, Kuniko melted in a puddle of submission. But, he remained unimpressed. Does she think I'm that naïve?

'Well, I'll manage somehow,' Kuniko said. 'I don't have much choice.'

'That's true. But what'll we do about a guarantor for your loan now that your husband is gone?' Though Tetsuya had only worked there for a couple of years, his old company had been fairly reputable, having a listing on the stock exchange, and it was for this reason that Million Consumers had been willing to lend Kuniko the ¥800,000. She seemed to be under the impression that she simply had to say the magic words and money would appear, like rubbing Aladdin's lamp. But the truth was, without her husband – common-law or otherwise – as guarantor, they would never have lent her anything. Since this partner of hers had quit his job and disappeared, they had effectively lost their only real prospect for collecting on the debt. Her stupidity made him want to scream. What kind of fool would lend money to a cow like you?

'But I can't think of anyone I could ask to do that,' said Kuniko rather sheepishly. She had apparently given no thought to the matter.

'Your parents live in Hokkaido, don't they?' He was looking at the original loan application which he'd brought with him. Kuniko had filled in an address and place of employment for her parents, but the column for 'other relatives' was blank.

'Yes, my father is in Hokkaido, but he's been quite ill.'

'I'm sure if he knew that his daughter needed help, he wouldn't refuse.'

'No, I'm afraid that's out of the question. He's been in and out of the hospital, and he doesn't have any money, anyway.'

'Well then, someone else. It doesn't matter who it is, a relative, a friend. As long as we have a signature and their seal.'

'I'm afraid there isn't anyone.'

'Well, that is awkward,' said Jumonji with an exaggerated sigh. 'You're still making payments on your car, aren't you?'

'Yes, for two . . . no, three more years.'

'What about another loan?' he asked.

'I'm trying to avoid that.' The casual way she answered was amazing enough, but Jumonji noticed that no sooner had the words left her mouth than she seemed to pale. Forgetting the cigarette in her hand, she stared at the waitress in the pink uniform who walked by carrying a steak. As he watched her, a film of oily sweat appeared on Kuniko's forehead. Odd, he thought.

'Are you okay?' he asked.

'Oh, yes,' she said. 'It's just that the sight of meat makes me a bit queasy.'

'Are you a vegetarian?'

'No, but I'm a bit sensitive when it comes to meat.'

'Oh, I wouldn't have thought of you as sensitive,' he said, unable to pretend otherwise. He smiled apologetically afterward, but he knew that he was beyond caring about her feelings. The only thing that mattered now was how to get his money back from this dumb bitch who didn't even seem to realise how much trouble she was in. If she couldn't pay, he'd put her to work in a bar somewhere – but then again, with that face and body, she wouldn't bring in much. The best plan was probably to find some other loan shark, preferably one who was none too bright, to lend her the money to repay his loan; but now that her husband was gone, that wasn't going to be easy. So the next step was to find the husband, but when he thought about the problems that presented, it made him want to spit.

Suddenly, Kuniko looked up. 'But you know, there's a good chance I *will* have some money coming in,' she said. 'And I'm going to start looking for a day job right now.'

'Money from where?' he asked. 'Different work?'

'Well, something like that.'

'About how much?'

'At least ¥200,000.' So now suddenly she's rich? Maybe she's just bluffing, he thought, studying her eyes as they shifted about, unable to settle. They had an odd, slightly feral look to them.

In the course of his work collecting bad debts, Jumonji had seen any number of dangerous and desperate people. He'd seen men resort to fraud or robbery when they couldn't repay their debts, and they tended to lash out when pushed into a corner. But Kuniko didn't seem like that type; what he sensed in her was something messier, more suppressed. Come to think of it, it was a look he'd seen once before. He searched his memory and came up with the face of a woman who, in the wake of a visit he and his associates had paid her, had written a letter listing all her endless grievances and then thrown her child off a bridge before killing herself. People like that were blind to their own faults, having convinced themselves that everyone around them was out to get them. Once you developed that kind of paranoia, you didn't care what innocent bystander you dragged down with you.

Recognising this creepy side to her, Jumonji looked away, focusing instead on the bunched leggings and tempting thighs of the high-school girls who sat puffing cigarettes at another table.

'Jumonji-san, I think it could be as much as ¥500,000,' said Kuniko with a little giggle.

'Are you talking about a regular income?'

'Not exactly, but I think something like that could be arranged.' So, she seemed to have some secret source of cash, maybe some old man she was playing along. But personally he didn't care how she got the money, as long as she made her payments, and he decided he wouldn't bother to find out any more about her. If she could come up with a guarantor, he'd simply keep an eye on the account.

'Okay. Since you're no longer behind, we'll leave it at that. Why don't you stop by the office tomorrow or the day after and drop this off with the signature and seal of your new guarantor,' he said, handing her a form.

'Do I really have to have one, if I've got that money coming in?' she asked him with a pout.

'I'm sorry, but I have to insist. Try to find someone tonight or tomorrow.'

Kuniko nodded reluctantly.

'I'll be going then,' said Jumonji.

'Oh,' she said, still staring at her lap. The tip of her tongue ran back and forth across her mouth, as if she were tasting her lipstick.

'Excuse me.' Picking up the bill, he stood to go. When Kuniko looked up, he could tell immediately how disappointed she was that he hadn't offered to drive her home, but he turned on his heel and walked away, regretting even having to pay for her coffee. As he stood there in the entrance to the restaurant, he flicked some lint from his suit, as though to brush off the dirt he always felt these deadbeats left on him when he had to meet them.

It wasn't that he disliked the job. Most of the people he dealt with knew they were never going to dodge a debt completely and were just trying to buy time. In those cases, you simply had to stay one jump ahead of them, and when you caught them they usually coughed up the money. There was even something entertaining about the chase.

When he reached his second-hand Cima in the vast suburban parking lot, he found that there was a black Gloria with tinted windows parked in the next space. Reaching into his pocket for his key, he began to unlock the door, but as he did so the window of the Gloria slid down and a man poked his head out.

'Akira? Is that you?' It was Soga, somebody who had been two years ahead of him at middle school in Adachi Ward. After he'd left school, he'd joined a motorcycle gang, and after that a yakuza group, or so Jumonji had heard.

'Soga-san,' he said, turning to face the car. 'It's been a long time.' They had run into each other five years ago at a bar in Adachi, but he hadn't seen him since. Soga was as thin as ever, and his narrow face was pale, as if he had liver problems. Five years ago he'd seemed like your average punk, but now he was looking fairly prosperous. His hair was smoothed back neatly from his forehead. The collar of his rust-red shirt stuck up stylishly from his sky-blue suit.

Grinning broadly, Soga got out of his car. 'What the hell are you doing way out here in the sticks? Some kind of powwow?'

'I'm not in a gang any more,' Jumonji told him. 'I've got my own business now.'

'Business? What kind of business?' He leaned over, hands stuffed deep in his pockets, and peered into Jumonji's car. It was empty except for a neatly folded road map. 'You got a strap in there?' he asked.

'That was a long time ago,' Jumonji said, remembering the way they'd hung out the window as they cruised the streets.

'And the hair. You trying to look like a teenager?' said Soga, eyeing his hairstyle, which was parted down the middle and combed back.

'No,' he muttered.

'How clean *are* you?' said Soga, grabbing the lapels of his jacket and bringing his face close.

'I'm running a loan business.'

'Loan sharking? That's more like it. You always were more

interested in money than anything else. I guess we all wind up doing what comes naturally.'

Jumonji leaned back to escape Soga's grip. 'And you? What are you up to?'

'A little of this,' he said, making a sign with his fingers; it was the sign used to identify a gang that was active in Adachi Ward.

'That figures,' said Jumonji, smiling nervously. 'And what are you doing out here?'

'Oh, nothing much,' said Soga, looking over at one corner of the parking lot. Jumonji followed his gaze and saw two men standing by their cars, apparently dealing with the aftermath of a rear-end collision. One of them, the older of the two, was looking contrite, hanging his head, while the other, who was dressed in a loud shirt, shouted at him. There was a big dent in the rear fender of one of the cars.

'An accident?' Jumonji asked.

'You could say that. He took it in the ass, so to speak.'

'I get the picture.' Come to think of it, he'd been hearing about a gang that specialised in faking accidents moving into the area. He'd even received an email list of their licence-plate numbers from someone he knew in the business. Their racket was to find a likely victim and then jam on the brakes right in front of him. Once they'd been hit from behind, they would wait for the other driver to jump out and then, depending on how he reacted, figure out the best way to screw money out of him. Jumonji was familiar with the way these groups operated, he just hadn't realised that the new gang was Soga's. 'I'd heard rumours,' he said.

'People like to talk,' Soga sneered. 'But this is just your garden-variety accident. That asshole hit us. We're innocent victims.'

While they were talking, Kuniko had come out of the restaurant and was now standing there, looking nervously in their direction. When she realised Jumonji had seen her, she turned away. Well, if this lit a fire under her to find a guarantor, then he was glad he'd run into Soga.

'Soga-san, we'll be heading to the hospital,' said one of the guys who had been in the 'accident'. He had come over to report. His partner was still crouching by the cars, dramatically clutching his neck. The older man stood over him, talking frantically. Jumonji felt no pity for such an easy mark. An asshole was always an asshole.

'Good, good,' said Soga, nodding expansively. 'Akira, do you have a card?' he added, holding out his bony hand.

'I do,' Jumonji said, taking one from his jacket pocket and handing it to him with mock formality.

'Jumonji?' Soga read. 'Since when have you been "Jumonji"?' His real name was Akira Yamada, but it had always seemed too ordinary, so he'd taken the name of his favourite bike racer.

'I guess it does sound a bit funny,' he said.

'Funny? It's downright weird. You'd think you were an actor. . . . But I guess you always did like the flashy stuff. Shit, why not?' Laughing, Soga stuffed the card into his breast pocket. 'It was lucky, running into you like this. We'll keep in touch now, see more of each other.'

'Sounds good to me,' Jumonji said, trying to seem enthusiastic. It was hard to believe that at one time they'd belonged to the same biker gang.

'I could even lend you some muscle for the collection side of business,' Soga added.

'If I'm ever short-handed, I'll be sure to ask,' said Jumonji. 'But it's mostly small-time stuff that we can handle ourselves.' In point of fact, his customers *were* small potatoes, and if you leaned on them too much, they sometimes vanished, leaving you with nothing. But they were weak, and being weak they mostly needed just a little reminder now and then. The trick was to find the right balance.

'Well, suit yourself. But I have to tell you, I'm not sure I like seeing you looking so clean and proper.' He patted Jumonji on the cheek. 'You're a piece of work, you are, but I can always use someone smart like you. Kids these days are just plain stupid, and it makes my life hell. They could all use a few years in the gang to straighten them out.' He glared in the direction of his aides.

'In the meantime, you wouldn't have any money-making proposition you could put me on to, would you?' Jumonji asked, bringing up a subject that was almost always on his mind.

'Same old Akira,' Soga said. Looking suddenly serious, he turned back toward his car. A young man with dyed-blond hair, apparently his driver and bodyguard, had been waiting the whole time by the door. Jumonji stood there until they had gone and then climbed into his own car and pulled out of the parking lot. He had no interest in borrowing someone else's goons, but if there was money to be made, he was more than willing. After all, you could never have too much of it.

On a street behind Higashi Yamato Station there was a nearly deserted sushi restaurant that specialised in take-out. The awning was dirty and the delivery van was muddy, and behind the shop a young employee was using a toilet brush to scrub out the rice buckets. It was the kind of place the health department loved to shut down. And next to it, up a staircase that had a prefab smell to it, was Jumonji's office. He charged up the creaky stairs and opened the plywood door marked with a white name plate reading 'Million Consumers Centre.'

'Welcome back, boss,' the two employees chimed as he came through the door. The office was sparse: one computer and a few phone lines. In front of them sat a bored-looking young man and a middle-aged woman whose hair was done up in a wild style usually worn by women half her age.

'What's up?' Jumonji asked.

'Things are usually pretty quiet after lunch,' said the man. It was probably useless, but Jumonji told him to find out where Kuniko's husband had gone. 'It won't be easy,' the man warned.

'Well, if it looks like it's going to cost money, just forget it.' The young man looked relieved, having apparently given up already. The woman studied her bright red fingernails a moment, then stood up from her desk.

'Boss, do you mind if I go home early today – only stay till five?'

'No problem,' said Jumonji. He'd considered getting rid of this employee and replacing her with someone younger, but in the end it didn't seem worth it. At least this one had a knack for hooking the customers. Then maybe it was the man he should be firing? He sat for a while staring out the window and wondering why Kuniko was expecting to come into some money. Money was all he could think about lately, and his curiosity was aroused. Beyond the grassy plot next to the station that would soon be a new building, the summer sun was sinking from sight.

7

He could hear the murmur of insects here and there, damp, quiet sounds, like the grass swaying in the night fog. It was so different from São Paolo, where the insects sang like bells ringing in the parched summer air. Kazuo Miyamori crouched in the thick grass, his arms clasped around his knees. For some time now, a small swarm of mosquitoes had been buzzing around him. He was sure they had already bitten him several times on the bare arms below the sleeves of his T-shirt, but he was not going to move – he would not fail the test he had set himself. He often created these trials; he was afraid that without them he would quickly become a bad person.

As he sat listening in the dark, he realised that he could hear not only the insects but the quiet sound of flowing water. It wasn't a pleasant ripple, nor was it the rushing of a current; the sound he could hear was the murky gurgling of a thick, dense ooze. Kazuo knew that it was the stinking stream in the nearby covered ditch: a solid stream of sewage, mixed with bits of junk and perhaps the occasional dead animal, flowing somewhere underground.

The summer grass rustled in a sudden breeze, and the rusty shutter behind his back rattled as if it were coming to life. The lonely sound reminded him that there was a cavernous space in the empty factory behind the shutters. He had pushed her up against them – the memory made cold sweat run down his back. What had he done? What kind of monster had he been last night? As soon as he abandoned his trials, he became just another nasty human being. He picked a stalk from the foxtail grass growing around him and flicked at it with his finger.

In 1953, when emigration had resumed after the war, Kazuo Miyamori's father had left Miyazaki Prefecture and crossed over to Brazil. He was nineteen at the time. Thanks to an introduction from a relative, he had found a job on a Japanese-owned farm in the suburbs of São Paolo, and there he hoped to make his fortune. But he soon discovered that there was a big difference between the attitudes of the Japanese who had been educated in a relatively liberal post-war Japan and the more traditional pre-war immigrants who had suffered in Brazil. Before long, Kazuo's free-spirited father left the farm and headed for São Paolo, though he didn't know a soul in the city.

In São Paolo, he was taken in not by the Japanese immigrants with whom he had blood ties, but by a kindly Brazilian barber who put him to work as his apprentice. By the time he was thirty, Kazuo's father had taken over the shop, and as soon as he'd settled into his new life, he married a beautiful mixed-blood woman – a mulatto, as they were known in Brazil. In short order, the couple had a child, Roberto Kazuo. But when Kazuo was ten, his father had been killed in an accident, and so he had learned little of the language or culture of his native country. About the only things Japanese his father had left behind were Kazuo's citizenship and his name.

After graduating from high school in São Paolo, Kazuo had gone to work in a print shop. One day he noticed a poster that read 'Workers Wanted for Jobs in Japan. Great Opportunity!' He'd heard that Brazilians of Japanese descent who had Japanese citizenship didn't even need a visa and could choose how long they wanted to stay. It was said that the economy was so good and workers in such short supply that you could find a job anywhere.

Kazuo asked an acquaintance about the situation in Japan and was told that it was the most prosperous country in the world. The stores were full of every imaginable product, and the weekly salary there was nearly as much as he made in a month at the print shop in São Paolo. Kazuo had always been proud of his Japanese heritage, and if the opportunity ever arose, he thought he'd like to see the place his ancestors had come from.

A few years later, he ran into the man he had consulted about Japan, who this time was driving a brand-new car, having just returned to Brazil after spending two years working in a Japanese car factory. Kazuo was jealous. The economic situation in Brazil was bad, with no prospects of improving, and he could only dream of owning a car on the little he made at the print shop. He decided then and there that he, too, would go to work in Japan. If he could last two years, he could get a car for himself, and if he stayed longer, he might even earn enough for a house – and he would see his father's homeland into the bargain.

He had worried that his mother would be against his going, but when he told her what he was thinking, she agreed almost at once. Though he didn't know the language or the culture, his blood was half Japanese, she told him, so the people there would treat him as part of the family. That was only natural. There were successful Brazilian Japanese who had managed to send their children to college and secure a place for them among the country's elite, but Kazuo's situation was different. He was the son of a barber from the poor part of town, and it made all the sense in the world for him to go abroad to seek his fortune. Then he could return to Brazil with his savings and make a success of himself. He would be following in the footsteps of the man whose independent spirit he'd inherited.

Kazuo quit the print shop where he had worked for six years, and six months ago he had arrived at Narita Airport. It had been an emotional moment, with him thinking of his father coming all alone to Brazil at the age of nineteen. Kazuo was twenty-five when he arrived in Japan as a guest worker on a two-year contract.

But he soon found that the land of his forefathers didn't pay much attention to the fact that its blood was running in his veins. At the airport, on the streets, he knew he was seen as a *gaijin*, a foreigner, and it burned him up. 'I'm half Japanese,' he wanted to shout. 'I'm a Japanese citizen.' But to these people, anyone who didn't share their facial features, who didn't speak their language, just wasn't one of them. In the end, he decided the Japanese as a whole tended to judge most things by their appearance; and the idea of fellowship, which his mother had taken for granted and which involved going beyond appearances, was something few people here were actually willing to follow up on. The day he realised that his face and physique would forever consign him to the status of a *gaijin*, Kazuo gave up on Japan. It didn't help matters that his job at the boxed-lunch factory was less interesting than the work he'd done at the print shop back in Brazil. It was mindless, back-breaking work that seemed designed to break your spirit, too.

So he had decided to think of his time in Japan as a spiritual test – a two-year test to see whether he could save up the money for a car. Kazuo's mother was a devout Catholic, but his was a different kind of spiritual discipline. Not God but his own willpower would give him the strength, the self-control to reach his goal. But last night, for the first time in a long while, he had let his self-control slip. He put the stalk of grass in his mouth and raised his eyes. Compared to Brazil, there were almost no stars in the sky.

Yesterday had been his day off. The Brazilian employees at the factory were on a five-day cycle, four days on and one off. This odd schedule numbed the body's internal clock, which was normally set to rest at the weekend, and made the workers feel exhausted when their day off came around. So, though he'd been looking forward to the break, Kazuo had been tempted just to spend the whole day in bed. He felt dull and heavy; perhaps, he thought, because he'd never experienced the rainy season in Japan before. The humid air plastered his black, glossy hair to his head and made his dark skin look lifeless. Wet laundry stayed wet; his spirits remained damp. In the end he decided to go and do some shopping in a town known as Little Brazil on the border between Gunma and Saitama prefectures. The trip would have been quick by car, but Kazuo didn't have a licence or a car. By train and bus, it took nearly two hours.

He stood in the aisles of the bookstore in the Brazilian Plaza and read soccer magazines. Then he bought a few ingredients he needed to make Brazilian food and looked in at the video store. By the time he should have been heading back to Musashi Murayama, he was thoroughly homesick. He missed São Paolo, missed everything about Brazil. Deciding to linger a bit longer, he stopped in at a restaurant and began drinking Brazilian beer. None of his friends from the factory were there, but as he sat drinking with these Brazilian strangers, he could almost imagine he was in a bar in downtown São Paolo.

The place he worked for had a dormitory for foreign workers near the factory. Two men could rent a single room with a small kitchen. Kazuo lived with a man named Alberto, but when he stumbled in drunk around nine, the room was dark. Alberto must have gone out for something to eat. Relaxed from his day off and the beer he'd drunk, Kazuo crawled into the upper bunk and dozed off.

It was about an hour later that he woke to the sound of heavy breathing. Alberto and his girlfriend must have come back while he was sleeping and they were going at it in the bottom bunk. Apparently they had no idea that Kazuo was sleeping above them, or if they did, it wasn't dampening their enthusiasm. It had been a long time since Kazuo had heard a woman in the throes of passion, and by the time he'd covered his ears, it was already too late – somewhere inside him the fuse had been lit. For all that he'd tried to keep the gunpowder away from sparks, he'd never been able to get rid of the fuse. And once it was lit, the powder was sure to explode. He lay writhing silently on the upper bunk, his hands trying desperately to cover his mouth, to plug his ears.

When the time came to go to work, Alberto and his friend got dressed and left the place, kissing noisily the whole time. Kazuo stumbled out a few minutes later and set off through the dark streets in search of a woman. He had never felt so pent up in his whole life, as if he might die if he couldn't find some release. He was scared to think that his self-imposed trials would probably make the explosion worse. But he couldn't stop himself.

He walked along the ill-lit street that led from the dormitory to the factory. It was a lonely stretch of road, lined with an abandoned factory and a bowling alley that had gone out of business. It occurred to him that if he waited here, one or two of the part-timers would come by. He knew that most of them were as old as his mother, or older, but at the moment he didn't care. Still, it was late, and no one came. Part of him was relieved, but another part felt the violent disappointment of the hunter whose prey has slipped away. He watched the empty road with mixed emotions . . . and then suddenly a woman had come hurrying along.

She seemed to be lost in thought, and even when he came up and tried to speak to her, she didn't notice him. That was why he had grabbed her arm, almost without thinking. As she pushed him away, he could see the look of horror in her eyes, even in the dark, and somehow that had made him want to drag her with him into the thick grass.

Would he have been lying if he said that he had no intention of raping her? He only wanted her to hold him, so he could feel her softness next to his body. But when she began to resist, he suddenly wanted to force her down, to pin her there. That was when she told him that she knew who he was.

'You're Miyamori, aren't you?' she'd said in that cold, hard voice of hers, and fear had gripped him. Now that he was close to her, he realised that he knew her, too: it was the tall woman who seldom laughed, the one who was always with the good-looking girl. He had often thought that anyone who looked that gloomy must be suffering nearly as much as he was. His fear gave way to guilt about the crime he was committing.

When she had suddenly proposed that they meet again later, 'just the two of them', his heart had leapt. For just an instant, he'd felt he was falling in love with this woman, despite the fact that she was so much older. But then he had realised that she would say anything to escape from him, and he felt a black anger welling up inside. He was just lonely – what was so wrong with that? Why couldn't she humour him? He didn't want to rape her; he just wanted her to be nice to him. Overwhelmed with longing and unable to control himself, he pushed her up against the shutter and kissed her.

How shameful it had been. He buried his face in his hands at the memory. But what happened later had been worse. When she had pushed him off and fled, he'd been terrified that she would report him to the management or to the police. He remembered that there'd been talk of a man stalking women in the area. The rumour had even reached the Brazilians, and some of the women seemed to talk of little else, forming their own theories about who it could be. It wasn't Kazuo, of course, but how was he going to explain that to this woman? He had to apologise to her – as soon as possible.

He had waited there by the factory all night. It had started to rain – that gentle Japanese rain which he found so depressing – and he went back to his room to get his only umbrella. He'd waited for the woman at the entrance to the factory, but when she eventually appeared, she seemed icy cold, oblivious to the fact that he was soaked to the skin from standing in the rain. He hadn't been able to apologise properly, let alone explain to her that he wasn't the stalker. But why should she forgive him? If it had been his girlfriend or his mother, he'd have killed any man who did what he'd done to her. He decided that the only thing to do was to keep apologising until the woman forgave him. It would be his new and most difficult test. And so he had waited again, starting at the appointed hour of 9.00, crouching motionless here in the grass. He doubted she would come, but he would keep their appointment.

All at once he heard the sound of footsteps coming from the direction of the parking lot. Startled, he turned to look and saw a tall figure coming toward him. Recognising her, he could feel his pulse quicken as he crouched in the shadows. He thought she would simply pass on by, but she stopped by the grass where he was hiding. Could she really be coming to meet him? He felt a rush of joy.

But his excitement vanished almost immediately as he watched her pull something from her bag and drop it through one of the holes in the concrete slabs that covered the drainage ditch. From the sound, Kazuo could tell that whatever she'd dropped must have been made of metal. The dull splash was soon followed by a clinking sound as it landed on the bottom. But what could she be throwing into this filthy stream? Was she doing this on purpose because she knew he was hiding here? No, he was sure she hadn't noticed him. He could always come back in the morning, after it got light, to see what it was.

As soon as she had disappeared from sight, he stretched his numb legs and straightened up. As the blood began to flow again, his mosquito bites started to itch. Scratching violently, he glanced at his watch. It was already 11.30, and he should be getting to work himself. The thought that this woman would be standing there on the line filled him with a mixture of hope and fear. Tonight, for the first time, he had discovered a real emotion in the midst of his long, dull test.

He saw her the minute he entered the lounge. She was standing by the drink-vending machines next to the door, whispering to the older woman who was often with her. She was wearing jeans and a faded denim shirt, and her arms were folded tightly across her chest. It was the same sort of sloppy outfit she always wore, but Kazuo was surprised how different she looked from this morning, after the long shift. He stared at her and she stared back, but he wilted under her sharp gaze.

'Good morning,' he murmured, but she ignored him. The other person, however, the short, older one, smiled and nodded at him. This woman was one of the best workers in the factory, and even among the Brazilians she was known as the Skipper. Wanting to say something more to them, Kazuo searched through the Japanese words he knew; but while he was thinking, they went into the changing area. Disappointed, he followed them and began looking for the hanger that held his own uniform. He changed quickly and joined the usual group of Brazilians in one corner of the lounge. Trying to be inconspicuous, he lit a cigarette and glanced over at the women's side of the changing room.

There were no curtains shielding the changing area, just the street clothes and uniforms hanging in rows, so the women were clearly visible as they put on their work clothes. He could see her stern profile and the deep creases that spread out from the corners of her clenched mouth. She was obviously a good bit older than he'd imagined, probably about the same age as his mother, who had just turned forty-six. He had never met a woman whose thoughts were so impossible to guess. The pretty girls he'd been with in the past were still more to his taste, but he found himself strangely attracted to this mysterious older woman.

He watched as she stepped out of her jeans. The fingers holding his cigarette trembled almost imperceptibly and he lowered his eyes for a moment. But unable to resist, he looked up and found her staring straight at him. She had finished putting on her work pants, and her jeans lay in a heap at her feet. Kazuo blushed, but then realised that she was looking right through him at the wall beyond, her face completely blank. He knew that something had changed in her since this morning, if only because her anger toward him had faded away. Now she didn't seem to be thinking about him at all, which was even worse.

The woman and her friend returned to the lounge, work caps in hand, and passed by without a word, apparently heading straight down to the factory floor; but as they went, Kazuo quickly memorised the shape of the characters on her name tag. Then, when nearly everyone had gone down, he pulled her time card from the rack and went to look for one of the Brazilians who knew Japanese.

'How do you read this?' he asked.

'Masako Katori,' the man answered. Kazuo thanked him. 'You fancy her or something? A bit old for you, isn't she?' The man had left Japan for Brazil more than thirty years earlier but had come back recently to work here.

'I owe her something,' Kazuo said with a serious look.

'Money?' the man laughed. If only it were that simple, Kazuo thought, going back to return the time card.

From the minute he knew her name, she became someone special for him. As he placed her time card back in the slot, he noted that her schedule gave her every Saturday off. He also noticed that she hadn't punched in until 11.59 last night, no doubt because of him, but otherwise there was no sign of any connection between them. Spotting the shapeless pair of sneakers in the cubby-hole labelled with her name, he imagined that they must still be warm from her feet.

After quickly washing and disinfecting his hands, he passed through the health inspector's checkpoint and walked slowly down the stairs that led to the plant. He knew that the women would be clustered at the bottom, waiting for the doors to open. They all looked alike in their uniforms, with only their eyes visible between their hats and masks, but he looked down the line for Masako, then realised she was right in front of him, standing slightly apart and staring at something. When he followed her gaze, he was surprised to find that it led to one of the blue plastic buckets they used to collect garbage. Was there something in it that bothered her? He craned his neck to peer in, but it contained nothing but scraps of food. She gave him a chilling look when he turned around.

'Excuse me,' he said, determined to talk to her.

'What?' Her low voice was muffled by the mask.

'I was . . . sorry,' he said, blurting out the only words he could remember. 'I want . . . to talk,' he added in his halting Japanese.

But before he could tell whether she had even heard this last part, she turned and faced the door, her expression hard, forbidding. It was a shock to be ignored like that, especially since he'd only been trying to make her understand, and he felt utterly miserable.

The doors opened and the part-timers filed in to begin scrubbing their hands. Kazuo was assigned to one of the carts that delivered food to the assembly lines, so he headed for the kitchen.

It was odd, but work that had been such a grind up to this point now seemed almost fun. His job tonight was to take the heavy vats of cold rice to the machine at the head of the line. The work was hard and carried some responsibility, since the whole line would stop if the rice didn't arrive on time. But it meant that he would get to see Masako with the woman they called the Skipper at their usual stations by the rice machine. And when he brought in the first load of rice, there they were, directing operations for the middle line.

'Hurry up!' the Skipper called, '– it's about to run out.' Kazuo lifted the heavy vat with both hands and dumped the rice into the machine. Masako never glanced up from the stack of containers she was feeding to the Skipper. This allowed him to study her profile from close up, and though only her eyes were uncovered, he could tell they looked troubled. The Skipper, too, who was usually shouting or laughing or both, seemed more subdued tonight. Kazuo noticed as well that neither the good-looker nor the fat woman who usually worked with them was on the line.

8

'Where were you, Mom?' a familiar but unexpected voice had called out as Yoshie arrived back from Masako's house, utterly worn out. Yoshie tugged off her shoes and ran inside – her daughter Kazue had come home. She had never told her friends at the factory, but she actually had two children. The reason she'd never mentioned the older one was that Yoshie herself could barely stand the girl, even though she was her own daughter.

Kazue would be twenty-one now. She had quit school and run off with an older man when she was eighteen, and Yoshie hadn't heard a word from her since. This was the first time she'd been home in over three years. Yoshie sighed loudly, feeling both relieved to see her again and wary of the trouble she knew she could cause; also wondering what other surprises the day had in store for her after what she'd already been through. She studied Kazue's face, trying to hide her shock and apprehension.

The girl's dyed-brown hair fell straight down almost to her waist, and tugging at the ends of it was a small boy who was staring up at Yoshie. This must be the child she'd heard rumours about a couple of years ago, her first grandchild. He looked exactly like his useless father, and none too cute at that. He was thin and pale, with a line of snot running down from his nose. The boy's dad was a loser who had hung around the neighbourhood, never able to hold down a regular job; and now his child was watching her with a knowing sort of look, as if he'd guessed what she was thinking.

'Where have you been all this time?' Yoshie asked. 'You never even called, and now you just show up like this and expect me to be thrilled?' She had perhaps been a bit blunter than she'd meant to be, but the time for caring or even getting angry had long since passed. Her only real worry now was that her other daughter, Miki, would end up just like this one. If Kazue came back for good, she was bound to be a bad influence on Miki. And then there was the little matter of what had happened earlier this morning, and the details still to be taken care of.

'What do you mean, "Where have you been"? Your daughter comes home after three years and that's all you can say? No "Welcome home"? No "How nice to see you"? This is your grandson!' Kazue's eyebrows – pencil thin, the way high school girls were wearing them – arched dramatically. She was still trying to keep up with all the teenage fashions, but her hard life had visibly aged her. Like her child, she wore cheap, well-worn clothes that looked slightly soiled.

'My grandson? I don't even know his name,' Yoshie said, her voice thick with resentment.

'It's Issey. You know, like the designer.'

'Never heard of him.'

'Fine welcome this is, after three whole years!' As her tone grew more aggressive, Yoshie was reminded of old times. 'What's wrong with you, anyway? You look like hell.'

'I'm working the night shift at a boxed-lunch factory.'

'And you're just getting home now?'

'No, I stopped off to see a friend.' She suddenly remembered the bags full of Kenji that she'd brought home with her. The smaller bags had been collected in one sturdy shopping bag, which she now quickly hid away in the kitchen.

'So when do you sleep? You'll ruin your health if you keep that up.' Kazue's concern was blatantly superficial. When she'd been living here, she had hated having to look after the old woman in their cramped little house – just as Miki did now – and that, in part, had led to her leaving home. But there was no point in dragging up all their old battles. Why did everything unpleasant and inconvenient and difficult seem to be happening all at once? Yoshie had always made it a rule to be patient and diligent whenever possible, but this rude and slovenly girl of hers was more than she could take.

'And just who do you think would look after your grandmother? If I worked days, she'd be all alone. And when have you ever lifted a finger to help?'

'Drop it,' said Kazue.

'I do it because I've got no other choice. . . . How is she, anyway?' Yoshie added, peering into the back room. She had run off to Masako's after feeding the old woman breakfast and changing her diaper, and now suddenly she was worried. Her mother-in-law was lying quietly in the dim room, but she was awake and had apparently been listening to their conversation. 'I'm sorry I'm so late,' Yoshie told her.

She heard the old woman grunt, then say, 'Where have you been? I thought you'd left me to die.'

Yoshie was suddenly livid. How can they all be so selfish? Do they think I'm a robot? 'That would have been fine with me!' she yelled at her. 'And when you died, I'd cut you up and throw you out with the garbage! Starting with that ugly old head of yours!'

Without missing a beat, the old woman began sobbing loudly, though there were few tears in evidence. For good effect she threw in a mumbled line or two from a sutra. 'Now we know what you're really like,' she blubbered. 'You're wicked! You seem so quiet and nice, but underneath there's pure evil. I'm living in the devil's house!'

And now we know what *you're* really like too, thought Yoshie, still smouldering as she stood staring at the faded flower pattern on the light summer blanket. But as her anger gradually subsided, she felt a sharp pang of regret. Why had she said that? Perhaps this whole experience had changed her. It was all Masako's fault for getting her involved in this mess. No, it was Yayoi's for killing her husband in the first place. But it was her fault, too, for having been willing to go along with it just for the money. That was it: it was all because she was broke.

Kazue, who had been slumped against the low table, listening in silence, now spoke up. 'Come on. Yelling at each other isn't going to solve anything.'

'You're right about that,' said Yoshie, the tension draining from her body. She walked back into the living room, though she could still hear her mother-in-law sobbing.

'I changed her diaper earlier,' Kazue said, apparently intent on playing the part of peacemaker.

'Oh? Thanks,' said Yoshie, sitting down at the table. The floor was strewn with the boy's tiny toy cars. Still feeling angry, she swept a pile of miniature police cruisers and ambulances under the table; but the child wouldn't know, since he'd gone into Miki's room to play.

'Have you applied to the city for someone to help?' Kazue asked. 'They have people who come to your house.'

'I've asked, but it's only three hours a week and I could barely do the shopping in that amount of time.' Her head was beginning to hurt from lack of sleep, but she braced herself and asked the question that was uppermost in her mind. 'So, just why is it you're showing up now?'

'Well,' said Kazue, slowly licking her lips. Yoshie remembered that she had a habit of doing this when she was about to tell a lie. 'The boy's daddy has gone to Osaka to work, and I'm thinking I should get a job myself. So I'm wondering if you can lend me some money.'

'I haven't got any. If he's in Osaka, why don't you go, too, and all live there?'

'But I don't know where he is,' said Kazue. Yoshie sat staring at her, mouth hanging open. So he's left them, and she's come crawling back here with the kid. But how were they ever going to manage with two more in this tiny place?

'But . . . can't you put him in day-care and get a job?' she said, beginning to panic.

'That's exactly what I'm planning to do, which is why I need a loan right now.' She held out her hand. 'Please. You must have something put away. And I was talking with the lady next door while I was waiting for you; she said they're going to tear this place down and build a new building. Maybe when the new apartment's ready, we could come live with you?'

'And how do you think I'm going to get by while they're building?'

'Mom, please!' she screamed. 'You've got the welfare and your salary, and Miki could get a job. And they'd have to put us on some kind of support. Please! I don't even have enough to buy Issey a hamburger!' She was begging now, tears welling up in her eyes. The boy came toddling in and stared curiously at his sobbing mother. Yoshie reached into her pocket and pulled out the money she'd found in Kenji's wallet: ¥28,000.

'Here, take this,' she said. 'It'll have to do for now. I'm broke myself – I had to borrow just to pay for Miki's school trip.'

'You've saved my life,' said Kazue, tucking the money carefully away. Then, as if she'd got what she came for, she abruptly stood up. 'Right, I'm off to look for a job.'

'Where are you living?' Yoshie asked.

'In Minami Senju, but it's a million miles from anywhere and the train fare is killing me.' She stepped out into the entrance hall and slipped into the cheap, cork-soled sandals she'd left by the door.

'What about him?' Yoshie said, nodding at the boy.

'Mom, I hate to ask, but would you mind taking care of him for a while?'

'Now hold on. . . .'

'Please! I'll be back to get him soon,' she said, as though referring to a suitcase. She opened the door, but the boy suddenly realised he was being left behind and called after her.

'Mama, where are you going?'

'Issey, you be a good boy for your grandmother. I'll be back soon.'

Yoshie said nothing as she stared blankly at her daughter's retreating figure. She'd suspected something of the kind all along, so she wasn't even particularly surprised. To judge from the way she skipped out the door, Kazue felt liberated, and there were no signs of guilt about leaving the child. It was as if she'd just dumped something inconvenient in this dirty house and then cut loose. Yoshie felt a twinge of jealousy.

'Mama, Mama.' One of the toy cars fell from his hand as the boy stood calling after her.

'Come here and let Granny hold you,' said Yoshie, reaching out for the child.

'No!' he screamed. Pushing her away with unexpected force, he threw himself down on the floor in a storm of tears. The faint weeping continued in the bedroom as well.

Will they ever stop, Yoshie wondered, clearing away the toys strewn across the tatami and lying down. She closed her eyes and listened to them cry, but the boy soon stopped and gathered up his cars to play, mumbling all the while to himself. He was obviously used to being left with other people, yet Yoshie found it hard to feel much pity for him. It was herself she felt sorry for. She suddenly realised there were tears running down her cheeks, and the thing that made her saddest was the way she had parted with the money she'd taken from poor, dead Kenji. She felt that she had crossed a line and there was no going back – perhaps the same way Yayoi had felt when she'd killed the man.

Over Miki's protests, Yoshie managed to leave the boy at home and get to the factory on time. Masako was waiting for her in the lounge, and they stood for a moment looking at one another in silence. The strong emotions of the morning had drained from Masako's face, leaving just a grim mask. Maybe this was the real Masako, Yoshie thought, feeling a bit daunted. She wondered how she must look to her.

'How are you feeling, Skipper?' Masako asked. Her expression was rigid, but there was warmth in her voice.

'Awful,' she said, though she knew she couldn't explain that her long-lost daughter had turned up, dropped off her child, and left with Kenji's money.

'Sleep much?' Masako asked. Her questions were always short and to the point. Though she hadn't slept at all, Yoshie nodded. 'And the garbage?'

'No problem. I spread it around on my way here.'

'Thanks. I knew you'd manage, Skipper. But I'm a little worried about Kuniko.'

'I know what you mean.' She glanced nervously around the lounge. The shift would be starting soon, but there was no sign of her.

'She's not here,' said Masako.

'The shock must have gotten to her.'

'I hate to say it, but I suppose I'll have to go check on her.'

'I suppose so.'

'But I think she's a bit scared of me,' said Masako.

'Still, we can't afford to have her talking,' Yoshie said, staring idly at the 'no change' light flashing on the vending machine. If they were found out, it was all over. She could feel herself going cold with fear. A warning light was flashing somewhere, telling her that everything could soon come crashing down around her.

'But she's in this, too, so I don't think she'll go running to the police. Still, she's weak, and that can be dangerous.' Masako fell silent, a deep crease appearing between her eyes.

'Well, I'll leave it up to you.' Yoshie couldn't help adding – too desperate to care about appearances – 'But do you think Yayoi will be able to manage the money?' Although she was used to taking care of things at home and here at the factory, she was beginning to see how comforting it could be to rely on Masako's strength. And if Masako could be trusted to deal with the rest of it, all she'd have to worry about personally was the money.

'Everything's set,' said Masako. 'She'll get it from her parents. And I think she's going to file a missing persons report tomorrow.'

While the two of them were whispering together, one of the Brazilian workers came up to say hello. The young man was apparently part Japanese, but his solid build made him seem completely foreign. Yoshie returned the greeting, but Masako made a point of ignoring him.

'Why did you do that?' said Yoshie, upset that she should be so rude.

'Do what?'

'Treat him like that,' she said, glancing at the young man, who stood for a moment looking puzzled before going into the changing room. Without answering, Masako changed the subject.

'Do you know where Kuniko lives?' she asked.

'I'm sure she said something about a city housing project in Kodaira.' Yoshie watched as Masako seemed to unfold a map in her head and make plans for the morning. It was all a job to her, she thought, a job that had to be done well. But then she realised how quickly the money had made her, too, forget her scruples. The shame was almost more than she could stand.

'You know,' she murmured, 'we're all heading straight to hell.'

'Yes,' said Masako, giving her a bleak look. 'It's like riding downhill with no brakes.'

'You mean, there's no way to stop?'

'No, you stop all right – when you crash.'

What would they crash into, Yoshie wondered. What was waiting for them around the next corner? The thought made her tremble.

Crows

1

As Yayoi stood in the kitchen peeling potatoes for dinner, she was distracted by a shaft of sunlight shining directly through the window. She raised her hand to shield her eyes and looked away. There was a short period every year, around the longest days of summer, when the sun would shine in through the kitchen window for a few minutes just before it set. For one moment, Yayoi felt that the light was a sign that the gods were judging her. It was so bright, like a laser beam that would burn out the evil part of her. But that would mean burning out *every part*. Every part of her had wanted Kenji dead.

Still, only a corner of her mind thought like this; the rest was becoming more and more convinced that Kenji had simply vanished into the darkness after that night when they had loaded him into Masako's trunk. Whenever the children asked what had happened to Papa, Yayoi found herself wondering the same thing, unable now to see much beyond the thick darkness. It had only been three days ago, but for reasons she didn't understand herself, her memory of strangling him was steadily receding.

Still avoiding the sunlight, she closed the home-made cotton curtains and then stood for a moment, pressing on her eyes until they adjusted to the dark. She had tried to distract herself with housework and looking after the children, but her worries kept pushing up into her head like bubbles from the bottom of a pond. At the moment, however, her biggest worry was a new one: Kuniko.

*

Yesterday afternoon, Kuniko had arrived unannounced.

'Yayoi?' She had recognised the voice on the intercom and opened the door for her. Kuniko was dressed in the sort of sleeveless white mini-dress that was in fashion, with white high heels to match, but the flashy outfit looked all wrong on her pale, flabby body.

'Kuniko,' she stammered, surprised by the sudden visit and unsure whether to invite her in. At least the children were away at the day-care centre.

'You're looking *very* well,' Kuniko said, exaggerating her own surprise. The tone was meant to show Yayoi that she knew exactly what she'd done. Yayoi suddenly felt queasy; but perhaps that was only to be expected in the circumstances.

'Thanks,' she said, still hesitating. 'What can I do for you?'

'Well, you haven't been at work the last few days, so I thought I'd just stop by to see how you're doing.'

'That's nice of you.' What's she up to, Yayoi wondered. It's not like her to go out of her way like this. She studied Kuniko's bulging eyes, but the thick ring of eyeliner obscured any signs of her true feelings. In the meantime, Kuniko had grabbed hold of the door, ignoring Yayoi's obvious reluctance.

'Mind if I come in?'

Having no choice, Yayoi opened the door and let her into the entrance hall. Once inside, Kuniko looked around curiously.

'So where did you kill him?' she asked, her voice dropping to a whisper.

'What?!'

Kuniko stared at her. 'I said "Where'd you kill him?"' At the factory, she played a junior role and adopted a more deferential tone, but as she stood here now, leering at Yayoi, she seemed almost a different person.

'I'm not sure what you mean,' Yayoi said at last. Her palms

were beginning to sweat.

'Don't play dumb with me. Don't forget, I stuffed his stinking body in those bags and lugged them all over the city.' Feeling exhausted, Yayoi suddenly wished Masako were here to see what had come of taking this woman into their confidence. Kuniko stepped out of her shoes and up on to the floor, her damp feet making a sucking sound on the wood. 'So where'd you do it? You see those pictures all the time . . . crime-scene photos. They say that after a murder there's a sort of aura for a while.' Kuniko was unaware that she was standing on the exact spot where Kenji had died. Yayoi planted herself in front of this larger woman, determined not to let her get further into the house.

'So why are you here?' she said. 'You didn't come all this way just for that.'

'It's hot in here. Don't you have air-conditioning?' Brushing Yayoi aside, she made her way through to the small living room. The air-conditioner was kept off to save money, and the room was stifling. 'Penny-pinching, eh?'

Yayoi was suddenly aware that the neighbours might hear through the open windows, so she ran after Kuniko to switch on the air-conditioner and then went around shutting up the house. Kuniko planted herself where she could feel the cool air and watched with an amused look as Yayoi fluttered about. Large beads of sweat glistened on her forehead.

'Now tell me, why are you here?' Yayoi said finally, unable to hide her alarm.

'I have to admit, I was shocked,' Kuniko said, her tone almost scornful. 'You're so cute and all, and then to find out you killed your husband. I guess there's no telling about people. But killing your own children's father . . . now that's something. What will you do if they find out later that you killed their dad? Have you thought about that?'

'Stop! I don't want to hear this,' Yayoi shouted, covering her ears. As she did so, Kuniko grabbed her arm with her sweaty hand. Yayoi struggled to get free, but Kuniko was too strong.

'You may not want to hear, but you're going to. Do you understand? I held those pieces of your husband just like I'm holding you now, and then I stuffed them into garbage bags. D'you have any idea how bad that was? Do you?!'

'I do, I do. . .' Yayoi muttered.

'No, you don't!' she shrieked, grabbing her other arm.

'Stop!' Yayoi pleaded, but her grip seemed to tighten even more.

'You know what happened, don't you? They cut him up! Do you know what that means? How hard that was? You hardly even saw him – after you killed him. But I saw him, and God knows how many times I threw up from seeing him . . . and feeling him, and smelling him! It was horrible, horrible. I don't think I'll ever be the same!'

'Please,' said Yayoi. 'No more, please.'

'But there *is* more, plenty more, and you have to hear it! D'you think I did this because I owed you a favour or something?'

'I'm sorry,' Yayoi murmured, crouching down like an animal. Kuniko let go of her with a spiteful laugh.

'Fine,' she said. 'That's not why I came, anyway. I wanted to know if you're really going to pay the Skipper and me.'

'Yes, of course I'll pay you.' So that's why she's here. Feeling slightly relieved, she dropped her arms and watched warily as Kuniko stood drying off under the air-conditioner. As she studied her, Yayoi was sure she'd lied when she said she was twenty-nine; Kuniko had to be older than her. What kind of lousy friend would be vain enough to lie to you about something like that?

'When?' Kuniko said.

'I haven't got the money now,' said Yayoi. 'I have to borrow it from my parents, and that's going to take time.'

'And am I really getting ¥100,000?'

'That's what Masako said . . .' Yayoi mumbled. 'Something like that.' At the mention of Masako's name, Kuniko folded her arms across her ample stomach with an annoyed look. Her voice grew suddenly coarser.

'And just how much are you paying Masako?'

'She said she doesn't want anything.'

'I don't get her,' Kuniko said, looking sceptical. 'What makes her think she can act so high and mighty?'

'But without her . . .'

'Yeah, yeah, I know,' she nodded impatiently, interrupting her. 'Anyway, I'm wondering whether you can give me ¥500,000 instead.'

Yayoi gulped, unsure how to deal with this new demand. 'I couldn't come up with that much now,' she told her.

'When can you?'

'I'll have to ask my father. It could take a couple of weeks, maybe longer. And I might have to give it to you bit by bit.' She hung back from any commitment, worried especially that Yoshie would complain if she found out that Kuniko was now getting more than she was. Kuniko appeared to think over what she'd said for a moment.

'Okay. We can work that out later. In the meantime, could you sign this for me?' She extracted a sheet of paper from her vinyl tote bag and put it on the dining-room table.

'What is it?' Yayoi asked.

'A guarantor's contract.' Pulling out a chair, Kuniko sat down and lit one of her menthol cigarettes. Yayoi put an ashtray on the table in front of her and hesitantly picked up the paper. It seemed to be a contract from somewhere called the Million Consumers Centre for a loan that carried a forty-percent interest rate. There was lots of small print about 'compounded delinquency charges' and other things she didn't understand, with the line for 'guarantor' left blank. A circle had been drawn around it lightly in pencil to indicate where Yayoi was supposed to sign.

'Why do you want me to sign?' she said.

'I just need a name. Don't worry, I'm not asking you to co-sign the loan, just be the guarantor. Seems we're sort of in the same boat. My husband disappeared, too, so I have to have someone else to sign it. They said anybody will do . . . even a murderer.' Yayoi frowned at the last bit.

'What do you mean, your husband disappeared?'

'It's none of your business. But at least I didn't kill him,' she said with a snicker.

'I don't know . . .'

'Look, you're not taking over the payments. It's not a big deal – really. You paying me the ¥500,000 is the main thing, signing this doesn't count. Just do it.'

Vaguely reassured by her explanation, Yayoi signed the paper. If she didn't, she was afraid Kuniko might never leave; and it would soon be time to go get the boys. She didn't want her coming around again when they were home.

'Here,' she said, handing her the contract.

'Thanks,' said Kuniko, stubbing out her cigarette. Her business finished, she stood up to go. Yayoi followed her to the door and watched as she slipped into her white shoes. As she was about to leave, Kuniko turned around as if suddenly remembering something. 'What does it feel like? Killing someone?' she asked. Yayoi said nothing, staring intently at the spreading sweat stains on Kuniko's dress. She had only just realised that she was being blackmailed. 'What does it feel like?' Kuniko insisted.

'I don't know,' she murmured.

'You do. Go on, tell me.'

Yayoi's voice dropped to a whisper. 'The only thing that went through my head was that it served him right.' Kuniko took a step backward, eyeing her nervously and grabbing the corner of the shoe cupboard to keep her balance as one of her heels wobbled. 'I did it right here,' Yayoi said, stamping her foot. Kuniko looked down at the spot, her eyes wide. As Yayoi watched her, she was surprised to realise that what she'd done could scare even a thick-skinned character like Kuniko. It made her see how numb she'd been inside since the night of the murder.

'Are you coming back to work soon?' Kuniko asked, straightening up and trying to recapture her superior tone.

'I want to, but Masako thinks I should stay home a bit longer.'

'Masako, Masako, Masako! Are you two lesbians or something?' Kuniko turned and left without another word. Get out, you pig! Yayoi thought, watching from the doorway – from the exact spot where she had killed her husband three days earlier.

She went back into the house and picked up the telephone to call Masako. She wanted to discuss what had just happened, but as the phone started to ring, she hung up, aware that her friend would probably be mad at her for having signed that document.

So the day had ended without her talking to anyone else. But today she wondered if it really mattered that Masako would be mad at her. She still needed to let her know what had happened yesterday with Kuniko. Yayoi put the potatoes in a bowl to soak and went to the phone. Just as she was about to make her call, though, the buzzer on the intercom sounded. Startled, she let out a little squeal, thinking that it might be Kuniko again, but when she picked up the receiver it was a slightly hoarse man's voice.

'Excuse me, ma'am. I'm from the Musashi Yamato police station,' he said.

'Oh? Yes?' she stammered, her heart beginning to pound.

'Is that you, Mrs Yamamoto?' the voice asked. Despite his polite tone of voice, Yayoi felt a surge of panic. Why would the police be coming so soon? Had something happened? Had Kuniko gone straight to the police last night and told them everything? It was all over! They knew! She wanted to run out the back door and never stop running. 'I've got a few questions to ask you,' the voice on the intercom said.

'I'll be right there,' she managed to answer, trying to collect herself as she went out to the hall. She opened the door to find a greying, slightly shabby man with his coat over his arm smiling amiably at her. It was Inspector Iguchi from the Public Safety Division.

'So your husband still hasn't shown up?' he said. She had met him before, when she went to file the missing persons report. The clerk who should have dealt with the form had been away from his desk, so Iguchi had politely explained the process to her and taken her paperwork. He had also answered the phone when she first called, so Yayoi had begun to feel comfortable with him.

'No, not yet,' she said, fighting to keep her anxiety under control.

'I see,' said Iguchi, his manner growing more serious. 'I'm afraid I have to tell you that pieces of a man's body were found this morning in Koganei Park.' As he spoke, Yayoi began to feel faint, as if the blood had suddenly drained from her head. She clutched at the door, certain that it was all over, that she'd been found out. But she soon realised that Iguchi had taken her panic to be shock at the news.

'Now don't worry,' he added in a hurry. 'We don't know that it's your husband. We're just checking all the missing person cases in the area.'

'Oh, I see.' Yayoi managed a relieved smile, but she knew that it had to be Kenji and she could feel the panic rising again.

'Would you mind if we come in for a moment?' Iguchi said, pushing open the door with his foot and sliding his thin frame past her in one motion. As he did so, Yayoi could see several officers in blue uniform waiting behind him. 'It's dark in here,' he commented. The curtains were drawn again to block out the afternoon sun, and after the bright outdoor light, there was something slightly odd about it. Feeling self-conscious, Yayoi ran to open the curtains. The sun had sunk lower, and it dyed the ceiling bright red.

'The windows face west,' Yayoi said, as though apologising for the fact. Iguchi, meanwhile, had spotted the soaking potatoes.

'It must get hot in here,' he said, taking out his handkerchief to wipe his face. Yayoi turned on the air-conditioner and hurried around closing the windows, just as she had done the day before with Kuniko. 'Please don't trouble yourself,' Iguchi told her. He looked around, studying the room, and when his gaze settled on her again, she felt it in the pit of her stomach – the one place that bore the mark of her battle with Kenji, the one place she would never let them see. She wrapped her arms around herself and stood waiting, frozen, unable to move.

'We'd like the name of the dentist your husband used,' Iguchi continued. 'And we'd like to take his fingerprints and palm print, if you don't mind.'

'He went to Dr Harada, across from the station,' Yayoi said, her voice emerging in a hoarse whisper. Iguchi wrote down the information in his notebook as the team of investigators stood behind him waiting for instructions.

'Would you have a glass or some other object that your husband used recently?' Iguchi asked.

'Yes,' said Yayoi. Her legs wobbled as she led the men back to the bathroom and pointed at Kenji's things. They immediately began sprinkling white powder around in search of fingerprints. When she returned to the living room, she was surprised to find Iguchi staring blankly at the tricycle in the garden.

'You've got small children?' he asked.

'Yes, two boys, three and five,' said Yayoi.

'Have they gone out to play?'

'No, they go to a day-care centre.'

'So, you have a job?' he said. 'What do you do?'

'I used to work at a cash register in a supermarket, but now I'm on the night shift at a boxed-lunch factory.'

'The night shift? That must be tough.' His tone was sympathetic.

'It can be,' she said, 'but I do get some sleep while the children are in day-care.'

'I see. I understand that's becoming quite a common arrangement. . . . And is that your cat?' he added, pointing out at the yard. Startled, Yayoi looked out and saw Milk crouching next to the tricycle, staring at the house. His white coat already looked ruffled and dirty.

'Yes, it is.'

'Don't you want to let it in?' he asked, apparently worried that he had made her shut up the house to turn on the air-conditioner.

'No, he likes being out,' she muttered, her voice betraying the anger she felt at the cat's refusing to come back inside. Iguchi glanced at his watch, appearing not to notice.

'I imagine you'll be needing to go get your children soon.'

'Yes. . . . Incidentally,' she added, working up the courage to ask the question that had been on her mind, 'what's a "palm print"?'

'The palm of the hand has a print, just like the fingers,' he explained. 'There were no fingerprints on the body we found in the park – seems they'd been removed – but there was a complete palm that we might be able to use for identification. I'm hoping it's not your husband, but I have to tell you that the blood type and general age seem to match his.'

'You said the body had been cut up?' Yayoi murmured.

'Yes,' said Iguchi, his manner becoming more official. 'They found fifteen separate pieces in the park, each one about this large.' He held up his hands to show her. 'Together, the pieces are about one-fifth of the whole body. They're searching the park now for the rest. It seems they found them because of the crows.'

'Crows?' she said, sounding bewildered.

'Yes, one of the ladies who works in the park was going through a garbage can looking for scraps to feed the crows when she came across these bags. If she hadn't, I doubt they'd ever have been found.'

'If it is Kenji,' said Yayoi, making a desperate effort to keep from trembling, 'why would anyone want to do this to him?' Iguchi ignored her question and asked another of his own.

'Has your husband been involved in any kind of trouble lately? Borrowed money perhaps?'

'Not that I know of.'

'And when does he usually come home at night?'

'He's always back before I have to leave for work.'

'Does he gamble or go to bars?' Yayoi thought of the baccarat game Kenji had mentioned, but she decided against mentioning it.

'Not that I know about,' she said. 'Though lately he has been drinking a bit more than usual.'

'I'm sorry to have to ask this, but do the two of you fight often?'

'From time to time, like everyone else; but he wa . . . is good to the kids, he's a good husband.' She fell silent, having barely stopped herself from using the past tense. But then it occurred to her that Kenji really had been a good father, and she felt tears welling up in her eyes. Iguchi stood up, uncomfortable with the show of emotion.

'I'm sorry,' he said. 'If this does turn out to be your husband, we'll be wanting you to come down to the station.'

'I understand,' said Yayoi.

'But let's hope we're wrong,' he said. 'Your kids are so young. . .' Yayoi looked up to find him staring out at the tricycle again. Milk was still sitting nearby.

*

As soon as they were gone, Yayoi phoned Masako, this time without a moment's hesitation.

'What happened?' Masako said, guessing it was an emergency from her voice. Yayoi told her what they'd found in the park. 'It's Kuniko,' said Masako, sounding defeated. 'I must have been out of my mind to trust someone like her. But who'd have thought it would all depend on a bunch of crows?'

'What should I do?' said Yayoi.

'If they take a palm print, they're sure to find out it's him. But you've got to go on pretending you don't know anything about it. There's no other way. He never came home that night; the last time you saw him was when he left for the office that morning. You two were getting along fine.'

'But what if they find someone who saw him coming home?' Yayoi said, the hysteria mounting in her voice.

'You told me no one saw him.'

'Yes, but . . .'

'Pull yourself together,' said Masako. 'We knew something like this could happen.'

'But what if someone saw us carrying him out to the car?' said Yayoi. Masako fell silent, as she often did when she was thinking; but when she finally answered, her words weren't reassuring.

'I don't know what we'd do then.'

'But one thing I can't let them know about is the bruise.'

'Obviously not. But you've got an alibi for that night, and you don't drive so they'd have no reason to think you could have left the body in the park. It'll all work out. You went to work as usual, and you took the kids to day-care the next day.'

'That's right, and I talked to that woman out by the garbage that morning,' she added, as if to reassure herself.

'Try to relax,' Masako said. 'I don't think there's anything to connect you to my house, and even if they search your bathroom, they're not going to find anything.'

'That's right,' Yayoi said again, then suddenly remembered the other worry she'd wanted to discuss with her. 'But there is one other thing. Kuniko showed up here yesterday and tried to blackmail me.'

'What are you talking about?'

'She wants half a million instead of ¥100,000.'

'I'm not surprised. It's just like her. She screws up and then wants to be rewarded for it.'

'She also made me sign as guarantor on a loan.'

'What loan?'

'I'm not sure, but it looked like one of those loan-sharking schemes.' This news seemed to catch Masako off guard and she was quiet again for a long while. As Yayoi waited, clutching the phone, she was sure that her friend would be furious with her, but when she spoke again her voice was calm.

'This could be real trouble,' she said. 'If the news gets out about your husband and the lender comes forward with the contract, anybody will be able to figure out that Kuniko was blackmailing you. There's no reason for you to guarantee a loan for her otherwise.'

'That's true,' Yayoi murmured.

'But maybe they won't notice your name since you're only the guarantor. She's not asking you to pay the loan for her. She's a fool, but I don't think she'd go that far.'

'She knew I didn't have the money even if she asked, so she had me sign instead.' Yayoi wasn't quite sure what Kuniko had wanted of her, but she found Masako's calm tone reassuring.

'It just occurred to me that there might be one advantage to having the body identified,' Masako said.

'What?'

'You'll get the insurance. He had life insurance, didn't he?' Of course he did, thought Yayoi, utterly amazed. Kenji had a policy worth fifty million yen. Just when things were looking hopeless, they'd suddenly taken an unexpected turn. She sat holding the phone in the gathering gloom, thinking over the possibilities.

2

Masako checked her watch as soon as she'd hung up. It was 5.20. She didn't have to go to the factory tonight, and she didn't know when her husband or her son would be home. She should have been able to spend the evening relaxing, but suddenly this new threat was looming. Things were happening more quickly than she'd expected. It had all gone smoothly so far, but now came the pitfalls; one false step and they might be swallowed up for ever. She sat for a moment, trying to focus her powers of concentration as if she were sharpening a pencil to a fine point.

Eventually she picked up the remote and switched on the television. She ran through the channels looking for the news, but it was still too early. Perhaps there had been something in the evening edition of the paper that she'd overlooked. Turning off the TV, she gathered up the sheets of newspaper she'd left scattered on the sofa. She found what she was looking for at the bottom of the third page: a small item with the headline 'Dismembered Body Found in Park'. Why hadn't she seen it before? It was just more proof that she'd been sloppy. Resolving to be more careful from now on, she read through the article.

It said that early that morning a park maintenance worker had found a plastic bag containing parts of a human body in a trash can. A police search had turned up a total of fifteen bags from other trash containers, all filled with parts of the body of an adult male. That was all it said, but from the location and the number of bags it was obvious that it was the share she'd made Kuniko take with her. She'd simply dumped them in the trash cans in the park.

It had been a big mistake to drag that woman into this; she had never trusted her, so why had she given her such an important assignment? Masako sat chewing at her fingernails – an old habit she thought she'd broken – blaming herself for the whole mess.

Now that they'd found the bags, it was just a matter of time before they identified the body as Kenji's. There was no way to undo what she'd done, but she probably still needed to warn Kuniko to avoid any more mistakes – maybe even threaten her. But before she did this, she ought to let Yoshie know what had happened. Yoshie was probably planning to go to work again today, so she had to get to her soon. Masako and the others usually took off the Friday night to Saturday morning shift instead of Sunday, because the pay was ten per cent higher for working Sunday. But Yoshie usually worked Saturday as well, needing the extra money.

Almost as soon as Masako rang the yellowed plastic bell, Yoshie's door opened with a harsh creak.

'Oh, hello,' Yoshie said, her face appearing through a cloud of steam. She must be making soup, Masako thought, sniffing the smell of broth mixed with the faint hint of cleanser that always seemed to linger in Yoshie's house.

'Can you come out a minute, Skipper?' she whispered. She could see Miki sitting in the tiny room just beyond the entrance hall, clutching her knees like a child as she stared at a cartoon on the TV. She never turned to look at the visitor.

'Sure,' said Yoshie. 'Why?' Seeming to realise something had happened, her face had gone pale. Masako noticed how bone-tired she looked. Turning away, she took a step back and waited for Yoshie to join her outside.

The tiny area next to the door had been planted with vegetables, and Masako stared curiously at the bright red tomatoes hanging heavily from the vines.

'Sorry,' said Yoshie, coming up behind her a moment later. 'What's so interesting?'

'Your tomatoes. You've got a real green thumb.'

'If I had the space, I've often thought I'd like to grow my own rice,' she said, laughing as she surveyed the little patch of garden tucked under the eaves. 'I get kind of sick of them, but tomatoes do seem to like it here. They're incredibly sweet. Take some with you.' She twisted a particularly large one off the vine and put it on Masako's outstretched palm. Masako stood looking at it for a second, thinking how plump and healthy it seemed, despite having been grown next to this run-down house by this run-down woman. 'So what's up?' Yoshie said, looking at her expectantly.

'Have you seen the evening paper?' Masako asked, turning toward her.

'We don't get a paper,' she said, looking slightly embarrassed.

'Oh? They found some of the bags in Koganei Park.'

'Koganei Park? Those aren't mine!' she blurted out.

'I know. It must be Kuniko. Anyway, the police showed up at Yayoi's house because she's reported Kenji missing.'

'Do they already know it's him?'

'Not yet,' said Masako. Yoshie looked worried, and the rings under her eyes were even more pronounced than they'd been the last time she'd seen her at the factory.

'What'll we do?' There was a hint of panic in her voice. 'They'll find out.'

'They're bound to find out it's him,' Masako agreed.

'So what should we do?'

'Were you planning to go to work?'

'I was,' said Yoshie, sounding ambivalent. 'But I'm not sure I want to be the only one there tonight.'

'You should go,' Masako told her. 'We need to go on acting as if nothing's happened. Do you think anyone knows you came over to my house that day?' Yoshie thought for a moment before shaking her head emphatically. 'Well, we have to keep that from coming out. I'm sure they're going to suspect Yayoi, so we have to make sure they don't find out she and Kenji were having problems, or that he hit her. If they do, we'll all end up like this,' she added, pressing her wrists together as though they were handcuffed.

'I know,' Yoshie gulped, eyeing her bony arms. Just then, a tiny boy tottered up and wrapped himself around Yoshie's ankles.

'Granny,' the thin child murmured as he clutched at the worn knees of her pants. He had apparently followed her out of the house wearing nothing but a diaper.

'Who's this?' Masako asked.

'My grandchild,' said Yoshie uncomfortably. She grabbed the boy's hand to keep him from running off.

'You've got a grandchild? This is the first I've heard of it.' She rubbed the boy's head, hiding her surprise. As her fingers ran through the soft hair, she remembered how Nobuki's hair had felt long ago.

'I've never told you, but I have another daughter. It's hers.'

'Are you looking after him?'

'Yes,' she sighed, looking down at the child. He was reaching up for the tomato that Masako was still holding. When she handed it to him, he sniffed at the red skin for a moment and then rubbed it against his cheek.

'Sweet,' Masako whispered as she watched him.

'You know,' Yoshie said, 'after what's happened, having him here is almost more than I can take.'

'It's always hard when they're this small. He's still in diapers, right?'

'I've got two to change now,' Yoshie laughed, the weight of this human custody showing in her eyes. Masako looked at her for a moment longer.

'Okay. If something else comes up, I'll drop by.'

'Masako,' she said, stopping her as she was about to go. 'What did you do with the head?' Her voice was barely audible, as if she were afraid even to let the child hear. The boy, however, was paying no attention as he studied the tomato held carefully in his outstretched hands. Masako glanced around before answering.

'I buried it the next day. It should be okay.'

'Where did you go?'

'It's better if you don't know,' she said, turning to walk back to her car which she'd left parked at the end of the alley. She had decided not to tell her about Kuniko's attempt to blackmail Yayoi, or about the insurance money. There was no point in worrying her any more, she told herself. But the truth was, Masako didn't really trust anyone now.

She could hear a horn tooting somewhere nearby, the sound tofu trucks use to advertise their wares, and, through the open windows around her, the sound of dishes rattling and televisions blaring. It was the hour when the women of the city bustled around their kitchens. Masako thought of her own neat, empty kitchen and her bathroom where the deed had been done. It occurred to her that lately she felt more at home in a dry, scoured bathroom than a busy, homey kitchen.

She used the map she kept in the car to locate Kuniko's apartment complex in the neighbouring town of Kodaira. The rows of ageing wooden mailboxes lining the entrance to the building were decorated with scraps of children's stickers and hastily plastered signs forbidding advertisers to leave pornographic leaflets. The names of the current occupants seemed to be written over those of previous tenants, suggesting the building had a high turnover rate. In some cases, they hadn't even bothered with a new nameplate, simply crossing out the old name with a stroke of a marker pen and writing in the new one next to it. Checking the boxes, Masako found that Kuniko lived on the fifth floor.

She rode up in an elevator that was nearly as derelict as the mailboxes, and stood at Kuniko's door. She buzzed the intercom but there was no answer. Since her car was parked outside, she was probably just out shopping. Deciding to wait for her, Masako stood off to one side of the passageway, making herself inconspicuous. She watched the bugs buzzing around the pale fluorescent light. Every so often, one would fly frantically against the bulb and then drop to the floor. She lit a cigarette and counted the dead insects as she waited.

Twenty minutes later, Kuniko came trundling down the passage dangling bags from the local convenience store. Despite the heat and humidity, she was dressed in style, all in black, and seemed to be in a very good mood, almost humming as she came. As Masako watched her approach, she thought of the crows in the park.

'Oh! What are you doing here?' Kuniko shrieked when she noticed her standing in the shadows.

'We need to talk.'

'Now? What about?' She looked disgruntled as she studied Masako's face.

'Yes, now! Thanks to you we're in deep trouble.' Masako grabbed the newspaper that was tucked into the mail slot and shoved it in her face. The clatter of the mailbox snapping shut echoed down the passage.

'What are you talking about?' Kuniko said, glancing nervously around her.

'See for yourself,' Masako hissed. Kuniko fumbled for her key, clearly frightened by the way she glared at her.

'The place is a mess, but you'll have to come in. We can't talk about this out here.' Masako followed her into the apartment and looked around for a moment. The furniture and decorations were an odd mixture of the crude and the refined, much like the occupant herself. 'I hope this won't take long,' Kuniko said, giving her an uneasy glance as she turned on the air-conditioner.

'Don't worry, it won't.' Masako opened the paper and pointed at the article. Kuniko dropped her grocery bags on the floor and scanned the page. Masako noticed a twitch in her cheek under the caked layers of foundation. 'They're yours, aren't they? Who else would have left them in a park?'

'It seemed like a perfect place to me.'

'You are so *dumb*! They're fussy about the trash in parks. That's why I said to leave them in a neighbourhood.'

'That's still no reason to call me stupid.' Kuniko formed her lips into a pout.

'Stupid is as stupid does. Thanks to you, the police showed up at Yayoi's place.'

'What? Already?' Her pout turned to a look of shock.

'Yes! They aren't sure it's him yet, but that won't take long. All hell's going to break loose tomorrow, and if they find out she did it, we're all going down together.' Kuniko stood staring at her, as though her brain had frozen. Masako stared back. 'You know what this means, don't you? Even if, by some miracle, they didn't find out we were involved, if they arrest Yayoi you'll never see your money.' At this, Kuniko finally seemed to grasp the situation. 'But it gets worse,' Masako went on. 'For you, the real problem is that guarantor's contract you made her sign. You're already an accomplice, with her husband all chopped up in pieces, but now you tried to blackmail her as well.'

'Blackmail!? I never meant . . .'

'Never meant to what? You threatened her, didn't you?'

'But I didn't know what else to do. I just thought she might be able to help. We're all in this together, aren't we? After what I did for her . . .' Kuniko sputtered on incoherently, sweat showing on her dull-witted face. Masako stared coldly at her. Her biggest worry now was that Kuniko's loan shark would find out about the insurance money. She doubted someone like that would care much about the murder itself, but he might come snooping around if he got wind of that kind of money.

'What do you mean, "all in this together"? You've never cared about anyone but yourself.' She thrust out her hand. 'Where's the contract? Get it – now.'

'But I already took it in,' said Kuniko, glancing nervously at her watch.

'Where?'

'A place called the Million Consumers Centre, right across from the station.'

'A loan shark. Call them up, right now, and tell them you want the contract back.' Her tone was so threatening that Kuniko seemed on the verge of tears.

'But that's impossible.'

'Impossible or not, it's got to be done. This will be all over the TV and papers tomorrow, and then your friendly lender is bound to pay you a visit.'

'Okay.' Still seeming reluctant, she pulled a business card out of her purse and picked up the phone. Masako noticed that it was covered with stickers, just like the mailboxes in the lobby. 'This is Kuniko Jonouchi,' she said into it. 'I was wondering whether you might be willing to return the contract I brought in a few minutes ago.' Masako stood listening while the man at the other end refused the request.

'Tell him to wait and you'll be right over,' she whispered, reaching out to cover the mouthpiece. After she'd hung up, Kuniko's legs seemed to give out and she crumpled to the floor.

'Do I have to go?' she asked.

'What do you think?'

'But why?'

'Because this whole mess is your fault.'

'But I didn't chop him up!' she squealed.

'Shut up!' Masako yelled, fighting back the urge to punch her. Kuniko had begun to sob.

'How much did you borrow from them?'

'Five hundred thousand . . . this time.' Masako knew the routine: she'd probably tried to borrow a somewhat smaller sum, but when they'd looked into her credit status they'd lent her more than she could handle. She'd had a feeling for some time that Kuniko was having trouble keeping up with the interest payments on her loans.

'You usually don't need a guarantor for that kind of money. I think you've been suckered.'

'But he told me I'd have to pay them back right away if I didn't have one.' Kuniko was whining again.

'And you believed him?' Masako muttered.

Kuniko looked amazed. 'But he was so nice and polite. I was expecting a yakuza, but he was just a regular guy. He even thanked me when I brought him the contract.'

'They change the act depending on the audience. They knew they could get around you with a little sweet talk.' Masako made no effort to hide her contempt.

'You seem to know all about it.'

'And you seem to know nothing at all. But we haven't got time for this. Let's go.' She turned away and stepped quickly into her tennis shoes. The heels had been crushed down and she worked her toes in as if they were slippers. Kuniko followed her, still sulking.

The lights were off in the Million Consumers Centre, but Masako climbed the stairs and knocked on the flimsy door.

'It's open!' a voice called from inside.

They entered the darkened office and found a man slouched on a sofa near the window, smoking a cigarette. The grimy table in front of him was littered with a crumpled newspaper and sticky cans of coffee.

'Hello,' he said, smiling and getting to his feet. 'Come in.' His grey suit and dark-red tie seemed too stylish for the shabby office, but the dyed-brown hair fitted right in. From his slightly flustered reaction, Masako guessed that he hadn't been expecting to see Kuniko, despite the phone call.

'Jumonji-san,' Kuniko said, 'it turns out that the lady who signed the guarantor form I gave you has changed her mind and wants it back.'

'And is this the lady?' Jumonji asked, turning warily to Masako.

'No, but I'm her friend. She's married and she doesn't want to get involved in something like this. Could you please return it?'

'I'm sorry, but we can't do that.'

'Then at least let me see it,' said Masako.

'All right,' he murmured, beginning to sound disgruntled. He opened a drawer in his desk and handed a sheet of paper to Masako. She scanned it for a minute.

'There's no legal provision for a separate guarantor, not unless you required it from the beginning. I'd like to see the original promissory note, please.' At this, Jumonji's expression hardened. He pulled another paper from the file and pointed out a section to Masako.

'It says right here that "a guarantor can be required in the event of a substantial change in the borrower's credit status". Well, Jonouchi-san's husband quit his job and ran off somewhere; I think we could call that a "substantial change".'

'Call it what you like,' Masako said with a smile. 'But the fact is, she's only been late once on her payments, and then only by one day. That's hardly a reason to impose a clause like this.'

Jumonji hadn't apparently expected a counter-punch and stood staring at her with open amazement. Kuniko glanced around nervously, as if expecting someone to come up and attack them. Jumonji looked at Masako for a moment longer.

'Have we met somewhere?' he said at last.

'No,' said Masako, shaking her head.

'No, maybe not.' His tone had softened a bit but he continued to stare at her. 'I have to tell you, we have real doubts about the repayment of this loan.'

'I'll make sure she pays,' said Masako, as if stating a flat fact.

'Then you're willing to serve as guarantor?'

'No, but I'll see you get your money, even if I have to take her somewhere else to get another loan to cover yours.'

'Fine,' said Jumonji, apparently giving in. 'But I'll be keeping an eye on Jonouchi-san's payments.' He went back to the couch and sat down. Kuniko stood staring at Masako, apparently shocked that she'd been able to extract the contract so easily.

'We'll be going then,' Masako said, trying to hustle her out the door.

'Now I remember,' Jumonji spoke up just as they were going. 'You're Masako Katori, aren't you?' Masako wheeled around, and abruptly remembered a younger Jumonji, a punk with a razor cut. He'd worked as a debt collector for a sub-subcontractor to her company. A lot had changed, including the less flashy name he'd used back then which she'd long since forgotten, but the shrewd eyes were unmistakable.

'Now that you mention it . . .' she stammered. 'But you've changed your name.'

'I'll even change the rules in her case,' he laughed, 'if you're willing to vouch for her.'

'How do you know him?' Kuniko said. She'd gone down the stairs ahead of her but turned back to face her, unable to hide her curiosity.

'I used to see him at my old job,' Masako said.

'What job?'

'I worked in the financial sector.'

'For a loan shark?' she asked, but Masako refused to say any more. Kuniko stood looking at her a moment longer but then made a dash for it, as though she couldn't wait to get off the dark, empty streets. Yet it was just those dingy alleys that Masako now felt like hiding in, after seeing that shadow from the past. She too was scared. What was next? Where could she run to?

3

Why was it you could talk to dead people in your dreams? In the midst of a fitful sleep, Masako dreamed that her dead father was standing in the garden staring at the bare lawn. He was wearing a light summer kimono like the one he'd worn in the hospital as he was dying from a malignant tumour on his jaw. The sky was heavily overcast. When he noticed Masako standing on the veranda, his face, deformed from the repeated operations, seemed to relax.

'What are you doing?' she asked.

'I was thinking of going out.' In his last days, her father had become almost incapable of speech, but in the dream his voice was clear.

'But someone will be coming soon,' she'd said. She had no idea who it was, but she'd run around the house getting things ready. The garden had been from the old home her father had rented in Hachioji, but the house itself was the new one she and Yoshiki had built, and tugging at the leg of her jeans was Nobuki, who was once again a toddler.

'Then we'll have to clean the bathroom,' her father said. A shiver went down her spine. Somehow she knew that the bathroom was stuffed with Kenji's hair; but how did her father know? It must be because he was dead, too. She pulled herself away from Nobuki's tiny hands and tried to think of an excuse to feed her father; but while she was at it, the old man came tottering toward her on his sticklike legs. She could see his face now, sunken and pale, just as it had been in death. 'Masako,' he said. 'Please kill me.' The voice was close to her ear now, and she woke up with a gasp.

That was the last thing he had said to her. He'd been in too much pain to speak, or even eat, but he had managed to choke out these words. The voice had been lost somewhere in her memory until now, but as it came back to her, she shook with fear, as if she'd heard a ghost.

'Masako.'

Yoshiki was standing by the bed. He almost never came into the room while she was there, and she stared at him now, half in wonder, as she tried to rouse herself from her dream.

'Have a look at this,' he said, pointing at an article in the newspaper he was holding. 'Isn't this someone you know?' She sat up and took the paper from him. At the top of the third page was a headline that read 'Dismembered Body in Park Identified as Musashi Murayama Office Worker'. Just as she'd predicted, they had figured out it was Kenji sometime last night. But somehow seeing it in print made the whole thing seem less real. Wondering why that should be so, she read through the article.

'On the night he disappeared, the victim's wife, Yayoi, had gone to her part-time job at a nearby factory. The police are trying to determine Yamamoto's movements after he left work that evening,' the paper said. There were no additional details, just a repeat of the previous article which had focused on the most lurid fact: dismembered body parts found in garbage.

'You do know her, don't you?' Yoshiki said.

'I do, but how did you know?'

'A Yamamoto has called here from time to time, saying she's from the factory. And the article says she works a night shift. Yours is about the only one around here.' Had he heard Yayoi's call that night? Masako studied his eyes for a clue, but he turned away, apparently embarrassed to have seemed so excited. 'I just thought you'd want to know,' he said.

'Thanks.'

'Who could have done something like that? Somebody had a grudge against him, apparently.'

'I doubt it was that,' Masako said. 'But I don't know.'

'But you know her pretty well, don't you? Shouldn't you go and see how she's doing?' He looked at her curiously, evidently surprised at how calmly she seemed to be taking the whole thing.

'I wonder,' she answered vaguely, pretending to look over the newspaper which was still lying on the bed. Yoshiki eyed her curiously for a moment and then went to take a suit out of the closet. He rarely went to work on Saturdays but today seemed to be an exception. Realising he was getting ready to leave, Masako jumped up and began making the bed.

'Are you sure you don't need to go over there?' he repeated, without turning around. 'The place must be swarming with police and reporters, and I bet she'd appreciate seeing a familiar face.'

'I doubt she needs one more person bothering her.' Without answering, Yoshiki pulled off his T-shirt. Masako stood looking at his bare back, taking in the sagging muscles and sallow skin. He stiffened, seeming to sense her eyes on him.

She had long since forgotten what it was like to sleep with Yoshiki. Now, they merely inhabited the same house, performing their prescribed roles. They were no longer husband and wife, nor even father and mother. They simply went on – automatically, faithfully – going to work, taking care of the house and, in Masako's mind, gradually going to pieces. Yoshiki slipped on his shirt and turned to look at her.

'At least call her,' he said. 'Why be so unfriendly?' Masako thought for a moment, realising that her anxiety about appearing to have any connection to the crime might be blinding her to how she would normally act.

'I guess I should,' she said, still sounding reluctant. Yoshiki looked at her.

'Once you decide something doesn't concern you, you just cut yourself off,' he said.

'I don't mean to.' She realised he must have noticed the change in her since the night she'd gone to Yayoi's.

'Sorry I butted in,' he said, frowning as though at the taste of something bitter. They stared silently at one another for a moment until Masako looked down and began straightening the quilt.

'You were moaning in your sleep just before you woke up,' he added as he was tightening his tie.

'I was having a nightmare,' she said, noting that his tie didn't match his suit.

'About what?'

'My father was in it, and he could talk.' Yoshiki grunted, stuffing his wallet and train pass into his pants pocket. He'd always liked her father, so she could only conclude that his refusal to pursue the subject meant he had given up trying to reach her. He probably no longer even felt the need to do so. Nor did she, perhaps. She took her time tucking in the edges of the quilt, thinking about all the things the two of them had lost.

After he'd gone, Masako called Yayoi's house.

'The Yamamotos',' a voice said wearily. It sounded like Yayoi, yet different somehow, older.

'My name's Katori. May I speak to Yayoi?'

'I'm afraid she's sleeping at the moment. May I ask what you're calling about?'

'I work with Yayoi at the factory, and I read what happened in the newspaper. I was worried about her.'

'That's very kind of you. She's stunned by all this, of course. She's been in bed since last night.' The woman sounded as though she had already given this speech a number of times. There must have been countless calls since this morning – relatives, Kenji's co-workers, Yayoi's friends, neighbours, and no doubt the media. She was simply repeating what she'd told everyone else, like the message on an answering machine.

'Are you her mother?' Masako asked.

'Yes,' the woman said almost curtly, apparently anxious to avoid giving out unnecessary information.

'You must be devastated. Well, we're all thinking about you,' Masako said, cutting the conversation short. At least she would remember that Masako had called. That should be enough. But it would have been strange not to call at all. Now all she had to do was concentrate on keeping the rest from coming to light.

As she was hanging up, Nobuki came down from his room and, after eating his breakfast in silence, went out. To work? To play? Masako didn't know. Once she was alone, she turned on the TV and surfed the news programmes. They all had the same story that she'd read in the paper, so apparently there hadn't been any new developments.

Yoshie called a few minutes later, her voice almost a whisper. Masako knew that, unlike her own quiet night, Yoshie had been to work and was now taking a break from caring for her mother-in-law to make the call.

'It's just like you said. I turned on the TV and there it was.' She sounded gloomy.

'The police will show up at the factory before long,' Masako said.

'Do you think they'll find our bags?'

'I doubt it,' she said.

'But what should we tell them?'

'Just say that Yayoi hasn't been to work since that night so you don't know anything about it.'

'I guess that's right,' Yoshie murmured. She asked the same

questions over and over, and she seemed to repeat the answers to herself just as often. Masako was getting a little fed up with the constant calls. Catching the sound of the child's voice whining in the background, she remembered her dream. The feeling of Nobuki's hands tugging at her pants had seemed so real. It was probably because she'd seen Yoshie's grandson. If she analysed each element of the dream, perhaps it would lose its power to frighten her. 'So, I'll see you tonight.' Yoshie's worried voice interrupted her train of thought. Masako hung up.

There had been no call from Kuniko. Maybe she'd been scared off by Masako's threats and would behave herself for a while. As she started the laundry, Masako thought about Jumonji, whom she'd seen last night for the first time in so many years. The racket he was running usually made a pile of money for a few years and then folded. She had no idea what would happen with Kuniko's loan, nor did she much care, but it could be trouble if Jumonji read the newspapers and recognised the name on the contract.

What sort of man was this Jumonji? For the first time in a long while, Masako allowed herself to dredge up memories of her former job. There was nothing from that period she wanted to recall, and yet as she poured detergent into the washing machine and watched it dissolve into a swirling foam, her thoughts travelled back.

The first thing that came to mind about her old job was warming sake for the New Year's party. The party was an annual event at T Credit and Loan, the company Masako had joined straight out of high school and where she had worked for over twenty-two years. They used to invite the executives of the companies they did business with and the senior officers of the agricultural co-ops who were their principal depositors, and give a party on the day before work resumed after the New Year's holiday. All the female employees were required to come to work that day dressed in traditional kimonos, though in practice the rule only applied to the younger ones.

The other women worked behind the scenes at the party, making hors d'oeuvres, washing glasses, and warming sake. The men did the heavy work, bringing in the beer and setting up the furniture in the hall, but the women were busy the whole day, starting early with preparations and ending late after cleaning up. But probably the worst part of it was knowing that their vacation, which officially lasted from the close of business on 30 December until the morning of 4 January, actually ended a day early as a result. Attendance was mandatory, though it wasn't treated as a regular workday.

Masako, who at some point had become the oldest woman in the company, was kept behind the scenes in the kitchen. The role actually suited her well enough since she wasn't fond of being on display, but hour after hour in the small room heating up sake made her queasy and light-headed. And when her male co-workers got drunk and came to recruit the other women to pour drinks, Masako was left shorthanded. As she struggled, often by herself, to keep up with the glasses and the empty sake pots, her labours came to seem more absurd than sad. In the worst years, she was even made to clean up the pools of vomit left by her drunken colleagues. More than a few women had quit the company in despair after seeing how unfairly Masako was treated as the senior female employee.

Still, the party was just one day a year and she could manage to put up with it. What bothered her much more was that the effort she put in all the other days was never recognised and after all these years she had never been promoted or given more than the rudimentary clerical work she'd done since the day she first came to work there. Though she punched in at 8.00 a.m. and stayed until 9.00 almost every evening, she continued to do the same boring work year after year; and no matter how hard she tried or how well she did her job, she played no more than a supporting role, with all the important decisions left to her male colleagues. The men who had entered the company around the same time she did had all received extensive training and had long since been promoted to section head or better, and now even the younger men were being promoted to positions above her.

One day she'd happened to see the salary figures for a man who had been with the company exactly as long as she had, and she nearly went berserk. He was making two million yen more than her, when she, after twenty years of service, was earning only ¥4,600,000 a year. After thinking long and hard about it, she had gone straight to the section head, a man who also joined the company the same year as her, and asked to be promoted to a management position and given the same work as the male employees.

The blatant harassment had begun the next day. First, they must have misrepresented her demands to the other women in the company since they suddenly began giving her the cold shoulder. The word had apparently gone out that she was determined to get ahead and didn't care what happened to the rest of them. They stopped inviting her to the monthly dinner at which all the women got together, and she found herself completely isolated.

The men, on the other hand, were constantly after her, making sure she was the only one asked to serve tea when guests came to the office, and swamping her with copying. As a result, she found it difficult to get her own work done and ended up putting in even more overtime. Inevitably, the quality of her work suffered, and this was reflected in poor evaluations. Poor evaluations meant, in turn, that she was ineligible for promotion – which had apparently been their strategy from the beginning.

Still, she'd been determined to stick it out. She stayed at the office till all hours of the night and took home what she couldn't finish. Nobuki, who was still in elementary school, had been sensitive to his mother's stress and gone through a bad patch, and Yoshiki had furiously demanded that she quit her job. Masako felt as if she were a ping-pong ball, bouncing back and forth between her family and her office and totally alone in both places. There was nowhere to hide and no way out.

Not long afterward she had discovered a major mistake that her boss had made, and when she'd pointed it out, the man had suddenly lashed out at her. Her 'boss' was in fact several years younger and utterly incompetent.

'You keep your trap shut, you!' he'd bawled at her; he even gave her a slap. This happened after work, so that no one else could hear, but the incident had left a deep scar on her. Why did the simple fact of being a man make him so important? Was it because he'd graduated from college? Didn't her experience and her ambition count for anything in a place like this? She'd often thought of finding another job, but she liked finance and had stayed on. After this incident, however, she realised that she'd come to the end.

The humiliating assault had occurred just at the height of the bubble economy. It had been a period of frenzied business for the banks and loan companies, with money being thrown at customers almost without a credit check. For years, even clients Masako knew to be bad risks had been given loans, and when the bubble finally burst, this all became a mountain of bad debt. Land prices tumbled and stocks with them, and more repossessed properties went on the auction block daily. But the auction prices never matched the value of the original loans, and losses mounted.

In that environment, it became increasingly difficult to raise capital, and eventually a bigger firm backed by a large agricultural co-operative had stepped in to take control of Masako's company. Rumours of a merger began to circulate, and there was talk of a major restructuring and layoffs. Masako, as the oldest female employee, was the most vulnerable, and she knew she'd done nothing to endear herself to the management. She was hardly surprised when an order came from the personnel office transferring her to an outlying branch. It was just a year before Nobuki was due to take his entrance exams for high school; if she took the transfer, she would have to leave Yoshiki on his own with her son. She simply couldn't. When she refused, they naturally asked for her resignation. The blow hadn't really hit her until she heard that when they announced her retirement at the office, there had been applause.

Jumonji had begun showing up at her company after the economy turned sour and the number of delinquent accounts began to multiply. In order to put pressure on customers who were behind on their payments, even the banks had employed men like him. In good times, they had been only too eager to make risky loans, but now they were too worried to bother about appearances. Masako had disapproved of both the reckless lending and the hardball tactics, and somehow she had imagined that Jumonji shared her feelings – even while he was making the collections. She'd never talked to him outside the office, but she was fairly sure she'd seen a look of disrespect or even dislike in his eyes as he'd laughed along with the arrogant regular employees.

Masako suddenly realised that the buzzer on the washing machine was signaling the end of the cycle, but she'd been so lost in thought that she'd neglected to put in the laundry. Dissolved in a whirlpool, drained, rinsed and spun dry – it was precisely what they'd done to her. A pointless spin cycle, she thought, laughing out loud.

4

Jumonji woke up with his arm tingling. He slid it out from under the woman's slender neck and flexed his fingers. Woken by the sudden movement, she opened her eyes and looked at him from under her impossibly thin eyebrows – the face uncannily like a child's and a middle-aged woman's at the same time.

'What's the matter?' she asked. He looked at the clock by the bed: nearly 8.00 a.m. The summer sunlight was already streaming in through the thin curtains, heating the air in the small bedroom.

'Time to get up,' he said.

'No,' she murmured, clinging to him.

'Don't you have class?' She was probably still in her first year of high school – a girl, really, not a woman at all – but he was only interested in the young ones, so to him she was a woman.

'It's Saturday,' she said. 'I'll just skip it.'

'But I've got things to do. Get up.' The girl scowled a moment and then yawned. As she did so, Jumonji glanced at the inside of her mouth. It was pink; in fact her whole childish body was a study in pink and white. Taking a last, lingering look, he pulled himself out of bed and turned on the air-conditioner. A tongue of stale, dusty air licked his face. 'Make breakfast,' he told her.

'No way,' she mumbled.

'You're a woman, make me something to eat.'

'I don't know how,' she said, a hint of a smile playing around her mouth.

'Dope. That's nothing to be proud of.'

'Don't call me a dope,' she pouted, taking a cigarette from Jumonji's pack. 'You old men all sound alike.'

'Old?!' he barked, cut to the quick. 'I'm thirty-one.' She gave a snicker.

'Like I said, old.'

'Well, how old is your father?' he asked, thinking this would prove that he was still young. He was beginning to get annoyed.

'Forty-one.'

'Just ten years older than me?' he said, suddenly feeling his age. He went to take a piss in the bathroom and then wash up. He thought she would at least have put the kettle on by the time he'd finished, but when he opened the door, her dyed, honey-coloured hair was still spread out across the sheets.

'Get up!' he shouted. 'And get out of here.'

'Asshole!' she shouted back, kicking her plump legs in the air. 'Dirty old fart.'

'How old's your mother?' Jumonji asked suddenly.

'Forty-three,' she said. 'A bit older than my dad.'

'Women are useless after twenty.'

'You're screwy,' she told him. 'My mother's still young – and beautiful.' Jumonji laughed, feeling as though he'd somehow scored a point by having no interest in older women. It never occurred to him that his attitude was itself childish. Ignoring the girl, he lit a cigarette and picked up the morning paper. As he sat down on the bed, she scowled at him with a very grown-up look, reminding him again how much he disliked older women. He wondered how this one would look in a few years' time, trying to imagine her mother's face. Taking her chin in his hand, he lifted her head and stared into her eyes. 'What?' she said. 'Don't do that.'

'Why not?'

'Stop it. What are you looking at?'

'I was just thinking that you'll be old too some day.'

'So what?' she said, shaking free from his hand. 'Why d'you have to be so mean this early in the morning? It's getting me down.'

Forty-three. Masako Katori, whom he'd seen yesterday for the first time in years, must be about that old. She was as thin as ever and even scarier than before, but he had to admit she made a strong impression.

Masako Katori had worked for T Credit and Loan, which used to be in Tanashi City. 'Used to be' because it was one of those places that had specialised in real-estate loans during the boom years and had been eaten up by a bigger company when most of its accounts proved uncollectable after the bust. Back then it had subcontracted collections to the security firm Jumonji had been working for at the time. He had vivid memories of Masako from his frequent visits there.

She was always at her computer terminal, neatly dressed in a grey suit that seemed to have just come back from the cleaners. She didn't wear flashy make-up the way the other women in the office did, or flirt with visitors. She just sat there and worked. There was something about her that seemed serious and unapproachable, though it was probably this professional manner that made the guys in his own company, at least, respect her.

Jumonji had little interest in the office politics of the place in those days, but he did remember hearing rumours that Masako, who had been there for over twenty years, had become something of a pain – and that she was likely to be laid off soon. His instincts told him there was more to it than that. There had always been a barrier around the woman that kept other people at a distance, a sign that marked her as someone at war with the world. It was perhaps only natural that he, as an outsider and something of a hired thug, should be able to read the sign. Birds of a feather, they always say. And people who couldn't read the sign made a point of picking on her, it seemed.

But what really puzzled him now was what Masako Katori was doing hanging around with a loser like that Jonouchi woman.

*

'I'm hungry.' The girl's voice interrupted Jumonji's train of thought. 'Let's go get something at McDonald's.'

'Hang on a minute,' he said, opening his forgotten newspaper.

'You can bring that with you,' she suggested, wrapping her arms around him.

'Shut up,' he said, twisting away. The headline on the lead story had caught his attention, particularly the mention of Musashi Murayama. He read the account of the dismembered body found in a nearby park, stopping when he came to the words 'his wife, Yayoi'. Where had he heard that name? Wasn't that the name on the guarantor's contract? His memory was vague since Masako had retrieved the contract before he'd had a chance to check up on the woman, but he was almost certain that *had* been the name.

'Yuck!' said the girl, who had been reading the paper over his shoulder. 'I was just in that park. How gross!' She tried to snatch the paper away. 'There's this skateboarder who kept telling me to come watch.'

'Shut up!' he said, pulling the paper away from her and starting to read the article again from the beginning. He remembered that Kuniko Jonouchi had said something about working the night shift at a boxed-lunch factory – the same place this Yayoi Yamamoto worked. She must be the one on the contract. But why was Jonouchi asking the wife of a murdered man to be the guarantor on her loan? The whole thing sounded fishy. It seemed likely that Masako had gone out of her way to get the contract because something had happened to the wife – and like an idiot, he'd just handed it over.

'Shit!' he said aloud. He read the article again. Since the victim hadn't come home on Tuesday night, the police suspected that he was murdered that day and his body was cut up soon afterward. But they hadn't identified him until last night. If that was the case, then maybe Masako had just been worried about the man's wife and wanted to help her out, as a friend. There was nothing particularly strange in that. But why had Jonouchi gone to someone whose husband was missing to ask her to guarantee her loan? And why had the wife agreed? If your husband's missing, you ought to be too worried to think about anything else. And what was Masako Katori really up to in all this? She wasn't the type to lose much sleep over other people's troubles. A cloud of questions swirled in Jumonji's head.

He'd have to look into the matter, he thought, tossing the paper on to the dusty carpet. The girl, a bit intimidated by his manner, had been watching him quietly. Now she reached out timidly for the paper and began scanning the TV listings. His mind was elsewhere as he watched her. He'd caught the smell of money and it excited him.

Young people these days borrowed money from the nearest cash machine, and that meant the loan-sharking racket had just about played itself out. His Million Consumers Centre probably wouldn't last another year, and he had pretty much decided that he'd have to start an escort service to make ends meet. But now this. . . . He felt as if a great big roll of cash had suddenly dropped in his lap. He took a deep breath.

'I'm hungry,' the girl whined, another pout forming on her lips. 'Let's go eat.'

'Okay,' he said. 'Let's go.' His sudden change of mood seemed to surprise her.

5

Yayoi could tell that people were sympathetic and suspicious at the same time, and she felt like a tennis ball being batted back and forth between two strong emotions. But how should a tennis ball behave? She had absolutely no idea.

Inspector Iguchi, head of the Public Safety Division at the Musashi Yamato station, had been quite sympathetic the night he'd come to say that the palm print on the hand found in the park had been identified as Kenji's, but since then he seemed to have become more suspicious. He had shown up at her door again to tell her they were handing things over to central headquarters, and that they were setting up an investigation unit at the local station, so they'd be needing her cooperation there. His face this time bore little resemblance to the quiet man who had stared out at the tricycle in her garden. The change was chilling, but she knew that these were just the opening moves.

That evening after 10.00 p.m., two detectives, one from the local station and one from headquarters, had come around, and both looked even less reassuring than Iguchi.

'I'm Kinugasa from Central Investigation,' one of them said, flashing the ID in his black leather notebook. He was obviously in his late forties but perhaps trying to look younger in a faded black polo shirt and khakis. His stocky build, thick neck, and closely cropped head made him look more like a thug than a cop. Yayoi had no idea what or where 'Central Investigation' might be, but she knew it was hard not to start shaking now that she was face to face with its representative.

The other man was thin and chinless and introduced himself as Imai, a detective from the local station. He was younger than Kinugasa and he let the other do the talking while he took notes. As soon as they were in the house, they asked Yayoi's father, who had been standing behind her looking worried, to take the boys out somewhere. Her parents had been horrified when she'd called them with the news and had driven in from Kofu that first night. The younger boy was sleepy and reluctant to leave, while the older one seemed almost frozen with tension, but her parents managed to get them both ready and out the door. It was clear that it never occurred to them that their daughter could be a suspect. To them, it was simply as though some terrible accident had happened.

'I know this must be a difficult time for you,' Imai said as soon as they were gone, 'but we need to ask you some questions.' Yayoi led them into the living room. She sighed as they sat down. The ceiling felt lower and heavier than usual. It seemed unfair somehow that she should have to deal with these two serious-looking men, just when she'd got rid of Kenji and his constant gripes and had started life over with her boys.

'What was it you wanted to know . . .?' she said, her voice trailing off into silence. Kinugasa said nothing for a moment, taking his time to study her quite openly. If he really bore down on me, Yayoi thought, I'd probably give in soon enough. She stiffened instinctively as he opened his mouth to speak, and was almost disappointed when his voice came out higher and gentler than she'd expected, his breath smelling of nicotine.

'If you'll cooperate with us, I'm sure we'll catch whoever did this in no time.'

'Of course,' she said. He looked at her, running his tongue across his thick lips. He's probably wondering why I'm not crying, she thought. She would have liked to oblige, but her eyes were dry.

'I'm told that you left for work before your husband got home on the night of the murder. You must have been anxious about leaving your children alone in the house, worried about a fire or an earthquake?' His narrow eyes grew narrower, and it wasn't until much later that Yayoi realised that this was how he smiled.

'He was always . . .' She had started to say that he was always late so she was used to it, but she stammered to a halt. If she told them that, they'd realise that she and Kenji hadn't been getting along. 'He was always home on time, but he was late that day for the first time. I was very worried but I went to work. Of course, it made me mad to find he wasn't here when I got back.'

'Why was that?' Kinugasa asked, pulling a brown plastic

notebook from the back pocket of his pants and jotting something down.

'Why was I mad?' she said, suddenly annoyed. 'Have either of you gentlemen got children?'

'Yes,' said Kinugasa. 'A daughter in college and one in high school. You have kids, Imai?'

'Yes,' said Imai. 'Two in elementary school and one in kindergarten.'

'Then you can understand how upset I was leaving two little kids alone all night. My first reaction was to be angry.' Kinugasa added something to his notes. Imai sat silently, his notebook open, letting the older man run the interview.

'So you were mad at your husband?' Kinugasa said.

'Of course I was. He knew I had to go to work but he was still late. . . .' Realising that her resentment toward Kenji was on the verge of bursting out, she stopped. 'I mean, I *thought* he was late,' she corrected herself. Her shoulders drooped, as if it had just dawned on her that he wouldn't be coming home at all. Never mind that you killed him, a voice whispered deep inside her, but she ignored it.

'Yes, of course,' said Kinugasa. 'But had this kind of thing happened before?'

'Not coming home?'

'Yes.'

'No, never. Once in a while he would go out drinking and he wouldn't be home by the time I had to leave for work, but he always hurried back as soon as he could.'

'Most men have to go out once in a while,' Kinugasa said, nodding agreeably. 'And sometimes it gets late.'

'I realised that, and I felt sorry for him. He was always good to me.' Liar! Liar! she screamed to herself. He never once hurried back, and I was always left worrying and wondering whether I'd have to leave the children alone. He knew how much I hated going to work before he got home, but he hated seeing me so much that he stayed away till I was gone. He was horrible! . . . Horrible!

'Then if this was the first time he'd ever spent the night away from home, why were you angry? I would have thought you'd be worried.'

'I thought he was out having fun,' she said, her voice almost a whisper.

'Did you and your husband fight?'

'From time to time.'

'About what?'

'Usually about nothing at all.'

'I guess that's right. Married people usually fight about the dumbest kind of things. Okay then, could you run through the events of that day for us one more time? Your husband left for work at the normal time?'

'Yes, that's right.'

'And what was he wearing?'

'Just what he always wore, a suit. . . .' As soon as the words were out of her mouth, Yayoi remembered that Kenji hadn't had his jacket when he'd come home that night. Maybe it was still somewhere in the house, or maybe he'd been so drunk he'd dropped it somewhere along the way. She had completely forgotten about it. A feeling of panic mounted in her chest and it became difficult to breathe, but she willed herself to stay calm.

'Are you all right?' Kinugasa asked, his eyes narrowing again. There was something disconcerting about the contradiction between his gruff appearance and his gentle voice.

'Sorry,' she murmured. 'I was just thinking that it was the last time I saw him.'

'It's hard when it happens so suddenly like that,' Kinugasa said, glancing over at Imai. 'We see this kind of thing all the time, but we still never get used to it. Isn't that right, Imai?'

'That's right.' They seemed so sympathetic, but she knew they were just waiting for her to slip up. But she wouldn't! She'd find some way to get through this. She'd been over it all in her head countless times and she knew her part by heart. Still, whenever suspicious eyes were watching her, she felt as though they could see right through to her bruise. Part of her even wanted to bare her chest and expose her pain . . . but that was a dangerous temptation. She suddenly realised she was wringing her hands as if she were wringing an invisible towel, hoping to squeeze from it the will-power she needed to help her hold out. Will-power was what she needed now if she was going to keep her freedom.

'I'm sorry,' she said. 'I'm just not myself.'

'No, no,' Kinugasa said, trying to sound sympathetic. 'It's like this for everybody. We understand how you feel, ma'am. You're actually holding up better than most. Usually, we get a lot of tears and howling, makes it hard to talk.' He waited for her to collect herself.

'He was wearing a white shirt,' she said at last. 'And a dark tie.' Her tone grew clinical and dry as she described Kenji's clothes. 'Black shoes.'

'What colour was his suit?'

'Light grey.'

'Light grey,' Kinugasa said, making a note. 'Do you know what brand it was?'

'I don't know the brand, but we get all his clothes at a discount place called Minami.'

'His shoes, too?'

'No, but I think he got them from another place here in the neighbourhood.'

'Do you know where?' Imai asked.

'It's called the Tokyo Shoe Centre, I think.'

'And his underwear?' Imai added.

'I bought it at the supermarket.' She said this looking down in embarrassment.

'We can go into all that tomorrow,' said Kinugasa, cutting him short. 'We just need the basics today.' Imai looked annoyed but held off. 'What time did your husband leave for work?'

'The same time as always, early enough to catch the 7.45 for Shinjuku.'

'And you didn't see or hear from him after that?'

'No,' Yayoi said, pressing her hands to her face. Kinugasa looked around the room as if he were just noticing where he was. It was strewn with the toys and books the grandparents had brought for the children.

'Where did your folks take the kids?' he asked.

'Out to get something to eat.'

'It's getting late.' Knowing that she'd want to keep the interview private, he glanced at his watch and saw that it was already past 11.00. 'We should probably try to wrap this up.'

'Could you tell us where your husband was from, and where your parents live?' Imai asked, looking up from his notebook.

'My husband was from Gunma. His mother and father should be arriving soon. I'm originally from Yamanashi.'

'Had you told his parents that he was missing?' Imai said.

'No . . .' she stammered. 'I hadn't.'

'Why not?' Kinugasa said, rubbing his hands through his short hair.

'I'm not sure. I suppose because the people at his office kept telling me that men did this kind of thing from time to time and that he'd be home soon. It seemed better not to make a fuss about it.' Imai stared at his notebook with a puzzled look.

'But Yamamoto-san, it was Tuesday night when your husband didn't come home, and you had already called about filing a report by Wednesday evening. We actually logged the case on Thursday morning, all of which is pretty quick for this kind of thing. Since you were so quick to tell us, why didn't you call his parents? Wouldn't they usually be the first people you'd talk to?'

'I suppose so, but neither of our families was in favour of our marriage, so I haven't seen much of them over the years.'

'Would you mind telling us why they were against it?' Kinugasa asked.

'I'm not sure I know myself,' Yayoi said. 'I guess my parents made it clear they weren't very fond of Kenji and that made his mother angry. . . .' The truth was that Yayoi had never got along with her mother-in-law and there had been very little communication between them. Even now, she was dreading her arrival and the fuss she would make. Yayoi even wondered whether the hatred she'd ended up feeling for Kenji wasn't due partly to the fact that he was that woman's son.

'But why did your parents dislike your husband?' Kinugasa asked.

'That's hard to say.' She hesitated a moment. 'I'm their only daughter, and I guess they must have had high expectations of the man they wanted me to marry.'

'Probably so,' Kinugasa said. 'Especially since their daughter is such a good-looking woman, if you don't mind my saying so.'

'No, it wasn't that,' she said, as if stating a known fact.

'No? Then what was the reason?' He had suddenly adopted a fatherly tone. Go ahead, he seemed to be saying, you can tell me anything, anything at all. Yayoi had been feeling more and more uncomfortable as the interview had progressed into areas she hadn't anticipated. They seemed to be interested in every aspect of her relationship with Kenji, and they were developing a picture of them as a couple and drawing conclusions from it.

'My husband was fond of gambling before we got married,' she said. 'He bet on horse races, bike races, that kind of thing. He'd even had loans to cover his gambling debts, but he paid them off. My parents found out about it and said they were against us getting married. But he gave it up as soon as we got involved.' The two men exchanged a glance at the mention of gambling, and Kinugasa's next question had a new intensity.

'And recently?'

Yayoi wondered for a moment whether she should tell them about the baccarat. Had Masako said not to mention it? She couldn't remember. She paused, afraid that if she told them about the gambling they'd find out that he'd been beating her up.

'Go on,' Kinugasa urged. 'You can tell us.'

'Well . . .'

'He'd started again, hadn't he?'

'I think so,' she said, shivering slightly. 'He mentioned something about "baccarat".' Although she didn't know it yet, this one word would prove to be her salvation.

'Baccarat? Did he say where he'd been playing?'

'I think it was Shinjuku,' she said in a small voice.

'Thank you,' said Kinugasa. 'We appreciate your telling us this. I think now we're sure to get his killer.'

'I wonder . . .' Yayoi stammered, sensing that the questions were coming to an end, '. . . do you think I could see my husband?' Neither detective had mentioned the subject of viewing the body.

'We thought we'd ask your brother-in-law to identify him, but I'm not sure it would be a good idea for you to come along,' Kinugasa told her, fishing some black-and-white photographs out of an envelope in his briefcase. He held them close to his chest like a poker hand, and selected one to put down on the table in front of her. 'If you're really considering going, it might be a good idea to have a look at these before you decide.'

Yayoi reached out and gingerly picked up the picture. It showed a plastic bag and a lump of mutilated flesh. The only thing recognisable was a hand – Kenji's hand – with the pads of the fingers sliced off in blackened circles. She gasped, and for a moment she was overcome with loathing for Masako and the others. This was just too gruesome. She knew she'd killed him, and then asked them to get rid of the body; she knew she was being unreasonable. But now that she saw Kenji's disfigured body with her own eyes, she couldn't stop the wave of indignation that swept over her. Tears welled up in her eyes and she buried her face in her arms.

'I'm sorry,' Kinugasa said, patting her gently on the shoulder. 'I know this is hard, but you have to be strong. Your children are going to need you.' The detectives seemed almost relieved to see the tears. A moment later, Yayoi looked up and wiped her eyes with the back of her hand. She felt utterly lost. Kuniko had been right when she'd told her that she couldn't possibly understand. It was true, she couldn't. It had been simpler to tell herself that Kenji had just gone off somewhere.

'Are you all right?' Kinugasa asked.

'Yes, I'm sorry.'

'We'd like you to come down to the station tomorrow,' he told her, standing to leave. 'We've got a few more things to go over.'

'Of course,' Yayoi murmured. There was more? When would it stop? But even now, Imai was looking slowly through his notebook, still sitting there in front of her.

'I'm sorry,' he said, glancing up, 'but there's one thing I forgot to ask about.'

'Yes?' she said, eyeing him through her tears. He studied her a moment.

'About what time did you get home from the factory the morning after your husband disappeared? Could you run through that day for us, please.'

'I finished work at 5.30, changed, and got home a little before 6.00.'

'Do you always come straight home?' he asked softly.

'Usually,' Yayoi said. She was conscious that she still hadn't recovered from the shock of the pictures and needed to choose her words carefully. 'Sometimes I stay and chat with friends for a while, but since Kenji hadn't been back that night, I was worried and came right home.'

'Of course,' Imai said, nodding for her to continue.

'Then I napped for a couple of hours before I took the children to the day-care centre.'

'It was raining, wasn't it? Did you take the car?'

'No, we don't own a car, and I don't drive. I take them on the bike.' She noticed another quick exchange of glances. The fact that she had never learned to drive was going to be to her advantage.

'And then . . .' Imai prompted.

'I got back here around 9:30 and talked to one of the neighbours for a while out by the garbage bins. I did the laundry and cleaned up around the house, and then around 11.00 I fell asleep again. At 1.00, there was a call from my husband's office saying he hadn't shown up for work. I was stunned, to say the least.' As she ran through all this again, the lines flowed smoothly; she began to relax, and she realised how wrong she'd been to resent Masako, even for a moment.

'Thank you,' Imai said, closing his notebook with a snap. Kinugasa had been standing impatiently with his arms folded. As she followed them to the entrance and watched them scuff back into their shoes, she could sense that their suspicions were fading again, giving way to a new wave of sympathy.

'We'll see you again tomorrow,' Kinugasa said before shutting the door behind him. When they were gone, Yayoi looked at her watch. Kenji's mother and brother would be here soon. She swallowed, steeling herself for her mother-in-law's tears. But now she could use her own tears as a defense. This interview with the detectives had been a good rehearsal for what was to come. The tension and confusion seemed to have melted away. Suddenly realising that she was standing just where Kenji had died, she gave a little jump.

Dark Dreams

1

Another blazing afternoon. Mitsuyoshi Satake stood looking out through the blinds, arms folded across his chest. From his second-floor window, the city outside seemed to be divided between the places brilliantly lit by the midsummer sun and those sunk in shadow. The leaves on the trees lining the road seemed to glow, the area beneath them just a smear of black. The figures of people hurrying along looked luminous, trailing dark shadows. The white lines of the crosswalk warped in the heat, and Satake flinched at the sight of them, remembering the unpleasant feeling of one's shoes sinking into the hot asphalt.

Just in front of him loomed the cluster of skyscrapers near the west exit to Shinjuku Station. The vertical strips of cloudless blue sky between the towers were almost too bright to look at, and he closed his eyes; but the image lingered on his retinas. He closed the blinds and turned away, waiting for his eyes to adjust to the dimmer light. The apartment was just two small rooms floored with old tatami mats and divided by faded sliding doors. The air-conditioner was turned up high, and in the middle of one room a large TV flickered in the gloom. There was almost no other furniture. A small kitchen opened off the entrance hall, but since Satake never used it, there were no pans or dishes. All told, it seemed an austere dwelling for a man who dressed the way Satake did.

In fact, while he was at home, Satake's appearance matched his apartment: a white shirt over grey pants worn through at the knees. This was his preferred way of dressing. But whenever he went out, he was obliged to think about how he looked to the rest of the world, and so found himself playing the role of Mitsuyoshi Satake, club owner.

Rolling up his sleeves, he washed his hands and face in the lukewarm water from the faucet, then dried off with a towel and sat down in front of the TV, folding his legs under him. The dubbed version of an old American movie flickered across the screen, but his eyes wandered away and he sat in a daze, running his hands through his close-cropped hair. He didn't really want to watch anything; he just wanted to bathe in the meaningless artificial light.

Satake hated summer. It wasn't the heat that bothered him so much as the various signs of the season in the back streets of the city that brought back memories with them. It was during summer vacation in his second year of high school that he'd hit his father hard enough to break his jaw, and then left home. That event, which had changed his life for ever, had taken place in a room just like this one, in August, with the air-conditioner groaning just as it was doing now.

Engulfed in the hot stench of the city, he found that the boundary between his inner and outer selves seemed to dissolve. The fetid air seeped in through his pores and soiled what was inside, while his simmering emotions leaked out of his body into the streets. In Tokyo, in summer, he felt threatened by the city, so it had always seemed better to avoid the whole season as much as possible, avoid the waves of withering heat that swept through the streets.

The return of this feeling was always a sign that the rainy season had ended and summer had started in earnest. To chase it out of his apartment, he stood up and went into the other room, where he opened the window and, before the fumes and noise could get in, pulled out the storm shutters and slammed them shut. As they slid into place, the interior fell into darkness and

Satake sank on to the discoloured tatami with a sense of relief. The room contained a dresser and a neatly folded futon. The corners of the futon were perfect angles, almost as if a schoolboy's triangle had been inserted in them, and the whole place brought to mind a prison cell – except, of course, for the television. In prison, Satake had suffered not only from memories of the woman he had killed but from the small, airless space in which he was confined. When he got out, he had avoided moving into a large concrete apartment block where he would have felt hemmed in, opting instead for this drafty old wooden building. For much the same reason, the television, his link to the outside world, stayed on all day.

He went back and sat in front of it now, in the formal posture that had been required in jail. There were no storm shutters on the windows in this room, so the sunlight continued to filter through the blinds. He muted the volume, leaving only the rumble of cars outside on Yamate Avenue and the hum of the air-conditioner. Lighting a cigarette, he peered through the smoke at the screen without really knowing what he was watching. A talk show had just started, and the host, looking serious, was using a flip chart to illustrate his topic. Satake gathered that it was a special programme devoted to a police case that was getting a lot of attention – something about a dismembered body that had been discovered last week in a park out in the suburbs. Having no interest in the subject, he folded his arms around his head to shield himself from the world outside. But just then the cell phone lying next to him began to ring, as if it had realised what he was doing. He hesitated, half resenting this other outside link, but finally spoke into the receiver.

'Satake,' he said, his voice low and gruff. He was reluctant to speak to anyone today, with the heat threatening to stir up his carefully suppressed memories; but he also felt a need for some distraction. This restless, ambivalent mood left him irritated; it was like his feelings about the city in summer – he hated the sweltering streets, but he knew he could never live anywhere else.

'Honey, it's me,' said a voice. The call was from Anna. Satake glanced at the Rolex on his wrist: exactly 1.00 p.m. About time they should be starting their rounds. He paused for a moment, wondering whether he should stay home on such a blistering day.

'What's up?' he asked at last. 'The beauty shop?'

'No, it's too hot. I was wondering if we could go to the pool instead.'

'The pool? Now?'

'Yes. Come with me!' The scent of chlorine and suntan oil came back to him – not the sort of summer memories he was avoiding, but he would still have preferred to say no.

'It's a bit late, isn't it? Wouldn't it be better to go on your day off?'

'But it's so crowded on Sunday. Can't we go today? Anna wants to swim!'

'Okay, okay. We'll go,' Satake said, suddenly decisive. He hung up and lit another cigarette, squinting at the muted TV. On the screen was the tense face of a woman who must have been the victim's wife. She was wearing a faded T-shirt and jeans. Her hair was pulled back in a simple bun, and she wore almost no make-up. Satake studied the face. Realising that she was much better-looking than he would have expected, he switched almost automatically to his professional mode, appraising the woman with an expert's eye. She was in her early thirties, he concluded, but with a little work on the make-up the face would still find buyers. What struck him most about her, however, was how calm she seemed despite the fact that her husband had been murdered. A caption scrolled across the bottom of the screen: 'The wife of murder victim Kenji Yamamoto'; but the name meant nothing to him. He'd long since forgotten that he had kicked a man named Yamamoto out of his club that night and beaten him on the stairs.

At the moment, he was much more concerned about the boiling summer afternoon that awaited him and a vague sense of foreboding it gave him. If he'd had this sort of premonition on that other day years ago, perhaps he might have escaped, might never have met that woman, and his life would have been different. Today, the same misgivings were stirring, but he had no idea why.

Ten minutes later, he was hurrying toward the parking lot where he kept his car. Through his sunglasses, the highway in the distance shimmered like a mirage. His skin, accustomed to the cool, dark apartment, began to sweat at the first assault from the heat and intense sunlight. He wiped his forehead with the back of his hand as he stood waiting for his car to appear from the parking-lot elevator. As soon as he had closed the door, he turned on the air-conditioning, but he could still feel the heat in the leather-covered steering wheel.

Satake was used to Anna's random demands. One day she wanted him to take her shopping; the next, he had to find her a new hairdresser, or a new vet. She constantly had him chasing around the city, but he understood that it was her way of testing his affections. He smiled to himself as he guided the car through the traffic, amused by this beautiful, whimsical child.

When he rang the bell on the intercom, the door opened almost immediately, as if she'd been waiting for him. She was wearing a yellow hat with a wide brim and a matching yellow sundress. She pursed her lips in mock displeasure as she fumbled with the straps on her black enamel sandals.

'What took you so long?'

'I can't help it if you come up with these hare-brained schemes all of a sudden,' Satake said, swinging open the door. He caught a whiff of the distinctive smell of Anna's apartment, a mixture of canine and cosmetics. 'Where do you want to go?' he asked.

'To the pool, of course!' she cried, rushing out of the place. She ran to the railing, leaned out as far as she could, and stared up at the sky, as if reassuring herself that the day was still blazing hot. She could barely contain her excitement at the prospect of the outing, and seemed completely oblivious to Satake's darker mood.

'But which pool? The Keio Plaza? The New Otani?'

'Hotels cost a fortune,' she said. Even when she was spending Satake's money, Anna tended to avoid unnecessary extravagance.

'Where then?' he said, setting off toward the elevator.

'The city pool's fine,' she said. '¥400 for both of us.'

There was no denying that the city pool was cheap, but it was also noisy and crowded. Still, if that's what she wanted, it was fine with him. All he wanted to do was survive the heat; if he could please Anna at the same time, all the better.

The pool was swarming with elementary-school groups and young couples. A row of trees lined the top part of the gently terraced poolside, and Satake waited in the shade until Anna emerged from the changing room in her bright red swimsuit.

'Honey!' she called, waving. He studied her body as she ran toward him. It was perfect, except perhaps for the fact that her skin seemed too white for a swimming pool. The breasts and hips were firm and high, the legs long. There was just enough flesh on the thighs, and yet the overall effect was sleek. 'Aren't you going to swim?' she said, taking a deep breath, as if to smell the chlorine.

'I'll watch you from here.'

'Why?' she said, tugging on his arm. 'Come on, get in!'

'You go ahead. Don't be too long – we can only stay an hour or so.'

'Is that all?'

'We've been through that. You've got to leave time for the hairdresser.' Anna made an irritated gesture but then seemed to think better of it and ran off toward the pool. On the way down the terrace, she picked up a beach ball and began playing catch with a group of little girls. Satake smiled. She was such a sweet thing. All he really needed was to be with her, to take care of her. He couldn't deny that she was a comfort to him. Still, she wasn't able to quiet the hum of the past that the sudden onset of summer had set up in his head. He closed his eyes behind his sunglasses.

When he opened them, Anna was no longer playing by the pool. He found her a moment later, waving her long white arms at him from the middle of the wide expanse of blue water, lost in a sea of splashing, shouting children. Satisfied that he had seen her, she began swimming down the pool, practising her awkward crawl. Satake watched as a young man followed her and struck up a conversation underneath the diving board. He closed his eyes again.

A few minutes later, she was standing next to him, dripping wet. She twisted her thick black hair over her head. Satake noticed that the young man was watching them. He wore a pony-tail and one earring.

'You're being watched,' he said.

'He was talking to me in the pool.'

'Who is he?'

'He says he's in a band.' She sounded blasé, but turned her head slightly to gauge Satake's reaction. Satake gazed at the drops of water sliding down her arms and legs, savouring her youth, her beauty.

'Go swim with him. You've still got some time.'

'Why would I want to?' she said, giving him a disappointed look.

'He was hitting on you, wasn't he?'

'You won't mind?'

'Not as long as you show up for work.'

'Oh,' she said. It was as though a bubble of innocence had burst. Throwing aside her towel, she ran back to where the man was lying by the pool. As he sat up to greet her, obviously delighted, he turned to look at Satake in disbelief.

Anna was quiet on the way home from the pool.

'I'll drop you off at the hairdresser's,' he told her.

'But you don't need to pick me up,' she said.

'Why?'

'I'll get a cab.'

'Fine. I'll take a shower and look in at the club.' After letting her out at her usual spot, he pulled on to Yamate Avenue. The sun was low, shining right in his eyes. The sunset in summer always reminded Satake of something, a memory so intense it made him wince. Back in the heat of his room, he stared at the shadows of the Shinjuku towers beginning to stretch across the street outside his window. That feeling, the uncontrollable irritation, was returning again.

When he made his entrance at Mika that evening, all the hostesses turned toward the door in their standard greeting. For a moment, their faces held the plastic smiles reserved for the clientele, but when they realised who it was, their smiles faded. Satake looked around the empty room.

'What the hell's going on? This the slack season?' he said to Chin, the floor manager, who was standing at his shoulder.

'It's still early,' said Chin, quickly rolling down his sleeves. Satake, who was strict about his employees' appearance, noticed that his bow-tie was crooked and his black pants wrinkled.

'You're a mess,' he said, pulling roughly on the tie.

'Sorry,' Chin muttered, wandering off. Sensing that Satake was in a lousy mood, Reika, the manager, hurried over from the kitchen. She was wearing a black dress with a string of pearls – as if she were going to a funeral, he noted sourly.

'Satake-san, good evening. I'm afraid things are a bit slow, what with the heat and all.'

'What do you mean, a bit slow? Have you been making calls? I just don't believe you can't drum up *any* business at all!' His eyes swept the room again before settling on the vases. 'And get some new flowers!' he shouted.

In general, Satake kept a low profile in his own clubs; but tonight was different. The way he scowled sent Chin scooting over to the nearest vase of badly wilted mauve bellflowers. The hostesses looked back and forth nervously between Satake and the vase.

'A number of regulars said they'll be in later,' Reika said, trying to soothe him.

'You can't run a business like that, waiting like some fucking princess for people to show up. Get out on the street and drag them in!'

'I was just going to do that,' Reika said, laughing amiably, but she made no move to go, obviously reluctant to face the heat outside. Holding in his anger, Satake looked around again. He'd had a feeling that something was missing – and now realised what it was.

'Where's Anna?' he asked.

'She called to say she'd be taking the night off.'

'Did she say why?'

'She said she'd got too much sun at the pool and wasn't feeling well.'

'Okay,' he muttered. 'I'll be back later.'

The relief was apparent on her face. Satake noticed that the whole place seemed to relax as he walked out the door, still struggling to control his rage.

Outside, he was instantly engulfed in the sweltering air of Kabuki-cho. Though the sun had set, the heat and humidity lingered, as though the whole city were in a steam bath; the heat was trapped inside, as if building under the skin of a grimy, middle-aged man with clogged pores. Satake let out a groan as he climbed the stairs to the next floor, a bit more slowly than usual. Things had got slack at Mika, and he would have to do something about it.

When he opened the door to Playground, Kunimatsu headed over to greet him. Satake was relieved to see a number of businessmen around the tables.

'You're early this evening,' Kunimatsu said, glancing down at Satake's clothes. Realising that patches of sweat were showing on his silver-grey jacket, he slipped it off, but the black silk shirt underneath was soaked through and clung to the lines of muscle on his chest. 'Is it hot in here?' Kunimatsu asked him uneasily as he picked up the jacket.

'No, it's fine,' said Satake, taking out his cigarettes. A young dealer who was practising at an empty table before going on duty looked up at them. Satake noticed the hint of a sneer that crept into his expression when he saw the limp jacket. 'What's the new guy's name?' he asked Kunimatsu.

'Yanagi.'

'Tell him to watch himself in front of the customers. Nobody wants to see a dealer pulling faces like that.'

'I'll tell him,' Kunimatsu murmured, backing away as if to distance himself from his unusually bad mood. Satake stood and finished his cigarette. Almost before he'd stubbed it out, one of the bunnies came over to change the ashtray, and he lit another. The staff seemed to be watching him nervously, paying more attention to him than to the customers; and somehow, though it was his own club, for the first time he felt very out of place.

'Can I bother you for a minute?' said Kunimatsu, coming back over.

'What's up?'

'There's something I wanted to show you.' Satake followed his manager's tall, tuxedo-clad form to a small room at the back of the club that served as his office. 'A customer left this,' he said, taking a grey suit coat from the locker. Satake noticed the silver jacket he'd just removed on another hanger. 'I was wondering what we should do with it.'

'No one's claimed it?' Satake asked, taking the coat. It was lightweight wool, obviously cheap.

'Look at this,' said Kunimatsu, pointing at a label sewn into the pocket. 'Yamamoto' had been machine embroidered in yellow thread.

'Yamamoto?'

'Don't you remember? The guy you chased off at the beginning of last week.'

'Oh, him,' said Satake, recalling the man who had been bothering Anna.

'He hasn't been back to get it. What should we do?'

'Throw it out.'

'You don't think he'll be around at some point looking for it?'

'He's not coming back,' said Satake. 'And if he does show up, just tell him we never saw it.'

'I'll do that,' said Kunimatsu with a small nod. He seemed to have something more he wanted to say, but thought better of it.

After discussing the recent receipts for a few minutes, Satake left the office. Kunimatsu hurried after him, still trying to humour him. A couple of flashy young women, apparently hostesses from the neighbourhood, had come to gamble. The sight of their artificially tanned skin made Satake think of his own top girl.

'I'm going to check up on Anna,' he said. 'I'll be back later.' Kunimatsu bowed politely, but Satake couldn't help noticing the way he relaxed as he saw him out the door. At moments like these, when he saw how nervous his employees seemed to be around him, he wondered whether they had somehow found out about his past.

He had been a model of self-control, had worked so hard to keep his dark side sealed away. But he knew that even a hint of what he'd done would terrify other people. Still, only he and the woman herself knew the truth about what had happened, and no one else could understand what he'd been up to. It had been Satake's misfortune to taste the forbidden fruit when he was twenty-six, and he'd been cut off from the normal world ever since.

Something seemed odd when he got to Anna's apartment. There was no answer when he rang the intercom. He was just taking out his cell phone to call her number when a voice finally came crackling from the speaker.

'Who is it?'

'It's me,' Satake said.

'Honey?'

'Are you okay? I want to see you for a second.'

'Okay,' she muttered. He could hear her unchaining the door – funny, he thought, she never used the chain. 'I'm sorry I didn't show up for work,' she said once the door was open. She was wearing shorts and a T-shirt and looking a bit pale. Satake glanced down at the floor of the entrance hall. A pair of fashionable sneakers lay next to Anna's shoes.

'The guy from the pool?' he asked. Her eyes followed Satake's to the shoes and she blushed. 'I don't mind if you fool around, but you can't let it get in the way of work. And no love affairs.'

She shrank back and stared at him, as if in shock.

'You mean you don't care?'

'Not particularly,' he said. In an instant, her eyes filled with tears. Satake noticed, but it seemed more of a nuisance than anything else. She was sweet, even apart from her value at the club, but for him she was just a fancy pet he liked to spoil. Like the skin that covered their bodies, his relationship with her was all on the surface. 'Just don't play hookey on me any more,' he told her.

As she turned without a word and went back inside, it occurred to him that this little fling and his reaction to it might give her ideas about moving to another club. He closed the door behind him as gently as he could. On the way back, he wondered to himself why everything seemed to be going wrong today. He felt edgy, volatile, as if the seal to his past had somehow been broken. He willed himself to keep his memories locked away.

He decided to skip another visit to Mika and headed straight up to Playground.

'How is she?' Kunimatsu asked, opening the door for him. 'I heard she took the night off.'

'It's nothing serious. I'm sure she'll be back at work tomorrow.'

'That's good. And I understand things have picked up downstairs since you stopped in earlier.'

'Glad to hear it,' said Satake, feeling slightly relieved. He did another quick check of the customers in the club: fifteen in all, half businessmen and the others connected with Shinjuku's night life. Of these, half were regulars at the club. Not a bad crowd, all told. Satake pronounced himself satisfied. Now he only needed to figure out what to do about the little crisis over Anna. It wouldn't do to have her moving to another club because of a silly thing like this.

It was just as he'd regained his composure and settled down to think through this problem that the door opened and two new customers walked in. They were ordinary enough – middle-aged men in short-sleeved shirts – and Satake almost had the feeling that he'd seen them somewhere before, though he couldn't have said where. Company men? Shop owners? But they looked around inquisitively, their eyes sharper than the average player's. Satake, who could usually size up a customer at a glance, was at a loss.

'Welcome, gentlemen,' Kunimatsu called out, walking over to greet them. He showed them to a table and, at their request, began explaining the game and the house rules. When he'd finished, one of the two men reached into his breast pocket and pulled out a black leather notebook.

'We're from the Metropolitan Police Department,' he said, holding up his ID. 'I'd like to ask you all to remain where you are. We want to talk to the manager.' A hush fell over the club, and Kunimatsu glanced sheepishly at Satake.

So was this the premonition he'd had since morning? Of course they looked familiar – like every other cop he'd ever seen. He picked up a chip lying on the table and crushed it between his fingers to keep from laughing out loud.

2

Satake thought he'd heard wrong when a new detective came into the interrogation room and introduced himself. 'Kinugasa,' he said, 'from Central Investigation.'

'What do you mean, "Central Investigation"?' he said. 'What's this all about?'

'What do you think it's about?' Kinugasa laughed. He was stocky and tough-looking, with those staring eyes detectives seemed to have – not Satake's favourite type. 'I want to ask you about another case we're working on.'

'What other case?' They'd already held him for over a week on nothing more than suspicion of operating an unlicensed gambling establishment, and now the big boys from Central were checking in. What did they want? He had to admit, they had him spooked, but he couldn't let them know that. 'What does Central want with a small-time gambling charge? What other case?'

'A little murder and dismemberment,' Kinugasa said. Pulling a disposable lighter from the pocket of his faded black polo shirt, he lit a cigarette and took a long, appreciative drag as he watched

Satake's reaction.

'Dismemberment?'

'You look a bit worried,' he said. Satake was wearing a blue shirt that Reika had sent him. He didn't much care for the colour, but the black silk shirt he'd been wearing when they arrested him had been soaked in sweat.

'Not particularly,' he laughed.

'Not particularly what? You don't have much to laugh about, asshole. So start talking.' Kinugasa exchanged a weary glance with the other detective from the Shinjuku station. 'Or are you so used to being in the slammer it doesn't even bother you?'

'Now hold on a minute,' he interrupted. 'I don't have any idea what you're talking about.' This was getting serious. It hadn't been a real raid at all. He'd been convinced all along that they were just making an example of him because his club was making money; but now it began to dawn on him that Central had planned the whole thing. Somehow, without realising it, he'd wandered into some kind of deep shit, and he was sure that it wasn't going to be easy getting back out.

'Don't give me that crap,' Kinugasa said. 'You remember a guy named Kenji Yamamoto who used to come into your place? Well, he's the victim. Don't tell me you didn't know that.'

'Kenji Yamamoto? Never heard of him.' Satake cocked his head to one side and stared back. From the window of the interrogation room, the Shinjuku skyscrapers were visible, and between them the tall strips of summer sky. Satake shut his eyes, blinded by the brilliant light. His apartment was somewhere nearby – how he longed to get out of here and hide himself away in his own dark room.

'Then maybe you recognise this?' said Kinugasa, taking a grey jacket out of a wrinkled department store bag that lay on the desk. Satake nearly choked: it was the jacket he'd told his manager to get rid of on the night of the raid.

'I've seen it. Some guy left it at the club.' He swallowed. So someone had cut up that idiot. He vaguely remembered the reports in the newspapers and on TV mentioning the name Yamamoto. The outline of what they were thinking began to take shape. He looked up to see the detectives smirking at him.

'So tell us, Satake. What happened to this "guy"?'

'How should I know?'

'You really don't know?' Kinugasa gave a high, almost girlish laugh. Shithead! Satake thought, a rush of blood making his head spin; but the self-control he'd learned since getting out of jail helped steady him.

'I really don't,' he said, managing to sound half-convincing. Kinugasa pulled a notebook from his bulging hip pocket and slowly began flipping the pages.

'We have several witnesses who saw you and the victim going at it outside the door of Playground around 10.00 p.m. on the night of 20 July – a Tuesday, if I'm not mistaken. They saw you kicking him down the stairs.'

'That's . . . more or less what happened.'

'More or less. . . . And what happened after that?'

'I don't know.'

'You do know,' said Kinugasa. 'The guy disappeared. What we want to know is what you did after the fight.' Satake searched his memory but came up blank. He might have gone straight home, or he might have hung around a while at the club. He decided the latter option sounded more promising.

'I had work to finish up, so I went back in the club.'

'Not according to your employees. They told us you left right after dealing with Yamamoto.'

'Is that right? Then I must have gone home to bed,' said Satake. Kinugasa folded his arms, apparently amused.

'So which was it?'

'Home to bed.'

'But they told us you always stick around until the place closes. Why would you leave early that one night? Doesn't it strike you as a bit strange?'

'I was tired, so I went home and went to bed early.' That was the truth. He remembered now that he'd felt pooped after the run-in with Yamamoto and had gone straight home without checking in at either club. He'd fallen asleep watching TV. It would have been better if he'd stuck around Playground, but it was a bit late now for regrets.

'Were you alone?'

'Of course.'

'And what made you so tired?'

'I was at a pachinko place all morning and then chauffeured one of the girls at the club around. I had a meeting with Kunimatsu, the casino manager – it was a full day's work.'

'And what was the meeting with Kunimatsu about? About how to get rid of the victim, wasn't it? That's what Kunimatsu told us.'

'That's ridiculous,' said Satake. 'Where do you come up with this stuff? I run a nice little club and a casino, end of story.'

'Don't fuck with me!' Kinugasa bawled, suddenly turning nasty. 'Nice little club and casino, my ass. We know about your record, about that woman you raped and murdered. How many times was it you stabbed her? Twenty? Thirty? And the whole time, you were fucking her brains out. Am I right? That how you get your jollies, Satake? You're a freak, you are. I nearly threw up just reading the transcripts. How the fuck did an animal like you get out after just seven years? Can you explain that to me?'

Satake could feel the sweat begin to well out of every pore on his body. The lid on his private hell, the lid he'd worked so hard to keep shut, was being pried off as he watched. The face of the woman in her death throes came back to him. The old, dark dreams that he'd thought were dead crept up his spine like an icy hand.

'That make you sweat?' Kinugasa said. 'Make you hot?'

'No . . . it's just that . . .'

'Spit it out. You'll feel better.'

'You're barking up the wrong tree. I'm a changed man.'

'That's what they all say. But in my experience, men who kill for pleasure don't stop after the first time.'

For pleasure? The words hit Satake like a sledgehammer, but he returned Kinugasa's taunting, come-off-it look. It wasn't for pleasure! he wanted to scream. The pleasure had come from sharing in the woman's death. At that moment, he'd felt nothing but love for her. That was why she was the only woman he'd ever have, why he was bound to her for life. He'd taken no 'pleasure' in killing her; what he'd felt couldn't be explained away by a single word. But how could he explain?

'You're wrong,' he said, staring down at his lap.

'Could be,' said Kinugasa. 'But we're going to do our damnedest to prove we're right. You don't have to tell us a thing.' He patted him on the shoulder, as though patting a dog. Satake twisted away to avoid his meaty hand.

'I really didn't do anything,' he said. 'I just warned the guy to keep away from the club. He'd fallen for my top girl and he was following her around. I told him to leave her alone. This is the first I've heard about what happened to him.'

'Maybe your "warning" is different from other people's,' said Kinugasa.

'What do you mean?'

'You tell me. What did you do after you beat the shit out of him?'

'That's ridiculous.'

'What's so ridiculous? You kill a woman, you're a pimp, and you beat up your customers. Is it so hard to imagine you might chop them up, too? And you've got no alibi either. You're the one who's ridiculous.' When Satake said nothing, Kinugasa lit another cigarette. 'Satake,' he hissed, blowing smoke in his face. 'Who'd you get to do it?'

'Do what?'

'You've got those Chinese guys working in your club. What does the Chinese mob charge for a job like that? What's the going rate these days? Finger-sized bits – like so much sushi – what'd they charge you for that?'

'You're out of your mind,' said Satake.

'The weeklies are saying it costs around ¥100,000. That sound right to you? At that rate, you could get ten guys hacked up on just what you walk around with.'

'I don't have that kind of money,' Satake laughed, amazed that the cop could be so unrealistic.

'You drive a Benz, don't you?'

'That's just for show. But I wouldn't throw away my money on something as stupid as that.'

'You might if you realised what would happen if you're convicted of murder again. This time around they'll go for the death penalty.' When he saw how serious Kinugasa was, Satake knew he'd already decided he was guilty. They really believed he'd killed a man and had somebody cut him up. How was he going to get out of this? Not without a lot of good luck. The spectre of a tiny prison cell made him prickle with sweat again. Noticing how uncomfortable he was, the other detective, who had been quiet so far, spoke up.

'Satake, has it occurred to you what this must be like for the guy's widow? She works nights in a boxed-lunch factory and still takes care of two kids.'

'His widow?' he muttered, remembering the woman he'd seen on TV. She'd been a lot prettier than he'd have expected a creep like that to be hitched to.

'Young kids,' said the detective. 'But you wouldn't understand, not having any of your own. She'll have it rough.'

'I'm sure she will, but that's got nothing to do with me.'

'Doesn't it?!' the man barked.

'That's right.'

'You can sit here with a straight face and tell me you're not somehow mixed up in this?'

'I'm telling you I didn't do anything and I don't know anything about it.' Kinugasa was quietly studying his reactions as the exchange dragged on. Sensing that he was being watched, Satake turned to stare at him. An idea was beginning to take shape in his head: maybe it was that woman, the wife, who had killed him. How could she be so calm when she'd just found out that her husband was dead and that somebody had made mincemeat of him? Something about that face on the TV had bothered him, like biting into a grain of sand in the middle of an oyster. He'd seen something written there, something you could never read unless you'd had the same experience – call it a sense of fulfilment. She had the motive. Her husband was running after Anna and spending all his time and money at Mika. He'd only had a glimpse on the tube, but the Yamamotos didn't seem rich. So naturally she'd have hated him.

'The wife,' he said aloud. 'What about her? Are you sure she didn't do it?'

This made even Kinugasa flip. 'You worry about your own sorry ass, Satake! She's got an alibi. My money's on you, all the way.'

So they've already given up on her, he thought, and this guy is looking for me to take the fall. He had to admit that it didn't look good. 'I'm sorry to disappoint you,' he said, 'but I really didn't do it. I swear to you.'

'Lying bastard,' Kinugasa roared.

'Fucking cop,' Satake muttered, leaning down to spit under the desk. While he was at it, Kinugasa caught him on the side of the head with a swing of his elbow.

'Don't mess with me,' the cop warned him. But Satake didn't

need any warning: he knew they could pin anything on you if they wanted to. And this time the stakes were high: maybe even his life was on the line. He found himself shaking with rage and fear. If he ever got out of this place, he swore he'd get even with the real murderer. For now at least, he figured that had to be the wife.

He knew enough about how things worked to realise that this little affair would probably cost him both of his clubs, and the thought nearly killed him. He'd slaved away in the ten years since he'd got out of jail, built up so much, and now to get mixed up in something like this . . . He should have known that summer would get the better of him; it was in the cards, he'd seen it coming.

It suddenly seemed dark, and looking up he saw that a bank of black clouds had sprung up over Shinjuku. The leaves on the zelkova trees outside were rattling in the wind, a portent of an evening shower.

That night, in his cell at the detention centre, Satake dreamed about the woman. She was lying in front of him, a pleading look on her face. 'Hospital, hospital . . .' she seemed to be saying. He put his finger in the wounds he'd made on her body, sliding it in up to the knuckle, but the woman seemed not to notice and merely whispered over and over, 'Hospital.' His hand was drenched in blood. He wiped it on her cheek, and as he did so, he realised that the face of this woman, marked with her own blood, had taken on an unearthly kind of beauty.

'Take me to the . . . hospital.'

'They can't help you. It's over.' In response, the woman grabbed hold of his bloody hand with startling strength and pulled it toward her neck, as though urging him to kill her quickly. He stroked her hair instead. 'Not yet,' he said.

The look of utter despair in her eyes made his heart contract with both pity and delight. Not yet. You can't die yet. Not before we come together. . . . He held her tighter, his whole body slippery with blood.

He opened his eyes. He was dripping with blood – or so it seemed for a moment until he realised he was covered with sweat. He glanced over at his cellmate, a cheque forger, who lay rigid in the next bunk, pretending to be asleep. Ignoring him, Satake sat up in bed. It was the first time he'd dreamed of her in ten years, and it excited him. He could still feel her lingering nearby. His eyes searched the dark corners of the cell, eager to find her.

3

She remembered her first ride on the national railroad, on a winter day four years ago. It was evening and the car was packed. For Anna, who wasn't used to the crowds, it was like being absorbed by a foreign body. Under a relentless assault from elbows and bags, she was driven far into the car. Somehow she managed to find a strap to grab and stood staring out the window at the burnt orange of the winter sunset. As the light flared, the buildings in the foreground seemed to recede into shadow, vanishing from sight as the train passed. She twisted around from time to time, worried that she would miss her stop or that she wouldn't be able to get to the door because of the crush of people.

Suddenly, she realised that voices speaking her own language were rising out of the crowd. Someone nearby was speaking in the familiar tones of Shanghai. Feeling comforted, she scanned the faces around her to see who it was; but then, listening more closely, she realised it was Japanese she'd been hearing, with its various similar sounds. And she felt a stab of real loneliness, the loneliness of the traveller adrift in a foreign country. Though the faces and voices resembled her own, she was alone in a world where no one knew her. When she looked out the window again, the sun had set and she found herself staring at her own reflection in the dark glass: she saw a forlorn young woman in a dowdy coat looking back at her, and the sight filled her with a sense of utter isolation. She had been nineteen at the time. To be sure, this wasn't the first time she'd felt overwhelmed by the economic prosperity of Japan or the frenetic activity of the city, but her loneliness at that moment was like nothing she'd ever felt before.

If she had come to Japan to learn, as her student visa suggested, she might have been able to put up with these feelings. But Anna had come with the sole aim of making money, and the only tools she'd brought with her were her youth and her beauty. She'd come with great expectations, attracted by the ease of it all, spurred on by the broker's promises of the riches to be earned in Japan; and in the end, it had been this love of ease that had undermined a bright, sensible girl like her. Anna had been a good student at school, and had even thought of going on to university. But now here she was, making easy money just for spending time with Japanese men. She knew there was something sleazy about the whole business, but she couldn't help herself.

Her father was a taxi driver, and her mother sold vegetables at the market. Every evening, they came home to tell each other about the day's successes, about the money they'd made by cunning and grit. That was the way of the Shanghai wage earner. But Anna felt that she could never report her own successes to her serious, hard-working parents. And here in Tokyo, though she took a secret pride in her Shanghai heritage and her own looks, she usually felt intimidated by the self-confidence of the rich young Japanese women. Self-confidence was something she lacked. It all seemed so unfair. And it was when she felt most frustrated with her situation, most insecure and lonely, that she saw herself as she did that time before – as a frightened country girl lost in the big city.

During her first months in Japan, she had gone dutifully to the language school recommended by the broker who arranged for her visa, working nights in a club in Yotsuya to support herself. She studied hard and, thanks to her good ear, she was soon able to get the drift of most conversations and communicate in broken Japanese. She also learned how to dress like the fashionable young women she saw in the department stores. Nevertheless, she could never quite shake the feeling she'd experienced that day on the train; no matter how hard she tried to ignore it, it always seemed to be lurking nearby, like a stray cat.

Still, what mattered was the money. The quicker she earned it, the sooner she could go back to Shanghai, where she planned to get rich running a fashion boutique. Days were spent at the language school, nights at the club. But in spite of all her efforts, she never managed to save much. Prices were high and it cost her more to live in Japan than she'd expected. It seemed as though she'd been here for ever, but she still had less than a quarter of the amount needed to open her shop; at this rate she'd never get home. Anna felt trapped, and the feeling filled her days with a vague anxiety, like a hairline crack that threatens to break up a delicate teacup. She lived with the fear that some day she would break, too. And then she met Satake.

He was a fairly regular customer at the bar where she worked, a man who was conspicuously generous with his tips despite the fact that he never drank. She noticed that the manager of the club seemed a bit wary of him. Still, they had assigned him one of the most popular girls, and Anna had concluded that he was out of her league. The next time he stopped in, however, he had asked for her to join him at his table.

'I'm Anna. Pleased to meet you.'

Satake seemed different from the other customers, who tended to be either self-conscious and shy or too full of themselves. He closed his eyes, as if enjoying the sound of Anna's voice, then opened them and studied the movement of her lips as she talked, like one of the teachers at her Japanese school. It made her nervous, as if she'd just been called on in class.

'Scotch and water?' she asked. As she mixed a very weak drink for him, she glanced up at his face. He was in his late thirties, swarthy, with close-cropped hair. Small, up-turned eyes and full lips. Though he wasn't exactly handsome, there was a composure in his face that made it appealing. But his clothes were ridiculously loud. A slick black designer suit that ill suited his sturdy frame, topped off with a gaudy tie. A gold Rolex and a gold Cartier lighter. The effect was almost comic, and strikingly at odds with the mournful look in his eyes.

His eyes. His eyes were like well-water. Anna remembered a photo she'd seen in a magazine somewhere of a dark pool hidden away in a high mountain valley. The water was steel grey, still and cold, and Anna had imagined that its depths sheltered strange creatures in the tangles of water grass. No swimmer would go near a pool like that, nor any boat. At night, the black crater would suck up the starlight, while its strange inhabitants watched unnoticed from the depths. Maybe the man beside her had chosen his shiny costume to keep people from looking into his own dark pool.

Anna examined his hands. He wore no jewellery, but his skin was smooth as if he'd never done any manual labour. For a man's hands, they were beautifully shaped. She couldn't imagine what he did to earn his living. Since he didn't seem to fit into any of the usual categories, she wondered if he could be one of those 'yakuza' she'd heard of. The thought gave her a half-curious, half-creepy feeling.

'Anna?' he said. He put a cigarette in his mouth and studied her face in silence for what seemed ages. There wasn't so much as a ripple on the surface of the pool. No matter how long he looked at her, there was no trace of either approval or disappointment in his eyes. His voice was soft and kind, however, and Anna thought she'd like to hear it again some time.

Realising he had a cigarette in his mouth, she remembered what she'd been taught and picked up a lighter, but she nearly dropped it again in her rush to play the part of the good bar girl. Her clumsiness seemed to make him relax.

'No need to be nervous,' he said.

'Sorry.'

'I'd guess you're around twenty?'

'Yes,' Anna nodded. She had turned twenty the month before.

'Did you pick out this outfit?' he asked, looking at her clothes.

'No,' she said. She was wearing a cheap, bright red dress that she'd been given by another girl from the bar who shared the same apartment. 'Someone gave it to me.'

'I thought so,' said Satake. 'It doesn't suit you.'

Then buy me one that does! – that was the sort of thing she would learn to say only later. That night she had just smiled vaguely to cover her embarrassment. Nor could she have imagined that Satake was amusing himself by picturing her as a paper doll he could deck out in an array of pretty paper dresses.

'I'm never quite sure what to wear,' she said.

'You'd look good in just about anything,' he said. She was used to crude, childish customers who said the first thing that came into their heads, but she could tell even then that he wasn't like them. He was quiet for a moment while he finished his cigarette.

'You were checking me over before,' he said eventually. 'What do you think I do?'

'Are you in business?'

'No,' he said, shaking his head with mock seriousness.

'Then are you a yakuza?' For the first time since she'd sat down, Satake laughed. Anna caught a glimpse of strong white teeth.

'Not exactly,' he said. 'Though you're not far off. I'm a pimp.'

'Pimp?' said Anna. 'What does that mean, "pimp"?' Satake produced an expensive pen from his breast pocket and wrote the characters on his napkin. Anna frowned as she read them.

'I sell women,' he said.

'To who?'

'To men who want to buy them.'

In other words, a scout for prostitutes. She was reduced to silence, stunned that he could admit this so openly.

'Do you like men, Anna?' he asked, his eyes on her fingers as she held the napkin. She looked puzzled.

'I like nice men,' she said.

'What kind of nice men?'

'Men like Tony Leung. He's an actor from Hong Kong.'

'If a man like that wanted you, would you mind being sold to him?'

'I suppose not,' she said, as if turning the problem over in her mind. 'But why would a man like Tony Leung want me? I'm not even that pretty.'

'You're wrong,' he contradicted her. 'You're the most beautiful woman I've ever seen.'

'Liar,' Anna laughed, unable to believe what she was hearing. She wasn't even among the top ten girls in a little club like this one.

'I never lie,' he said.

'But . . .' she murmured.

'You just lack confidence,' he said. 'If you come to work for me, I'll have you believing that you're as beautiful as you really are.'

'But I don't want to be a prostitute,' she said, pouting slightly.

'That was just a joke. I run a club, just like this one.'

But if it was just another club, Anna thought, what was the point? A look of disappointment crossed her face at the thought of more years working in Japan. As Satake watched her, his elegant fingers flicked at the drops of condensation that had formed on his glass, flicking them on to his coaster where they mottled the white paper. Anna had the odd feeling that she'd made the drink just so that he could practice this little stunt.

'Don't you like this kind of work?' he asked at last.

'No, it's not that,' she said, glancing nervously at the woman who ran the club. Satake noticed the look.

'I know it's hard to make this sort of decision,' he said. 'But you came here to make money, didn't you? Then why not really make some? You're wasting a wonderful gift.'

'Gift?'

'A beautiful person has a gift, just like a writer or a painter. It's not something that's given to everybody; it's a special favour. But writers and painters have to work to develop their gifts, and so do you. That's your duty. In a sense, you're a kind of artist yourself, at least that's the way I look at it. But at the moment, you're neglecting your duty.' As she listened to his soft voice, Anna felt almost giddy. But when she looked up, she realised that he was probably just trying to lure her away to his club. The management at her current place had warned her about men like this.

Satake sighed, guessing what was going through her mind. 'You're wasting yourself here,' he said, smiling at her.

'But I don't have any gift,' she said.

'You do. And if you start using it, things will work out just the way you planned them.'

'But . . .'

'And when they do, you'll see,' he said.

'See what?'

'Your fate,' he said.

'Why?' she murmured.

'Because fate is what happens to you in spite of all your plans.' Satake said this quite seriously and then slipped a neatly folded ¥10,000 bill into her hand. She glanced away as she took the bill, feeling that she'd caught a glimpse of something deep down in the pool of his eyes, something she shouldn't have seen.

'Thank you,' she said.

'I'll see you again,' he said; then, as if he had abruptly lost interest in her, he glanced over at the manager and signalled her to get him another girl. Having become suddenly extraneous, Anna moved on to another table. She felt disappointed, in part at her own lukewarm response which she blamed for Satake's loss of interest. She'd half believed him when he said that she'd be prettier if she went to work for him. And if what he said was true, she might even see what 'fate' held in store for her. Had she missed a chance to make something of herself? She regretted her own timidity.

When she got back to her apartment, she took out the bill he'd given her. Unfolding it, she found the name 'Mika' and a telephone number written inside.

After she moved to his club, Satake had taught her a great many things about older Japanese men. That it was often better to make them think you didn't speak much Japanese. That they preferred quiet, conservative girls with nice manners. It was best to let them think you were still in school and that you worked as a hostess just for pocket money. Emphasise the fact that you're a student – most men have a thing about schoolgirls. Even if they know it's a lie, they like to feel they're financially superior, and it makes them more likely to tip well. And above all, try to give the impression that you come from a good family in Shanghai. This they find reassuring. Satake also gave her explicit instructions about the sort of clothes and make-up that would appeal to them. In Shanghai, men might appreciate a woman who insisted on equal rights, but not here.

When Anna still had doubts about the Japanese way of doing things, Satake told her to think of the whole thing as an act, a role she played to succeed in her chosen profession. After that, she learned quickly. She didn't have to become that sort of woman; she just had to perform, as part of her job. Anything for the job. This was something her parents would have understood. And in time she discovered that she did have a gift, exactly as Satake had said. The more she played the part, the more attractive she became. His discriminating eye had been right.

Before long, she'd become the top hostess at Mika; and as her popularity grew, she became more confident. With self-confidence came the determination to make a success of herself in her new 'career'. At last she'd found a way of keeping loneliness, her old stray cat, firmly at bay.

She took to calling Satake 'honey', and in return he made no secret of the fact that she was his special pet. When she realised that he hadn't tried to fix her up with a well-heeled customer the way he was always doing for the other girls, she decided that it was proof that he was in love with her. But no sooner had she come to this conclusion than he called to say he'd found someone.

'He's just the right type,' he told her over the phone.

'What type?'

'He's nice and he's rich.' Of course, the man in question wasn't Tony Leung. He wasn't good-looking and he wasn't particularly young, just very wealthy. Practically every time she saw him, he would hand her a million yen. The maths were simple: if she met him ten times, she'd have ten million – more than enough to live on for a whole year. Soon she'd be rich herself. By the time she actually passed the goal she'd set when she came to Japan, she had forgotten all about Tony Leung.

But the man who had supplanted the handsome actor in her affections wasn't her wealthy patron, it was Satake himself. She found herself intrigued by what she'd glimpsed in his eyes when they first met. He'd said fate was something that happened in spite of our best plans. Then what had happened in his case? She had a feeling – one that aroused a nervous excitement in her – that she of all people might be able to find out; after all, she was his 'number one'. She would have liked to see for herself what sort of creatures lived down there at the bottom of that pool, and catch them with her own bare hands.

In the end, though, she realised that the more she tried to learn about him, the less he allowed her to see. He seemed to guard every aspect of his life with great care. He never let anyone come to his apartment, for example. Once, Chin, the floor manager at Mika, had told her that he'd spotted a man who looked like Satake in front of a run-down old apartment building in West Shinjuku; but instead of the flashy designer clothes the boss favoured, the man was shabbily dressed. He'd come out to dump some garbage, dressed in ragged pants and a sweater that was worn through at the elbows. He could have been any old tired drudge, but as Chin watched, the guy began cleaning up around the garbage can with a surly look on his face, and from the way he moved, he realised that it had to be Satake. The whole episode had come as quite a shock, he told Anna – had even scared him a bit.

'Here at the club, he's so cool. He may not say much, but you know you can depend on him. If that was the real Satake I saw, then it's almost like he's schizy. It gives me the creeps to think that everything he does here is just an act. But why should he have to put on an act for us, anyway? What's he hiding? You get the feeling he doesn't trust us. But how can you live if you don't trust anyone? Maybe it means that you really don't trust yourself?'

Satake was a mystery, a puzzle waiting to be solved. When the rest of the staff at Mika heard the story, the boss's secret life became a topic of endless discussion. Everyone seemed to have his own opinion about what sort of man he was, but no one felt you could trust him much. Anna, though, couldn't bring herself to agree with Chin that it was Satake who didn't trust anybody. Still, she found herself feeling jealous of his secrets, and even ended up thinking that there must be another woman involved. Perhaps it was only with *her* that he could really be himself. . . .

One day, she finally got up the nerve to ask him straight out, 'Honey, do you live with someone?' Satake hesitated a second, staring at her in surprise, which she took as proof that she'd guessed right. 'Who is it?' she pressed.

'No one,' he said with a laugh. But the light in his eyes had seemed to die at that moment, like the time at the end of the night when they turned off the lights at the club. 'I've never lived with a woman.'

'Then don't you like women?' she said. It was reassuring that there had never been talk of a woman in Satake's life, but now she was suddenly afraid he might be gay.

'Sure I do,' he said, 'especially beautiful ones like you. They're like the best of all presents.' As he said this, he took her hand and began stroking her long, slender fingers, but the way he did it was as if he were getting the feel of some delicate instrument. Besides which, when he'd said that he liked women, she had a feeling he meant nothing more than an aesthetic appreciation.

'Presents from who?' she asked.

'From the gods, to men everywhere,' he said.

'Do girls get presents, too?' she asked, meaning getting a man like him for herself. But he seemed not to understand.

'I suppose so. Someone like Tony Leung? How'd you like that?'

'Not much,' she said, giving him a reproachful look. Anna wanted to touch a man's heart, not just his body. And there was just one heart she wanted, just one that made her own beat faster. Unfortunately, the 'beautiful women' Satake said he liked were nothing more than valuable objects, not living, breathing people with feelings of their own. She doubted he had any use for a woman's heart. And if that were the case, then one 'beautiful woman' was as good as the next, which made it all the more unfair that there was only one man in the whole world she cared about. 'So if a woman is good-looking, that's enough for you?' she asked.

'That's enough for any man,' he said. Anna stopped the questions then, having sensed that, deep inside the man she loved, there was something badly damaged. Perhaps a woman had hurt him in the past. The thought filled her with sympathy for him; it also gave her the comfort of daydreaming about how she would heal his broken heart.

That day at the pool, however, Anna had been shaken awake from her daydream. At first she'd been delighted that he'd given in and come swimming with her, but her heart sank at his reaction when that boy made a play for her. Satake had practically winked his encouragement, like an understanding uncle, which could only mean that he had no idea she was in love with him. It was this realisation that made her do something she'd never done before: invite a man home to her apartment – her own modest form of rebellion. But even then Satake had given no indication that he had any feelings for her.

'I don't mind if you fool around,' he'd said, 'as long as it doesn't get in the way of work or go on too long.' She would never forget how he'd sounded as he told her this – as though she were a product to be sold in his store, a toy to attract the men who came shopping. If he'd been especially nice to her, it was only because she did exactly as she was told, played the role of money-making doll to perfection.

She found it hard to sleep that night, conscious as she was that the crack in her self-confidence which she thought had been repaired was opening up again. But the next morning brought an even greater shock.

Chin had called early. 'Anna, Satake-san has been picked up on a gambling charge. Since you were out last night, I thought you'd want to know.'

'What do you mean, "picked up"?' she said.

'Arrested, by the police,' he said. 'They got Kunimatsu and the other people at Playground, too. We're not going to open today. If the police come around asking questions, just say you don't know anything.' Then he hung up.

Before she got the call, Anna had decided that she was going to confront Satake and force him to tell her whether she meant anything to him. She'd made up her mind that if the answer was not the one she wanted to hear, she would quit. Now she suddenly had nothing to do, so she went straight to the city pool and got badly sunburnt there.

That night, as she sat staring at her blistering skin, she remembered their trip to the pool the day before. Perhaps it was unfair to think that he just saw her as merchandise. Wasn't it possible that he was holding back because of the difference in their ages? Why would he bother to do so much for her, if she hadn't mattered much to him? No, it was wrong of her to doubt him, with all the evidence she had. And gradually the good, kind, docile Anna surfaced once again, and she found herself loving him even more than before.

The next day, the employees who had been arrested during the raid came back. They all assumed that Satake would be released as well, but he was the only one who remained in custody. The clubs stayed closed for a week. She heard that Reika had gone to see the boss in prison and he'd told her to announce an early summer holiday.

Anna spent her days at the pool. Baked in the sun, her skin turned the colour of ripe wheat, and she looked more beautiful than ever. When she passed men on the street, they turned to stare after her, and at the pool they seemed to cluster around her like flies. She was sure Satake would have enjoyed this change in her, and it seemed a shame he was missing it.

One evening, Reika came by her apartment. 'I've got something important to tell you,' she said.

'What about?'

'About Satake-san. It looks as though this might drag on a while.' Reika always spoke to Anna in Mandarin; since she was from Taiwan, she couldn't speak the Shanghai dialect.

'Why?'

'It seems there's more to it than just a gambling charge. I've asked around a bit, and I hear it has something to do with that murder case, the dismemberment.'

'What's "dismemberment"?' Anna asked, pushing away the dog that was barking at her feet. Reika lit a cigarette and gave her a searching look.

'You don't know?' she said. 'Three weeks ago, they found a body that had been cut up in pieces. The victim turned out to be that guy named Yamamoto who used to come to the club.' Anna gave a start.

'You mean the one who was always after me?'

'Seems hard to believe, doesn't it?'

He had asked for her whenever he showed up there, and he never took his eyes off her once she sat down at his table. He'd hold her hand, and when he got a little drunk, he'd try to push her down on the couch. But it wasn't his persistence that bothered her as much as the lonely look she'd seen in his eyes. If men wanted to play, she was willing enough, but a lonely man held no attraction for her at all. So when he'd disappeared, she'd been delighted and then promptly forgotten all about him.

'The police are bound to show up here soon. You might be better off moving,' Reika said, looking around at her expensive apartment.

'Why would they come here?'

'They think Satake killed him because he wouldn't leave you alone. And then asked one of the Chinese gangs to get rid of the body.'

'He would never do something like that,' Anna said.

'Still, he was seen beating him up outside Playground.'

'I know, but that's all he did.'

'Maybe,' Reika said, dropping her voice, 'but did you know that he once killed a woman?' Anna felt her throat contract, and her mouth was suddenly too dry to swallow. 'And do you know how he killed her? I was shocked when I found out, and I'm sure the girls at the club would quit if they knew.'

'Why? What did he do?' Anna asked, remembering the strange light that seemed to shine from somewhere deep in Satake's eyes.

'They say he used to work as an aide to a big yakuza boss who ran the prostitution and drug rackets around here. Satake-san sometimes collected debts for the gang, or hunted down girls who tried to get out of the business. Well, one day they found out that a woman was stealing their girls and setting them up at another club. Satake caught her and locked her up in his room. Then, they say he tortured her to death.'

'What do you mean, "tortured her"?' Anna was unable to control the tremour in her voice. She was suddenly reminded of a trip her family had made to Nanjing when she was a child and the horrible mannequins she'd seen at the War Museum. Was this what lay at the bottom of Satake's pool? His horrible past?

'It was really bad – brutal,' Reika said, arching her sharply drawn eyebrows. 'He stripped her and beat her; then he raped her. Then, it seems he kept stabbing her to keep her from losing consciousness. And when she was covered with blood, he raped her again. They say her teeth were broken and her body was covered with bruises. Even the other yakuza were shocked, and wanted nothing to do with him after that.'

Anna let out a long, mournful wail. At some point, while she was still crying, Reika went home, leaving her alone with the toy poodle which sat watching her, wagging its tail.

'Jewel,' she sobbed. The dog barked happily, thinking the

entreaty was an invitation to play. She remembered when she'd bought it. She'd wanted to indulge herself with something special, for her and no one else, so she'd gone to a pet shop and picked out the prettiest dog she could find. Maybe it was the same with men: they wanted women the same way she'd wanted the poodle, and she meant no more to Satake than the dog did to her.

She knew she could never go down into that dark pool now – but it still made her want to cry her eyes out.

4

It was the fourth day after the newspapers began featuring the incident that the police showed up at Masako's house. She had already been interviewed briefly at the factory, and she had prepared herself for the likelihood that they would come here as well. After all, it was common knowledge that she was Yayoi's closest friend. Still, she was fairly confident that they would never find out that Kenji's body had been cut up in her bathroom. If she didn't know herself why she had helped Yayoi, why would anyone else ever suspect her?

'I'm really sorry to bother you. I know how tired you must be.' It was the young man named Imai who had been with the detective at the factory interview. He must have had some idea what it meant to work a night shift, since he seemed genuinely sorry. Masako glanced at her watch and saw that it was barely 9.00 a.m.

'No, don't worry about it. I'll get some sleep later.'

'Thanks,' he said. 'But it really is a strange schedule you people keep. Doesn't it cause problems for your family?' Perhaps because Masako had been frank herself, he seemed to feel that he could begin prying without the usual formalities. He might be young and inexperienced, but she still had to be careful.

'You get used to it,' she said.

'I suppose so. But don't your husband and son worry about you being out all night?'

'I've never really thought about it.' She led him into the living room, wondering to herself if they ever even noticed she was gone.

'I'm sure they do,' Imai insisted. 'Men are like that. It must bother them to have you out that late.' Masako decided against making tea and sat down directly across from him. For such a young man, he certainly seemed to have conservative ideas, she thought. He was wearing a white polo shirt and carrying a light-brown jacket. He put the latter down on the chair next to him. 'Did you consult your husband when you were deciding to work nights?'

'Consult? No, not exactly. Though he did say he thought it might be hard.' That was a lie. Yoshiki had said nothing when she'd announced her decision, and Nobuki hadn't said anything at all to her for as long as she could remember.

'Really?' said Imai, as though he didn't quite believe her. He gave her a puzzled look as he opened his memo pad. 'I'm asking because your situation is the same as Yamamoto-san's, and I guess I find it hard to understand why any husband who worked regular hours himself wouldn't be against his wife working nights.' Startled by this line of reasoning, Masako looked up.

'Why do you say that?' she asked.

'Well, for one thing, you'd be on opposite schedules. How would you have any kind of life together if you were always passing each other on the way out the door? And I guess any man would wonder what his wife was doing, up and about in the middle of the night. It seems to me that a day job would be much better for everyone involved.' Masako took a deep breath. She gathered that Imai suspected Yayoi of getting up to something with other men – probably par for the course for a detective's imagination.

'In Yayoi's case,' she said, 'she'd already been fired from a day job because of the children. The way she explained it to me, she didn't have any other options.'

'That's what she told us, too. But I still don't see how a night job could be worth it.'

'It isn't,' Masako said, interrupting his train of thought. His persistence got on her nerves. 'The one good thing about it is that it pays twenty-five per cent more than the day shift.'

'I don't see how that could be enough to make a difference,' he said.

'Maybe not. But if you had the choice of spending three hours less on the job for the same pay, it might make sense.'

'I see your point,' he said, though it was obvious he didn't.

'I suppose it's hard to understand if you've never had a part-time job.'

'Not many men do,' he said, failing to see the irony in this admission.

'If you did, I think you'd see that it's only natural to want to make a little extra pay for a little less work.'

'Even if it means living your life out of sync with the rest of the world?'

'Even then.'

'Okay, then perhaps you could tell me why Yamamoto-san in particular was willing to put up with this kind of life.'

'I suppose she needed the money,' said Masako.

'Couldn't they get by on what her husband made?'

'I don't really know, but I assume they couldn't.'

'Wasn't it really because her husband was fooling around? Wasn't she doing it to get back at him, and because she wanted to avoid having to see him?'

'I wouldn't know about that,' said Masako. 'She never said anything about her husband, and as far as I know, it would've been a luxury she couldn't afford.'

'Luxury?'

'You said she was doing it to get back at him, but from what I could see she was too busy with those kids and her job to bother about anything as frivolous as revenge.'

Imai nodded. 'I'm sorry – I spoke out of turn. It's just that we've learned that her husband had used up all their savings.'

'Really?' said Masako, making an effort to look as though she were hearing this for the first time. 'Doing what?'

'As far as we can tell, he was a regular at a hostess club and he played baccarat almost every night. . . . So I'll get to the point here. We've been told that you're Yamamoto-san's closest friend at the factory, so I need to ask you what you know about the couple's relationship.'

'I don't know much at all. She hardly ever talked about it.'

'But don't women usually tell one another this kind of thing?' he said, eyeing her doubtfully.

'I suppose some women do,' Masako said. 'But Yayoi isn't that type.'

'I see. That's to her credit. But her neighbours tell us they often heard them arguing.'

'Is that so? I'm afraid I don't know anything about it.' She suddenly wondered whether Imai already knew that she'd been at Yayoi's house that night, and she glanced at him nervously. He looked back calmly, as if still trying to size her up.

'As far as we can tell, he'd been playing around a lot lately and they weren't getting along. At least that's what his colleagues at work told us. It seems he'd been complaining about her to them, saying that she flew off the handle so easily that he tried to avoid getting home until after she'd left for work. Yet his wife insists that he'd never been late until the night he disappeared. Odd, isn't it? Why would she need to lie about something like that? Did she ever mention it to you?'

'Never,' Masako said, shaking her head. 'Then you think she

might be involved?' she fired back.

'Not at all!' Imai insisted, fluttering his hands. 'It's just that I've been trying to think of things from her point of view. Here she is, slaving away on the night shift while her husband is out throwing away their hard-earned money on women and cards, stumbling home every night drunk. It's like she'd been bailing out a sinking ship only to find out that he'd been pumping water in. She must have felt pretty helpless. Most men would have refused to let their wives work at night, but he seemed to encourage it. I can't help thinking there must have been some bad blood there somewhere.'

'I see what you mean, but Yayoi never said anything about it to me.' It struck her as almost comic how perfectly he had reconstructed the situation.

'So you'd have to say that she's just incredibly long-suffering.'

'You'd have to, yes,' she agreed.

'Katori-san,' he said, looking up from his notes. 'When a woman's put in that kind of position, would she go looking for a lover?'

'I suppose some women would. But not Yayoi, she's not the type.'

'Then she wasn't involved with someone at the factory?'

'No, I'm quite sure she wasn't,' Masako said flatly, realising that this was what Imai had wanted to ask her from the beginning.

'Someone not at the factory then?'

'I don't know,' she said. Imai hesitated for a moment before continuing.

'The fact is, I've found out that five men were off from work that night. Is any of them particularly friendly with Yamamoto-san?' He turned his notebook so she could see, and her heart started pounding at the sight of Kazuo Miyamori's name at the end of the list. She shook her head gravely.

'No, none of them,' she said. 'Yayoi isn't like that.'

'I see. . . .'

'In other words,' she interrupted, 'you think Yayoi had a lover and he murdered her husband?'

'No, no!' Imai said, frowning in embarrassment. 'Not at all. I didn't mean to imply . . .' And yet it was clear that that was the scenario he probably had in mind. Yayoi must have had an accomplice, a man, who'd helped her kill Kenji and dispose of the body.

'Yayoi was a good wife, and she's a good mother. I can't think of any other way to describe her.' As she was saying it, Masako realised that she really believed it to be the case; and it was exactly because she had been such a model wife that the discovery of Kenji's betrayal had set her off, had driven her to kill him. If only she'd *had* a lover, perhaps none of this would ever have happened. In that sense, Imai's theory seemed completely off the mark.

'I'm sure you're right,' he said, though he went on flipping through his notes, apparently reluctant to abandon his theory. Masako went to the refrigerator and got a pitcher of cold barley tea, and poured out a glass for him. As he drained it in large gulps, the sight of his bobbing Adam's apple reminded her of Nobuki's – and Kenji's, too. She watched a moment longer, almost in a trance, then slowly turned away. 'I'm sorry,' Imai said when he'd finished drinking, 'but I have to ask, just as a formality. Could you tell me what you were doing last Wednesday from the early morning until about midday?' He set his glass down on the table and cleared his throat as he looked up at her.

'I went to work as usual. I saw Yayoi there. And when I was done, I came home about the same time as always.'

'But you got to work later than usual that night,' he said, glancing at his notes. He'd noticed that she'd punched in at the last possible moment. The care he'd taken with his research surprised her, but she tried not to let it show.

'I guess that's right,' she said, nodding. 'I remember that the traffic was bad.'

'Is that so?' he said. 'So you drive from here to Musashi Murayama? In the Corolla parked outside?' He gestured toward the door with his pen.

'That's right,' she said.

'Does anyone else drive that car?' he asked.

'No, not usually.' She'd cleaned the trunk as carefully as she could, but if they really started snooping around there's no telling what they'd turn up. She lit a cigarette to hide her anxiety. Fortunately, her hand didn't tremble.

'And what did you do after work?' he asked.

'I got home before 6.00 and got breakfast ready for my husband and son. After we ate, they left for work and I did the laundry and cleaning. A little after 9.00, I went to bed. That's pretty much the standard routine.'

'Did you talk to Yamamoto-san that morning?'

'No, not after we said goodbye at the factory.'

At that moment, an unexpected voice broke into their conversation: 'Didn't she call that night?' Startled, Masako turned and found her son standing in the doorway. Her jaw dropped when she realised he had just spoken to her. He hadn't come out of his room this morning, and she'd completely forgotten he was in the house.

'And who's this?' Imai asked quite calmly.

'My son,' Masako murmured. Imai bowed slightly in Nobuki's direction and then looked curiously back and forth between mother and son.

'About what time did she call?' he asked.

Masako stared at Nobuki without answering. It had been more than a year since she'd heard her son's voice, and now he was suddenly speaking up about that phone call. She could only assume that it was some form of revenge – but what had she done to deserve it?

'Katori-san,' Imai repeated. 'What time was it?'

'I'm sorry,' she said, coming back to earth. 'It's been a long time since I've heard him say anything.' At the prospect of becoming the topic of conversation, Nobuki frowned and turned to go.

'What were you saying?' Imai called after him.

'Nothing!' Nobuki yelled, slamming the living-room door behind him and dashing out of the house.

'I'm sorry,' Masako said again, adopting the tone of a worried parent. 'He's been giving us the silent treatment ever since he dropped out of high school.'

'It's a tough age,' Imai said. 'I used to work in the Juvenile Division, so I've seen it all.'

'I almost fainted when I heard him speak.'

'Maybe it was the shock of hearing about the murder that snapped him out of it.' He sounded sympathetic, but he was obviously keen to get back to his question.

'She did call,' Masako told him. 'On Tuesday night, I think.'

'Tuesday. That would be the twentieth. About what time?' He'd perked up now. Masako appeared to think for a moment.

'Just after 11.00. She said her husband hadn't come home yet and she didn't know what to do. I think I told her to go to work and try not to worry.'

'But hadn't this sort of thing happened before? Why would she have picked that particular night to call you?'

'I'd never heard anything about it happening before. She'd always said that he got home by 11.30. That night her son seemed to be having trouble settling down and she was worried.'

'Why was that?'

'She said he was upset because the cat had disappeared.' Masako said the first thing that came into her head, noting that she would have to make sure later that her story agreed with Yayoi's. At least the part about the cat was true.

'I see,' Imai said, still sounding dubious. At that moment the buzzer on the washing machine went off, announcing the end of the cycle. 'What's that?' he asked.

'The washing machine.'

'Oh? Would you mind if I had a look at your bathroom?' he said, standing up. Masako felt a chill run down her spine but nodded and smiled weakly.

'No, go ahead.'

'We're thinking about remodelling,' he said, 'and I'm trying to see how other people have their bathrooms set up.'

'Come have a look then,' she said, leading him toward the back of the house. He followed, glancing around as he went.

'This is nice. How long have you been here?'

'About three years now,' she told him, opening the door to the bathroom.

'This is great,' he said, craning his neck to look around. 'It's really spacious.' Masako decided he was probably considering the possibility that Kenji's body had been cut up here. Warning lights began to flash.

The tour of the bathroom finished, Imai was slipping into his shapeless shoes when he turned back toward her. 'Is your son usually at home?' he asked. Though Nobuki kept very regular hours at his job, Masako decided to risk a small lie.

'Sometimes in, sometimes out. He does as he pleases.'

'I see.' Imai sounded slightly disappointed. He thanked her politely and left without another word.

As soon as he was gone, Masako went up to Nobuki's room. From his window, she could see the street out in front. She peeked through the curtains and saw Imai studying her house from the empty lot across the street. But it wasn't the house itself he was looking at; it was her car.

When she was sure he wasn't around, Masako phoned Yayoi for the first time since the story had come out in the paper.

'Hello,' said a quiet voice. Masako was relieved it was Yayoi herself who answered.

'It's me. Can you talk?'

'Masako!' she cried in obvious delight. 'Yes, there's nobody here.'

'I'd have thought his family or your mother would still be there.'

'My mother-in-law's at the police station, and Kenji's brother had to go home. My mother's out doing the grocery shopping.' Masako could tell from her voice that she was feeling more relaxed now that her parents were there to take care of her.

'Are the police snooping around?'

'They haven't been here much in the last few days.' She sounded almost cheerful, as if she were talking about someone else's problems. 'They found Kenji's jacket at a casino in Kabuki-cho and they're busy with that.' A ray of sunshine, Masako thought with some relief, but the news made her all the more wary of the detective who had paid her a visit.

'Watch out for the one named Imai,' she said.

'The tall one? I will. But he seems nice enough.'

'Nice?' Masako said, dismayed that she could be so naïve. 'There's no such thing as a nice detective.'

'But they're all pretty sympathetic.'

Could she really be so dense, Masako wondered, almost angry now.

'They found out you called me that night,' she said. 'I told them you said your son was upset because the cat had disappeared.'

'You're good,' said Yayoi, giggling quietly. Masako could feel gooseflesh rising on her arms as she realised there was no trace of guilt in her voice at all.

'Make sure you tell them the same thing.'

'Don't worry. You know, I've got a feeling this is all going to work out.'

'Don't get overconfident,' Masako told her.

'I won't. . . . By the way, a reporter from one of the talk shows is coming the day after tomorrow.'

'This soon after the funeral?'

'I told them I didn't want to be on, but they kept pushing.'

'It's asking for trouble,' said Masako. 'Tell them you changed your mind. You don't know who'll be watching.'

'I don't want to do it. It was my mother who answered the phone, and they talked her into it. They said it wouldn't last more than a couple of minutes.'

Masako wound up the conversation quickly, feeling suddenly depressed. It occurred to her that it would have been better to have Yayoi help get rid of the body. She seemed to be forgetting that she was the killer. Still, maybe this lack of any sense of her own guilt made her able to cope better with the suspicion. But what depressed Masako more was remembering the way Nobuki had betrayed her. The first time he'd opened his mouth in over a year – and it was to the police . . .! She knew he was punishing her for having let him keep his distance, but did she really deserve it? In her own mind at least, she'd been doing all she could, both at work and at home; and how did her son repay her? By stabbing her in the back. A wail of misery rose in her throat, and she shut her eyes tight, digging her fingers into the upholstery of the sofa to keep from crying out loud.

Once, a while ago, she'd compared her career at the credit union to an empty, spinning washing machine, but now she realised it had probably been much the same at home. If that were the case, then what had been the point of her life? Why had she worked all these years? What had she been doing? It made her want to howl when she saw what she'd become – a lost, worn-out woman. That was why she'd chosen the night shift. She could sleep away the day and work at night, keep herself moving, tire herself out, and give herself no time to think. But this life at odds with her family had only increased the unhappiness and the anger. And now they couldn't help her, not Yoshiki, not Nobuki, not anyone.

She could see now why she'd crossed over the line. She hadn't understood that she'd sought this other world out of despair. That was her motive for helping Yayoi. But what had been waiting for her on the other side? Nothing. She stared down at her white hands still gripping the sofa. If they came now and arrested her, they'd never be able to find out why she'd done it; they'd find no trace of what had spurred her on. She could hear the sound of doors closing behind her, leaving her utterly alone.

5

Imai mopped the sweat from his face as he walked along the narrow street. It had probably once been a path between rice fields, but now it was lined with small, ageing houses that had been left behind as the rest of the area was developed. By the looks of the badly dented tin roofs, the splintering wood of the doors, and the rusty gutters, Imai guessed the houses had been built more than thirty years ago. They looked flimsy and unsafe, as if a single match would send them all up in flames.

Kinugasa, the detective from Central Investigation, was convinced that Kenji Yamamoto had been killed by the man whose casino Yamamoto had visited the night he disappeared, and who was now locked up in the Shinjuku station. But Imai disagreed and was continuing the investigation here on his own. The discovery that the club owner had a prior record sent Kinugasa running off to Kabuki-cho, but something still drew Imai back to the wife, Yayoi Yamamoto. He couldn't quite put his finger on it, but something – gut instinct, maybe – made him think that she held the key to the case.

He stopped in the middle of the street and took out his notebook. As he flipped through the pages, he ran over the facts in his head. A group of schoolchildren, their heads still wet from the pool, stared curiously at him as they passed.

Suppose Mrs Yamamoto *had* killed her husband. The neighbours said they fought constantly, so she seemed to have sufficient motive. Anyone was capable of murder in a fit of passion. Still, she was on the small side, even for a woman, and it would have been difficult for her to do it unless he was sleeping or drunk. But they knew he'd left the casino in Shinkuku by about 10.00 p.m., and even if he'd come straight home, it would have taken him more than an hour and the effects of any alcohol he'd drunk would have worn off a bit. If they'd had a fight that was bad enough to end in murder, the neighbours should have heard something, or the kids. And they had no witness who could place the victim either on the train or at the station – as if he'd just vanished after leaving Shinjuku.

Still, for the sake of argument, suppose the wife had managed to kill him and had gone off to her job as though nothing had happened. Then, who had gone to work on the body? The bathroom at the victim's house was too small, and the crime lab hadn't turned up anything. So, let's assume some of her friends at work decided to help her. He knew that women were capable of this; in fact, they seemed to have a certain affinity for it – for the whole dismemberment thing. He'd been doing some checking into the records and had turned up two common features in past incidents involving women and chopped-up bodies. One was that the crimes tended to be unpremeditated, almost haphazard in origin, and the other was that they tended to bring out a feminine solidarity.

When a woman commits an unpremeditated murder, her first problem is what to do with the body. In general, she isn't strong enough to move it by herself, so she's often left with no choice but to cut it up. Men sometimes cut up bodies, too, but they usually do it to conceal the victim's identity or because it gives them some kind of sick thrill; women do it because they can't carry it whole. That was how you knew the crime wasn't premeditated. There was the case of a hairdresser who was murdered in Fukuoka; the woman who did it told the police that after she'd killed her, almost accidentally it seemed, she hadn't been able to move the body, so she'd carved her up and carried off the pieces.

It also seemed that women who had some shared experience tended to become accomplices in this sort of thing out of sympathy for the murderer. He'd found one case where a mother had decided that her daughter had been justified in killing her drunk and violent husband, so she decided to help her cut up and dispose of the body; and in another, two close friends had murdered one of their husbands, chopped him up in little pieces, and tossed them all in a river. The man must have been pretty annoying, since even after they were arrested the women insisted they'd done nothing wrong.

With all the time they spent in the kitchen, no doubt women were more used to dealing with meat and blood. They knew how to handle knives, and what to do with the garbage. And perhaps because they had the experience of childbirth, they seemed to feel more closely connected to the whole process of life and death, which might give them the nerve to go through with it. These were qualifications almost every woman possessed – even his own wife, he laughed to himself.

Then suppose that the woman he'd just interviewed, Masako Katori, had decided to help her friend get rid of the body. He pictured her calm, intelligent face again, and her large bathroom. She had a driver's licence, and she'd had a call from Mrs Yamamoto that evening. Suppose it had been a desperate call for help from a woman who had just killed her husband. Katori had stopped off on her way to work and loaded the body into her car. But the two of them had shown up at the factory as if nothing had happened, as had the rest of their little group, Yoshie Azuma and Kuniko Jonouchi. It all seemed too gutsy, too well planned – which shot holes in his theory that the murder itself was unpremeditated.

According to her deposition, Mrs Yamamoto had gone home the next morning and spent the day there, and the neighbours seemed to confirm this. So it was unlikely that she'd had a hand in cutting up the body. Was it possible that Masako Katori had brought the body home and cut it up by herself or, more likely, with the other women in the group? But that left the wife taking it easy at home while the others were going through hell. Why would they have been willing to do something like that for her? It wasn't as if they had a grudge against the man, either. There was no way that a smart woman like Katori would have been prepared to run such a risk.

In this case, there also didn't seem to be much basis for the 'sisterhood' idea that tended to drive these things. Yayoi and Masako didn't have that much in common. First of all, there was a significant difference in their ages, and Yayoi still had small children at home. Then you had their economic circumstances: the Yamamotos were apparently just barely scraping by, but the Katoris, while not exactly rich, seemed quite comfortable – to the point that Imai had questioned Masako's motives for working the night shift. Her husband worked for a first-rate company, and they lived in a brand-new house – nice enough to make Imai himself envious, cramped as his own family was in their city-owned housing. No doubt Masako had problems of her own, especially with her son, but he was almost grown up and would soon be off her hands. Surely they could get along well enough without her salary. . . . At any rate, there was almost nothing to connect her to Mrs Yamamoto except the job at the factory.

Then maybe the whole thing was about money. He remembered how miffed Katori had been when he'd said he thought it was absurd for women to work at night. She seemed particularly concerned about the difference in salary. It was possible that Yamamoto had promised to pay for her help. She knew she needed an alibi, so she'd asked her friend to take care of the body in return for some sort of pay-off; and she could have made the same offer to Azuma and Jonouchi. But where would Yamamoto get that kind of money? Her husband's life insurance – he suddenly remembered hearing she was due to benefit. Had she been planning to use that? Maybe she'd told them about it to get them to go along with the scheme. But then why had they cut up the body? In order to get the insurance money, they needed a positive ID on the victim. Another dead end. And then there was the problem of a motive; his pet theory seemed to run aground on that reef as well. He remembered how shocked Yamamoto had looked when they'd shown her the photos of her husband's body. A look like that wasn't something you could fake. He knew real horror when he saw it – and there was no way she'd cut up the body herself. But no one reported seeing Katori's red Corolla near the Yamamoto house that night, and it hadn't been seen at Koganei Park either. Reluctantly, he found himself giving up on this theory.

That left his fall-back position: that the wife had a lover who was in it with her. She was undeniably good-looking, so it wouldn't be surprising if she'd become involved with another man. But he hadn't been able to turn up any information along this line. He glanced over the places he'd highlighted in his notes, the things that had bothered him during the investigation. First, the fact that the neighbours said the Yamamotos were always quarrelling. Then, their finding that the couple no longer shared a bedroom. Followed by the fact that the older boy had originally said that he'd heard his father come home that night (though his mother insisted it was just a dream). And finally there was the cat, which had refused to come back into the house after the night in question. . . .

'The cat . . .' he said aloud, suddenly looking around. A brown tabby was watching him warily as it crouched among the evening primroses running riot in the garden of one of the shabby cottages. He stared for a moment at its yellow eyes. What had the Yamamotos' cat seen that night? What had made it so frightened it was no longer willing to set foot in the house? Too bad there was no way to question a cat.

It was still blazing hot. He wiped his face with his wrinkled handkerchief and started walking again. A little further down the road, he found an old-style candy shop. He bought a can of cold oolong tea and drained it on the spot. The owner, a heavy-set man approaching middle age, was watching television at the back of the shop.

'Would you know where the Azumas live?' Imai asked him. The man pointed toward the house on the corner. 'I understand the husband's no longer alive.'

'That's right,' the man said. 'He died some time back. The widow takes care of his invalid mother, and now she's got a grandchild living there, too. They were in today for some candy.'

'Is that right?' Imai said, wondering whether a woman in such circumstances would have had the energy to get mixed up in something like this. He could feel his theory evaporating like mist on a sunny morning.

'Excuse me,' Imai called. As he pulled open the door to the Azuma house, he was assailed by a powerful smell of excrement. From the entrance, he could see all the way through the tiny house. Yoshie Azuma was in the midst of changing an old woman's diaper. 'I'm sorry to bother you,' he said.

'Who is it?' Yoshie called.

'The name's Imai, from the Musashi Yamato police station.'

'A detective? I'm afraid I'm a bit tied up at the moment. Could you come back later?' Imai hesitated but then decided he'd rather not have to make the long, hot walk again.

'Would you mind if I just ask you a few questions while I'm here?'

'Fine with me,' she replied, looking around at him. Her hair was dishevelled and her forehead covered with sweat. 'If you can stand the smell.'

'Don't worry about me,' he told her. 'I'm sorry to catch you at such a bad time.'

'Are you here to ask about Yayoi?'

'I'm told you're close friends.'

'Not particularly close. She's a lot younger.' Yoshie grunted as she hoisted the old woman's legs and began wiping her with toilet paper. Embarrassed, Imai looked down and found himself staring at a pair of tiny shoes decorated with a cartoon character. He glanced into the dark, cramped kitchen to his right and realised that a child was crouching on the floor drinking from a juice carton. The grandchild. Well, this much was certain: the body hadn't been cut up here. He wouldn't need to find an excuse to check out the bath.

'Had you noticed anything odd about Yamamoto-san lately?' he asked.

'I'm sorry, but I don't know anything about that.' She had finished wiping and was putting on a fresh diaper.

'Then perhaps you could tell me what kind of person she is.'

'She's pretty straight, so I'm sure this must have shaken her up.' Imai decided that the quaver in her voice was due to exertion.

'I was told she took a fall at the factory the day before her husband disappeared.'

'You've done your homework,' she said, looking up at him. 'That's right. She slipped on some sauce.'

'Could you say what might have caused the fall? Was she preoccupied about something?'

'I don't think so,' said Yoshie, sounding tired. 'You don't have to be "preoccupied" to slip in a place like that.' She gathered up the soiled diaper and got to her feet. Leaving it at the entrance to the kitchen where the child was still playing, she straightened up and turned to face him. 'Was there something else?'

'What were you doing on Wednesday morning?' he asked abruptly.

'The same thing I'm doing now.'

'All day?'

'All day.'

After making his apologies, Imai fled the house as fast as he could. There was something indecent in suspecting a woman who spent her nights at work and then came home to that. When he and Kinugasa had questioned her at the factory, her answers had seemed hesitant, almost suspicious, but not today.

So that left the last member of the group, Kuniko Jonouchi, though Imai was beginning to feel discouraged. He stopped in at the candy store for another oolong tea.

'Was she home?' the man there asked.

'She was a bit busy. By the way, did you notice whether Azuma-san went out somewhere last Wednesday?'

'Wednesday?' he said, eyeing him suspiciously.

Imai showed him his badge. 'She works with a woman whose husband was the victim in that murder-dismemberment.'

'You're kidding!' the man said, his eyes lighting up. 'Horrible business, that is. Now that you mention it, I did read that she worked at the factory.'

'And Azuma-san? Last Wednesday?'

'She sticks pretty close to home,' said the shopkeeper, clearly curious about why he should be investigating his neighbour. Imai left the store without another word, beginning to feel that he was wasting his time.

He stopped for some cold noodles at a restaurant across from Higashi Yamato Station, so it was well after noon when he reached Kuniko Jonouchi's apartment. He pressed the button on the intercom, but no one answered. After ringing several more times, he was just about to give up and head back to the station when a disgruntled woman's voice came crackling over the speaker.

'Who is it?' Imai identified himself and the door opened almost immediately, revealing a sour, groggy face.

'I'm sorry to wake you up,' he said, noting the apprehension that his sudden visit seemed to produce. 'Are you usually asleep at this time of day?' he asked, looking around the apartment.

'Yes,' she said, 'I work nights.'

'Is your husband at work?'

'Uh, yes. . . ,' Kuniko muttered.

'Where?' Imai asked, sensing that a quick barrage of questions might be effective in this case.

'To tell the truth, he quit his job . . . and moved out.'

'Moved out?' Imai repeated. There was no reason to suspect that this could have anything to do with the Yamamoto business, but his professional curiosity had been aroused. 'Do you mind if I ask why?'

'No particular reason,' she told him. 'We just weren't getting along.' As she fumbled in her bag for a cigarette, he could see her breasts swaying loose under the baggy T-shirt. Apparently, she hadn't bothered to get dressed before she answered the door. Noticing the unmade bed in the apartment beyond her, it occurred to him that most men would find it depressing to live with a woman like this. She'd found her cigarette now and tucked it in the corner of her mouth as she looked up at him.

'I understand that you're friendly with Yamamoto-san, and I

wanted to ask you a few questions.'

'Friendly?' she said. 'Not particularly.'

'Really? I had the impression that you two and Azuma and Katori-san were kind of a team at the factory.'

'At work, yes, I guess you could say that. But Yayoi's a bit stuck-up – I suppose because she's good-looking – and we aren't exactly "friendly".'

'I see,' Imai said, sensing her barely concealed hostility. It was interesting that she apparently felt no sympathy for a woman whose husband had just been murdered – and interesting that both she and Azuma denied being friendly with Yamamoto. Something didn't smell right. Word at the factory was that the four of them worked every shift together and then stayed around to chat afterward. Everything he knew about such cases told him that women in this kind of situation would be more than usually sympathetic. 'Then you don't see much of her outside of work?'

'Not much at all.' Getting to her feet, she went to the refrigerator and filled a glass from a bottle of mineral water. 'Would you like some? It's just tap water.'

'No thanks.' He'd caught a glimpse of the contents of the refrigerator as she pulled out the bottle. There was almost nothing to suggest that a woman kept house here, no groceries, no leftovers, not even a bottle of juice. Didn't she eat here? Come to think of it, the whole set-up was a bit strange. Her clothes and accessories looked expensive, but there wasn't a single book or a CD anywhere to be seen and the apartment itself was as basic as it could be. 'Do you cook at all?' he found himself asking as he glanced at the empty fast-food boxes scattered around the room.

'Can't stand it,' Kuniko said. She twisted her face into an exaggerated grimace, but then made a show of looking embarrassed. A real clown, Imai thought.

'I've got a question or two to ask about the Yamamoto case,' he said. 'I understand you weren't at work Wednesday night, and I was wondering if you could tell me why?'

'Wednesday?' Kuniko gulped, her plump hand going to her chest.

'Late Tuesday night to Wednesday morning. Her husband went missing that night and the body was discovered on Friday. I was just curious about why you missed work that night.'

'I believe I had a stomach ache,' she said, sounding a bit rattled. Imai paused for a moment.

'Do you know whether Yamamoto-san had a boyfriend?' he said eventually.

'I doubt it,' she answered with a shrug.

'And how about Katori-san?'

'Masako?' she screeched, apparently startled that he should have mentioned her.

'Yes. Masako Katori.'

'Not likely, not a scary woman like her.'

'You think she's scary?'

'Not scary exactly. . . .' Kuniko fell silent, at a loss for another word. Imai waited, satisfied that she'd meant what she said but a bit puzzled that she found the woman frightening. 'At any rate, I'm thinking of quitting,' she added, changing the subject. 'It's a bit creepy after Yayoi's trouble, almost like the place is jinxed.'

'I can see that,' said Imai, nodding. 'Then you're looking for work?'

'I'm thinking of getting a day job. There's that pervert who's been bothering us and the whole place seems to be going to hell.'

'Pervert?' he said, pulling out his notebook at the prospect of new information. 'At the factory?'

'He's tricky, they haven't been able to catch him.'

'I doubt it's got anything to do with Yamamoto-san's husband, but could you tell me what you know about it?' Imai said, suddenly eager. Kuniko launched into an account of the assaults that had begun in April. As he went on taking notes, Imai thought again how hard it was for these women working nights.

When he left Kuniko's apartment building, the long rays of the afternoon sun were beating down on the concrete parking lot. He sighed, thinking about the long walk to the bus-stop in the scorching heat and the sweaty wait once he got there. The line of shiny cars parked by the building caught his eye, and among them, the flashiest of all, a dark green Volkswagen cabriolet. He thought it strange that anyone who lived here should have a car like that, but he never guessed that it might belong to the seemingly hard-up woman in the apartment he'd just left.

So, he'd come to a dead end. He would have to start over and try interviewing the five men who had been absent from the factory on Tuesday night. He could begin doing it tomorrow, but if that didn't pan out, he'd have to admit defeat and tag along with Kinugasa. He frowned to himself as he marched off into the steamy afternoon.

6

Kazuo Miyamori was sprawled on the upper bunk, studying his Japanese textbook. In addition to the trial of working in the factory, he had set himself two new tests: one was to get Masako's complete forgiveness, and the other, to learn enough Japanese to accomplish that. But these new tasks were different from the simple, repetitive chore of delivering rice to the assembly line; they had a certain attraction to them.

'My name is Kazuo Miyamori.'

'My hobby is watching soccer.'

'Do you like soccer?'

'What sort of food do you like?'

'I like you.'

He lay on his stomach, whispering each sentence over and over until his eyes wandered to the narrow strip of window visible from this angle. The brilliant orange of a summer sunset lit up the clouds hanging below a band of deep indigo. As he watched, the light faded from the clouds and the sky darkened; he wanted night to come quickly, so he could see Masako again.

He hadn't talked to her since that day. It would be too painful if he tried to say something and she ignored him. But he had gone back later and retrieved what she'd thrown into the drainage ditch that night. He fished a silver key from under his pillow and squeezed it in his hand. The cool metal gradually warmed in his palm, and he smiled to himself, thinking that this was just how his heart had warmed to Masako.

If he were to tell any of the other men, they'd laugh at the idea of falling for a woman who was so much older. They'd probably tell him to pick one of the Brazilian women. So no one needed to know. Perhaps he was the only one who could sense the special quality this woman seemed to have; and perhaps she was the only one who could understand what was special in Kazuo. If he could just get to know her, he was sure they'd understand one another. He grasped the key as if it were a charm capable of making his wish come true.

He had strung the key on a silver chain and begun wearing it around his neck. It was such an ordinary object, he doubted even Masako would realise it was the key she'd thrown down the drain. Although he was twenty-five, the little charm made him feel like a high-school boy in the throes of his first crush; and it never occurred to him that his feelings might be nothing more than an attempt to find some comfort in the inhospitable country his father had come from. All he knew was that he was unlikely to find another woman like her, even in Brazil.

*

Kazuo had gone back to the culvert early the next morning. Unlike the Japanese women who worked part-time in the factory, the Brazilian employees generally didn't get off until 6.00 a.m. From then until 9.00 when the day shift came on, the factory was completely deserted. Kazuo had taken advantage of this gap to search the drain.

He was fairly sure he knew where to look, and he was very curious to know what Masako could have dropped down that hole. From the sound it had made hitting the bottom, he guessed it must have been a metal object that wouldn't have washed away. He waited until the last few students and office workers had hurried by on the way to the station, and then used all his strength to drag one section of the concrete cover off the ditch. The morning sunlight sparkled on the surface of the sluggish, murky water which, until now, had flowed quietly in the dark. Kazuo peered into the hole. The water was black and foul but shallower than he'd imagined. Somewhat reassured, he quickly slipped over the edge and dunked his feet, tennis shoes and all, into the stream. Dark, pungent muck splashed up on his jeans, and as he sank ankle deep in the mud he realised he had ruined his Nikes. Still, he bent down low enough to see a metal key holder decorated with a black leather insert that had become wedged under a crushed plastic bottle. He reached down into the lukewarm water and pulled it out. The corners of the leather insert were rubbed white; the holder contained a single silver key. As the sunlight glinted off it, Kazuo saw that it was an ordinary house key. It struck him as odd that Masako should take such pains to dispose of something like this, but these thoughts were soon forgotten in the pleasure of having recovered something that had belonged to her. He detached the key and slipped it into his pocket before throwing the ruined holder away.

*

That evening, he arrived at work earlier than usual and lingered by the door waiting for Masako to appear. He would have liked to wait for her along the route from the parking lot, to see her coming by the deserted factory, but he knew that was out of the question. He mustn't scare her any more than he already had. No, that wasn't right, he realised, smiling to himself: *he* was the one who was scared, scared of doing something to make her dislike him even more – it was this he dreaded more than anything else.

He stood next to Komada, the health inspector, pretending to be checking his time card as he kept watch. At last she appeared, at the usual time, her tall frame bending quickly to put her black bag down on the red industrial carpet as she slipped out of her tennis shoes. For a moment she glanced up at Kazuo, but, as before, her gaze seemed to pass through him, fixing on some point on the wall beyond. Nevertheless, with that one look, Kazuo felt a sort of simple, basic pleasure, like watching the sun rise.

She retrieved her bag and greeted Komada before turning her back to let her run the roller over her clothing – an oversized green polo shirt and a pair of jeans. Breathing slowly and evenly to control the throbbing he felt when she was near him, Kazuo took advantage of the health inspector's drill to stare at her figure. The careless way she dressed looked almost masculine, but he liked her slimness and the way her face seemed to have been stripped of any excess. As she passed by he steeled himself and spoke to her.

'Good morning.'

'Good morning,' she said with a look of surprise. As she disappeared into the lounge, he closed his hand around the key that hung from his neck and said a word of thanks. She had said good morning! Just then, the office door opened, as if someone had been waiting for him to finish this little formality.

'Miyamori. I'm glad you're here. Could I see you a moment?' The plant manager beckoned to him from the door. At this hour, there was usually no one in the office but the elderly watchman. Kazuo was surprised to see the manager here so late but even more surprised to find that an interpreter was waiting for him when he entered the place. 'Could you come back here at midnight? The police want to ask you a few questions.' Having made this request for the interpreter to relay to Kazuo, he turned toward the reception area at the back of the office where one of the Japanese employees was being questioned by a thin-looking man, apparently a detective.

'The police?' Kazuo said.

'Yes, that's him over there.'

'He wants to talk to me?'

'That's right.'

Kazuo's heart skipped a beat. Masako had reported him. The room seemed to go dark as he realised he'd been fingered. He knew it had been self-centred to ask her not to tell, but he never thought she could lie to him like that. He'd been an idiot to think she would let him off the hook.

'Okay . . .' he muttered in Portuguese. Despondently, he made his way back to the lounge. Masako stood there on her own, smoking a cigarette by the vending machines. Neither the woman they called the Skipper nor the fat one named Kuniko had shown up yet, so she apparently had nobody to talk to; and ever since the pretty one, Yayoi, had stopped coming to work, something about Masako seemed different, as though she'd cut herself off from everyone and everything. Still, Kazuo couldn't stop himself from going up to talk to her, his voice shaking with anger.

'Masako-san.' She turned to look at him, and he struggled to make his meaning clear in Japanese. 'Did you tell them?'

'Tell them what?' She folded her thin arms in front of her and stared at him, her eyes wide with surprise.

'The police . . . have come.'

'The police? Come about what?'

'You promised, didn't you?' he managed to say, and then stopped, watching her eyes. She pressed her lips together, returning his stare, but said nothing. Eventually he turned, his shoulders drooping, and headed for the changing area. He would probably be arrested and lose his job, but he was much more upset by the idea that Masako had broken her word to him.

If they were going to question him at midnight, just as he was due to start work, he would need to change now. He found the hanger that held his uniform. Since they were forbidden to wear any jewellery or other personal effects on the factory floor, he removed the chain that held the key and carefully slipped it into his pants pocket. Clutching the blue work cap that the Brazilian employees wore, he returned to the lounge. Masako was standing just where he'd left her, apparently waiting for him. She too had changed while he was gone, but wisps of hair stuck out from her net, suggesting she had hurried.

'Wait,' she said, catching hold of his beefy arm as he passed, but he ignored her and headed for the office. If she had reported him, then the trials were over, and the purpose of his life was gone. But as he walked, he remembered how her hand had felt for that split second when it touched his arm, and he pulled himself back from the brink. This, too, he decided, was a trial, one she herself had set him, and like the others it would have to be endured. The key felt cool against his thigh, as if to remind him it was still there. He knocked at the office door, which opened almost immediately. The Brazilian interpreter and the detective were waiting for him. As his heart began to pound, he slipped his hand into his pocket and closed it around the key.

'Imai,' the detective said, showing him his badge.

'Roberto Kazuo Miyamori,' he said in reply. The detective was tall and chinless. He looked friendly enough, but he had a penetrating stare.

'Are you a Japanese citizen?' he asked.

'Yes. My father was Japanese, my mother's Brazilian.'

'You must get your good looks from her,' he laughed. Kazuo stared at him coldly, sensing that the remark could be taken as a slur. 'I'm sorry to drag you in like this, but I've got a few questions to ask you. I've arranged with the factory to have this time counted as regular work.'

'I see,' Kazuo said, tensing as the detective prepared to start. But the question that came was completely unexpected.

'Do you know Yayoi Yamamoto?' Taken aback, Kazuo glanced at the interpreter, who indicated he was expected to answer.

'Yes, I know her,' he nodded, unsure what Imai meant by the question.

'Then you know what happened to her husband?'

'Yes, I've heard rumours.' What did this have to do with him?

'Had you met her husband?'

'No, never.'

'Then have you ever spoken to Yamamoto-san herself?'

'I say "hello" to her once in a while, but that's about it. What's this all about, anyway?' The interpreter apparently decided against translating Kazuo's question and the detective continued.

'I understand you were off last Tuesday. Would you mind telling me what you did that night?'

'Do you think I'm involved in this?' Kazuo asked, upset at being dragged into something he knew nothing about.

'No, no,' Imai assured him. 'We're just trying to talk to everyone who was friendly with Yamamoto-san, particularly if they were off work that night.' Kazuo still didn't understand why he was being questioned, but he began to outline what he could remember of that night.

'I slept until about noon. Then I went out to Oizumi-machi. I spent the rest of the day at the Brazilian Plaza they have there, and I was back in my room asleep by about 9.00.'

'But your roommate says that you never came home that

evening,' the man said, checking his notes with a sceptical look.

'Alberto didn't notice I was there when he came back with his girlfriend,' Kazuo protested. 'But I was asleep in my bed.'

'But how could he not have noticed you were there?'

'Because I was on the top bunk.' Kazuo looked uncomfortable, remembering what had happened that night.

'So he brought his girlfriend back to the room but never realised you were up there,' the detective laughed, finally seeming to understand. Embarrassed, Kazuo glanced nervously around the empty office. He stared at the line of desks, each with its computer neatly housed in a clear plastic cover. He had wanted to learn how to use a computer when he came to Japan, but somehow he'd ended up here, hauling rice to an assembly line. The whole situation suddenly struck him as crazy, absurd. 'So did you spend the rest of the night in your room?' the man asked.

Kazuo hesitated. That was the night he had grabbed Masako and then wandered around afterward in a fit of remorse. It had started to rain, so he'd gone back to his room at dawn for an umbrella. But that was after Alberto had left for work. Then he'd gone back to wait for Masako.

'I went out for a walk,' he said.

'In the middle of the night? Where did you go?'

'I came here, to the factory.'

'Why here?'

'No reason. I just didn't want to be in my room.'

'How old are you?' he asked with an almost sympathetic look.

'Twenty-five,' Kazuo told him. Imai nodded thoughtfully, as if he had just realised something, but said nothing as he flipped through his notes. 'Can I go now?' Kazuo asked, finding the silence unbearable. The detective held up his hand, indicating he still had a few questions.

'Someone told me that a number of women have been assaulted near the factory,' he said. 'Did you know about that?'

Here it comes, thought Kazuo, clasping the key in his pocket.

'I've heard rumours,' he replied. 'But would you mind if I asked who mentioned this?'

'I suppose I can tell you,' Imai said with some amusement. 'It was Ms Jonouchi, one of the part-timers.' Kazuo released the key from his sweaty palm, overwhelmed with gratitude that it hadn't been Masako. He would have to apologise to her later. 'This has nothing to do with the Yamamoto case, but I wonder if you could tell me whether there's talk among the Brazilian workers about these attacks. Who the victims are, and who might be responsible.'

'Not that I've heard,' Kazuo said, his tone quite final. He looked up at the clock on the wall as he slipped his cap on his head.

'Thank you,' Imai said, realising the interview had come to an end.

The line was already moving when Kazuo reached the factory floor, and a neatly stacked pile of finished meals was growing at the far end. With both Kuniko and the Skipper absent, Masako was doing the rice at the head of the line. After the rumours started about Yayoi's husband, their group had broken up. He was puzzled by this, but at the same time happy that Masako no longer had so many friends around. If he hurried to get changed after the shift ended, he might be able to talk to her.

It had been a perfect chance, but he'd been forced to do fifteen minutes of overtime and Masako, like the other part-timers, was already gone when he got to the lounge, well after 6.00 a.m. As he left the factory, the early morning sun lit up the grey wall of the car factory. It seemed a shame that on such a beautiful summer day he had to go back to his room and curl up in the dark like an animal. He pulled his black cap from his pocket and gloomily tugged it down over his eyes. But when he looked up, he stopped in shock: Masako was standing right where he'd waited for her that morning in the rain.

'Miyamori-san,' she said, her face pale with fatigue as she came up to him. Unconsciously, he reached for the chain and slipped the key out over his T-shirt. It was all thanks to the key. Masako glanced at the silver object as it lay now against the white shirt, but, unaware that it was the one she'd thrown away, quickly looked back at Kazuo's face. 'In the lounge last night, what did you mean?' she said, seeming to assume he could understand her Japanese.

He bowed his head, as he knew was appropriate. 'I'm sorry. I made a mistake.' Masako went on looking at him, apparently not satisfied.

'I haven't told anyone what you did,' she said.

Kazuo nodded. 'I know.'

'The police wanted to ask about Yayoi's husband, didn't they?' she said, then turned and began walking toward the parking lot. Kazuo followed a couple of metres behind, conscious that the Brazilian employees were beginning to leave the factory, chatting noisily among themselves. Masako marched briskly away, as though no one else were with her.

By the time the Brazilians turned off toward their dormitory, Masako and Kazuo were passing the abandoned factory. The fresh smell of summer grass barely masked the stench of the drain, but the heat would soon bring it out; in a few hours, the road would be parched and dusty and the grass would wilt under the blazing sun.

Kazuo saw her glance at the culvert and then stop, as if frozen, at the sight of the section of the concrete cover he had removed. He was confused at the look of panic that was spreading on her face. Maybe he should tell her what he'd done, but he found it difficult to admit that he'd gone poking around in the mud for something she'd discarded, and he kept quiet, his hands thrust in his pockets. Masako's pale face seemed to get paler as she edged up to the hole and peered in. Kazuo watched her from behind, and when he finally got up the nerve to speak, he found himself making the sharp enquiry he'd heard so many times from Nakayama, the foreman at the factory.

'What the hell are you doing?' He knew it sounded rough, but it was the only phrase in his limited stock that seemed to fit the situation. Masako spun around. Her eyes met his and then dropped to the key that hung on his chest.

'Is that your key?' she said. Kazuo nodded slowly, then shook his head. He couldn't lie to her. 'You didn't fish it out of there, did you?' she said, looking angry at his vague response. He spread his arms and shrugged. There was nothing to do but tell the truth.

'I did.'

'Why?' she asked, coming toward him. She was tall, just slightly shorter than Kazuo, and he shrank away from her, clutching the key in both hands to keep her from taking it. 'How did you know? Were you there again that night?' She stabbed her finger toward the grass where he'd been hiding. Just at that moment a large beetle flew out of the undergrowth, as if her finger had pointed a laser there. Kazuo nodded. 'But why?'

'I was waiting for you.'

'Why?'

'You promised to come . . . didn't you?'

'I did not.' She stretched out her hand. 'Now give it back.'

'I won't,' he said, still clutching the key.

'Why would you want something like that?' she said, resting her hands on her hips and studying him.

Don't you understand? Do you want to force me to say it?

'Give it back,' she repeated. 'I need it. It's important.' He understood well enough what she was saying, but he couldn't comply. If it was so important, then she shouldn't have thrown it away. She only wanted it back because he had it now, kept close to his body.

'I won't,' he said. Masako stood there, her lips compressed as she appeared to be considering what to do next. Her anguish made him take her hand. It was so thin it seemed to disappear in his. 'I like you,' he said.

'What?' she said, staring open-eyed at him. 'Because of what happened that night?' He wanted to tell her that he felt she would understand, but no words came. Frustrated, he repeated the one phrase he knew, as if it were a Japanese lesson.

'I like you.'

'I'm afraid that doesn't work for me,' she said, pulling her hand away. Kazuo felt a wave of disappointment. She left him standing by the ditch and walked down the road. He started to follow her but saw rejection in the set of her back; he stopped, letting the sadness wash over him as he watched her go.

7

The factory parking lot appeared to be level but was actually built on a gentle slope. In the dark it was barely noticeable, but at dawn, after a night of exhausting work, the ground sometimes seemed to warp under one's feet. Feeling slightly dizzy now, Masako rested her hands on the roof of the Corolla to steady herself. The metal was covered with drops of condensation from the cool night air, and her palms were instantly wet, as if she'd dipped them in a pool of water. She wiped them on her jeans.

How could he say that? Still, she knew he was serious. Remembering how he had followed her like a lost dog, she turned to look back as she had before, but this time he was gone. She knew he was hurt, and it worried her that he'd recovered the key. But what disturbed her most was the depth of his feelings. She had no need for such emotions any more. She'd left them behind. She understood that she'd chosen her path out of the same sense of isolation that had driven her to help Yayoi.

She had crossed a line that day. She had cut up a man's body and scattered it across the city. And even if she could erase the memory of what she'd done, she could never go back to the way she'd been.

With barely any warning, a wave of nausea rose up in her and she vomited beside the car; but the nausea stayed with her. She dropped to her knees, tears streaming from her eyes, as the yellow bile poured out of her mouth.

Wiping her face with a tissue, Masako started the car. Instead of heading home, she turned on to the Shin-Oume Expressway and headed west, in the direction of Lake Sayama. There was no other traffic at this early hour, but she down-shifted and slowed as the road became curvy climbing into the mountains. Except for one old man on a motorbike, she passed nobody at all.

Eventually she came out on a bridge above the dam spanning the valley. Lake Sayama, backed up behind the dam, spread out before her. The land around the lake had been levelled, and the whole area looked artificial, like an alpine Disneyland. She remembered that, as a child, her son had been reduced to tears by the sight of this lake; he'd been convinced that a dinosaur was going to rise up out of the water, and he had pressed his face against her and refused to look. Masako laughed to herself at the memory.

The surface of the lake glinted in the morning sunlight, hurting her tired eyes. Squinting, she turned off toward the UNESCO Village. A few more minutes along the mountain road and the spot came into view. She pulled on to the grassy roadside and stopped the car. Kenji's head was buried in a place she'd found five minutes into the woods from here.

She got out, locked the car, and made her way through the trees. It was obviously dangerous to have come back, but her legs moved automatically, drawing her into the forest. Finding the enormous zelkova tree she'd used as a landmark, she stood beneath it and stared at a patch of ground a few metres away. A small mound of fresh earth was visible in the undergrowth, the only sign of what she'd done. Summer was reaching its peak and the woods smelt of life, richer and fuller even than when she'd been here ten days ago. She pictured Kenji's head turning to pulp in the ground, becoming part of the earth. Becoming food for worms and insects. It was a gruesome thought, but also somehow comforting – she had given the head to the creatures underground.

The light filtering obliquely through the branches hurt her eyes. Shielding them with her hands, she stared for a long time at the mound as that day came back to her.

She remembered bringing the head into the woods in search of a place to bury it. She had double-bagged it, but it was so heavy she'd been afraid the bottom would rip out. Juggling a shovel in the other hand had been no mean feat. She'd stopped any number of times to wipe her face with her cotton work gloves, shifting the bag each time to give her arms a rest. And each time she did this, she could feel Kenji's jaw poking into her, making her skin crawl. She shivered now recalling the sensation.

There was a movie she'd seen once, *Bring Me the Head of Alfredo Garcia,* in which a man was racing across Mexico with a severed head, trying to keep it from rotting in the heat. She could still picture the actor's face, the fury and distress it showed, and it occurred to her that she must have looked much the same as she buried the head here ten days ago. Anger – that was what she'd felt. She had no idea who or what she was angry at, but at least she'd put a name to her emotion. Perhaps, though, she was angry at herself for being so utterly alone that she couldn't get help from anyone else. Perhaps she was furious with herself for rushing headlong into this whole mess. But now she realised that the anger had been liberating, and something had changed in her that morning.

When she emerged from the woods this second time, she sat in her car for a while smoking a cigarette. She would not be coming back here. Stubbing out the butt, she gave a little wave and put the car in gear.

Yoshiki and Nobuki had already left for work when she got home. The dirty dishes from the meals they'd eaten, no doubt separately, were left forlornly on the dining-room table. Feeling it was too much trouble to wash them, she stacked the dishes in the sink and then stood in the living room wondering whether to go straight to bed.

There was nothing she needed to do, nothing she needed to figure out; all she wanted was to rest her weary body. It suddenly occurred to her to wonder what Kazuo was doing now. Perhaps he was lying sleepless, tossing and turning in his darkened room. Or maybe he was still walking in endless circles around the grey walls of the car factory. As she pictured him on this solitary circuit, for the first time she felt a certain sympathy for him, a sense of the isolation they shared. She decided she would let him keep the key.

The phone rang. What a bother – it was barely 8.00 a.m. She lit a cigarette and tried to ignore the sound, but it kept on ringing.

'Masako?' a voice said when she answered. It was Yayoi.

'Hi. What's up?'

'I tried phoning earlier but you weren't back yet.'

'I had something to do on the way home.' She decided not to tell her where she'd been.

'Have you seen the morning paper?' Yayoi asked, her voice sounding eager.

'Not yet,' she said, glancing at the newspaper that had been left on the table. Yoshiki always folded it neatly after he read it.

'Take a look,' Yayoi told her. 'You're in for a surprise.'

'What?'

'Just look. I'll wait.' Her tone was urgent but she sounded almost cheerful. Masako put down the receiver and picked up the paper. She found the headline on the third page: 'Suspect Emerges in Koganei Park Dismemberment.' Skimming the article, she gathered that the owner of the casino Kenji had visited that night had been arrested on another charge and was being detained in connection with the case. Masako shivered, a bit nervous that things should be going so well.

'I read it,' she said, still holding the paper as she picked up the phone.

'We're pretty lucky, don't you think?'

'It's a bit early to start celebrating,' said Masako, conveying a note of caution.

'Who would have imagined it could all work out so neatly? The paper said they'd been fighting, but I already knew that.' Yayoi was apparently alone now, so she could speak freely.

'How did you know?'

'He had a cut on his lip when he came home, and his shirt was dirty. I wondered at the time whether he'd been in a fight.'

'I didn't notice anything,' Masako said, but she was aware that Yayoi was talking about a living person while she was referring to a corpse. At any rate, Yayoi didn't seem to be listening.

'I wonder if he'll get the death penalty.' Her voice was almost dreamy.

'I wouldn't count on it,' Masako told her. 'More than likely he'll be out soon for lack of evidence.'

'A shame, isn't it,' Yayoi murmured.

'Don't say that!'

'But he had another club, the one where Kenji fell for that slut.'

'And that makes him guilty of murder?!'

'I'm not saying that,' Yayoi protested. 'But he's hardly innocent.'

'Maybe you should ask yourself why your husband would fall in love with another woman,' Masako said, finishing her cigarette. The comment just slipped out, perhaps because of what had happened with Kazuo, and she wasn't really expecting an answer.

'Because he was bored with me,' Yayoi said flatly. 'I was no longer attractive to him.'

'You really think so?' Masako felt she would actually like to have asked Kenji this question were he still able to give an answer. If there was a reason why people were attracted to one another, she wished someone would tell her.

'But sometimes I think he could have been looking for a way to get back at me.'

'For what? I always thought you were the model wife.' There was a pause as Yayoi seemed to consider this.

'That's exactly what he hated,' she said at last.

'Why?'

'I suppose a woman becomes boring when she's good.'

'But why?' Masako repeated, as if lost in thought.

Yayoi sounded suddenly angry. 'I'm not sure myself – you'd have to ask Kenji.'

'I guess you're right,' Masako muttered, startled out of her daze by her tone of voice.

'What's got into you today?' Yayoi asked. 'You're not yourself.'

'I'm just tired.'

'Of course you are,' she said apologetically. 'Since I've started sleeping nights again, I've forgotten what it's like. How's the Skipper?'

'She wasn't there last night. Kuniko either. I think we're all exhausted.'

'From what?' Masako said nothing. 'Sorry. It's my fault, isn't it? . . . Oh! I've been meaning to tell you that I'll be getting all Kenji's insurance, so I'll be able to give them plenty.'

'How much?' Masako blurted out, caught off guard.

'A million each. Is that enough?'

'It's too much. Five hundred thousand each for the Skipper and Kuniko is ample. If I had my way, Kuniko wouldn't get a penny.'

'But won't they be mad? Especially since I'm getting fifty million.'

'There's no need to mention the insurance at all. Just hand them the money and leave it at that. But I wonder if you could give me two million instead?'

'Of course. . . ,' Yayoi said, sounding startled, since Masako had said all along she didn't want to be paid. 'But what made you change your mind?'

'I've decided I need to have some money of my own, just in case. I'd really appreciate it.'

'Of course,' she repeated. 'I owe you such a lot. How could I refuse?'

'Thanks,' said Masako. As she hung up the phone, she had a sense that she was emerging from her funk and might be able to fight her way through this after all. The police had a suspect, but there was no way of telling whether he was thought to be the right man; it was certainly too soon to assume they were in the clear. Still, a slight sense of relief helped her fall quickly asleep.

8

It was late in August when Satake was released, after the typhoons had passed and the autumn winds had begun to blow. As he slowly made his way up the stairs, he found the landing littered with fliers for massage parlours and escort services, and he bent over to pick them up, crumpled them in a ball, and stuffed them in the pocket of his black jacket. It was a sign of neglect that would have been unthinkable when Mika and Playground were doing business. With two of its most prosperous tenants closed, the whole building seemed to be going downhill.

Sensing that someone was watching, he looked up. The bartender at the other club on the second floor was keeping a nervous eye on him from up there. Satake knew the man had testified that he'd had a fight with Yamamoto. He stared back, his hand still shoved in his pocket, and the man quickly shut the purple glass door. He was probably shocked Satake had got out so soon. Aware that the guy must still be watching him through the door, he climbed the last few steps and stood looking at the sign for Mika. For once, its cord was neatly wound and it had been pushed back in the corner. On the door was a notice: 'Closed for Remodelling.'

Satake had been arrested on charges of operating an unlicensed gambling establishment and soliciting for prostitution. In the end, only the gambling charge had been made to stick, and when no hard evidence turned up to support the theory that he was involved in the Yamamoto murder, they had been forced to release him. Knowing how bull headed the police could be, Satake felt lucky to have got away, but there was no denying that the price had been high. The little kingdom he had built up from nothing over the last ten years lay in ruins; and worst of all, his past had been revealed and he had lost the trust of everyone around him. With his past exposed, it would be almost impossible now to go back to his old life.

Trying not to let it get him down, Satake climbed the stairs to the third floor. He had arranged to meet Kunimatsu at what had once been Playground; the club, which had been his prize possession, was already gone. The heavy, expensive door he'd had installed was still there, but the space was now occupied by a mahjong parlour called 'East Wind.' He opened the door carefully, conscious that what had once been his had passed into other hands. Inside, Kunimatsu sat alone, waiting for him.

'Satake-san,' he said, looking up from the one lighted mahjong table in the room. He was smiling, but he seemed to have lost weight and there were dark smudges under his eyes, perhaps because of the spotlight overhead.

'Long time no see,' Satake said, as his manager rose to his feet.

'And it hasn't been much fun for you, I'm afraid.'

'You back at the tiles?' Satake asked, remembering that when he'd first met Kunimatsu, he'd been working at a mahjong place in the Ginza. At the time, Kunimatsu, still in his twenties, spent his days hustling games and running errands for the management. Satake had been amused to see how this ordinary-looking youth was transformed into a seasoned gambler every time he sat down at a mahjong table. He'd been impressed by the depth of his experience in the business, despite his age, and when Satake had opened the casino, he had immediately recruited him as his manager.

'This game's had it,' said Kunimatsu, dusting talc on to the tiles with a practised hand. 'Kids these days learn it online.' There were six tables in the room, apparently rented from a local dealer, but with the exception of the one where Kunimatsu was sitting, they were all covered by white shrouds that reminded Satake of a wake. He nodded. Looking around the room, he remembered where the large baccarat table had been, where the customers had stood waiting for a slot to open – all just a month ago but long gone now. 'Anyway, it looks like I'll be out of a job again,' Kunimatsu laughed, putting the lid on the can of talc. Satake noticed that there were wrinkles now around his eyes.

'What do you mean?' he asked.

'This place is closing up already. They're opening a karaoke bar instead.'

'I guess that's the only way to make a buck these days.' There had been a karaoke machine at Mika, but Satake had never liked using it himself.

'Things are bad all over,' said Kunimatsu.

'We did well enough with baccarat.'

Kunimatsu nodded, a sad smile playing around his mouth. 'You've lost some weight,' he said, looking at Satake more carefully under the light. As he did this, Satake could see a hint of apprehension in his eyes. Like everyone else, he knew that Satake had killed a woman in the past and that he was somehow connected with the Yamamoto business. The world had turned suddenly cold. His creditors were recalling his loans, and he would have trouble from now on finding space to rent for any business venture. Why should Kunimatsu be any different from the rest of them? It infuriated him to think that no one would ever trust him again, but when he spoke, his voice was calm and measured.

'You think so?' he said. 'I didn't get much sleep in there.' In fact, he had barely slept the entire month.

'I can imagine. It must have been rough.' The police had let Kunimatsu go after questioning him on the gambling charge, but he'd been called back several more times about the murder, and he seemed to have some idea how things had gone for Satake.

'I'm sorry you got pulled into it,' Satake said.

'Not to worry. I had a crash course in the judicial system – though I guess I'm getting a bit old for school.' While he talked, Kunimatsu's fingers worked the tiles with a hustler's delicate touch, aligning them with a satisfying clatter and then turning them up one by one. Satake lit a cigarette and watched him in silence for a moment. He sucked the smoke deep into his lungs, savouring its effects after a month of forced abstinence. Satake had few vices. This was his great indulgence. 'I have to admit,' said Kunimatsu, glancing at him, 'it was a bit of a shock to hear what happened to Yamamoto.'

'I guess that's how you end up when you go poking your nose where it doesn't belong.'

'Like you said, "the card shark got bitten",' said Kunimatsu, laughing again.

'And I was right.'

'About Yamamoto?'

'No,' he laughed, 'about me.' Kunimatsu nodded, but it was hard to tell what he was thinking. He probably half-believed that Satake had killed Yamamoto; and if he hadn't gone running for cover, it was only because, unlike the hostesses, he had nowhere else to earn a living.

'It's a shame about Mika, though. There wasn't another club in Kabuki-cho that made money like that.'

'Not much I can do about it now,' said Satake. While he was locked up, he'd told the manager to put everyone on an extended 'summer vacation'; but almost all the employees had been Chinese, with nothing more than student visas, and they'd all gone elsewhere rather than risk getting involved with the police. Reika, the manager who reportedly had ties with the Chinese gangs, was the first to go, heading home to Taiwan at least for the time being. Chin, the floor manager, had apparently moved on to another club, but Satake had no idea where. Anna, who had long been pursued by headhunters from rival clubs, must have found other work as well; and the rest of the girls had either gone home, if they had visa problems, or had signed on at other clubs. What else could you expect in a place like Kabuki-cho? When business was booming, they came buzzing around like bees to a flower, but at the slightest sign of trouble, they were gone. And he could imagine that the news about his past had sent them packing with greater than usual haste.

'Will you be starting over?' Kunimatsu asked. Satake looked up at the ceiling. The chandeliers he had picked out himself were still there, though they were dark now. 'Is there a "New Mika" in our future?' his manager said, staring at his hands which were coated with talc.

'No. I've decided to sell the place, furniture and all.' Kunimatsu looked up at him, clearly surprised.

'That's too bad. Can I ask why?'

'There's something I have to do.'

'What's that?' said Kunimatsu, dusting the powder from his long fingers on to the tiles. 'Whatever it is, I'd like to help.' Without answering, Satake reached back and slowly began to rub his neck. He was having trouble working out the kinks from the sleepless nights in the cell, and if he ignored them they developed into a vicious migraine. 'So what is it?' Kunimatsu sounded impatient.

'I'm going to find out who really killed Yamamoto.'

'Sounds like fun,' Kunimatsu laughed, thinking he was joking. 'Like playing detective.'

'I'm serious,' Satake said, his hands still kneading his neck.

'But what are you going to do if you find him?'

'I'll figure that out when the time comes,' he murmured. He had already given some thought to the question, but he would keep his plans to himself. 'When the time comes,' he repeated.

'You have somebody in mind?' Kunimatsu asked, eyeing Satake nervously.

'At the moment, I'm betting on the wife.'

'The wife?' He looked surprised.

'But you can't tell anyone.'

'Of course.' Kunimatsu looked quickly away, as if he'd just caught a glimpse of the darkness in Satake's heart.

Satake left the club and wandered out to the main street. The late summer days were still brutally hot, but the nights had grown cool, and he appreciated the change as he made his way to a nearby building. It was brand new and cheaply built, all glass and steel; and according to the gaudy signs out front, it housed a collection of small clubs. He checked the name of the bar, 'Mato', on the directory and pressed the button in the elevator. As he opened the black door, the manager, dressed in black himself, came hurrying over.

'Good evening,' he said. But when he got closer he stopped, eyes wide. It was Chin.

'I see you landed on your feet,' Satake said. Chin smiled respectfully, but his expression was less obsequious now.

'Satake-san, it's a pleasure to see you. Are you here as a guest?'

'What else?' he said, smiling bitterly.

'And did you have a particular girl in mind?'

'I heard that Anna ended up here as well.' Chin glanced toward the back of the room and Satake's eyes followed. The place was smaller than Mika, but the Chinese decor and rosewood furniture were nice enough.

'I'll call her for you,' said Chin. 'But she's changed her name.'

'To what?'

'She's "Meiran" now.' The name sounded flat and ordinary to Satake's ears. The lady in charge, a Japanese woman in a kimono who knew Satake, looked up in surprise as he was led through the club.

'Satake-san,' she said. 'What a pleasure. Have things settled down at your place?'

'You might say that,' he told her.

'I understand Reika-san is still in Taiwan.'

'Could be. I haven't heard from her.'

'I suppose there could be some unpleasantness if she came back,' the woman said. Satake sensed she was referring to his own supposed connections with the Chinese mafia, but he decided to ignore the remark.

'I wouldn't know,' he said.

'Well, it's all been a terrible shame,' she said, looking uneasy, as if she'd realised she had offended him. He smiled vaguely, beginning to weary of the constant suspicions. A good-looking woman who might have been Anna was seated toward the back of the club, but from behind he couldn't be sure.

The table that Chin led him to was poorly situated, in the middle of the place, even though the preferred seats at the rear were mostly empty. The customers were taking turns at the karaoke machine, and after each performance, the hostesses would automatically applaud, like a troop of trained animals. Recoiling from the noise, Satake worked his way further along the couch. A young woman, whose only qualification seemed to be her youth, appeared at the table and began to chatter at him in broken Japanese, an artificial smile plastered on her face. Satake sat quietly downing glasses of cold oolong tea.

'When is Anna . . . I mean Meiran . . . going to be free?' he asked after a while, at which the girl abruptly stood up and moved to another table. From then on, he sat by himself, eventually nodding off in the comfort of a familiar environment. He was probably asleep for no more than a few minutes, but to Satake it felt like hours. There was no chance of his finding any real peace now, but these moments of rest were an escape, a chance for his body to relax.

He caught a whiff of perfume and opened his eyes to find Anna seated across from him. Her deeply tanned skin was set off by a white silk pants suit.

'Good evening, Satake-san,' she said. It had always been 'honey' before.

'How are you?' he asked.

'Quite well, thanks.' She smiled as she answered, but Satake could feel the wall that had gone up between them.

'That's some tan,' he said.

'I was at the pool every day.' She was quiet for a moment, perhaps remembering that it had all begun with their trip to the pool. Her hands seemed to move automatically, making two weak drinks from the bottle of Scotch they had brought without a word from him. She set one in front of him, though she knew he didn't drink.

'How are they treating you here?' he asked, studying her face.

'Well enough. I was top girl this week; the customers at Mika have all been coming around.'

'I'm glad to hear it.'

'And I've moved.'

'Where?'

'To Ikebukuro.' She didn't offer the address, and an awkward silence fell between them.

'Why did you kill that woman?' she asked suddenly. Taken by surprise, he stared into her brilliant eyes.

'I don't really know myself,' he said.

'Did you hate her?'

'No, it wasn't that.' In point of fact, she'd been an intelligent, rather impressive woman. But he felt it was useless trying to explain to someone as young as Anna that usually hatred was an emotion arising out of the desire to be accepted by another person, and it didn't apply in this case.

'How old was she?' Anna said.

'I'm not sure. In her mid-thirties, probably.'

'What was her name?'

'I don't remember any more.' He'd often heard it mentioned at the trial, but it was an ordinary one that had long since slipped his mind. He had no need for a symbol like a name when the woman's face and voice were sealed inside him.

'Didn't you care for her? Were you her lover?'

'No, I met her for the first time that night.'

'Then how could you have killed her like that?' she pressed. 'Reika-san told me what you did, how you tortured her beforehand. If you didn't love her – or hate her – how could you have done something like that?' Hearing the intensity in her voice, the people at neighbouring tables turned to look, then quickly looked away again, unnerved perhaps by what they'd heard of her question.

'I don't know,' he murmured. 'I really don't.'

'You were always so nice to me. Was Anna just taking her place?'

'No,' Satake said.

'But honey,' she said, 'how can there be two of you? The one who killed that woman, and the other one who's so good to me.' In her agitation, she'd reverted to calling him 'honey'. He opened his mouth to answer but she interrupted: 'I was just a pet to you, something to spoil. You had me dolled up, like a fancy poodle, so that you could sell me to your customers. That's how you got your kicks, turning me into your best product. If I hadn't let you, would you have killed me like you did that woman?'

'Of course not,' Satake said, taking out another cigarette and lighting it himself, which she would never have let him do before. 'You're beautiful. She was . . .' At a loss for the right word, he fell silent. She waited, watching him, but he couldn't go on.

'You say I'm beautiful, but the truth is, that's all I am to you. When I first heard what you'd done to that woman, I felt sorry for her. But I think maybe I'm just as sad. Do you know why, honey? Because you can't even hate me enough to do what you did to her. If you cared enough to do that, at least I'd know you felt something. But you don't, you can't. If you could, I don't think I'd mind dying. Once you killed her, you had nothing left for me but making me look nice. But nice is dull, and Anna's been unhappy. Anna's the really sad one, did you know that, honey?' Tears had welled up in her eyes, and as she finished speaking they ran down past her pretty nose and dropped on to the table. The people around them were staring now, and the lady in charge was watching with a worried expression.

'I won't bother you again,' Satake said. 'You get back to work and forget about all this.' Anna said nothing as he rose and paid the bill. Chin followed him to the door with a polite smile, but no one else came to see him off. Fair enough, he thought. This was no longer his world.

The day that detective had first questioned him, he'd realised that the woman who'd died was still clinging to him, despite the seventeen years that had passed. And now he was resigned to facing her, to exposing the memories he'd kept tightly sealed away, like prying loose the soft meat inside a cracked shell.

It had been a long time since he'd been alone in his own apartment; nearly four weeks, to be precise. As he opened the door, he was greeted by the musty smell of a room shut up too long in the summer heat. He also heard voices, and he hurried inside after slipping out of his shoes. A pale light was flickering in the darkness – the television had been left on. He had apparently forgotten to turn it off as he'd wandered out into that miserable, scorching day to meet Anna. And whoever had come to search the place later hadn't bothered to turn it off for him. He smiled bitterly, settling down in front of the set. The news was just ending.

Now that the summer was winding down, the buzzing in his head had begun to subside. He rose and went to open the window. The noise and fumes from Yamate Avenue rose to meet him, but the cool night air flowed in, replacing the stale air in the apartment. The lights of the skyscrapers shone starkly against the black sky. He was all right now, he told himself, filling his lungs with the dirty city air. There was just one more thing he had to do.

He opened the closet where he stuffed old newspapers before throwing them out. The newsprint was damp with humidity and beginning to yellow, but he flipped through the pages in search of articles about the Koganei Park murder. When he found something, he laid the paper out on the floor and took notes on a small pad. Once he was done, he sat back and smoked a cigarette as he went over what he'd written.

Then he got up off the floor and turned off the TV. He was ready to go out, go wandering through the back streets of the city. There was nothing to hang on to now, nothing to lose. He had crossed a deep river and the bridge had collapsed behind him. There was no way back. He felt an exhilaration that he hadn't known for years, not since his twenties when he'd been a gang boss's gofer. There was something oddly similar about this feeling of wandering without a destination and the realisation that there was no going back. Both promised a kind of liberation, he thought, smiling to himself.

Piece Work

1

Flat broke. No matter how much she tore up the apartment, all she could find was some loose change and a few thousand-yen bills in her purse. Kuniko had been staring at the wallet-sized calendar she'd got at Mister Minute for some time, but the longer she stared, the more unavoidable it looked: the due date on her loan from Jumonji. Masako had made a big show of telling him they'd get another loan to pay him, but since then it seemed she'd forgotten all about Kuniko's problems. And what had come of Yayoi's promise to pay her? So far, not one yen. The two of them had forced her to do that horrible thing, had dragged her into their crime, and then left her high and dry. Suddenly furious, she raked the pile of thick fashion magazines off the table in a flurry of glossy print. Then she sat for a while, turning the pages with her toes, lost in the dreamy ads for all her favourite luxury items, Chanel, Gucci, Prada . . . shoes, bags, the new fall fashions.

The magazines had been retrieved from the recycling bin. They had food stains here and there, but she didn't mind: at least they were free. Her newspaper subscription had lapsed, and she didn't go out in the car much any more because she couldn't afford gas. About the only amusements she had left were the soaps and talk shows on TV; so who was she to sniff at someone else's discarded magazines? Not knowing where Tetsuya had gone off to was one thing, but she'd missed a lot of shifts at the factory in August, so her pay cheque had been smaller than usual. No wonder she had no savings. Poverty just wasn't her thing, and the longer it went on, the louder she wanted to scream.

She'd looked through the want-ads with the idea of finding steady daytime work, but she knew those jobs didn't pay enough for her to keep up with her loan payments. Something in the night life, something maybe a little sleazy, would pay much better, yet having no confidence in her own appearance kept her from even considering this. So she had little choice but to stay at the factory, where she could earn a decent hourly wage on the night shift. She seemed to contain two contradictory impulses, like two sides of a coin: a longing to be rich, to dress up and flaunt herself; and a feeling of worthlessness that made her want to curl up in the dark where no one could see her.

Maybe she should just declare bankruptcy. She had toyed with the idea, but if she went ahead with it, she might be cut off from her precious credit cards for life. There was always the old solution of trying to live within her means – but she'd rather die than do that! She had never been much good at delaying gratification of any kind, so what hope did she have now, when the prospect of a big pay-off from Yayoi was dangling there in front of her?

She decided to call Yayoi right away. She'd been wanting to for some time, but the fear that the police might be hanging around had stopped her. Now, she was beyond caring.

'It's me, Kuniko.'

'Oh,' Yayoi murmured. It was clear her call wasn't welcome, but Kuniko forged ahead.

'The newspapers make it sound like you're in the clear.'

'About what?' Yayoi said. So she was still pretending. Kuniko could hear a cartoon blaring in the background and children's voices. They sounded pretty cheery for kids whose daddy had ended up like Kenji, she thought, her surliness extending even to two little boys.

'Don't play dumb with me,' she said. 'I saw where they arrested that guy who owns the casino.'

'Yes, I guess they did.'

'You guess they did? You don't deserve such dumb luck.'

'But I'm not the only one. I know I shouldn't say this, but if you hadn't left the bags in the park, none of this would ever have come out. Masako was pretty mad.' Yayoi was usually so docile, so easily cowed by bluster, that Kuniko was thrown off balance.

'Well . . . ,' she sputtered, 'you're a fine one to talk. I'm not the murderer around here.'

Muffling the receiver, Yayoi said, 'What is it you want? Has something happened?'

'Yes, it has. I'm broke! I need money. You said you'd pay me, but when? Could you at least give me some idea of a date?'

'Oh yes. I'm sorry, but I still can't say exactly. It should be in September, if you can wait that long.'

'September. . . ?' Kuniko gulped. 'You're getting it from your parents, aren't you? Why can't you just tell them you need it now?'

'I suppose I could,' she said, still sounding non-committal.

'And can you really give me ¥500,000?'

'That's what I promised.'

'Good,' she said, relieved on that score at least. 'But I'm still in a pinch. Could you let me have ¥50,000 right away?'

'If you can just wait a bit longer . . .' Her voice trailed off.

'Then what? Are you getting insurance or something?'

'No, of course not,' Yayoi stammered. 'He didn't have any insurance.'

'Then you're in the same boat as me: no husband and nothing but a part-time job to pay the bills. How do you think you'll get by?'

'To tell the truth, I haven't really thought about it much. I imagine I'll stay here and do the best I can. My mother thinks that's the best plan, at least for now.' This earnest answer to her rhetorical question irritated Kuniko.

'What about your parents?' she said.

'They'll help some, I'm sure. But there's only so much they can do.'

'That's not what Masako told us when she promised you'd pay.'

'I'm sorry,' Yayoi whispered.

'Well, I'm not asking for much. Your dad has a regular job – you should be able to get something out of him now.' Desperate to extract whatever she could, Kuniko continued to wheedle, but Yayoi simply repeated that she would have to wait, and eventually, realising that she was wasting the price of the call, Kuniko hung up.

Masako was next. Kuniko saw her every night at the factory, but they hardly said a word to each other. Ever since she'd learned that Masako knew Jumonji, she'd been more than usually wary of her. Despite her money problems, she still somehow associated herself more with the elegant world of her fashion magazines than the back streets where the likes of Masako and Jumonji hung out.

Nevertheless, the due date on the payment was almost up and she had to do something, no matter how risky. She'd already forgotten that a similar attitude had just recently got her involved in Yayoi's mess. She dialled Masako's number.

When Masako answered, there was none of the background noise she'd heard at Yayoi's place. Kuniko wondered what Masako did all by herself in that big, clean house. A chill ran down her spine at the memory of the scene in her bathroom. Did she shower on those tiles that had been splattered with blood? And what did she feel like when she settled into a tub that had held those awful bags? The thought made Masako seem even scarier.

'It's Kuniko . . .' she said in a breathy voice.

'Your payment's due, isn't it?' said Masako, dispensing with formalities. Apparently she hadn't forgotten.

'That's right. I'm wondering what I should do.'

'Don't ask me. It's your problem.'

'But didn't you say we'd get another loan to cover this one?' she whined, feeling she'd been misled.

'So go get one,' Masako told her. 'I'm sure you'll find someone dumb enough to lend you more money. Use that to pay off Jumonji and then go find another to pay off that one.'

'How does that solve anything? I'll just be running in circles.'

'What do you think you've been doing?'

'Don't say that! I'm asking you what I should do.'

'You are not. You don't want advice, you want money.' Kuniko winced at her scornful tone of voice.

'Then why don't you let me have some? Yayoi just tells me to wait.'

'I don't have any to lend. When things settle down, I'm sure Yayoi will come through. You'll just have to make do until then.'

'But how?'

'You're young and healthy. You figure it out.'

Kuniko slammed the receiver down. Some day, she'd get back at Masako, figure out how to make her sorry for treating her this way; but at the moment she couldn't think how, and it made her so angry she wanted to spit.

Just then, the intercom rang. Startled, she crouched down, wanting to curl up in a ball and hide, if just for today. She wrapped her arms around her head, breathing hard.

The buzzer rang again. Probably another detective. Worse yet, it could be the same one, that nosy Imai who'd come three weeks ago. She thought she'd managed to avoid telling him anything important, but she hated the way he looked at her. What if he said they had a witness who'd seen a green Golf at Koganei Park? What would she do then? She just couldn't face him again right now. Deciding to pretend she wasn't home, she lowered the volume on the television; but as she was doing this, someone began knocking on the door.

'Jonouchi-san? It's Jumonji from Million Consumers. Are you in there?'

'Yes,' she stammered into the intercom. 'I know the payment's coming up, but I still have a few days, don't I?'

'Of course,' said Jumonji, sounding pleased to have caught her in. 'I actually wanted to talk to you about something else.'

'About what?'

'I guarantee it will be worth your while. Could I come in for a minute?' Kuniko was still wary, but her curiosity got the better of her and she opened the door, to find him standing there holding a box of cakes. She shrank back, conscious of her thick legs in a pair of shorts. He was dressed more casually than usual, in chinos, sunglasses and a loud Hawaiian shirt – birds of paradise on a black background. 'Sorry to bother you like this,' he said, handing her the box, 'but there's something I'd like to discuss with you.' She hesitated, but his smile was beginning to work its magic.

'Come in,' she told him. He peered about curiously before sitting down at the dining-room table while she hurriedly picked up the magazines she'd strewn on the floor.

'Shall we have the cakes?' she suggested, bringing out plates and forks and an almost empty bottle of oolong tea. Then she told a lie. 'If it's about the payment, I'm all set to make it, the day after tomorrow, I think it was?'

'Actually, it has nothing to do with your loan. It's something else, something that's got me very curious.' He took a pack of cigarettes from his pocket and offered her one. She nearly pounced on it, having been unable to buy cigarettes lately, and he watched as she lit it and took a long, satisfied drag. 'You're welcome to keep the pack,' he told her.

'Thanks,' she said, putting it down in front of her.

'I get the feeling things are rather difficult for you now.'

'You might say that,' she sighed, no longer bothering to keep up a front. 'I haven't heard from my husband. . . .'

'I assumed you'd be heading off to work soon, so I wanted to catch you before you left. Actually, I wanted to talk to you about the lady who signed your guarantor's form the other day – Yamamoto-san.' Kuniko looked up at him with a start. He was watching her with a good-natured smile. 'I was reading the paper the next morning, and I got a shock when I realised she must be the wife of that guy who was found cut up in the park. And since then there's something that's been bothering me: why would she have signed as your guarantor when she was in the middle of all that?' His speech seemed well rehearsed.

'Because I asked her to. We're friends from the factory.'

'But why didn't you ask Katori-san? She worked at a credit union for more than twenty years, so she knows all about that kind of thing.'

'A credit union?' So that was Masako's secret past. Now that she thought about it, she could just picture her sitting at a computer terminal behind the counter at some two-bit bank.

'What I'd really like to know is why you'd choose Yamamoto-san to be a guarantor.'

'Why do you want to know?' The question was natural enough. Jumonji laughed, running his hands through his brown hair.

'Plain curiosity.'

'Because Yamamoto-san is nice. Katori-san isn't – it's as simple as that.'

'And it didn't matter to you that her husband was missing?'

'I didn't know that at the time.'

'It was pretty generous of her to agree, considering what she was going through.'

'Like I said, she's a nice person.'

'Okay. Then why did Katori-san come to get the form back?'

'You've got me,' Kuniko said. He wasn't here out of 'plain curiosity', that much was obvious. Sensing trouble, she began to feel panicky.

'Katori-san must have known the husband was missing,' he suggested, 'and thought it might look bad if her friend's name turned up on the form.'

'No. She thinks I'm an idiot. That's why she went to get it back.'

'It just doesn't add up,' he said, folding his hands behind his head and staring at the ceiling, as if he enjoyed playing the detective like this. Kuniko, on her side, was enjoying his company and soon forgot her earlier misgivings.

'I think I'll have a piece of cake,' she said.

'Go ahead, help yourself. This bakery's quite good. I have it on the best authority: a high-school girl.'

'Your girlfriend?' said Kuniko, a hint of coquetry in her voice. Fork poised, she stared into his dark-brown eyes.

'No, no,' he said, rubbing his face to cover mild embarrassment.

'I bet you could have any girl you want, even the young ones.'

'No, no, let's not exaggerate.' Kuniko concentrated on her cake for a moment, having already lost interest in trying to figure out why he'd come. Jumonji glanced at the date on his watch.

'How many payments do you have left on your loan?' he asked suddenly.

'. . . Eight,' said Kuniko, putting down her fork with a dismayed look.

'Eight payments? A bit more than ¥440,000, all told. I tell you what I'll do: if you tell me everything you know, I'll write off the loan.'

'Write it off?'

'Meaning you won't have to pay it back.' Kuniko pondered this inexplicable proposition for a second, until she realised she had a dollop of whipped cream on her mouth.

'Tell you everything I know about what?' she said, licking her lips.

'About what you ladies did.'

'But we didn't do anything.' She held her fork steady, but inside her head the scale on which she weighed everything in her life, calculating profit and loss, was going haywire.

'Nothing?' Jumonji said. 'Really? You see, I've had my people do some checking. They found out how friendly you are, you and Yamamoto-san and Katori-san, and one other lady, I believe. I'm guessing that the three of you felt sorry for Mrs Yamamoto and decided to help her out.'

'Help her out? No, we didn't do anything.' Kuniko put down her fork.

'You told me yourself that you had some money coming in soon,' he said, smirking. 'Did that have anything to do with this?'

'To do with what?'

'Don't play dumb with me,' he said – exactly what she'd said herself to Yayoi a while ago. 'With the Yamamoto murder.'

'But I read where they arrested that casino owner for that.'

'That's what the newspapers said, but something about the whole thing smells.'

'Smells? Like what?'

'Like a bunch of women helping out a friend.'

'But I told you, nobody helped anybody.'

'Then why did Mrs Yamamoto guarantee your loan at a time like that? Most people wouldn't want to do that even if they didn't have anything else to worry about. Why don't you just tell me, and then you can forget about the payments.'

'And what would you do if I did tell you?' The question slipped out before Kuniko could stop herself. For one second, his eyes shone with the satisfaction of having guessed correctly.

'I wouldn't do anything. I just need to satisfy my curiosity.'

'And if I won't tell you anything?'

'I still won't do anything. You'll just go on making your payments – when was the next one due? The day after tomorrow, wasn't it? Eight more payments of ¥55,200. You can handle that,

I'm sure.' I'm sure too, thought Kuniko – that I'm flat broke. She licked her lips, but the whipped cream was gone.

'How can I be sure you'll cancel the loan?' she said. Jumonji opened the briefcase that was resting on his lap and pulled out some papers: Kuniko's promissory note.

'I'll tear this up as soon as we're finished,' he said. Instantly, Kuniko's internal balance tipped in favour of the cancelled loan. If she could wipe out the payments to Jumonji, she could keep all the money she'd be getting from Yayoi for herself. Once she realised this, there was really no other option.

'Okay, I'll tell you.'

'Really? That's great,' he said, laughing a mirthless laugh.

The rest was easy. Kuniko actually enjoyed describing how Masako and Yayoi had forced her to go along with their plan. She would worry about the consequences later, for right now she felt she was getting even with them. She'd never been any good at deferring her pleasures, but for the moment at least she could defer the pain.

2

Jumonji sat on the bench in the playground in front of the apartment building. He put a cigarette in his mouth, but as he pulled his lighter from his pocket, he noticed that his hand was shaking. Laughing to himself, he tightened his grip and lit the cigarette. After the first drag, he looked up at the building and located the balcony of Kuniko's apartment. Other than the air-conditioning unit, it contained nothing but a messy stack of black garbage bags. So it all came down to the garbage, did it?

A dozen or so children, probably first or second graders, were playing tag in the fading light. They seemed almost frantic as they chased after one another, perhaps because they knew they'd soon have to be heading home, or because their summer vacation itself was drawing to a close, with the prospect of classes and endless homework awaiting them. Their cries pierced the air, and dirt flew in their wake. Finding all this youthful energy a bit overpowering, Jumonji slumped down on the bench.

Kuniko's story had excited him. It wasn't just that something he'd thought inconceivable was actually true; it was the shock of discovering that Masako Katori was at the centre of it all. Even with his own unsavoury background, he would have baulked at the job of getting rid of a body – let alone cutting one to pieces. He felt in awe of her. Who'd have thought a skinny old dame like that would have the nerve? It never once crossed his mind that she might have got herself into something she should have avoided.

'So cool!' he murmured to himself. His cigarette had burnt down and was about to scorch his fingers . . . the same way whatever he was getting into might burn him, too. He wanted to join up with her, do something risky – something cool. And profitable. He'd always hated working as a team, but he'd welcome the chance to team up with Masako. Above all else, he felt he could trust her.

He remembered catching sight of her years ago as he'd walked into a coffee shop near the credit union. The place was completely full and almost all the customers were fellow employees who had crowded around the tables regardless of who they'd come in with. But Masako had been sitting alone at a table for four by the window. He remembered thinking at the time that it was strange no one had joined her, and it was only later he'd learned that she was being ostracised. But there had been no sign then of the trouble she was going through. She'd sat alone, calmly sipping her coffee and reading the business paper she'd spread in front of her much as a man might. The other jerks crammed into their seats at the surrounding tables had looked stupid by comparison.

The memory of it made him clap his hands and laugh aloud. Startled, the children stopped for a moment and eyed him suspiciously, but he didn't care. Though he'd never felt the slightest hint of desire for an older woman, when it came to business, he had always trusted them far more than he did men. It occurred to him that this might even be the result of having met Masako at an impressionable age. He took his cell phone and address book out of his bag and, finding the number he wanted, pressed the buttons.

'Toyosumi head office.' They picked up almost immediately.

'This is Akira Jumonji. Could I speak with Soga-san?' The young man at the other end mumbled for him to wait and a recording of the 'Lovers Concerto' came on – not exactly what you'd expect from a yakuza office.

'Akira, is that you? They said it was somebody named Jumonji. Shit, boy, call yourself Yamada.' The tone was flat but Jumonji could tell he was being teased.

'I gave you my card, didn't I?' he said.

'Seeing the writing and knowing how to pronounce it are two different things.' Soga occasionally came out with the odd intelligent remark, despite the way he looked.

'There's something I want to ask your advice about,' Jumonji said. 'Could we get together some time soon?'

'Soon? How about now? We'll go for a drink. Ueno okay with you?' Jumonji checked his watch and agreed. He knew he was sticking his neck out, but he'd paid more than ¥440,000 for the information. He might as well get on with it.

They had agreed to meet at a quiet bar in Ueno that had been around for a number of years. When Jumonji arrived at the low, ivy-covered building, he found the two young men he'd seen that day in Musashi Murayama standing guard at the door. The dyed-blond, dense-looking one greeted him. Bodyguards – just in case;

Jumonji remembered that Soga had always liked playing the mob boss, even back in their biker days. Still, it would be a mistake to think of him as some puffed-up punk. Jumonji braced himself for what was to come.

As he entered the bar, Soga, cigarette in hand, waved to him from a dark table in the back. The room was panelled in wood that smelt of wax. An older man in a bow-tie stood behind the counter, his face expressionless as he worked the cocktail shaker. Soga sat alone, legs spread wide on a soft, green velvet chair.

'It was good running into you the other day,' Jumonji said. 'Sorry to be bothering you so soon.'

'No problem,' said Soga. 'I was going to call you up for a drink anyway. What are you having?'

'A beer.'

'This place is famous for its cocktails. The bartender's waiting; do him a favour and order one.'

'Okay then, I'll have a gin and tonic.' He eyed Soga as he named the first drink that came to mind. Soga was wearing a pale-green summer suit over an open-collar black shirt. 'You're looking sharp,' he added.

'This?' Laughing with pleasure, he pulled the jacket open to reveal the label. 'It's Italian, but a brand nobody ever heard of. They say the boss is supposed to wear Hermès or something, but it takes real style to find something like this.'

'It looks great.'

'The Hawaiian shirt's not bad either,' he told him, obviously pleased by the compliment. 'Is it vintage?'

'Actually, I got it at a discount shop out there in the sticks.'

'With a baby face like that, you could wear just about anything and the girls would still come running,' he laughed.

'Hey – flattery.' Soga seemed in no hurry to get down to business, and Jumonji found it difficult to steer the conversation around to his proposal. Soga suddenly changed the subject.

'You ever read Ryu Murakami's *Love and Pop*?' he asked.

'No,' said Jumonji, not sure what he was getting at. 'I don't read stuff like that.'

'You should.' Soga put out his cigarette and took a sip of his cocktail, an elaborate concoction in graduated shades of pink. 'That Murakami, he knows women.'

'I doubt I'd get it.'

'You'd get it. He's particularly into high-school girls, the kind that turn tricks for spending money.'

'That's what it's about?'

'That's what it's about,' he echoed, tapping his lips with a delicate finger.

'Then maybe I'll take a look. I'm into high-school girls myself.'

'It's not smut, you dope. He tells it like, from their side of things, really pulls you in.'

'Sounds interesting,' Jumonji muttered, looking down at the table and feeling utterly mystified by the course of the conversation. Just then, his gin and tonic arrived like a lifeboat drifting up to the table. Moving the sliver of lime to the coaster, he tipped his head back and took a long swallow.

'It is,' said Soga. 'You see, I got certain standards when I read a novel.'

'Such as?'

'I judge it by what it's got to do with my line of work.'

'And how's this one score?' Soga watched with some astonishment as Jumonji drained his glass.

'High marks. It's all about us, in a way.'

'In what way?'

'Murakami and these girls, they hate the old men, the ones who run this country. And you might say the kind of work we do starts from the same place – hating those old geezers. They're misfits, just like we're misfits. You see what I mean?'

'I suppose so,' said Jumonji.

'Misfits,' Soga repeated, almost shouting. 'You went to Adachi Middle School and joined a bike gang – that qualifies you right there. Now you're a loan shark and I'm yakuza. Still not exactly mainstream, not nice and proper, right? And it's all their fault, those old farts who call the shots, the ones who ruin everything. But we're all the same, you, me, Murakami, and those high-school girls – all completely cool. You see that, don't you?' Jumonji stared at Soga's sallow face, which looked almost haggard in the dim light. It was fortunate that he seemed to be in such a good mood, but as Jumonji listened patiently to him go on about this wacky stuff, he began to have doubts about the scheme he'd thought up and to question the wisdom of broaching the subject with him. No, the whole thing seemed implausible, scary even.

'What was it you wanted to talk about?' Soga said suddenly, apparently sensing his hesitation. He was trapped now.

'Actually, it's a business proposal, but a strange one,' Jumonji said, almost in spite of himself.

'Strange but profitable?'

'Maybe, if we can pull it off. At least I thought it might be. But I don't really know if it'd work.'

'Why don't you just tell me what it is? It's safe with me.' Soga slipped his hand into the front of his shirt and began to rub his chest, a habit he had when the talk turned serious.

'Soga-san,' said Jumonji, screwing up his courage, 'I think I've got the perfect way to get rid of stiffs.'

'What the hell are you talking about?' he said, his voice cracking slightly. The bartender was concentrating on making perfect, paper-thin slices of lemon, as if his life depended on it. In the silence that followed, Jumonji realised for the first time that an old rhythm-and-blues tune was playing quietly in the background. He'd been too nervous to notice, he thought, wiping his forehead.

'What I mean is, if somebody's got a body he needs to get rid of, I'd like to do it.'

'You?'

'Yes.'

'How? It's gotta be done without leaving any evidence, you realise?' There was a hint of interest in his jaundiced-looking eyes.

'I got to thinking,' said Jumonji. 'If you bury them, there's always the chance somebody will dig them up later, and if you toss them in the sea, they might start dredging. So I'm going to cut them up and throw them out with the garbage.'

'Sounds good, but it's easier said than done. You know what happened with that Koganei Park thing?' His voice had dropped; he was no longer an adolescent talking about books and clothes. His thin face had grown hard.

'Sure,' Jumonji said.

'They managed to get it cut up and then slipped up throwing it out. But d'you know how hard it is just to get that far? Do you have any idea how tough it'd be to cut up a body? It's hard enough just cutting off one finger.'

'I know. But if we can do it, I've thought up a way to get rid of the pieces so nobody will ever find them, a way to leave no shred of evidence.'

'How?' Soga leaned forward, his cocktail forgotten.

'My family lives in Fukuoka, near a huge garbage dump. Not one of those landfill jobs out in the harbour; this place has a great big incinerator and they burn everything that comes in. And the best part is, people who miss the garbage pick-up can bring their bags any time they feel like it. If we took the stuff there, it'd vanish without a trace.'

'And how would you get them to Fukuoka?'

'Pack them in boxes and ship them. Since my dad died, my mom lives there by herself. I could fly down and meet the shipment and take it to the dump.'

'Sounds like a lot of work,' Soga murmured, thinking it over.

'The hardest part would be cutting up the body, but I've got that figured out as well.'

'Meaning what?'

'Meaning I've got somebody who can handle it, somebody we can trust.'

'Does this guy work for you?'

'You might say that – but it's not a guy.'

'Your girlfriend?'

'No, but somebody I trust,' said Jumonji, sounding as confident as he could. As he was talking, Soga had grown visibly more interested, perhaps because he knew there was a need for the service.

'There might be something in it,' he said. Pulling his hand from his shirt, he reached for his drink. 'There are people who do this kind of work, but I hear they're expensive. If you'd got something like that on your hands, though, you'd want them to be reliable, right?'

'You know what they charge?' Jumonji asked.

'It depends. But it's risky work, so you can bet it's plenty. How much are you thinking?'

'I'm not sure, but it would have to be enough to make it worth my while.'

'Now don't go getting greedy on me,' Soga said, glaring at him.

'I was thinking about nine million,' said Jumonji with a sheepish smile.

'How about eight? You've got to undercut the competition.'

'I guess I could do it for that.'

'And since I'd be bringing you the business, I'd get half.'

'Isn't that a bit steep?' he said, frowning.

'Maybe it is,' Soga laughed. 'How about three mil?'

'You've got a deal.' Jumonji did a quick mental calculation as Soga nodded with satisfaction. If he got five million from the original eight, that would leave three for him and two for Masako. He would insist on their excluding Kuniko – she was far too big a risk. But he would give Masako and the other one, Yoshie, a share. Masako could figure out how to divide it up.

'Good,' said Soga. 'I get wind of this kind of thing from time to time, so when I hear of something, I'll let you know. But you've got to guarantee it's all handled right; if you mess up, it'll be my neck.'

'We'll be figuring it out as we go, but I think it should work.'

'Just one more question,' Soga said. 'Were you involved in the Koganei Park thing?'

'No, no,' said Jumonji, deflecting Soga's hunch with a shake of the head.

The wheels had been set in motion. All that he had to do now was convince Masako to go along with his plan.

3

Pink slices of ham. Red shoulder of beef shot through with whitish sinews. Pale pink pork. Fine-grained ground beef, red, pink and white. Dark red chicken gizzards outlined in yellowish fat.

Masako was pushing her shopping cart through the meat section at the supermarket. She felt distracted, unable to figure out what to buy, unsure even why she was here. She stopped and gazed at the stainless-steel frame holding the blue plastic shopping basket, a basket that was, of course, empty. That was it: she'd come to get something for dinner. But lately the effort of coming up with a menu and putting food on the table just seemed too much of a bother to keep doing.

Dinner on the table was somehow proof that their family still existed. She doubted Yoshiki would be particularly upset if she gave up cooking, despite all the years she'd been at it, but he would expect her to explain why she'd stopped. Since she had no explanation to offer, he would probably just conclude that she was lazy. As for Nobuki, after his outburst in front of the detective, he'd shut up like a clam again and she'd heard nothing more from him. The only thing he did at home was eat.

The two of them kept their own schedules, never consulting her, but on this one point they were amazingly regular, as if it were an article of faith: they always made it home for dinner. This almost childlike faith in her cooking struck her as odd. Left to her own devices, she would have eaten anything or nothing, but knowing how they depended on this meal, she found herself worrying over their special likes and dislikes, preparing something that would appeal to both of them. But in return they seemed completely unresponsive. Whatever ties had once bound them were all but gone, and only her prescribed role remained to hold her down. It all seemed so futile, like pouring water into a pot with a gaping hole. How much had already run out of the bottom? Everything that had seemed so normal and natural yesterday now struck her as strange.

A cold mist was rising from the meat cases, like poison gas escaping into the store. Wafts of frigid air blew against her. She rubbed the goose bumps on her arms, trying not to overreact, and picked up a package of sliced beef. But, realising the flesh looked like Kenji's, she let it drop back into the case. It was all Kenji – the tendons, the bones, the fat – it all made her sick. She'd never felt like this before; she was getting soft. Disappointed in herself, she decided to give up on dinner. She would just leave for work without eating anything, and her empty stomach would be her punishment – though punishment for what, she wasn't quite sure.

The warm, still air that preceded a typhoon was oppressive. The storm, a fairly large one, was bearing down on them now, signalling an end to summer. Masako looked up at the sky, listening to the wind wailing in the upper atmosphere. As she reached her red Corolla, she saw a familiar bicycle coming toward her across the supermarket parking lot.

'Skipper!' she called, waving to Yoshie.

'Didn't find much, did you?' Yoshie said, stopping her bike next to the car and eyeing the empty bag in Masako's hand.

'I gave up.'

'Why?'

'I guess I just didn't feel like making dinner.'

'And that's okay?' said Yoshie, shaking her head. Masako noticed that her hair seemed greyer than it had only a few weeks ago. 'What's wrong?'

'Nothing. I guess I'm just tired.'

'You're lucky you can just decide not to cook. If I did that, Issey and Granny would starve to death.'

'Is he still there?' Masako asked.

'He is, and I've no idea where his mother's gone. The old lady isn't popping off any time soon, and now I've got that brat whining day and night. I guess you could say I'm stuck.'

Having nothing to say to this, Masako leaned against the car and looked up at the lowering sky. As she listened to Yoshie's litany of woes, she felt as though they were all stuck in a long tunnel with no sign of the exit in sight. She just wanted out, to be free of everything. None of it mattered any more. Anyone who couldn't get out was doomed to a life of endless bitching – the life they were leading now.

'Summer's just about over,' she said.

'What are you talking about? It's September already; it's long gone.'

'I suppose so.'

'Are you going to work tonight?' Yoshie asked, sounding anxious. Masako glanced at her. The question had raised the spectre of Masako's quitting and it floated between them.

'I was planning on it,' she said.

'Good. You seem kind of out of it. I thought you might be thinking of deserting us.'

'Deserting you? What do you mean?' Taking a cigarette from her bag, Masako stood looking at her. A gust of wind tugged at her lustreless hair and she reached up with both hands to hold it down.

'Kuniko said you used to work at a credit union. You're not cut out for the factory.'

'Kuniko?' She suddenly remembered that the due date on Kuniko's loan had come and gone. How had she managed to make the payment without any extra income? If she'd found out about that banking job of hers, it could only mean she'd had a visit from Jumonji. Under pressure, the woman was capable of almost anything, and Masako realised she'd left her to her own devices too long. What had she done? 'I'll be there. And I'm not thinking of quitting,' she said.

'I'm glad,' said Yoshie, beaming.

'Skipper, does something seem different to you nowadays?'

'Different? What?' Yoshie looked around as if they were being watched.

'No, not that. I think we've probably shaken the police. I mean something different in you.' Yoshie thought for a moment but then gave her a sheepish look.

'No, I don't think so. But it may be because I keep telling myself that I was only helping out.'

'The same way you help out your mother-in-law and your grandson?'

'No, not like that,' Yoshie said, frowning. 'I wouldn't want them lumped together with what we did to Kenji. Still, I suppose they do have something in common, in the sense that I always seem to be doing the jobs nobody else is willing to do.' She stood for a moment, lost in thought. Her wrinkled forehead and pale skin made her look far older than she was.

'I know what you mean,' Masako said, tossing her cigarette on the ground and crushing it underfoot. 'I'll see you later.'

'What about you, though, Masako?'

'Nothing's different for me either,' she said, opening the car door. Yoshie pulled her bicycle out of the way.

'See you this evening,' said Yoshie. Masako climbed behind the wheel and waved at her through the windshield. Yoshie smiled and then swung herself up on the bike with surprising agility and pedalled off toward the supermarket. As she watched her go, Masako thought about what was happening to them. Even if Yoshie hadn't noticed it yet, the money she was going to get from Yayoi would eventually begin to work on her, like a chemical reaction. There was no malice in this observation – but facts were facts.

The phone was ringing when she got home. She threw her bag on the shoe cupboard and ran to answer it. She hadn't heard from Yayoi in more than a week and it was about time she should be calling.

'Katori-san?' said a man's voice. 'My name is Jumonji. I used to be called Yamada when we worked together.'

'Oh, it's you,' said Masako, surprised to be hearing from him. She pulled a chair over to the phone and sat down. Her whole body was sweaty from the rush to get the phone.

'It's been a while,' Jumonji said.

'What do you mean? – I saw you just the other day.'

'By happy chance,' he laughed.

'What do you want?' Fumbling for a cigarette, she remembered she'd left her bag in the hall. 'If this is going to take any time, you'll have to hold on a minute.'

'I'll wait,' he said. Masako went out and chained the door. If someone came home, this would give her a few extra seconds. She picked up her bag and went back to the phone.

'Sorry,' she said. 'Now what is it you want?'

'It's a bit difficult to discuss over the phone. I'd like to get together, if you don't mind.'

'What can't you talk about over the phone?' Masako had imagined it had something to do with Kuniko's loan. But perhaps she'd underestimated this little loan shark.

'It's a bit complicated,' he said. 'To be honest, there's a business proposal I want to make to you.'

'Hold on,' said Masako. 'I've got something to ask you first. Did Kuniko Jonouchi make her payment?'

'She made it, right on time.'

'Using what for money?'

'You might say she paid with information.' Jumonji's tone was casual, but Masako realised her fears had been justified.

'What information?' she asked.

'That's what I want to talk about.'

'Okay. Where do we meet?'

'You're going to work this evening, aren't you? Could we have dinner somewhere before?' Masako gave him directions to a Royal Host restaurant near the factory and told him to meet her there at 9.00.

So they weren't going to get away with it after all. She'd suspected as much ever since her conversation with Yoshie, but it depressed her to think that it was her own negligence in handling Kuniko that had been their undoing.

She could hear the sound of the chain rattling as someone tried to open the door. The buzzer on the intercom echoed angrily through the house. When she went out to the hall and unlatched the door, Nobuki appeared on the other side, fixing her with a sulky look. His black knit cap was pulled down over his eyes, despite the heat. Faded black T-shirt, baggy pants draped around his hips, Nike shoes.

'Hi,' Masako said. Nobuki slipped past her without a word. His strong young body was surprisingly supple. If he were still talking to her, she was sure the first thing he would have done was tell her not to put the chain on. He ran up to his room without so much as a glance in her direction. 'You're on your own for dinner tonight,' she called up the stairs after him. Her voice echoed through the empty rooms, as if her message were a rejection not just of the boy on the second floor but of the whole house.

Masako arrived at the Royal Host right at 9.00, but Jumonji was already there, standing by an inconspicuous table in the back. He held a wrinkled copy of the evening paper in his hand.

'Thanks for coming,' he said. Masako met his stare as she sat down across from him. He was casually dressed in a white polo shirt and a jacket. Masako wore what she always wore to work: jeans and one of Nobuki's old T-shirts.

'Good evening,' said a black-suited man who seemed to be the manager. He looked vaguely puzzled as he passed them their menus, probably wondering what they could possibly have in common. 'Enjoy your meal,' he said as he walked off.

'Have you eaten?' Jumonji asked. He had been drinking iced coffee while he waited. Masako thought for a moment, then shook her head.

'No, not yet.'

'Me either,' he said. 'Let's order.' Masako decided on spaghetti and Jumonji flagged down the man in the suit. He ordered spaghetti for himself as well and, without consulting Masako, told him to bring their coffee after the meal. 'It's been a long time,' he said, when the man had gone. 'It was great running into you like that after all these years.' His manner was fawning, and he seemed almost afraid to look her in the eye. Why should he be nervous?

'What is it you wanted to talk about?'

'I appreciate your making time,' he said, giving a slight shrug.

'You said you couldn't discuss it over the phone.'

'You haven't changed,' he said.

'What do you mean by that?' she asked, taking a sip of water. It was ice cold.

'You were always so businesslike.'

'And you could afford to be a little more that way yourself. Why don't you get to the point? I think I know what's coming anyway.' Masako recalled what he'd been like in the old days, when he helped out in the collection department. His look had been all biker punk, with part of his eyebrows shaved off and tightly permed hair; and there had been rumours that he was actually in a gang. He had cleaned up his act considerably since then, transforming himself into a fairly presentable young man, but it was still the same Jumonji.

'The point?' he said, scratching his head. 'You're amazing.' Just then, the waitress arrived with their spaghetti. Masako picked up her fork and began eating. She had planned to skip dinner and here she was sharing a meal with him – of all people. The thought made her smile to herself. 'What's so funny?' Jumonji asked.

'Nothing.' She suddenly realised why she had wanted to punish herself by going hungry: it was for suppressing her desire to be free. She wiped her mouth with the paper napkin when she'd finished the spaghetti. Jumonji had finished as well and immediately lit a cigarette.

'So what's this business you mentioned?' she said.

'Before we get to that, I want to offer my congratulations.'

'For what?'

'The whole thing was so cool,' he said, grinning at her, apparently without a hint of irony.

'What was so cool?'

'Koganei Park,' he whispered. Masako stared into his eyes, stock-still.

'So you know about that?'

'Yes.'

'Everything?'

'Pretty much.'

'Kuniko blabbed, didn't she? For a lousy ¥440,000.'

'You shouldn't blame her,' he said.

'Maybe not,' said Masako. 'Still I'm impressed that you figured it out.'

'Just my morbid curiosity, I guess,' he said. Masako stubbed her cigarette out among the butts in his overflowing ashtray. She'd lost.

'And the business proposition?' she asked.

Jumonji leaned forward, lowering his voice. 'I'm wondering whether you'd be interested in helping to dispose of some more bodies. It seems there's a fairly steady supply of people nobody wants found. We'd take care of them.' Masako stared at him, mute with amazement. She'd been expecting threats and blackmail, not a pitch for a start-up business. But then she should have realised that a group of poor housewives weren't exactly a likely target for extortion, unless it was for the insurance money. 'What do you think?' Jumonji said, looking at her in an almost deferential way.

'What have you got in mind?' she said.

'I would drum up the business. It involves a pretty rough crowd and I wouldn't want you to have to deal with that. Once we took delivery on a shipment, you would cut it up and then I'd get rid of it. I know a place with a huge incinerator, so it would all disappear without a trace.'

'Why can't you just throw it in there without cutting it up?'

'It wouldn't work. Shifting a whole body is too risky. Somebody would notice it before it got to the incinerator. But cut up in pieces so it looked like all the rest of the garbage, it should be okay. The other hitch is that we have to get it all the way to Fukuoka.'

'Are you planning to ship it?' Masako said, the look of amazement returning to her face. Was he really serious?

'Exactly,' he said. 'In five-kilo packages, say a dozen or so. Then I would fly down to meet them and take them to the dump. What could be simpler?'

'Then all you want me to do is cut them up?'

'That's right. Are you interested?' The coffee had arrived. Jumonji took a sip, desperately trying to read her expression. Masako noticed that there was something intelligent about his eyes.

'What made you think of all this?' she asked.

'I wanted to find something we could do together.'

'We? You and me?'

'I just thought it would be . . . cool, working with you.'

'I'm not sure I understand.'

'It doesn't matter. Just call it a quirk of mine.' He ran his fingers through the soft hair hanging over his ears. Masako turned and took a quick look at the nearly empty restaurant. No sign of anyone from the factory. At the cash register, the man in the black suit had dropped his formal expression and was chatting amiably with a young waitress. As Masako hesitated, Jumonji appeared to be getting anxious. 'This loan shark racket has a short life-span,' he said. 'A few years at most. By next year I'll be looking for something else. I just wanted to do something with a bit more kick to it. I guess you must think I'm flaky.'

'But would you really be making any money?' she interrupted. Jumonji nodded.

'A lot more than a two-bit loan shark,' he said.

'How much would your customers pay? – per unit, let's say.' Having decided she might be interested, Masako asked the obvious question. Jumonji's tongue flicked across his narrow, well-shaped lips as he debated how much to tell her. 'Don't beat about the bush,' she said. 'If we can't be frank about this, we can't work together.'

'Okay, I'll tell you. The source I spoke to promised eight

million. He wants three million of that for bringing in the business. That leaves five: what would you say to two for me and three for you?' Masako lit a cigarette.

'I won't do it for less than five,' she said, almost without missing a beat.

Jumonji choked. 'Five million?'

'Five million,' she repeated. 'You might think this is easy, but it's not. It's a dirty, stinking business, and you get nightmares afterward. You can't understand until you've done it. And you need a place to do it in, a bathroom. But I wouldn't want to use my house; it's too risky. Where were you thinking we'd do it?'

'Jonouchi-san told me you did the first one in your bathroom, so I was hoping we could use it again,' he said, looking dismayed.

'Why not at your place? You're single.'

'It's an apartment,' he said. 'The bath is too small.'

'But my place is almost impossible. We'd have to find a time when nobody else was home, and then get it in without the neighbours noticing. The "unit" comes with bits of telltale belongings; getting rid of those is tricky.' Masako stopped for a moment, remembering how the Brazilian had retrieved the key. Jumonji held his breath, waiting for her to continue. 'And it's virtually impossible for one person,' she said. 'And there's the clean-up afterward, which is almost as bad as the job itself. I couldn't do that at my house again for less than five million.' Jumonji picked up his empty coffee cup and put it to his lips, visibly perplexed. Realising the cup was empty, he signalled the waitress, who was still chatting with the manager, and she brought a pot of weak coffee over. When she'd gone, he spoke again.

'What if I get it into your house, take care of the clothes, and handle the disposal?'

'I think the problem is that three million is too much for your middle man. He's telling you eight, but you can bet he's charging ten. So he ends up with five million before we ever see anything. I assume we're talking about some yakuza friend of yours?'

'I see what you mean,' said Jumonji, finger at his lips as he considered what she'd said. 'You've got a point.' She hadn't exactly said he'd been taken, but that was the implication.

'So you'll either have to ask him to take a cut or figure out if he's really getting ten million, one or the other.'

'Okay. But how would you feel about a million five for me and three and a half for you?'

'No dice,' she said, glancing at her watch. It was nearly 11.00; time for her to be getting to work.

'Just give me a minute, would you?' he said, taking out his cell phone, apparently with the aim of conducting the negotiations on the spot. Masako took it as her cue to go to the bathroom. She stared at her face in the mirror there for a moment before pressing a paper towel to her oily forehead. What was she getting herself into? She felt anxious, but also a bit excited. Remembering she had a lipstick in her purse, she fished it out and applied a dab of red to her mouth, which produced a look of surprise when she got back to the table.

'What?' she said.

'Nothing. I think we worked it out.'

'That was quick.'

'I just appealed to his better instincts,' he laughed. Masako remembered that, with a little instruction, he'd been good enough at his job even in the old days.

'And what did you decide?'

'I told him we couldn't do it for eight, but he swore that until we'd proved we could deliver, that was the ceiling. So in the end he reduced the finder's fee to two million; which leaves two for me and four for you. The one condition is that if anything happens, we're on our own and he'll deny he's ever heard of us.'

'Of course he will, which is exactly why you should have asked for more right from the start.' Masako ran through the numbers again in her head. If Yoshie agreed to help her, she could pay her a million. Kuniko was definitely out; and she'd decide what to do about Yayoi later.

'What do you think?' He sounded more confident this time.

'You've got a deal,' said Masako.

'Great!' he said, sighing with relief.

'Just a couple more things.'

'Yes?'

'I'd prefer we use your car for the deliveries. And I want you to get a set of scalpels from a medical supply store. I'm not sure we could manage it again without better equipment.' Jumonji scratched his cheek as he listened to her requests.

'It's like being a butcher, isn't it?' he said.

'With meat and bone and steaming offal,' she added. Jumonji clenched his teeth. 'And there's just one more question I want to ask you. How did you get Kuniko to spill the beans?'

'I told her I'd cancel her loan,' he said, laughing cheerfully for the first time since they'd sat down. 'Her story cost me ¥440,000, so we need to do some brisk business to recoup my investment.'

'And you're okay with two million?' she asked.

'I am, if there's a decent turnover.'

'Do you really think there's that kind of demand?'

'There's only one way to find out,' he said. She found his enthusiasm appealing. Nodding, she put the money for her share of the bill on the table and stood up. The whole thing still seemed far-fetched to her – at least for the moment.

4

The wind, which before had been howling ominously in the upper reaches of the sky, had died down while she was in the restaurant, but now the air was warm and close, announcing the approach of the typhoon. With her hair plastered to her head, Masako found herself worrying how the weather would be in the morning, after the shift. She turned on the radio in the car, but she reached the factory before she could find a weather report.

In one corner of the parking lot, a small, prefabricated guardhouse was under construction. She stared at it for a moment, but her mind was elsewhere, preoccupied with Jumonji's proposal. Before fully realising what she was doing, she'd entered a new and very foreign world; and regardless of whether her decision had been the right one, she was excited by the mere fact of having made it. There was something almost amusing about the way her new concern had driven the familiar sights and sounds of the parking lot right out of her head.

As she slipped out of her tennis shoes in the entrance hall of the factory, she realised that a woman she didn't at first recognise was standing in front of her.

'Masako.' The voice was familiar – Yayoi's. Her shoulder-length hair had been cut short, revealing the graceful nape of her neck. Her eyebrows had been drawn on, narrow and arched, and she wore red lipstick. The change was startling, and it was more than just her appearance. The dreamy, ineffectual Yayoi was gone, replaced by a woman who seemed younger but more certain of herself.

'Sorry,' Masako said. 'You startled me. I didn't know who it was at first. You're a different person.'

'So they tell me.' She smiled bashfully, but even this familiar gesture seemed more confident. 'But you look different yourself. You're wearing make-up.'

'What?'

'The lipstick,' Yayoi said. Masako had completely forgotten that she'd put it on in the bathroom at the restaurant. When she touched her finger to her lips, it came away stained sticky red. 'Don't,' said Yayoi, taking her hand. 'You'll wipe it off. Leave it. It looks nice on you.'

'Are you starting back today?' Masako asked.

'No, I just came by to show my face. I brought some cakes and wanted to apologise to the boss and Komada-san for all the trouble I've caused.'

'Then you're heading home?'

'With the typhoon, I wanted to be home with the boys. They say it'll come inland by the morning.'

'Then you should get home.'

'I also paid Kuniko and the Skipper,' she whispered close to Masako's ear, pressing a thick brown envelope into her hand.

'What's this?' Masako asked. Ignoring the question, Yayoi gave a quick bow.

'I start again tomorrow. See you then,' she said, slipping past her through the door. Her whole manner was different, brisker and more self-assured than the old Yayoi. Masako ran after her as she marched across the green Astroturf and down the stairs.

'Wait,' she called. Yayoi turned, smiling brightly. 'What's in here?' said Masako, waving the envelope. Yayoi held up two fingers – the two million yen she'd promised. 'Did you get the insurance already?' Masako asked in a softer voice.

Yayoi shook her head: 'No, not yet. I told my parents I needed to pay off a loan. I didn't want you to have to wait any longer.'

'You didn't need to do that.'

'I prefer it this way. Kuniko was getting impatient, and I know how much the Skipper needs it. I just felt like it was time.'

'Still, it seems too soon.'

'I know, but this way I can finally feel free of the whole thing.' Masako had wanted to say that it was too soon for Yayoi to have changed so radically, but she knew the comment would have fallen on deaf ears. Masako herself had changed – it was natural enough that Yayoi should want to, too.

'I understand,' she said. 'Thanks.' Yayoi gave a quick wave and disappeared down the stairs into the humid darkness.

Masako went back inside. After the health inspection, she skirted the lounge and headed straight for the bathroom. Once she was safely in a stall, she opened the envelope. Inside she found two bundles of ¥10,000 bills, still in their bank wrappers. As she shoved them to the bottom of her bag, she realised that this toilet stall was the only place in the factory where you could find any privacy.

Back in the lounge, she found Yoshie and Kuniko sipping tea together. They had already changed for work and were talking quietly, but their faces betrayed a kind of giddy excitement.

'Did you see Yayoi?' Yoshie called, waving for Masako to join them.

'I ran into her on her way out.'

'Did you get it?'

'You mean money?'

'We got ¥500,000 apiece,' she said. Kuniko looked down, her cheeks flushed with pleasure. Hers will be gone in no time, Masako thought. And now that she's had a taste of easy money, there was no telling what she'd do next time. They would have to watch her.

'I imagine it was hard for her to come up with it,' said Kuniko.

'I'm sure it was. I told her we could wait, but she insisted,' Yoshie said, though she couldn't help still sounding cheerful at this sudden windfall.

'Then don't worry about it,' Masako said.

'And you don't mind?' asked Yoshie, giving her a concerned look. Masako shook her head and smiled. She had rationalised the fact that she was getting more – and hiding it from them – by telling herself that the money could be used, if necessary, for a getaway, or as working capital for this new business. Since she was going to use it for the good of the group, she had no qualms about keeping it secret in the meantime.

'It's fine,' she said.

'Well, we're grateful,' said Kuniko, clutching the bag that held her share as if someone might try to snatch it from her. Masako glanced at her, fighting to control her temper.

'This means you can repay your loans,' she said, her voice dripping with sarcasm. Kuniko smiled vaguely but said nothing. 'What are you going to do with it while you're downstairs?' she asked, as she was pulling back her hair and fastening it with a barrette.

'We were just talking about that,' Yoshie told her, looking around the room. 'We thought we'd ask someone to put it in a locker.' The only people entitled to lockers were the regular employees who'd been there three years or more, and the Brazilians, who were said to be more concerned about their privacy. But the number of regular employees was almost too small to count.

'Maybe I should ask Miyamori-san?' said Yoshie, turning again to look around her. She found Kazuo sitting in a corner of the room with the rest of the Brazilians. He was smoking a cigarette, his legs stretched out in front of him on the floor. His eyes seemed to avoid the corner where Masako and her friends were sitting.

'What about Komada-san?' Masako suggested. As health inspector, Komada was one of the few regular employees; but as she said her name, Masako realised it would be unwise to let her know they'd come into large sums of money. 'No, maybe not,' she corrected herself.

'No, I've got a feeling we can trust Miyamori to keep quiet about it,' Yoshie said. 'I'll go ask him.'

'Will he understand you?' Kuniko sounded sceptical, but Yoshie ignored her and got to her feet.

When he saw Yoshie approaching, Kazuo shot Masako a questioning glance. She could see the wounded look in his eyes as he waited to hear what Yoshie had to say. Masako would have preferred to avoid any dealings with him, but it was none of her business what those two did with their money.

Pretending to ignore the whole transaction, she went to change. She slipped into her white uniform and then shoved the envelope far down in the pocket of her work pants; it would be awkward, to say the least, if it fell out during the shift. Through the line of hangers, she could see Yoshie and Kazuo together. She had apparently just finished her explanation, and Kazuo rose and left the lounge with the two women in tow. The Brazilians had a line of lockers next to the bathroom.

As Masako was scrubbing her hands and arms at the sink in the hall, the other two came back.

'That's a relief,' Yoshie said, picking up the little brush Masako had been using. 'He's a nice guy.' Kuniko turned on the water at a spigot well down the line.

'Did he understand what you wanted?' Masako asked.

'He seemed to. We told him we had something valuable we wanted to store in his locker, and he agreed right away. He said he'd be a little late getting off work and to please wait for him. He was very polite.'

'I'm glad it worked out,' said Masako, looking up just in time to see him walk by on his way to the factory floor. His build was so different from Japanese men – the thick neck planted on a powerful chest. His deeply chiselled face looked straight ahead as he passed. A man who would have been in his element under the Latin American sun seemed sadly out of place in the white uniform and ridiculous cap of a Japansese night-shift worker. She wondered whether he still had the key; but what really puzzled her was why this young foreigner should be attracted to her at all.

*

Work on the line stopped earlier than usual that morning, due to the typhoon. The part-time women sighed gloomily as they looked out the window in the entrance. Dawn had brought the storm with it. The rain fell sideways in heavy sheets, and the spindly pagoda trees around the car factory across the way seemed ready to snap in the wind. The gutters on both sides of the road were flowing like small rivers.

Yoshie frowned as she stared out at the storm. 'I don't think I'll be able to ride a bike in this.'

'I can give you a lift,' Masako offered.

'Could you?' She looked relieved. 'I'd really appreciate it.' Pretending she hadn't heard this exchange, Kuniko busied herself with her time card. 'I hate to ask,' Yoshie added, 'but would you mind waiting till Miyamori-san finishes work?'

'Not a bit.'

'I'll meet you at the parking lot.'

'No, I'll go get the car and pick you up here.'

'Thanks,' said Yoshie, glaring at Kuniko's broad back as she marched obliviously down the hall.

Masako changed quickly and left the factory. The heavy skies of the night before had burst open, pelting the earth with rain and wind, but to her it seemed almost refreshing. Realising that her umbrella was useless, she closed it and decided to run the short distance to the parking lot. The rain fell in enormous drops, soaking her in a matter of seconds. She brushed the hair out of her eyes, worried only about the bag of money she clutched in front of her as she ran. When she reached the abandoned factory, she could see that the concrete cover on the culvert was still where Kazuo had left it. The sound of roaring water rose from the hole, and it crossed her mind that Kenji's other belongings – apart from the key – must have been washed away. As she ran on, buffeted by the wind, she pictured that torrent to herself, and a laugh rose in her throat. She too would be free! The very thought made her feel freer.

When she reached the Corolla, she slipped into the driver's seat without stopping to brush off her wet clothes. She found a rag she kept under the dashboard and wiped her arms. Her jeans, heavy with rain, seemed to tighten around her legs. She turned the windshield wipers to the highest setting to see if they could keep up with the downpour and switched on the defrost. The blast of cold air brought goose bumps to her damp skin.

Easing the car out of the parking lot, she retraced her way to the factory. As she pulled up in front, Kuniko was just coming down the stairs, as flashily dressed as usual in a baggy black T-shirt and flowered tights. She glanced at Masako's car, but then opened her blue umbrella and walked off in the storm without a word. Masako watched in the rear-view mirror as the wind pulled her along. Perhaps they could still work together at the factory, but she resolved never to have anything to do with her beyond that. And as she watched in the mirror, Kuniko seemed to fade into the flood, as if in response to the thought.

Yoshie was coming down the stairs now, and she was surprised to see Kazuo following her, his clear plastic umbrella held out over her head. His black cap was pulled down around his ears. Catching sight of Masako's car, Yoshie hurried over and tapped on the window.

'Sorry to bother you,' she said, squinting against the rain, 'but d'you mind opening the trunk?'

'Why?' said Masako.

'I think he's saying he'll put my bike in for me.' She pointed behind her and Masako found herself staring into Kazuo's clear, innocent eyes. Without a word, she pulled the lever that released the trunk. The top popped open, obscuring the view through the rear window. But just at that moment the wind picked up and the top began to flap alarmingly. Masako opened the door and hopped out into the pelting rain.

'You'll get soaked!' Yoshie called. 'Get in!' She had to yell to make herself heard over the howling wind.

'I'm already soaked!' Masako yelled back.

'Get in!' Kazuo said, coming over to her and pressing firmly on her shoulder. Having little choice, Masako crawled back inside. A moment later, Yoshie tumbled into the passenger seat.

'It's awful out there,' she said. Kazuo, who had apparently gone around to the bike racks behind the building, came back pushing Yoshie's bicycle. He picked it up with ease and started manoeuvring it into the trunk. It was a heavy old bike that Yoshie used mainly for shopping, but he somehow managed to load it so that only a bit of the front wheel protruded. Getting out to check, Masako could see that the trunk was almost shut; she should be able to drive.

'Get in,' she said. He looked up at her, his face as wet as if he'd been swimming. His white T-shirt clung to his body, and there on his chest hung the key. He raised a hand to shield it from her eyes.

'Thanks,' she said.

'You're welcome,' he answered, without smiling. The wind shrieked by and a branch tumbled between them.

'Get in,' she repeated. 'I'll give you a ride.' Shaking his head, he picked up the umbrella he'd left on the ground, opened it, and walked off toward the abandoned factory.

'What was that all about?' Yoshie said, turning to look at his receding figure when Masako had climbed back in the car.

'I'm not sure,' said Masako. She avoided looking in the mirror as she pulled away from the kerb.

'It was nice of him, though,' Yoshie murmured, wiping her face with a towel. 'I'm lost without that bike.' Masako said nothing, peering out at the road through the frantic rhythm of the wipers. She turned on her headlights when they pulled on to the highway, noticing that the other cars had theirs on as well. They crept along, the spray splashing from their tyres. Yoshie tried to suppress a yawn as she said apologetically, 'Sorry to bring you so far out of your way. And I'm afraid your trunk's getting wet.' Through the rear-view mirror, Masako could see the top of the trunk bobbing in time with the bouncing of the car. Inevitably the rain was getting in – and washing the place where Kenji had been.

'Not to worry,' she said. 'I've been meaning to clean it out.' Yoshie fell silent for a time. 'Skipper,' Masako said at last, her eyes still on the road. 'Would you be willing to do it one more time?'

'Do what?' Yoshie said, turning toward her with a shocked look.

'I think some work might be coming in.'

'Work? You mean do that again? Who for?' Her mouth was hanging open.

'Kuniko talked, and word got around. Now it looks like it might turn into a line of work.'

'She talked? Then somebody's blackmailing you?' Yoshie pressed her hands against the dashboard as if she were suddenly terrified by the way the car was being driven.

'No, they want to pay us for the same kind of job. There's no need for you to know the details; you can leave that to me. I just need to know whether you'd be willing to help me if it happens. I could pay you.'

'How much?' There was a quiver in her voice, but a hint of curiosity as well.

'A million,' Masako said. Yoshie sighed and then was quiet.

'For the same kind of work?' she asked after a moment.

'We don't have to get rid of it afterward. All we've got to do is cut it up at my house.' Yoshie gulped. Masako lit a cigarette and the car filled with smoke.

'I'll do it,' said Yoshie, coughing.

'Really?' Masako glanced at her. She looked pale and her lips were trembling.

'I'm desperate for money,' she said. 'And I'm willing to march into hell if I'm following you.'

Was that where they were headed, Masako wondered. She peered through the streaming windshield. Only the tail-lights of the cars ahead of them were visible. She could no longer feel the tyres on the road, and the car seemed to be floating along. It all seemed unreal, as if her talk with Yoshie were only a dream they were having together.

5

When the typhoon passed, the brilliant summer sky went with it, as if swept away by a broom, and in its place the colourless dome of autumn appeared. As the temperature fell, Yayoi's overheated emotions also began to cool – her anger and remorse, her hopes and fears. She lived with her boys now, and the new life had begun to seem normal. But the women in the neighbourhood, who at first had rallied around the tragic widow out of sympathy and curiosity, quickly withdrew as she turned into a self-confident single mother. She rarely went out now, except to the factory or to shuttle the children back and forth, and she began to feel strangely cut off.

Had she really changed so much? What had she done except cut her hair – and try to fill in as a father figure for the boys, now that Kenji was gone? Yayoi hadn't realised yet that she was changing gradually from within, having thrown off the shackle that Kenji had been and exchanged it for an internal one, the guilt of having killed her husband.

One morning, when it was her turn to clean up around the garbage collection site, Yayoi went out, broom and dustpan in hand, to do her bit. The local residents left their trash by a utility pole at the corner where the wall along the alley turned, the spot where Milk had been crouching the morning after she had killed Kenji. Yayoi looked up at the wall. The stray cats in the area often perched there, hoping to find the garbage unguarded. A dirty white one that might have been Milk and a large brown tabby were sitting on it, but they fled as Yayoi approached. Milk had never come home after that day and had now joined the ranks of the strays, but Yayoi had long since stopped caring. She went on with her work.

As she swept up the scraps of food and paper left behind by the garbage truck, she had the feeling that she was being watched by unfriendly eyes, neighbours staring out at her from behind their curtains. The thought made her increasingly edgy, until to her surprise she heard a pleasant voice.

'Excuse me.' Yayoi looked up to find a woman standing there with a friendly smile. There was no trace of the nosiness she'd come to expect; so maybe this one didn't know about her. She tried to remember if she'd seen her before. The woman appeared to be in her early thirties, straight hair and simple make-up, as if she worked in an office, but there was something hesitant about her, as though she'd not had much experience with the world. Yayoi liked her immediately.

'Are you new in the neighbourhood?' she asked.

'Yes, I've just moved into that building,' the woman said, turning toward a block of ageing apartments behind her. 'Is this where I leave my garbage?'

'Yes. The schedule's posted there.' Yayoi pointed at a sign attached to the pole.

'Thanks,' the woman said, pulling out a notepad and copying down the information. She was dressed to go out, but the white blouse and navy-blue skirt were simple and understated. She waited until Yayoi had finished her sweeping and was about to go before she spoke again.

'Do you always clean up here?' she asked.

'We take turns,' Yayoi said. 'I suppose yours will come up eventually. There's a neighbourhood circular that explains the system.'

'Thanks so much,' the woman said.

'If you can't manage it because you're working, I'd be happy to cover for you,' Yayoi offered.

'That's kind of you,' she said, looking rather surprised. 'But I'm not working at the moment.'

'You're married then?'

'No, I'm not, though I'm certainly old enough.' The laugh that came with this brought out fine wrinkles at the corners of her eyes. Yayoi decided they were about the same age. 'I just quit my job, and I'm unemployed at the moment.'

'Oh, I'm sorry.'

'Actually, I'm giving myself a treat: I've gone back to school.'

'Graduate school?' Yayoi said, realising she was being nosy. Still, she was just happy to be talking to someone. She had no real friends in the vicinity, and things had been strained at the factory since Kenji had died. It was fun to chat like this, even with a total stranger.

'No, nothing so grand. It's just something I've been wanting to do for a long time. I'm taking dyeing lessons. I'm hoping to make a living from it some day.'

'Then are you doing something part-time while you're learning?'

'No, I've got enough saved for two years of school – as long as I live like a pauper.' She laughed and turned back toward the dilapidated wooden apartment building, known in the area for being run-down but cheap.

Yayoi told her her name and said: 'We're the house at the end of the alley. Come by if you have any more questions about things like the garbage.'

'Thanks. I'm Yoko Morisaki. It was nice meeting you.' She sounded so relaxed, so normal. Yayoi wondered what she would think if she knew about Kenji.

The next day, after a late afternoon nap, Yayoi was in the kitchen making dinner when she heard the buzzer on the intercom.

'It's Yoko Morisaki,' said a cheerful voice. Running to open the door, Yayoi found her new friend holding a box of grapes. Once again her clothes and make-up were subdued and tasteful, and she seemed genuinely pleased to see her.

'Come in!' Yayoi said.

'I just wanted to stop by and thank you for being so kind yesterday.'

'There's no need to,' said Yayoi, taking the grapes and leading the way back to the living room. Since that night, the only people she'd had in the house were her parents, Kenji's relatives and co-workers, Kuniko, and the police. It was wonderful to have a guest she felt relaxed with.

'I didn't realise you had children,' Yoko said, glancing at the crayon drawings taped to the walls and the toy cars scattered in the hall.

'Yes, two boys. They're at day-care.'

'I envy you. I love kids; I hope you'll introduce us soon.'

'I'd love to,' said Yayoi. 'But I have to warn you, they're a bit wild. They'll tire you out.' Yoko sat down in the chair she was offered and stared at her for a moment.

'I would never have guessed you had two children. You look too young and pretty.'

'That's sweet of you,' said Yayoi, delighted to receive a compliment from a woman her own age. She hopped up to make some tea, which she served with the grapes.

'Is your husband at work?' Yoko asked, spooning sugar into her cup.

'My husband died two months ago,' Yayoi explained, pointing toward the picture of Kenji in the new household altar in the next room. The photo was a few years old, and Kenji looked young and happy – and unsuspecting.

'I'm so sorry,' said Yoko, turning a bit pale. 'I had no idea.'

'Of course you didn't. Don't think a thing of it.'

'Was he ill?' she asked timidly, as if she'd very little experience of people dying.

'No,' said Yayoi, searching the woman's face. 'You really don't know?'

'No.' Her eyes were wide as she shook her head.

'He got mixed up in some kind of trouble. Have you heard about what happened in Koganei Park?'

'You don't mean . . .' A look of acute embarrassment spread over her face. Apparently, she really hadn't known. She looked down at her lap, with tears in her eyes.

'What's wrong?' Yayoi said, surprised by the tears. 'Why are you crying?'

'I just feel so sorry for you.'

'Thank you,' Yayoi murmured, moved at what seemed like the first sign she'd seen of pure human sympathy. A lot of people had expressed their condolences after the incident, but she had always sensed an undercurrent of doubt. Kenji's relatives blamed her quite openly, and her own parents had gone home. She knew she could count on Masako, but being with her made her nervous, as though she might cut herself if she weren't careful. Yoshie was hopelessly old-fashioned and judgemental; and as for Kuniko, she never wanted to see her again. Having felt isolated from nearly everyone for some time, Yayoi was genuinely touched by her new friend's tears. 'I really appreciate having you here,' she told her. 'The neighbours have been keeping their distance, and I've been very lonely.'

'You've no reason to be thanking me,' said Yoko. 'I'm afraid I'm terribly ignorant about how the world works, and I often wind up saying the wrong thing. So I often don't say anything at all, out of fear of hurting somebody. To tell the truth, that's more or less why I quit my job and decided to take up dyeing. I thought I might be able to make a little world of my own there somehow.'

'I understand,' Yayoi said; and then, slowly, she began to tell the official version of what had happened to Kenji. Yoko listened quietly at first, as if slightly afraid, but as Yayoi spoke she seemed to relax, eventually coming out with a question.

'So that was the last time you saw him, when he left for the office that morning?'

'Yes.' At some point Yayoi had come to believe this herself.

'How sad,' she said.

'I never imagined something like this would happen, that I'd never see him again.'

'And have they caught the killer?'

'No, they don't even know who did it,' Yayoi said with a sigh. As she continued to construct her story, the fact that she had killed Kenji seemed less and less real.

'But they cut him up!' Yoko said indignantly. 'It must be someone awful, a monster.'

'I can't imagine who'd do something like that, either,' she agreed, remembering the photo the detectives had shown her of Kenji's severed hand. The hatred she'd felt for Masako at that moment reared its head again. How could they have gone that far? Some part of her told her she was being illogical, but as they talked, as she went over what had happened, her take on the incident began to change.

The telephone rang. It was probably Masako, she thought. Now that she had this nice new friend, she suddenly realised how tiresome it was to have to talk with a bossy know-it-all like Masako. She hesitated, unwilling to pick up the phone.

'Don't worry about me,' Yoko said, signalling her to answer.

Reluctantly, she complied.

'It's me, Kinugasa again,' said a familiar voice. He or Imai checked in each week to see how she was doing.

'Thanks for calling,' she said.

'How have things been going?'

'Well enough.'

'Are you back at work?'

'I am,' she told him. 'I have friends there, and I'm used to the routine, so I'm planning to stay on.'

'That sounds sensible.' His voice was quiet, soothing. 'And you leave the boys to fend for themselves?'

'Fend for themselves?' she repeated, struck by the disapproval in his choice of words.

'I didn't mean it like that,' he said. 'But what do you do with them?'

'I put them to bed before I go; I think they're safe enough.'

'Unless there's a fire or an earthquake. If something happens, you should call the local police station immediately.'

'I appreciate your concern. . . ,' she said.

'By the way, I hear that you'll be getting your husband's insurance.' He sounded happy for her, but she could hear a slight reservation in his tone. She glanced around and saw that Yoko, out of courtesy perhaps, had left her seat and was standing by the window staring out at a withered pot of morning glories that the children had brought home from day-care.

'Yes,' she said. 'I hadn't even realised he'd taken out a policy at his company. It was a shock, but I must say I'm grateful. I wasn't sure what I'd do, trying to raise these boys by myself.'

'Well, I'm happy for you,' said Kinugasa. 'I'm afraid there's some bad news, though. It seems the owner of that casino has disappeared. If you see any sign of him, please let us know right away.'

'What do you mean?' said Yayoi, raising her voice for the first time since she'd answered the phone. She wheeled around to find Yoko staring at her.

'Now don't get excited,' Kinugasa told her. 'He's just gone missing. It's a mistake on our part, but we're doing everything we can to locate him.'

'So you think he ran off because he's guilty?' Kinugasa said nothing for a moment, and in the background she could hear phones ringing and men's voices talking. She frowned, feeling that the smoky, masculine fug of the police station had somehow made its way into her home.

'We're looking for him,' he said eventually, 'so try not to worry. If something happens, call me directly.' With that, he hung up.

This was good news for all of them, Yayoi thought. She'd been disappointed when he was released for lack of evidence, but if he'd gone on the run he was as much as admitting he was guilty. She could relax again. When she put down the phone and went back to her chair, she looked quite cheerful.

'Good news?' Yoko asked, smiling herself.

'No, not really,' she said, trying to look serious again. Yoko seemed surprised by the sudden change of expression.

'Perhaps I should go,' she said.

'No, please. Stay a while.'

'Was the call about the case?'

'It seems the suspect disappeared.'

'Was that the police calling?' Yoko said, a hint of excitement in her voice.

'One of the detectives,' said Yayoi.

'It was? Wow . . . I mean. . . . I'm sorry.'

'That's all right,' Yayoi said, smiling. 'They're a bother, those men, always calling to see how I'm doing.'

'But don't you wish they'd hurry up and find who did it?'

'I certainly do,' said Yayoi forlornly. 'I don't know how much longer I can go on like this.'

'I don't blame you. But if he ran off like that, it must mean he did it.'

'Wouldn't that be wonderful?' The words slipped out of her mouth before she knew what she was saying, but fortunately Yoko seemed to take no notice and went on nodding in sympathy.

It was only a matter of time before a friendship developed between them. Yoko would often show up soon after Yayoi awoke from her nap, before she was quite ready to go get the boys and start dinner. Yoko said she was on her way home from school, and she usually brought some inexpensive dessert or snack. Yayoi's children liked her right away. Yukihiro told her about the cat, and she took them out to search for him in the neighbourhood.

'Yayoi-san,' Yoko said to her one day, somewhat hesitantly, 'why don't I stay here with the boys while you're at work?' Yayoi was amazed that someone she'd only just met should be so kind to her.

'I couldn't ask you to do that,' she said.

'You certainly could. I've got to sleep somewhere anyway, and I hate to think of little Yukihiro waking up alone at night, his papa gone and his mother off at work.' She seemed to have a soft spot for the younger boy, and he in turn was completely attached to her. So Yayoi, who had been feeling starved for simple human kindness, jumped at the offer.

'Then you have to agree to have dinner with us. I can't pay you, but at least we can feed you.'

'Thank you,' said Yoko, beginning to cry.

'What's wrong?'

'It's just that I'm so happy,' she said, wiping away the tears. 'I feel like I have a new family. I've been alone so long, I'd forgotten how nice it is to be with other people. That room gets so lonely. . .'

'I've been lonely, too. I lost my husband so suddenly, and since then I feel as though nobody understands what I'm going through.'

'I know how hard it must be.' Both in tears now, the two women embraced; but when Yayoi looked up, she saw her kids staring at them in amazement.

'Boys,' she laughed, wiping her cheek, 'Yoko-san is going to be staying with you at night from now on!'

It never occurred to her that Yoko would be the cause of a shouting match with Masako.

Masako's grilling had begun with, 'Who is that answering the phone at your house these days?'

'Her name is Yoko Morisaki. She's a neighbour, and she's been nice enough to look after the boys for me.'

'You mean she stays over at your house?'

'She's been sleeping there while I'm at work.'

'So she's living with you?' asked Masako in that analytical way of hers.

'No, it's nothing like that.' Yayoi sounded annoyed. 'She goes to school. When she's done, she comes over for dinner. Then she comes back when I leave for work.'

'And she stays with your kids all night for free?'

'I feed her dinner,' said Yayoi.

'She's pretty generous, wouldn't you say? You don't think she's after something?'

'No!' Yayoi protested. She couldn't allow anyone to make nasty insinuations like that about Yoko, not even Masako. 'She's just incredibly kind – and you're rather mean.'

'Mean or not, I'm just trying to remind you that you're the one who'll suffer most if we're found out.'

'I know, but . . .'

'But what?'

Yayoi was fed up with this cross-examination. Why did Masako always keep on hammering away at things?

'Why are you getting at me like this?' she said.

'I'm not,' a puzzled Masako replied. 'Why are you getting so angry?'

'I'm not angry!' Yayoi insisted. 'I'm just tired of all your questions. In fact, I've got a few of my own. What have you and the Skipper been cooking up? And why aren't you talking to Kuniko any more? Did something happen?' Masako frowned. She hadn't told her that Kuniko had talked to Jumonji, or that she was considering another 'job' as a result; and it never occurred to Yayoi that she was being kept in the dark because Masako considered her weak and unreliable.

'No – nothing,' Masako said. 'But are you sure that woman isn't after the insurance money or something?'

'Morisaki-san is not that kind of person!' Yayoi shouted, exploding at last. 'She's not like Kuniko!'

'Fine, fine. Forget I mentioned it.' Her outburst over, Masako subsided; and Yayoi, remembering her debt to her, was quick to apologise.

'I'm sorry, I just snapped. But I'm sure Yoko is all right.'

'But aren't you worried about her spending all that time with your kids?' said Masako, refusing to give up. 'One of them might say something.'

'They've forgotten all about that night,' Yayoi said, amazed at her persistence. 'They've never mentioned it again.' Masako sat and stared at the ceiling for a moment.

'You don't think that's because they know it would cause trouble for you?'

'No, that's not it,' she said, though the comment had hit home. 'I know them better than anybody, and I'm sure they've forgotten all about it.'

'I hope you're right.' Masako glanced at her. 'But you don't want to get sloppy in the late innings.'

'Late innings? Why do you say that?' To her mind, the game had ended, and they had won. 'Haven't you heard? The casino owner has disappeared, so it's all over.'

'What do you mean?' she snorted. 'I don't see how it will ever be over for you.'

'What a horrible thing to say!' Glancing around, she realised that Yoshie had come up quietly and was standing behind Masako, watching her with the same accusing eyes. Yayoi couldn't stand the way they seemed to be plotting something together, shutting her out of their plans, blaming her for everything, even though they were more than willing to take her money.

After work, she left the factory without talking to anyone. The dawn came later these days, and the darkness seemed to close in around her, reminding her how lonely she was. When she arrived home, Yoko and the boys were still asleep in the bedroom, though her friend must have heard her come in since she appeared a few moments later in her pyjamas.

'Good morning,' she said.

'Did I wake you?'

'Don't worry about it. I have to get an early start today so I should be up anyway.' She stretched sleepily but then seemed to realise that Yayoi was upset. 'You look pale. Did something happen?'

'No, it's nothing important – just an argument at work.' She couldn't mention, of course, that her defence of Yoko had been the cause.

'Who with?'

'A woman named Masako, the one who calls here all the time.'

'You mean the one who's always so curt? What did she say?' Yoko was flushed, as if she'd had the argument herself.

'Nothing much,' said Yayoi, dodging the question. 'It was all pretty silly.' She tied on her apron and began fixing breakfast.

In a quiet voice, Yoko asked: 'Why do you always sound so

meek when you're talking to her?'

'What?' she said, wheeling around. 'I do not.'

'Is she threatening you somehow?' There was a sharply inquisitive look in her eyes, the same look she'd seen in the other neighbours, but Yayoi forced herself to ignore it. Anyone else, she thought, but not Yoko.

6

The late-afternoon autumn sun cast a soft light on the bundles of money sitting on the table. They were so new and perfect, they looked unreal, like some jokey sort of paperweight. Nevertheless, there was more money there than she earned in a year at the factory, and after all her time at the credit union, she'd been making no more than twice this amount. Masako sat staring at the two million yen she'd received from Yayoi, mulling over the events of the past few months and the prospect of the 'business' to come.

Eventually, her thoughts turned to a hiding place for the money. Should she put it in the bank? But then she couldn't get to it in a hurry if something happened – and there would be a record of it. On the other hand, if she hid it somewhere in the house, there was always the chance somebody would find it there. While she was still weighing these options, the buzzer on the intercom sounded. She stuffed the money into a drawer under the sink before answering.

'I'm sorry to bother you,' said a woman's hesitant voice.

'Can I help you with something?' Masako asked.

'I'm thinking of buying the lot across the street, and I was wondering if I could ask you a few questions.' Having little choice, Masako went out to the hall and opened the door. A middle-aged woman in a dowdy lavender suit was standing outside looking embarrassed. Judging from her face, she was about the same age as Masako; but her figure had begun to spread, and her voice was high and slightly frantic sounding, as if she'd never learned to keep it under control. 'I'm sorry to barge in like this,' she said.

'That's all right.'

'I'm thinking of buying the lot across the street,' she repeated, pointing to a patch of bare earth directly opposite. There had been talk of a sale several times, but recently it had begun to look neglected.

'And how can I help you?' Masako said in her most businesslike voice.

'Well, I was wondering why that was the only lot that didn't sell, whether there was some problem with it.'

'I'm afraid I wouldn't know.'

'So you haven't heard of any kind of trouble connected with it? I'd hate to find out there was something wrong after we bought it.'

'I understand your concern,' Masako said, 'but I really have no idea. You might try asking the realtor.'

'I have, but he won't tell me anything.'

'Then perhaps there's nothing to tell.' Masako was beginning to get slightly annoyed.

'But now my husband says that the soil is too red.' Masako cocked her head to one side and stared at her visitor. This was the first she'd heard about red soil. 'It makes a bad foundation,' the woman added, sensing her impatience.

'It's the same foundation we have on our house.'

'Oh, I'm sorry,' she said, looking guilty. Masako turned away, to put an end to the conversation.

'I think it should be fine,' she told her.

'Then there's no problem with drainage or anything?'

'We're on a slight rise here, so the run-off is okay.'

'Yes, I suppose so,' the woman said, peering in toward the back of the house. 'Well, thank you very much.' She bowed and turned to go.

It had been a brief conversation, but it left Masako with an uncomfortable feeling. Especially when she remembered what a neighbour had told her when she'd stopped her on the street a few days earlier.

'Katori-san.' The older woman who lived in the house right behind hers taught flower-arranging there. She was straightforward and sensible and Masako got along with her better than with most of the other women in the neighbourhood. 'Do you have a minute?' she said, tugging at Masako's sleeve and lowering her voice. 'I wanted to tell you about something odd that happened the other day.'

'What was that?'

'Someone from your company came around asking a lot of questions.'

'My company?' Masako immediately assumed it must be Yoshiki's office, or perhaps a bank. Still, there was no reason for anyone to be investigating Yoshiki; and Nobuki wasn't old enough yet for that kind of thing.

'I'm sure he said he was from the factory,' she said, frowning doubtfully, 'but I thought it might be a detective agency or something like that. He asked all sorts of questions.'

'Such as?'

'Who lives with you, your daily routine, your reputation in the neighbourhood, that kind of thing. Of course, I didn't tell him anything, but he might have heard plenty from other sources,' she said, nodding toward the house next door where an old couple lived. When Nobuki was in middle school, they'd frequently complained that his stereo was too loud. They would probably have been only too glad to go into the details of Masako's life.

'Did he really go around asking everyone?' Masako said, suddenly uneasy.

'So it seems. I saw him snooping around your place and then ringing their doorbell. It's a bit worrying, isn't it?'

'Did he say why he was investigating us?'

'Now, that was the strange part. He said you were being considered as a full-time, regular employee.'

'Nonsense,' Masako muttered. Part-timers could only be promoted to semi-regular status, not to official full-time employment, and even for that kind of promotion you had to have three years of service. The man was obviously lying.

'What did he look like?' she asked.

'He was young, wore a nice suit.' Jumonji came immediately to mind, but they'd known each other for years and he had no reason to be checking into her background. It might be the police, but they wouldn't need to work undercover like that.

It was at that moment that Masako first sensed a presence, someone who was lurking just beyond the edge of her awareness. Not the police, though she was sure they were watching too, but some unknown party. It occurred to her that this woman, Morisaki, who had turned up so suddenly at Yayoi's place, might be connected in some way. The fact that Yayoi didn't seem at all suspicious was odd in itself – perhaps a sign of how good they were at keeping whatever they were planning secret. The police were too clumsy for it.

First Morisaki, then the young man, and now this dowdy woman asking about real estate. If they were all connected, then her opponent was working with a team of sorts. But who was it? And what did they have to gain from all this? She felt a sudden surge of fear, a fear of the unknown. She wondered for a moment whether she should let Yoshie and Yayoi know what she'd discovered, but having no firm proof, she decided against it.

*

When she got to work that night, Masako realised that the guardhouse in the parking lot had been completed. The tiny structure stood empty, its little window still dark. Getting out of her car, she stood staring at it as Kuniko's Golf came careening into the lot, raising a shower of gravel in its wake. Masako flinched, sensing the hostility in this manoeuvre.

It took Kuniko several tries to angle the car into the space, though even then it was crooked. Pulling sharply on the parking brake, she looked out the window at Masako.

'Good morning,' she said, with her usual mock politeness. She was wearing a new red leather jacket, no doubt acquired with her recent windfall.

Masako returned the greeting. Since they'd stopped waiting for each other out here, she'd seldom run into Kuniko on the way to work; and judging from the disappointed look on her face right now, she suspected Kuniko preferred it that way.

'You're early today,' said Kuniko.

'I guess I am.' Masako peered at her watch in the dim light; she was, in fact, almost ten minutes ahead of schedule.

'Do you know what that's about?' Kuniko said, nodding toward the guardhouse as she pulled up the top on her car.

'I suppose they're planning to have a guard out here.'

'I hear the police found out about that pervert and forced management to keep an eye on things.' It seemed more likely to Masako that they'd agreed to the guard only because people had been parking illegally in their lot.

'What a shame,' she said. 'Now you won't get a chance to meet him.'

'What do you mean by that?' said Kuniko, twisting her face into a look of open hostility. Her make-up was perfect, as if she were going shopping downtown, but to Masako the showy paint merely seemed to emphasise the flaws in her features.

'I see you're still driving that car,' she sneered, nodding toward the newly polished Golf. 'You should get yourself a bike, save your money.'

But Kuniko turned on her heel and walked off in a huff. Ignoring her, Masako stood rubbing her arms to warm them. It was a bit cooler tonight than usual, even for the beginning of October, and she found she could distinguish various smells in the cold, dry air: fried food from the factory, exhaust fumes, the grass growing around the lot, and the fragrant white olive trees. The last surviving insects were singing somewhere nearby.

She found a sweatshirt on the back seat of the car and pulled it on. Lighting another cigarette – she was almost never without one now – she waited for Kuniko's retreating red figure to disappear. A few minutes later, she heard the rumble of an engine and a large motorcycle pulled into the parking lot. The rear tyre skidded on the dirt and the headlight bounced up and down as the bike came toward her across the rough lot. Who was it? None of the part-timers came to work on a motorbike. Masako stared suspiciously as it pulled up next to her.

'Katori-san,' a voice called, and the rider lifted the visor of his helmet. It was Jumonji.

'What are you doing here? You nearly scared me to death.'

'I'm glad I caught you,' he said, cutting the engine. The parking lot suddenly fell silent, and even the bugs had stopped singing, startled perhaps by the noise. Jumonji set the bike's kickstand in one swift motion.

'What's up?' she said.

'We've got a job,' he told her. Her pulse had quickened at the surprise arrival of the bike, but now she found herself clasping her arms across her chest to control the pounding. She caught a whiff of the familiar smell of detergent from the sweatshirt that had been packed away since last spring; and it crossed her mind for a second that she was now leaving behind the sort of life that smell represented. She hugged herself tighter.

'That kind of job?' she said.

'What else? I had a call just now saying there was a body that needs to disappear. I was worried I wouldn't be able to get in touch with you, so I decided to come straight here . . . but I was afraid Jonouchi-san might recognise my car.' His voice had a quaver of excitement in it.

'So you used the bike,' Masako said.

'I haven't ridden it recently, and it took a while to get the engine started.' He pulled off the helmet, like an actor removing a wig, and smoothed his hair back with his usual gesture.

'What do you want me to do?' Masako asked.

'I'll go pick it up and bring it to your house. What time do you finish work?'

'Five thirty,' she said, tapping her foot.

'And what time do you get home?'

'A little after 6.00. But you'll have to wait until everyone's out of the house, around 9.00. Do you think you can get the clothes off before you bring it over?'

'I'll give it a try,' he said grimly.

'And can you shift it by yourself?'

'We'll see. . . . I bought some scalpels, so I'll bring them along.'

'Good,' said Masako, chewing her fingernails as she frantically tried to think of anything they might have forgotten. In the heat of the moment, nothing came to mind; and then she remembered something. 'And make sure you get the boxes.'

'Do you want big ones?'

'No, not really. We don't want them to attract attention, so get the kind they have at grocery stores. But make sure they're good and sturdy.'

'I should be able to pick up some tomorrow morning. Have you got plastic bags?'

'I bought some just in case,' she said. 'There's one other thing: what should I do if something goes wrong?' A number of possible hitches had suddenly come to mind: Yoshiki might decide to stay home from work, for example, or Nobuki might skip his shift.

'What could go wrong?' he asked, sounding alarmed.

'Well, what if the house isn't empty, for instance?'

'Then give me a call on my cell phone.' He pulled a business card out of the pocket of his jeans and handed it over. The phone number was printed on the card.

'All right,' she said. 'If something comes up, I'll call you by 8.30.'

'Otherwise, I'll see you around 9.00,' he said, holding out his hand. Masako stared at it for a moment and then reached out to shake it. It felt cold and rough in the chilly wind. 'See you, then,' he said, starting the engine. The low, powerful noise spread out across the empty lot, fading into the darkness beyond. At the last minute, Masako signalled him. 'Something else?' he said, raising the visor again.

'Somebody's been snooping around my place. Maybe from a detective agency.'

'What do you think it means?' he asked, clearly worried.

'I've no idea.'

'It's not the police, is it? We don't want to mess with that.' Masako's heart sank. Maybe they should lie low for a while. But it was too late for that.

'I don't know,' she said, 'but I say we go ahead.'

'I guess so,' he agreed. 'We've come too far to back out now. A lot of important people would lose face.' He made a neat turn and sped away, kicking up clumps of dirt behind him.

Left alone, Masako set off toward the factory, reviewing the procedure as she walked: first came the head; then the arms and legs; then, you opened the torso. . . . She could picture the whole gruesome, unnerving process. It suddenly occurred to her to wonder what shape the body would be in when it came to them, and this unnerved her all the more. Her knees began to shake, as if baulking at the idea of carrying her any nearer this horror, and it was difficult to walk. She stopped and stood in the dark, realising that what really spooked her wasn't the body she would soon be seeing but the unseen people who were out there somewhere, watching.

As she entered the lounge, Kuniko made a show of standing up and walking out without so much as glancing at her. Masako, however, had no time for that kind of behaviour, intent as she was on finding Yoshie. She found her soon afterward, in the changing room with Yayoi.

'Skipper,' she said, tapping her on the shoulder just as she was pulling up the zipper of her uniform. Yayoi, who was standing beside her, turned around as well, a look of cheerful innocence on her face. Masako had been meaning to leave her out of their plans this time, but when she saw that face – without a trace of the horror they had been through visible there – she felt a violent urge to make her tremble the way she had, just now out there in the night. She clenched her teeth, trying to resist it.

'What's up?' Yoshie said, but a look of consternation showed that she knew the answer almost before she asked the question.

'We've got a job,' Masako told her. Yoshie stared back, her lips tightening into a fine line. Masako decided she wouldn't mention her qualms about being watched; she was afraid Yoshie would lose her nerve, and she'd never be able to do the job alone.

'What are you two whispering about?' Yayoi said, pushing in between them.

Masako grabbed her by the wrist and said: 'Do you really want to know?' staring her right in the eye as she spoke.

'What is it? What are you doing?' she muttered in dismay. Masako wrapped her fingers around her elbow now instead.

'We're cutting – just about here. Another "job".' Yayoi backed away, her arm still in Masako's grasp. Yoshie glanced around, worried that someone might be looking, and signalled to Masako to be careful. But the other women in the room were paying them no attention as they glumly went on changing their clothes in anticipation of the hard night ahead.

'You're not serious,' Yayoi whispered, her voice breathless and high like a little girl's.

'Dead serious,' she was told. 'Do you want to join us? All you have to do is show up at my house.' When Masako let go, Yayoi's arm dropped limply to her side and her work cap fell to the floor. 'And another thing: make sure you get rid of that Morisaki woman if you do decide to come.'

Yayoi glared at her for a moment before hurrying away.

7

The body turned out to be a short, thin man, perhaps around sixty. He was bald, had all his own teeth, and had scars from operations on the right side of his belly and in the middle of his chest. The one on the chest was the larger of the two; the one on his stomach was apparently from an appendectomy. Judging from the purple flush on his face and the finger marks on his neck, he had probably been strangled. There were scratches on his cheeks and arms, suggesting he had put up a fight.

There was nothing to tell them what sort of work he had done, or who had killed him, or why. Stripped of his clothes, he was reduced to a lifeless piece of flesh with no links to his previous life. Nor did they need to trace any; all they had to do was carve him up, stuff the bits in bags, and pack the bags in boxes. If you could numb yourself to all the blood and gore, there was really very little difference between this job and the one they did at the factory.

Yoshie pulled the cuffs of her sweat pants up to her knees; Masako wore shorts and a T-shirt. They both wore aprons and gloves pilfered from the factory. Afraid of stepping on bone chips if they went barefoot, Masako was using her husband's rubber boots and had lent Yoshie a pair of her own. And again, there was little difference between these uniforms and the ones they used at work.

'These scalpels are great,' Yoshie said admiringly. The surgical instruments Jumonji had brought them were extremely effective. Unlike the sashimi knives they'd used on Kenji, the scalpels cut through the flesh almost effortlessly, like a new pair of scissors through cloth. Thanks to these improved tools, the work proceeded more quickly than they'd expected.

Unfortunately, they soon realised they wouldn't be able to use the power saw Jumonji had acquired for cutting the bones. During the trial run, it sent a fine mist of bone and flesh flying in their eyes. They would need goggles if they were going to use it in the future. As the work progressed, the room became saturated with blood, and the air was filled with a foul stench from the entrails, just as had happened with Kenji; but in the same way that the work seemed easier this time, the horror associated with it was somehow less acute.

'This must have been heart surgery.' Yoshie's eyes were red from lack of sleep as she traced her finger across the purple, wormlike scar on the man's chest. 'It seems a bit sad somehow: he managed to survive this operation and then ended up getting murdered.' Masako busied herself with sectioning an arm and leg while she listened to Yoshie's musings. The legs were different from Kenji's. While Kenji had been in the prime of life, the skin on this man was sallow and wrinkled, with almost no fat at all. Perhaps it was just her imagination, but she even had the feeling that the saw was cutting through something dry and hollow rather than through flesh and bone. 'It's a lot easier without the blade getting gummed up with fat,' Yoshie said, continuing her monologue as she worked. 'Not like the first one. The bags are lighter, too.'

'I bet he barely weighs fifty kilos,' Masako said.

'And I bet he was a rich old bastard,' she added, sounding very sure of herself.

'How in the world can you tell?'

'Just look at this notch on his finger here. He must have worn a huge ring, thick as a doughnut, studded with diamonds and rubies. Somebody must have yanked it off.'

'You've got an overactive imagination,' Masako laughed.

The morning had begun for Masako as though it were the continuation of a bad dream. Yoshie still hadn't arrived when Jumonji turned up on schedule just after 9.00, looking pale, and carried the body inside, wrapped in a blanket.

'That was pretty scary,' he said, rubbing his cheeks as if he was just back from the Arctic – despite the fact that it was fairly warm for an October morning.

'What was?' Masako asked as she spread a blue vinyl sheet on the bathroom tiles, the same sheet they had used for Kenji.

'This!' he said, gesturing at the corpse. 'It's the first time I've ever seen a dead body. But it wasn't just seeing it, I had to play nursemaid to it half the night. After I put it in the trunk, I went to a Denny's to kill time, and then drove around Roppongi.'

'Weren't you afraid you'd be stopped?'

'It crossed my mind,' he said, 'but I didn't want to be alone with it. I needed to be around people. I know everyone ends up like that when they die, but it still seemed like I had this zombie hidden in my trunk. I knew I was supposed to get the clothes off and all, but I just couldn't, not by myself. I couldn't even look at it till the sun came up. I guess I'm just a coward.' Masako, gazing at his pale face, understood what he'd been through. There was something about dead bodies that made the living recoil. She wondered how long it would take before a corpse came to seem like any other object.

'Where did you have to go to get it?' she asked, touching the bent fingers.

'I think it's probably better if you don't know. If something unexpected happened, it might prove awkward.'

'Like what?'

'I don't know,' he said. 'Something . . . unexpected.' He lifted the blanket very gingerly and peeked in at the face.

'You mean like the police?' Masako said.

'Not just the police.'

'Then who, for example?'

'The interested parties, so to speak; somebody looking for revenge.' Masako thought immediately of her unknown observer, but Jumonji seemed to mean people with a more mundane, professional connection with the corpse.

'I wonder why he was killed,' she said.

'His disappearing probably made someone else very rich. That's why they have to make sure the body never turns up.' That meant this man was worth several billion yen, at the very least. Masako stared at the dull, colourless skin on his bald head. If you could forget about the 'interested parties', a dead body really was something to be disposed of like any other kind of garbage. Garbage was a natural by-product of human life; and it was nobody else's business what got thrown away or who did the throwing. Though when the time came, you had to be willing to accept the fact that you, too, would be thrown out with the rest.

'Help me get the clothes off,' she said to him calmly.

'All right,' he said. Masako cut slits in the suit and began slipping it off the body, while a jittery Jumonji stuffed it into a bag.

'Was there a wallet or anything else?' she asked.

'No, they took everything like that. We got all that was left.'

'It really is just garbage, then,' she muttered to herself.

'I suppose you could say that,' Jumonji said, looking shocked.

'It's easier to think of it that way.'

'I guess I see what you mean.'

'Did you get the money?'

'I've got it right here,' he said. From his back pocket he produced a brown paper bag, the kind used for penny candy. 'It's exactly six million; I told them we couldn't do it unless we got the whole amount up front.'

'Well done,' she said. 'But what happens if, God forbid, the body's found later on?'

'Then we'll have to give the money back. But there are still some people who'll wind up with egg on their faces, and you can be sure they'll find other ways to make me pay.' His voice was shaky, as if he'd only just understood the risk he was running. 'So let's be as careful as possible,' he added.

'Okay,' said Masako. When they'd finished removing the clothes and laid out the naked body in the bathroom, Jumonji took four stacks of bills from the bag and set them in front of her.

'Why don't you take these now,' he said. The bills were dark and wrinkled and wrapped with rubber bands, not like the newly minted money she'd received from Yayoi. They reminded Masako of the cash that had changed hands at the credit union. Dirty business, dirty money, she thought.

Masako looked at the alarm clock she'd left on the washing machine in the dressing area outside the bathroom. It was almost noon. They were nearly done, and Jumonji should be back with the boxes soon. Her shoulders and hips felt stiff and heavy from crouching so long over the body – something she hadn't remembered on the first occasion, probably because she'd been so nervous. She also hadn't had any sleep since getting home from the factory, so she was keen to get this over with and lie down.

Straightening up, Yoshie reached around to massage her sore back but then hesitated, her arm suspended in mid-air. 'I can't even rub my own back without getting blood everywhere,' she said.

'Use a new pair of gloves.'

'I don't want to waste them.'

'Don't be silly,' Masako said, nodding toward the bundle of gloves she'd brought home from the factory. 'We've got plenty.'

'It looks like Yayoi's not coming,' Yoshie said as she peeled the bloody gloves off her hands.

'I suppose not,' said Masako. 'I wanted her to see what this is like, just once.'

'She seems to think we're guiltier than she is – even though she's the one who killed her husband.' Her voice was heavy with resentment. 'She looks down on us because we're doing this for money, but that's nothing compared to what she's done.' Just then, the intercom rang and Yoshie screamed in fright. 'Somebody's here. It must be your son.' Masako shook her head. Nobuki almost never came home at this hour.

'It's probably Jumonji,' she said.

'You're right,' said Yoshie, relaxing slightly. When Masako looked through the peephole, she saw Jumonji standing outside, struggling with an unwieldy load of boxes. She helped him carry them in, and they both went through to join Yoshie.

'I got them,' Jumonji told her.

'Just in time,' Yoshie said, adopting the tone she used with junior employees at the factory.

'How many do we need?' he asked. Masako held up eight fingers. The man had been small, and the bags were less bulky than they'd expected. Besides which, Jumonji had decided to carry the head and clothes, which could be most easily identified, rather than ship them.

'Eight?' he said, looking surprised. 'I would have guessed more.'

'Do you think anybody saw you?' Yoshie asked.

'I don't think so.'

'You didn't see anyone watching the house?' Masako added, giving him a searching look. It could be disastrous if those other, unknown people learned what they were up to.

'No one,' he said. 'Except . . .'

'Except who?'

'There was a woman standing in the lot across the way. Though she left as soon as she saw me.'

'What did she look like?'

'Plump, middle-aged,' he said. Obviously the woman who had come with questions about the lot.

'Did she seem to be watching the house?' Masako said.

'No, I think she was just looking around. Otherwise, I only saw a couple of other people, probably out shopping. I don't think they noticed anything.' It had been a mistake to insist that he use his own car; next time, her Corolla would be less conspicuous.

They loaded the boxes in the car, and as soon as it was done Jumonji drove away.

'Like the foreman wheeling away a stack of boxed lunches,' said Yoshie, which made them burst out laughing. Then they took turns cleaning up in the shower, and scrubbed the bathroom. Realising that Yoshie was beginning to worry about the time, Masako went to get her share of the money.

'Your fee,' she said as she gave it to her. Holding it at arm's length, as if it were filthy, Yoshie quickly stuffed it in the bottom of her bag.

'Thanks,' she said, sounding relieved.

'What are you planning to do with it?'

'I thought I'd use it to send Miki to junior college,' she explained, smoothing back her tangled hair. 'How about you?'

'I'm not sure.' Masako now had five million of her own, but she didn't know what she'd wanted it for.

'I have to ask you this,' Yoshie said, hesitating a moment, 'but don't take it the wrong way.'

'What?'

'Did you get a million, too?'

'Of course,' said Masako, looking her straight in the eye. Yoshie reached into her bag and pulled out the stack of bills.

'Then I want to pay back the money I owe you.' Masako had forgotten she'd lent her money for her daughter's school trip. Yoshie peeled off eight ¥10,000 bills and bowed as she handed them over. 'I still owe you ¥3000, but I don't have change. Can I give it to you at work?'

'Sure,' said Masako. A loan was a loan. Yoshie looked at her a moment longer, perhaps half expecting her to refuse the money, but when it became clear she wasn't going to, she stood up.

'I'll see you tonight,' she said.

'Tonight,' said Masako. They were used to the night shift, and it felt wrong somehow to be working during the day.

Apartment 412

1

When she woke in the evening, Masako felt vaguely sad. The early sunset, signalling the onset of winter, was depressing. She lay in bed, watching as the light in the room gradually faded, leaving her in the dark. This was the sort of moment that made the night shift seem unbearable, and made it seem almost inevitable that so many of the women who worked it should end up slightly crazy. But it wasn't the winter dark that led to depression so much as the strain of living a life turned upside down from the normal, everyday world.

How many busy, 'normal' mornings had there been in her life? Always the first one up, in order to make breakfast for everyone, to pack lunches. Hanging the laundry up to dry, getting dressed, putting Nobuki through his paces, getting him off to day care. Constantly keeping an eye on the clock on the wall or sneaking a peek at her watch; working like a dog at the office. No time to read the newspaper, let alone a novel; cutting back on sleep to have time to get everything else done; and then, when the rare vacation rolled around, catching up on the endless laundry and cleaning. Busy, 'normal' days, free from loneliness or guilt.

She had no desire to go back to them, no desire to change the way things were now. When stones lying warm in the sun were turned over, they exposed the cold, damp earth underneath; and that was where Masako had burrowed deep. There was no trace of warmth in this dark earth, yet for a bug curled up tight in it, it was a peaceful and familiar world. She closed her eyes. Perhaps because her sleep was so shallow and irregular, her body felt heavy and she never seemed to recover from the exhaustion of the factory. Eventually, she descended slowly into unconsciousness, as if dragged down by gravity, and soon she was dreaming.

She was going down in the old elevator at T Credit and Loan, staring at the familiar, pale-green panelling. The panels were pockmarked from innumerable collisions with the cart used to move cash around the building. Masako herself had lugged heavy bags of coins from this elevator more times than she could count. The elevator stopped at the second floor, which housed the finance office – her old workplace. The doors opened and she gazed into the dark, empty room for a moment. It was all so familiar she could have found her way around with her eyes closed, but she had no more business here now.

Just as she pressed the button to close the doors, a man slipped into the elevator with her. It was Kenji, who she'd thought was dead. She suddenly found it hard to breathe. He was wearing a white shirt, grey pants and a plain tie: the same outfit he'd been wearing that day. He greeted her politely and then stood with his back to her, facing the door. She studied the nape of his neck, which was partly covered by his shaggy hair, but then drew back in horror, realising that without thinking she'd been checking for scars from the cuts that she'd made there.

The elevator was painfully slow, but at last it reached the ground floor and the doors opened. Kenji walked off into the dark, disappearing in the area where the reception desk should have been. Masako could feel her body breaking out in a cold sweat as she stood alone in the elevator, wondering whether she should follow him into the blackness.

It was then, when she made up her mind and stepped off the elevator, that somebody jumped out at her from the dark. Before she could get away, long arms had closed around her from behind and she couldn't move. She tried to scream for help but her voice died in her throat. The man's hands tightened around her neck. She tried to struggle, but her limbs seemed paralysed. Sweat began to flow from her pores, as if her frustration and terror were seeping from her body. The fingers tightened, and Masako went rigid with fear. But then, slowly, the warmth of his hands, the rough breathing on her neck, began to arouse a buried impulse in her: the urge to surrender, to relax and allow herself to die. Abruptly, her fear began to dissipate, as if floating weightlessly away, and in its place came a sense of blissful pleasure. She cried out in delight.

She opened her eyes and found herself lying face up in bed. Her hand moved to her chest, feeling the throb of her heart. It wasn't the first erotic dream she'd had, of course, but it was the first time that her pleasure had been so inextricably linked to fear. She lay for a while in the dark, frozen by the discovery of this scene that had been hidden in her subconscious. Who was the man in the dream? As she tried to remember exactly how his arms had felt around her, she considered the possibilities. It wasn't Kenji. He had appeared as a ghost who lured her on toward her fears. It wasn't Yoshiki, either. He had never raised a hand against her in all their years together. Nor did the arms feel like the Brazilian's, Kazuo. Then she could only assume it was that unseen figure watching her, who had taken shape in her dream. But what did it mean that her fear had been tied to such intense sexual pleasure? She lay for a moment, lost in a sensation she had nearly forgotten.

She got up and turned on the light. Pulling back the curtains, she sat down at the dressing table. Her face frowned at her from the mirror, pale and sickly in the fluorescent light. It had changed since that day; she knew it herself. The lines between her eyebrows had deepened, and her eyes had a more piercing look. She seemed older, probably. But her lips were slightly parted, as if she were about to call someone's name. What was going on? She raised her hand to cover her mouth, but there was no hiding the light shining in her eyes.

A noise brought her back to reality. Probably just Yoshiki or Nobuki coming home. She checked the clock by the bed: nearly 8.00 p.m. She quickly combed her hair, threw a cardigan around her shoulders, and left the room. The sound of the washing machine could be heard from the bathroom. Yoshiki was apparently doing his laundry after work. For several years now, he had been washing his own underwear and other clothes.

She knocked at the door to his room. There was no answer, but she opened the door and found him sitting with his back to her, still in his dress shirt, listening to music on his headphones. The room was small to begin with, but it seemed impossibly crowded after he had moved in a bed, bookshelves, and a desk, setting himself up like a student in a dorm room. She tapped him on the shoulder. Startled, he pulled off the headphones and turned to look at her.

'Are you sick?' he said, eyeing her pyjamas.

'No, I just overslept.' Feeling a sudden chill, she began buttoning her sweater.

'Overslept? It's eight o'clock,' he said in a flat voice. 'It always sounds strange, put that way.' His comment came from across the divide, from the daylight world.

'I know,' said Masako, leaning on the window-sill. 'It does sound strange.' She could hear classical music seeping from the headphones lying on the bed, but the piece was unfamiliar.

'You've stopped making dinner,' Yoshiki observed, without looking at her.

'Yes,' she said.

'Why?'

'I just decided not to.'

'It's fine with me,' he said, refraining from pressing for a reason. 'But what are *you* doing for dinner?'

'I just eat whatever we have.'

'And we can just fend for ourselves?' he asked with a twisted smile.

'I suppose so.' It was better to be honest. 'I'm sorry, but I thought you'd get things you wanted.'

'But why stop?' he said.

'I guess you could say I'm turning into a bug. I just want to be left alone to curl up out of sight, somewhere underground.'

'That might be okay if you *were* a bug, but . . .'

'You think I'm better off as a woman?'

'I suppose so.'

'I think you'd be happier as a bug, too.'

'What do you mean?' he said, giving her a puzzled look.

'In a way, that's what you are already. You've shut yourself away in your own little world. After work you come in here and ignore us – you might as well be living in a rooming house.' She waved her hand around at the place.

'Yes, well . . . ,' he said, picking up the headphones. The conversation had taken a turn he preferred not to pursue.

Masako stood staring at him. He had changed since they'd first met: his hair was thinner, and greyer. He'd lost weight as well, and he constantly smelt of alcohol. But more than the physical changes, she was struck by the sense that his search for whatever it was – some sort of personal integrity – had become more desperate. Even back in the old days, Yoshiki had valued his freedom more than other people and had wanted to live with a certain level of intensity. His work had claimed much of his time even then, but when he was free, he had been a warm and generous man. Masako, who had been young and naive in those days, felt lucky to have his love; and in turn, she had loved and trusted him.

But now, when he could escape from work it seemed that he also wanted to escape his family. The world around him was so manifestly corrupt; his job – unspeakably so. But even Masako kept him from the freedom he needed, and now Nobuki, too, had failed. The more he focused on his own integrity, the less tolerant he apparently became of those who failed to live up to his standards. But if his solution was to hide away, to give up on everyone and everything, then he'd wind up a hermit. And Masako had no intention of living with a hermit. It occurred to her that this resolve was related somehow to the pleasure she'd felt in her dream just now. Something inside her had been set free.

'Why don't we sleep together any more?' she asked, raising her voice to be heard through the headphones.

'What?' he said, pulling them from his ears again.

'Why do you want to be in here alone?'

'I guess that's it: I want to be alone,' he said, staring at the perfectly aligned spines of the books on his shelves.

'But we all want to be alone,' she said.

'I suppose so.'

'Why did you stop sleeping with me?'

'It just happened,' he said, flinching slightly and looking away. 'You seemed tired, too.'

'I suppose I was.' Masako was trying to recall the circumstances – four or five years ago it would be now – that had made them retreat to separate rooms. But it hadn't been any one thing, just an accumulation of trivial grievances whose details she'd long forgotten.

'Sex isn't the only thing that links two people to one another,' he said.

'I know that,' she murmured. 'But you seem to be rejecting everything else as well, as if you couldn't stand having anything to do with Nobuki and me.'

'You were the one who decided to take that night shift,' he said, sounding vaguely indignant.

'I had to,' she said. 'You know I'd never have found another job in my field.'

'You can believe that if you want to,' Yoshiki said, looking her in the eye now, 'but you know you could have found something in accounting at a smaller company. The fact is, you were hurt, and you weren't willing to risk letting it happen again.' It was hardly surprising that someone as intuitive as Yoshiki should have sensed this; and Masako suspected that he had even felt the pain with her.

'So you're saying things began to go wrong when I started working nights?'

'No, but I think it's obvious that we both wanted to be alone.' Masako realised that he was right, that they had chosen separate paths. There was nothing particularly tragic in that, but it did make her feel lonely. They were silent for a moment.

'Would it surprise you if I left?' she asked at last.

'I suppose it would if you just disappeared. I'm sure I'd worry.'

'But you wouldn't come looking for me?'

Yoshiki thought for a moment. 'Probably not,' he said, putting the headphones back over his ears to show that the conversation was over. Masako stared at him. She had made up her mind to leave this house, and the encouragement she'd needed was hidden beneath the bed she'd just left, in a box among her nightclothes: five million yen in cash. Opening the door as quietly as she could, she stepped out into the corridor. There she found Nobuki, standing in the dark. He looked flustered at her sudden appearance, but held his ground. Masako closed the door to Yoshiki's room behind her.

'Were you listening?' she said. Nobuki looked away in confusion but said nothing. 'You may think you can escape everything unpleasant in life just by keeping your mouth shut,' she told him, looking up at his eyes, 'but it doesn't work that way.' He was taller than her now. Was it really possible that this huge boy had come out of her own body? She had watched him gradually retreat from her, but now she found that she was the one who was about to break the bond. 'There's a good chance I'll be leaving,' she said. 'But you're grown up now. You should do as you see fit. Go back to school if you want to; or just get out of here if that would suit you better. You'll have to make those decisions for yourself.' She gazed at his hollow cheeks, searching for a sign that he might say something; but though his lips trembled for a moment, no words emerged. Then, as she turned and started down the corridor, a great bellow, hoarse with adolescent anguish, broke over her back.

'Thanks for nothing, bitch!' It was the second time she'd heard his voice this year. It sounded older, more a man's voice now than a boy's. She turned back to look at him. There were tears in his eyes, but when she tried again to speak to him, he turned with a violent lurch and charged up the stairs. Her chest ached, but she knew she didn't really want to find a way back.

For the first time in some months, she headed toward Yayoi's house on her way to work. Dry leaves blown up from the road brushed the windshield with a pleasant swishing sound. Feeling a cold draught from the window, she began to put it up; but a beetle flew in just then and began buzzing around the dark interior. She was reminded of the night she'd driven down this road trying to decide whether she should help Yayoi or not, when the scent of gardenias had drifted in for a moment. It had been only last summer, but it seemed years ago now.

There was a noise from the back seat. She knew it was probably nothing more than the map book sliding to the floor, but she couldn't shake the feeling that it was really Kenji, who had decided to join her on this visit to his wife.

'Glad you could come along,' she said aloud, glancing back into the darkness. She had seen him so often in her dreams that he'd come to seem almost like an old friend. They would go together to check up on this woman, Yoko Morisaki, who was staying with Yayoi's boys while she went to work.

Just as she'd done on the night she picked up the body, Masako pulled into the alley in front of Yayoi's house and parked. A warm yellow light was coming through the curtains in the living-room window. She rang the buzzer on the intercom, and Yayoi's anxious voice answered.

'It's Masako,' she told her. 'I'm sorry to bother you so late.' Yayoi gave a cry of surprise, and a moment later Masako could hear the sound of footsteps hurrying toward the door.

'Is something the matter?' Yayoi said. Damp strands of hair were hanging on her forehead, as if she'd just got out of the bath.

'Can I come in a minute?' Masako said. As she stepped into the cramped entrance hall and closed the door behind her, her eyes were drawn involuntarily to the spot where Kenji had sat that night. Realising what the look meant, Yayoi glanced away.

'It's early to be leaving for work,' she said.

'I know, but I needed to talk to you.' Yayoi's face hardened as she remembered the fight they'd had at the factory.

'What about?'

Masako peered beyond her toward the living room. 'What time does Morisaki-san come?' The children had apparently gone to bed. The sound of a news programme could be heard on the TV.

'I've been meaning to tell you,' Yayoi said, her face clouding over. 'She doesn't come here any more.'

'Why?' said Masako, feeling inexplicably apprehensive.

'About a week ago she suddenly announced she had to go back to the country. I tried to get her to change her mind, but she said she had no choice. The kids were heartbroken, and Yoko was almost crying, too.'

'Where was she from?'

'She never said exactly.' Yayoi was unable to hide the wounded look on her face. 'She just said she'd get in touch later. And I thought we were such good friends.'

'Look, you need to tell me exactly how you got to know her.' Yayoi gulped and then launched into the details of how she'd met Morisaki and how their friendship had developed. As she spoke, Masako became more convinced than ever that the woman had come to snoop around. Yayoi noticed the worried look on her face.

'Why are you so worked up about her?' she said. 'I think you're reading too much into it.'

'Maybe,' said Masako, 'but I think somebody's poking about trying to find out about us. I just want you to be careful.' She'd finally put her suspicions into words.

'Are you sure? . . . Who? Why?' Yayoi cried, as if at last she'd understood. Drops of water fell from her hair. 'Is it the police?'

'I don't think so.'

'Then who?'

Masako shook her head. 'I don't know. Which is why I'm worried.'

'Then you think Yoko was in on this?'

'Probably.' The odds were that the woman had already cleared out of her apartment, so there was little point in trying to trace her that way. But one thing was certain: whoever it was, they'd spent a good deal of money on renting an apartment just to be near Yayoi. It made her flesh creep to think that someone was willing to go to such lengths to spy on them.

'Maybe it was somebody from the insurance company,' Yayoi suggested.

'But haven't they already agreed to pay on the policy?'

'Yes. I should be getting the money next week.'

'Maybe that's what they're after,' Masako said. Yayoi rubbed her arms, as if warding off the cold.

'You think they're after me? What should I do?'

'They know you because you went on that TV programme. I think it might be better if you stopped coming to work. You need to lie low for a while.'

'You really think so?' she said, looking at her. 'But if I quit, those two will know I came into some money.' Masako returned her look, realising that a lot of what Yayoi had done up to this point had been prompted by uneasiness about Yoshie and Kuniko. She was struck by how calculating Yayoi had become since she'd got rid of Kenji.

'You don't have to worry about them,' she said.

'I suppose you're right.' She nodded, but there was still doubt in her eyes – doubt as to whether she could trust Masako herself, perhaps.

'I won't say anything,' Masako said, anticipating her concern.

'I know. Besides, you've already got the two million.' The words were like a slap, and Masako realised their argument at the factory was still in the air.

'A fair enough fee for carving up your husband,' she said. She held up her hand. 'I'll be going then.'

'Thanks for coming by,' Yayoi said.

As she was closing the car door, Yayoi came running out of the house. Masako opened the door on the passenger side.

'I almost forgot,' Yayoi said, slipping inside. Her hands reached up to smooth her damp hair, and a girlish smell of conditioner filled the car.

'What?'

'What did you mean the other night at the factory? What kind of "work" were you going to do? Another body?'

'I'm not telling you,' Masako said, starting the engine. The sound echoed through the quiet neighbourhood.

'Why not?' Yayoi said, biting her pretty lips. Masako stared at the windshield without looking at her, counting the dried leaves pinned under the wipers.

'I don't want to.'

'But why?'

'You don't need to know,' Masako said. 'Not an innocent lamb like you.'

Yayoi got out without another word. As Masako put the car in reverse and backed out of the alley, she could hear the sound of a door slamming.

2

It was late afternoon. As soon as she got out of bed, Kuniko turned on the TV. Then she had a boxed lunch – one of theirs, naturally – which she'd bought at the convenience store on the corner. It was a grilled beef lunch, probably made on the line next to hers, and she could immediately detect the hand of a novice in the way the meat was arranged on the rice. So much the better! New girls could never keep up with the pace of the conveyor belt, and the container was always getting away from them before they'd really finished smoothing the meat – which meant that the lunch contained a mound of twisted beef that was far bigger than the usual portion.

It was a sign, getting a lunch like this: it was going to be her lucky day. She spread out the pieces of meat, carefully counting each one. Eleven! It's amazing that Nakayama didn't blow a fuse, she chuckled to herself. The Skipper could completely cover the rice with just six pieces. The Skipper. . . . She seemed rather flush lately. She'd suddenly announced that she was sending her daughter to college, and then said they were looking for a new apartment. How could she afford all that on the ¥500,000 from Yayoi? It would cost nearly that just to move.

Maybe she'd had something stashed away? No, that was ridiculous. Kuniko knew how hard up she'd been before all this –

in fact, she'd often thought she would rather die than have to live the way Yoshie did. There was something fishy about the whole thing. She sat puzzling over this mystery, being more than usually keen when it came to money matters.

Her speculations developed into a theory: maybe Yayoi had secretly decided to pay Yoshie more than ¥500,000. Once she'd hit on this idea, there was no way to control her jealousy. She had always found the thought of anyone else's happiness almost unbearable, and she was easily convinced that she was getting a raw deal. Now these feelings fuelled her theory. Deciding that she would have to corner Yoshie – no, Yayoi – at the factory and grill her, she picked up her chopsticks and started wolfing down the meat.

In mid-mouthful, she stopped chewing for a moment and grinned, remembering that she still had ¥180,000 left of the money she'd received. After paying off the interest on various loans, she'd had plenty left over for the red leather jacket, a black skirt and a purple sweater. A pair of boots had caught her eye as well, but she'd decided to forgo them in favour of some new cosmetics. And she still had ¥180,000. Was there anything better than cash in your pocket? Wiping out Jumonji's loan had been a real stroke of luck.

She had absolutely no interest in knowing why Jumonji had wanted to find out their secret or how he had used the information. As long as it didn't come back to haunt her, what did it matter? It had crossed her mind that she'd go to jail if the whole thing ever came out, but now that the police seemed to have lost interest, that hardly seemed likely. Her part in it all, the whole mess – it all seemed like ancient history now. Except if she could still make it pay. . . . Threats, blackmail, anything for the bottom line!

She tossed the empty lunch container in the trash and went to wash her face, then sat down at her dressing table to apply her make-up for work. She pulled the wrapper off a new lipstick and tried it on. The new brown for autumn. The clerk at the make-up counter had persuaded her to buy it, but now she realised it made her pale, fleshy face look sinister. Her lips seemed to jump out at her. When she'd tried it on at the store, the woman had told her how nice it looked. How could she have believed her? ¥4,500 down the drain. She'd have been better off with an ¥800 lipstick from the supermarket. . . . Still, she might be able to make it work if she changed the kind of foundation she was using. Pleased with this new idea, she began leafing through her magazines for features on make-up. Yes, everything would be okay if she bought a new foundation . . . and the boots. She bought things to satisfy a need; and the new products themselves invariably led to new needs, in a gradually mounting spiral. But in the final analysis, this endless chase was the reason for Kuniko's existence – it *was* her whole existence.

Finishing with her make-up, she slipped on the new purple sweater and the new black skirt over a pair of black tights. Now this was more like it. As she gave herself a satisfied look in the mirror, she felt a sudden rush: she wanted a man. When was the last time she'd had sex? She pulled out the Mister Minute calendar. Tetsuya had left at the end of July, so it had been more than three months. He'd been a useless asshole, but there had been one upside to having him around. Feeling suddenly depressed, she threw herself down among the clothes strewn on the bed.

She wanted somebody to tell her how pretty she looked in all her new things. She wanted somebody to hold her. And not a wimp like Tetsuya; a real man – any man. Even a groper would do, even a one-night stand, if she could only get lucky enough to land one. Her longing grew uncontrollably, demanding satisfaction.

Just as her imagination had given rise to a whole series of suspicions about Yoshie, just as one product seemed to stimulate a need for lots more, now her sexual desire seemed to grow out of all proportion. She suddenly thought of Kazuo Miyamori. He was probably a few years younger than she was, but he was good-looking and well built – maybe because of the mixed blood – and she'd had her eye on him for some time. He'd been so nice and polite when they'd asked him to take care of their money. If he had to share that dorm room of his with a room-mate, you could bet he'd be getting a little horny. Confident in her reading of the situation, she decided she'd find an excuse to talk with him at the factory. Yes, that's what she'd do. Remembering again that she had money in her purse, she got up from the bed with her spirits restored.

Kuniko opened the car door. She decided to carry her jacket in order to show off the purple sweater. Since she'd just had her hair done, she would keep the top of the Golf up today. The one thing bothering her was the possibility of running into Masako in the parking lot. She couldn't stand the sight of the woman's face any more, and she certainly had no intention of working the same line with her. But the only way to avoid seeing her was to get to work a little early. The thought made Kuniko drive away more recklessly than usual.

When she reached the factory parking lot, a man was standing next to the new guardhouse there. A nightstick hung from the belt of his grey uniform, and a large flashlight was attached to the breast pocket. Kuniko got out of the car slowly, her mood somewhat dampened by the realisation that with the guard there she'd never get her date with the neighbourhood pervert – exactly as Masako had predicted. She glared at him as she shut the car door.

'Good evening,' the man said, bowing in her direction. Impressed by this show of gallantry, she looked at him more carefully. The guards at the factory were all retirees who were way over the hill, but this one was much younger. He was solidly built and looked quite sharp in his uniform. It was too dark in the lot to get a good look at his face, but she had a feeling she'd like it, too.

'Morning!' she almost shouted, buoyed up again. He seemed surprised by this hearty greeting, but only for a second.

'Are you headed for the factory?' he asked.

'Yes,' said Kuniko.

'Then I'll walk you there,' he said, coming over to her car. His voice was low and smooth.

'Will you really?' Kuniko purred, beginning to flirt in earnest.

'I'm supposed to walk everyone at least part of the way.'

'Each of us individually?'

'Yes, but just till we get past the old factory, where the light gets better.' The light from the guardhouse showed his profile for a moment. It was a plain enough face, though the thick lips were attractive. There was something strange about it, however, not a face that fell into any of her known categories.

'Still, I'd be glad for the company at least that far,' she said, congratulating herself on having worn her new outfit, and having spent the extra time on her make-up. She felt sure she looked especially good today. Hoping that something might come of this, she waited for a moment at the entrance to the lot while the guard removed his flashlight and shone it on the ground in front of her feet. The brightly lit circle of gravel faded at its fringes. She fell in step next to him, enjoying the idea that they were leaving on an adventure together, heading off down the dark road.

'Is that your own car?' the man said. His voice sounded brighter, as if his mood now matched hers.

'Yes.'

'Not bad,' he said, sounding quite impressed.

'Thanks,' Kuniko giggled, forgetting for the moment that she had three more years of payments to make on the car.

'How long have you had it?'

'Three years now. But it costs a fortune. It doesn't get very good . . . what's the word?'

'Mileage?' he said.

'That's it. It doesn't get good mileage.' She gave his arm a squeeze as she said this, and her heart skipped a beat as her hand met hard muscle.

'How many kilometres to the litre?' he asked.

'Oh, I don't know,' she said. 'But the man at the gas station says it's not so good.'

'They say the handling's a little sluggish, too.'

'You certainly seem to know a lot about it,' she said, smiling broadly. She felt a surge of happiness. 'Have you driven one?'

'Not me. Foreign cars are too rich for my blood.' The man smiled as he came to a stop in front of the abandoned factory. The dilapidated building had always struck her as rather creepy, but today it seemed to lend some atmosphere to the situation, like the fanciful ruins tricked up for an amusement park. 'This is as far as I go,' the guard said. Kuniko felt a bit disappointed that their walk had come to such a sudden end. 'You be careful now,' he added, giving a quick salute. 'And have a good shift.'

'Thanks!' said Kuniko as brightly as she could, delighted to have discovered such a promising prospect. Who knew where it might lead? And in response to this new stimulus, all her other fancies came bubbling to the surface. She'd buy a new suit as well, to match the boots. Black, of course – it made you look slimmer. She was in such a good mood now, nothing could bother her; and if she ran into Kazuo Miyamori, he'd just have to take a rain check.

Humming to herself, she changed into her soiled uniform, which she resolved to take home soon for a good washing. Yoshie then appeared in the changing room in her usual worn-out sweatshirt and a tired black sweater. On her chest, though, was a brand-new silver pin. Kuniko noticed it immediately, and her brain did a quick appraisal: at least ¥5,000, she decided. Much too fancy for the Skipper.

'You're early.' The look of dislike on Yoshie's face as she said this made Kuniko's blood boil, but she controlled herself.

'Good morning,' she answered in her politest manner. Then she tried flattery: 'That's a beautiful brooch.'

'This?' Yoshie said, with a faint smile. 'I decided I just had to have it. I've always wanted one like this, but I could never afford it. It was either this or getting my hair done, and I went for the brooch. It's a little present to myself.'

'With Yayoi's money?' Kuniko asked, dropping her voice.

'Yes,' said Yoshie, her face turning red. 'I suppose I should be ashamed of myself.'

'Not at all, I think it's lovely.' Having finished changing and knowing that Masako would be showing up any minute, she decided it was time to begin pumping her. 'Skipper,' she said, 'I wanted to ask you something about the money.'

Yoshie lowered her voice too and looked around the room before saying, 'What about it?'

'Did you really get the same amount I did?'

'What do you mean?' she said, looking annoyed.

'Nothing, nothing, it's just that I didn't do very much and I was afraid I took too much. I didn't want any hard feelings about getting the same as you did . . . since Masako originally said I'd be getting ¥100,000.'

'Don't worry about it,' Yoshie told her, patting her ample shoulder. 'We all had a bad time.'

'So you really got ¥500,000?'

'I really did,' Yoshie nodded. But Kuniko noticed she avoided her eyes. She's lying, she thought.

'Then how can you afford to be living so high on the hog?'

'High on the hog? What are you talking about?' she said, astonished.

'I'm talking about all the things you've been doing. It looks to me as though you got more than ¥500,000.'

'Even if I did, what business is it of yours?'

'None really, I suppose,' said Kuniko, giving Yoshie's brooch a vicious look. Yoshie glanced toward the lounge, as if searching for someone to rescue her, and her face relaxed into a relieved smile. Masako had just arrived, looking a bit smarter than usual herself, in a form-fitting black sweater and black pants.

'I don't believe it,' Kuniko said in an exaggerated whisper. 'She actually looks like a woman.' Masako, however, apparently missed the remark, as she went straight over to the ashtray near the vending machines to smoke a cigarette. While she puffed away, she stared gloomily at the notices taped to the wall. Kuniko studied the unfamiliar outfit. The two of them had pulled a fast one on her, she thought. Still, she couldn't confront Masako with it.

'See you later,' she said to Yoshie, picking up her work hat and hurrying out of the changing room. She slipped behind Masako, who was still facing the wall, and escaped out into the corridor. Yayoi was next, and she wouldn't rest until she got the truth out of her. . . .

But there was no sign of her. She waited, but she didn't come. She went to the entrance and was just about to check the time cards when she sensed there was someone behind her.

'Yayoi won't be coming,' Masako said. She had already changed into her uniform.

'What?'

'You heard me,' she said, pushing past her to punch her own card.

'Oh . . .' said Kuniko, hating herself for still being afraid of her, 'you mean, she won't be coming today, or won't be coming at all?'

'At all.'

'Why's that?'

'Maybe because she didn't like you blackmailing her,' Masako said as she was taking her ruined sneakers out of the shoe cupboard. They'd once been white, but had long since turned dark brown from all the grease and a particularly sticky sauce used for tempura lunches.

'You're horrible!' Kuniko bleated. 'I was just trying to . . .'

'Give it a rest!' said Masako, wheeling on her with eyes blazing. Kuniko froze.

'What d'you mean?' she muttered.

'You got your ¥500,000, and you sold us out to Jumonji for the price of your loan. What more do you want?' Kuniko's mouth dropped open. So she knew.

'How did you find out?'

'He told me, of course. Are you stupid as well as lazy?'

Kuniko, cheeks puffed out resentfully, knew it wasn't the first time she'd said this to her. 'No need to be so mean,' she complained.

'Mean? You're a lot worse than mean,' said Masako, clipping her with her elbow as she pushed by.

'Don't!' she squealed: it hurt to have that bony arm jabbing you through your clothes.

'Your big mouth's going to send us all to hell,' Masako spat out. 'But you've dug your own grave too, you fool!' And she stormed off toward the stairs that led down to the factory floor.

As she disappeared around the corner, Kuniko realised for the first time that she'd made a serious mistake. But as usual she couldn't blame herself for long. If things got too rough here at the factory, she would just have to find another job. It was a shame, just when she'd met that nice guard; but if push came to shove, she would have to put some distance between herself and the rest of them.

She looked at the wooden rack that held the time cards for the part-time workers. Two years she'd been here, and she'd finally got used to things. But if she had to go elsewhere, maybe she could find something less gruelling, somewhere pleasant that paid better, with nicer co-workers. Some place where they had nice men. There had to be a job like that somewhere. Maybe even something in the entertainment line – today she had the confidence to imagine even that. Yes, she'd start looking right away. Her itch for better things would spur her on, and there was the added incentive of getting free of the whole nasty mess.

After the shift, a weary Kuniko returned home to find a welcome surprise. She had parked her car in the lot and was walking past the rows of mailboxes by the door to her building when a man turned to look at her.

'Well, this is a coincidence,' he said. For a moment she didn't recognise him. 'We met last night at the parking lot,' he explained.

'I'm sorry!' she bubbled. 'I didn't realise! Isn't this amazing!' It was the guard. He was out of uniform now, dressed in a navy-blue jacket and grey work pants; and besides, she'd barely seen his face in the dark last night. He snapped shut the door of his wooden mailbox, still covered with stickers from the previous tenant's children, and turned to face her. Seen straight on, he was rather nice-looking, though there was still something strange – a bit scary, even – about him. She felt her heart race. The luck of the boxed lunch was still with her.

'Is this when you usually get home?' he said, unaware apparently of Kuniko's designs. He glanced at his watch – a cheap digital, she noted. 'That's a tough shift.'

'It is,' she said, 'but not any harder than yours.'

'But I've just started,' he said, 'so it hasn't really sunk in, I guess.' As he reached into the pocket of his jacket for a cigarette, his sleepy eyes glanced out the window at the late November sunrise. 'It must be hard on you ladies, though, especially now that it's so dark in the morning.'

'You get used to it.' Kuniko decided not to mention that she was quitting.

'I suppose so,' he said. 'By the way, I haven't introduced myself. The name's Sato.' He took his cigarette from his mouth and bowed politely.

'Kuniko Jonouchi,' she said, bowing back. 'I'm on the fifth floor.'

'Well, it's a pleasure to meet you,' he said, his straight white teeth showing when he smiled.

'The pleasure's mine,' said Kuniko. 'Do you live alone?' she added.

'To tell you the truth,' he said hesitantly, 'I'm divorced. I'm all by myself here.' Divorced! Her eyes twinkled with delight, though he didn't seem to notice. He looked away, apparently embarrassed.

'I see. Well, your secret's safe with me. You see, I'm in the same boat myself.' Sato gave her a surprised look. And hadn't she also seen a hint of satisfaction, of desire even, in his eyes? That settled it: she'd get the boots and the suit, and a gold necklace for good measure. She glanced past him to check the number on his mailbox. Apartment 412.

3

Something had been bothering her. Masako had thought about it the whole time she was cleaning the bathroom, but she still didn't have an answer. She scrubbed the grime from the tub and rinsed it with the shower hose until all the suds disappeared down the drain; but as she was finishing, perhaps because she was preoccupied, her hand slipped and she dropped the shower nozzle. It danced across the rim of the tub, writhing like a snake, and fell to the floor, spraying her with cold water. She grabbed it as quickly as she could, but she was already soaked. A chill ran through her body.

It had been raining since early afternoon, and the temperature had been falling. Cold enough to be late December. She wiped her face with the sleeve of her sweatshirt and closed the bathroom window, shutting out the cold air and the sound of the rain. Looking down at her wet clothes, she stood thinking for a moment as the chill from the tiles crept up through her legs.

She watched the water that had sprayed around the room form tiny rivulets and flow down the drain. Kenji's blood, and that of the old man, too, must already have been washed down the sewer and out to sea. The old man's body, wherever Jumonji had taken it, was probably nothing more than ashes now; and these, too, had probably washed away. As she listened to the rain, quieter now behind the closed window, she remembered the roar of the water in the culvert during the typhoon, and imagined the debris that had bobbed on the torrent, caught for a moment in the drain. Something was stuck like that in her head – but what? She ran over the events of the night before.

She had stopped off at Yayoi's on the way to work, so she'd been a bit later than usual getting to the factory parking area. She didn't like being late for work, but this Morisaki woman who had suddenly disappeared from Yayoi's place was on her mind. Was she after the insurance money? Or was it something else? Should she talk to Jumonji about it? Or could he be involved somehow? There was no one she could trust. She felt as though she were adrift at sea in the middle of the night; a sense of desolation.

She noticed that a light was on in the new guardhouse. There was no sign of the guard, but the light itself seemed like a beacon in the dark lot. Feeling relieved a little, she backed toward her space. Kuniko's Golf was already there.

The guard soon appeared, walking back from the direction of the factory. He stopped in front of the guardhouse and turned off his flashlight, but then seemed to realise that a new car had appeared in the lot, and turned it back on. He aimed it at her licence plate for a moment. The company had a record of their licence numbers, so he was probably checking hers against his list. Still, it seemed to take a bit longer than she would have expected. Masako switched off the engine and listened to the sound of his feet on the gravel as he made his way over to her car. He was tall and well built, approaching middle age.

'Good evening. Are you heading for work?' The voice was low and soft, quite easy on the ears. So much so that it occurred to her to wonder why its owner should have chosen such a solitary profession.

'Yes,' she said. The beam of his flashlight fell on her face and lingered there, again just a bit longer than was strictly necessary. It made her uncomfortable, especially since his face was hidden in shadow, and she held her arm up to block the light.

'Sorry about that,' he said. Masako locked her car and set off toward the factory. When she realised the guard was following a few steps behind, she spun around. 'I'm supposed to escort you,' he explained.

'Why's that?'

'It's a new policy. After all the trouble you ladies have been having out here.'

'I'll be okay by myself,' Masako announced.

'If something happened, though, I'd be in trouble.'

'I'm running late,' she said. 'I'll make it quick.' She turned and walked away, but the guard continued to follow her, lighting her way with his flashlight from a few steps back. Finally, she was unable to control her irritation and turned on him again. But when she did, she saw that she wasn't going to shake off that dark stare of his. For one moment, she had the feeling she'd seen him somewhere before. 'Have we met?' she started to say, but then realised how silly it sounded. 'No, I suppose not.'

His eyes gazed calmly out at her from under the brim of his hat, but his mouth seemed large, with fleshy lips. An odd face, she thought, looking away.

'It's dark,' he said. 'I'll see you as far as the factory.'

'Don't bother,' she said, flatly refusing his company. 'I'll be fine by myself.'

'Okay,' he said. As he turned to go, she thought she caught a glimpse of anger in his eyes. But what kind of man gets angry over something like that?

When she got back to the parking lot the next morning, he was already gone. But it had been enough to set her thinking.

Why should all these strange people suddenly be appearing around them? Nothing bothered her more than something she couldn't quite get a handle on. She went back to her bedroom and was just stripping off her wet clothes when the phone rang. Still in her underwear, she picked up the receiver.

'Hello?'

'It's Yoshie.'

'Skipper,' she said. 'What's up?'

'You've got to help me.'

'What happened?'

'Could you come over? I'm in a jam.' The skin on Masako's bare arms prickled, and though the heating hadn't been turned on yet, her goose bumps weren't just from the cold. It might be something serious, and she wished Yoshie would spell it out.

'Just tell me what it is,' she said.

'I can't talk about it here,' Yoshie murmured, apparently worried her mother-in-law might hear. 'And I can't get out right now.'

'All right,' Masako told her. 'I'll be right over.' She hung up and climbed into her jeans and a black sweater she'd bought recently. She'd begun to wear clothes that pleased her again, as she had when she was working at the credit union. She knew why: she was in the process of reassembling a self she'd thrown out long ago. But as the pieces came together again, she realised she was no longer the same woman, like a broken doll that could never quite be whole again.

Twenty minutes later, she was parking in the street next to Yoshie's alley. Putting up her umbrella, she picked her way through the puddles toward the shabby house. Yoshie was waiting for her, an old mustard-yellow cardigan pulled over her grey sweatsuit. She was pale, and looked as though she'd aged almost overnight. Picking up her own umbrella, she came to meet Masako halfway.

'Can we talk out here?' she said, her breath coming in white puffs of steam.

'Fine with me,' said Masako, peering out from under her umbrella.

'I'm sorry to make you come all the way here.'

'What happened?'

'The money's gone!' she gasped, tears welling up in her eyes. 'I had it hidden under the floorboards in the kitchen, but it's gone.'

'All of it? A million and a half?'

'Everything I had left. I paid you back and spent a little, but there was still ¥1,400,000.'

'Do you know who took it?'

'I think so,' Yoshie said, looking sheepish. 'I think it was Kazue.'

'Your older girl?'

'I'm almost sure. I went out shopping a few hours ago, and when I came back Issey was gone. At first I thought he might have gone out to play, but I realised he couldn't have, not in this rain.

So I started looking around, and all his clothes were gone, too. I asked Granny, and she said Kazue had come while I was out and took the boy away with her. That's when I checked the kitchen. . .' Yoshie looked shattered.

'Has she ever done anything like this before?'

'I'm afraid it's something of a habit with her,' she said, her face going red. 'I know I should have put it in the bank, but I couldn't risk having the welfare people find out I'd come into so much money.'

'Skipper,' Masako said, 'did anyone else know about it?'

'No. . . . Though I did mention to Miki that there'd be some money coming in.'

'Was that when you told her you could pay her tuition?'

'That's right. She was so happy about it.' Yoshie was in tears now. 'How could she?' she murmured. 'What kind of girl would steal her sister's tuition money?'

'Are you sure it wasn't Miki who took it?'

'Why would she steal her own money? No, I'm sure, especially with Issey disappearing like that. I'll bet Kazue called the house and Miki told her something about going to college. . . . To tell the truth, I miss Issey.' At the thought of her grandson, she began to cry even harder.

'But you're sure?' Masako pressed her. 'It couldn't have been somebody from outside?' She needed to know, though she hadn't told Yoshie her reasons yet.

'It had to be her. She's known about that hole under the floor since she was a kid.' If that was the case, then it probably was Kazue, Masako decided. And there was nothing to be done about it. She fell silent, staring at the worn, damp material of her down jacket. Her first thought had been that this might be another sign of that unseen stranger's hand.

'But what am I going to do?' Yoshie said. 'What can I do?' It was an old habit – repeating herself when she was upset.

'How should I know? There's probably nothing you can do.'

'Masako?' she said, her voice taking on a pleading tone.

'What?'

'Could you lend me something?' Masako looked at the desperate face staring out under the umbrella.

'How much?'

'A million? No, I could get by with ¥700,000.'

'I don't think so,' Masako told her, shaking her head.

'Please! I've put off moving as long as I can.' She pressed her hands together, cradling her umbrella in her arms.

'But you'd have no way to pay me back. It's bad policy to make loans like that.'

'You sound like a bank,' she said. 'But your money is just sitting there.'

Masako's voice hardened. 'That's none of your business.' Yoshie was silent for a moment.

'You're not really like that,' she murmured, her voice trembling.

'I'm learning to be,' Masako said.

'But you lent me the money for Miki's trip.'

'That was then and this is now. You screwed up, letting your own daughter rob you.'

'I know,' Yoshie said, looking defeated. Masako waited quietly in the awkward silence, flexing her chilled fingers as they clutched the umbrella.

'I won't lend you the money,' she said after a bit. 'But I'll give it to you.'

'What do you mean?' asked Yoshie, her face brightening.

'Consider it a present: one million.'

'But are you sure?'

'I'm sure. You've been a great help in all this. I'll bring it around soon.' She deserved that much, Masako thought.

'I don't know how to thank you. I won't forget this.' Yoshie made a bow, then stood there quietly for a moment. 'I was wondering,' she said.

'What?'

'Whether there'd be another job coming in.' Her face looked smaller to Masako as she squinted at her in the rain.

'Not at the moment,' she said.

'You'll be sure to call, won't you?'

'You're that desperate?' Masako's voice was subdued, but Yoshie, who knew nothing of her worries, seemed almost eager.

'Yes. I need the money, and that's the only way I can get it. I guess I'm even more desperate than poor Kazue.' She turned away and disappeared into the dingy, ageing house. The rain spilled from the broken gutter, splashing noisily on the ground below. Masako's jeans were wet far up the leg, and she could no longer keep from shivering. She had the strange feeling she often got when she was coming down with a cold: that everything around her demanded her attention.

4

The door to the balcony was wide open. Five degrees centigrade. The cold dawn air poured in, cooling the room to roughly the same temperature as outside. Satake pulled up the zipper on his navy-blue jacket. He lay stretched out on the bed in the grey work pants he'd worn all night. He wanted the windows open to let the cold air circulate through the rooms; but the north side, facing the passageway, was shut up tight.

Apartment 412. It was a cramped little place, long and narrow, running north and south. Two rooms and an eat-in kitchen. As in his apartment in Shinjuku, he had removed all the sliding doors to open up the space. There was no furniture except for a bed, positioned to look out at the skies above the Musashi plain.

The morning stars were visible now, but Satake couldn't see them. He lay with his eyes closed, his teeth clenched against the cold. He wasn't sleepy; he simply wanted no distractions as he tried to recall every detail of Masako Katori's face and voice. He lay in the cold, stitching together the fragments of his memory and then taking them apart again, over and over. Her face came floating up to him, lit by his flashlight there in the parking lot. The watchful eyes, the thin, determined lips, the taut cheeks. Satake smiled, remembering the shadow of fear that had crossed that face, lean with self-denial.

'Don't bother,' she'd said. 'I'll be fine by myself.' The low voice, rejecting everyone and everything, still echoed in his ears; the look of her as she walked away down that dark road. As he'd followed a few paces behind, it was another woman she called to mind; and when she'd turned again, her face illuminated in the beam of the flashlight, his body had shivered with pleasure at the sight of her, the irritated look, the fine lines on her forehead. She was so much like the other woman: the face, the voice, even the wrinkles.

That woman had been ten years older than Satake at the time. But he'd been wrong to think she'd died all those years ago; she hadn't, she'd been living here in secret, in this dull, dusty suburb – under another name. Masako Katori. She had felt it, too. She had started to ask if they'd met before, and that gave him his first glimpse of a crack in her hard protective shell. Fate, he whispered.

He thought back to that hot summer day, seventeen years ago, when he'd first seen the other woman on the streets of Shinjuku. Someone had been luring girls away from the clubs and massage parlours run by his gang. Whoever it was – and the person was rumoured to be a woman in her thirties who'd once been a hooker herself – was a slick operator. Satake had been violently offended by the idea that it was a woman jerking them around. In order to catch her, he had spent a good deal of time and energy planting bait – in the form of girls he trusted – around the neighbourhood; and at last he hooked her. She'd arranged to meet one of his decoys at a certain café. It was a muggy evening, with rain threatening.

He had watched her from the shadows as she approached the place, holding back so as not to scare her off. Her outfit was too flashy: a sleeveless blue mini-dress of some glossy synthetic fibre that clung to her slim figure so closely it made him hot just looking at it. She had white sandals on her bare feet; the nail polish was chipped and peeling. Short hair, and a body so thin he could see the strap of her black bra through the armhole of her dress. But the eyes told him he was looking at a strong, resourceful woman. And the eyes saw through him, spotting him almost instantly. She turned away from the café and ran off into the crowd.

Even now, after all these years, he could see the expression on her face at the moment she realised who he was. After a flash of anger at having fallen into his trap, she sneered at him, signalling her determination to escape. Despite the danger, she'd still found a few seconds to insult him; and it was that fleeting look that had set off an explosion in him. I'll track you down! I'll catch you and shake you like a rat till you're dead, he'd sworn. When he had laid the trap, he'd had no intention of killing her. He'd planned just to nab her and scare her a bit. But that look had released something in him that had lain hidden until then.

He'd been shocked even then at the way his excitement had mounted as he chased her through the streets. He knew he could simply catch up with her, but that would have been too easy. Better to reel her out, lull her into a sense of security, and then grab her. That would prolong the agony, make it all more interesting. As he loped through the warm, humid dusk, pushing past people on the street, his mood grew darker and more violent, his hand itching to grab her hair and drag her down from behind.

The woman was getting more desperate. She dashed through the traffic on Yasukuni Avenue and dodged down the stairs into a basement shopping arcade. She must have realised that she would be walking right into his back yard if she'd headed for Kabuki-cho. But he knew all of Shinjuku like the back of his hand. He pretended to let her slip away and then plunged into an underground garage. By running at full speed through a passage under the Oume Highway, he came out at the opposite end of the arcade; and just as she was emerging from a restroom where she'd hidden, sure that she had lost him, he grabbed her arm from behind. He could still remember the feel of her bare skin, damp with sweat from her dash through the summer streets.

Caught unawares, she turned on him with pure hatred and hissed, 'Fucking bastard! What a lousy trick.' The voice was low and raspy.

'You didn't think you'd get away, did you, bitch?'

'You don't scare me,' she said.

'Oh, but I will,' he said, nudging his knife into her side. He had to fight the urge to stab her on the spot. As the blade poked through her dress, she seemed to understand what he had in mind and fell silent. She allowed herself to be led back to his apartment without any tears or pleas for her life. He held her arm to keep her from running off again, aware of how little flesh there was on the bones inside. The skin on her face, too, seemed paper thin, but her eyes shone with light, like those of a stray cat. He could use a woman like this, find pleasure in her resistance; but he was startled and confused by these unfamiliar feelings. Women had been nothing much more than tools for his pleasure, so he'd always preferred them pretty and submissive.

When they reached his apartment, it was like a steam bath. He turned the air-conditioner to its coldest setting, drew the curtains, and turned on the lights. While the room was cooling down, he beat her about the face. He'd wanted to do this from the moment he'd seen her. As he hit her, instead of begging for mercy she seemed to grow more angry and defiant; and her hatred made her all the more attractive to him. He wanted to go on hurting her for ever. Finally, when her face was swollen beyond recognition, he tied her to the bed and raped her – over and over again; he never knew how long they stayed there, with only the sound of the air-conditioner groaning in the background.

Their bodies were smeared with sweat and blood. The leather belts binding her wrists cut into the skin, sending new trickles of red snaking down her arms. As he sucked at her swollen lips, his mouth filled with the metallic taste of blood. At some point, the knife he had used to prod her in the arcade appeared in his hand. He was inside her, his lips pressed to hers, when she suddenly cried out. At that moment the hatred seemed to drain from her eyes and she surrendered to him, but he was overcome with grief and frustration that he couldn't get deeper into her. He realised that he was stabbing the knife into her side. From her screams, he could tell that she had reached her climax, and he came inside her with a rush of intense pleasure.

It had been hell on earth. He stabbed her body here and there, then worked his finger into the wounds. But the more he tried to find a way in, the more impossible he realised it was. He held her then, wild with frustration and desire, willing their flesh to melt together, seeking a way to crawl into her, whispering all the while that he loved her, he loved her. And as they lay there, joined together in this bloody union, hell had gradually become heaven. But heaven or hell, it was a moment only the two of them could understand, a thing nobody else could presume to judge.

The experience had changed him. The person he'd been before vanished without a trace, and a new one appeared in its place. The woman had been the dividing line between the old Satake and this other one. He had never expected to meet anyone like her. She was the one thing he hadn't planned on, the one factor he couldn't control – in short, his fate. And now the cold, dark vision of her that he'd felt creeping up his spine began to fade; and in its place, Masako Katori seemed to reach out to him, beckoning him toward heaven . . . and hell.

As he stared up at the stars, he could imagine her, still working the line at the factory; he could picture her lonely figure as she moved about the cold concrete floor. Inside, she was probably feeling relieved, even a bit proud of herself for having fooled the police – just as the other woman must have congratulated herself on giving him the slip. But she wouldn't celebrate for long. He was sure those watchful eyes would flash with the same kind of fury when he finally caught her. Blood would pour down her hollow cheeks when he beat her. As the memory of her eyes, squinting from the glare of his flashlight, floated up before him, he could feel himself honing his desire, sharpening his murderous instinct like a blade ground against a well-oiled whetstone.

He imagined how Masako must have mobilised their little group to help the wife get rid of the body. The wife lacked the guts and brains it would have taken. Satake had quickly lost interest in her as soon as he'd discovered the connection with Masako. He had no further use for her – except as a source of insurance money. He might have known to expect no more from the wife of a creep like Yamamoto. He didn't give a shit about their little domestic drama, the quarrels, the murder, the remorse. He didn't give a shit about any of them. Nothing shut down his emotions like contempt.

Now that he had found Masako, he'd all but forgotten why he'd been looking for revenge in the first place. He reached his hands over his head and felt the sturdy metal frame of the bed. It was icy cold from the winter wind blowing in through the windows, and his palms grew numb from gripping it. He would strip her and tie her here. Gag her and torture her, with the windows wide open. The cold would bring out taut little goose bumps on her skin, stiff enough to scrape with his knife, like grains of millet. And if she screamed, he could always go to work on her belly, hollow it out with his blade. Let her scream for mercy – he would never spare her. He knew a woman like that could take it.

Perhaps, at the very end, she would whisper in his ear the way the other one had done, 'Hospital.' A word that marked the split in his mind between the desire to keep her alive and the temptation to share her death. At that moment, she had seemed dearer to him than anything else in the world. Never had he experienced an emotion of this power: the joy and sorrow of sharing in her death. He began to tremble at the memory of her voice, and for the first time since he'd left prison all those years ago, his cock began to stiffen. Tugging at the zipper on his pants, he pulled it free and gripped it. His breath came white and ragged in the icy air as his hand began to move.

The sky was just growing light in the east when Satake got up from his bed. He gazed at the purple silhouettes of the hills shimmering at the horizon, and above them a crimson cloud that seemed to retreat in the face of the rising sun. The ghostly figure of Mount Fuji soared above the hills. It would soon be time for Masako to be heading home, her eyes puffy and red from lack of sleep. Each detail was so clear it was as if he could reach out and touch her: the disgruntled look, the way she smoked her cigarette, her heavy step on the dirt of the parking lot. He even knew exactly how her face must have looked as he'd followed her on that dark road. He could see her eyes, brimming with annoyance and hostility – exactly like those other eyes.

Get some sleep then. We'll meet again soon, and you'll know your fate. But until then, sleep in peace. He looked out in the direction of her house. As the sun rose higher in the sky, he closed the door to the balcony and drew the black curtains, restoring the night to his apartment.

5

The garbled sound of a loudspeaker filtered into the room, an advertisement for some unfamiliar product. Satake opened his eyes and looked at the watch that was still strapped to his wrist: 3.00 p.m. He smoked a cigarette as he stared at the panels on the ceiling, trying to decide whether the murky brown stains were real or a trick played by the light from the cracks in the curtains. Turning on the light next to the bed, he looked down at the mound of paper on the floor. The carpet was mottled with food stains from the previous tenant, but the reports were in order and neatly stacked: the results of the investigation he'd asked a detective agency to make. Yayoi, Yoshie, Kuniko and Masako. The pile had grown in recent days after the trail had led from Kuniko and Masako to Jumonji. The investigation had already cost him nearly ten million yen.

He lit another cigarette and gathered up the stack of papers, reading once again through material he'd almost memorised by now. First, the report from Yoko Morisaki, who had managed to work her way into the Yamamoto household.

<u>The older Yamamoto boy (age 5):</u> 'That night [when Yamamoto disappeared] I heard Papa come home. I thought I heard Mama go out and say something to him, but the next morning she said I must have been dreaming, so I wasn't sure any more. But the night before, I know they had a fight and Papa hit Mama. I remember because I couldn't sleep I was so scared. I saw the bruise Mama got that night when we were in the bath.'

The younger boy (age 3): 'Mama and Papa had a lot of fights. I'm usually in bed so I don't know but they were always yelling when he came home. I'd get down under, like I'm asleep. I don't remember that night [when Yamamoto disappeared]. But Milk [the cat] ran away. After that he won't come home. I don't know why.'

A neighbour (age 46): 'She's so pretty that when I heard she'd started working nights I assumed there was a man involved. To tell the truth, we often heard them screaming at each other in the middle of the night or early in the morning. She looks even prettier now that he's gone – which raised some eyebrows around here.'

A neighbour (age 37): 'I heard a rumour that the cat still comes when the kids call it, but it won't have anything to do with their mother. They say it bolts at the sight of her. When we heard it had run away that night, everybody assumed it must have seen something. It gives me the creeps to think she might have cut him up in there and let his blood and guts run down the drain.'

******

Yamamoto-san is not favourably viewed in the neighbourhood, mostly because of the transformation she underwent after the incident. Suspicions were aroused by her apparent lack of feeling and the perception that she seemed to be liberated by the loss of her husband – also by the fact that she seems even better-looking than before.

During my stay in her house I saw ample evidence that she was glad her husband was dead. I also had the chance to observe her as she learned from the police that a prime suspect had disappeared, and it was clear that she considered this good news.

Perhaps because she felt the police were preoccupied with this suspect, she seemed to relax and all but forget about the incident. When I casually asked about the bruise on her stomach that her son had mentioned, she told me quite simply that her husband had hit her, but she offered no further explanation.

Perhaps because she is expecting to receive her husband's insurance settlement, she has recently begun talking about quitting her job at the factory. However, when her friends from work call the house, especially Masako Katori, she adopts a highly deferential tone with them. She seems almost frightened of Katori.

I discovered no hard evidence, nor even any rumours, of a love affair.

At the end of November, an insurance settlement of ¥50,000,000 is due to be deposited in Yayoi Yamamoto's bank account.

REPORT ON MASAKO KATORI

A neighbour (age 68): 'She seems to get along well enough with her husband – he works for a construction company, I think – although I have to say I've never seen them go out together. They say her son [age 17] isn't on speaking terms with them. His music used to bother us, but lately he's been very quiet. When you run into him on the street, he seems moody and never says a word. Masako isn't particularly sociable either, but she does nod and say hello. She's rather strange, though, and she doesn't seem to take very good care of herself.'

A young woman (age 18) studying for her entrance exams who lives across the street: 'You can't miss her: she leaves in the middle of the night and comes back every morning at the crack of dawn. I can see their house from my desk, so you could say I'm watching all day long. That morning [the day after Yamamoto disappeared], two women came to see her. One was on a bike and the other in a green car. I think they went home around noon.'

A local house owner (age 75): 'That morning [the day after Yamamoto disappeared], a young woman came out of the Katori house and tried to leave the garbage she was carrying in my cans. I gave her a piece of my mind and sent her packing. The bags looked heavy, easily ten kilos apiece. She didn't put up much of a fight; just ran off with them as quick as she could go. Katori-san herself would never try a stunt like that.'

Factory manager (age 31): 'She's worked here about two years. She takes her job seriously and she's one of our best workers. I heard she used to work as an accountant, so I'm considering upgrading her to regular employee status. She's a leader on the line, though her skills seem rather wasted there. She's friendly with Yoshie Azuma, Yayoi Yamamoto and Kuniko Jonouchi. They always used to work as a team, though since that business with Yamamoto's husband, they seem to have split up. Of the four, only Katori and Azuma still come to work on a regular basis.'

Former co-worker at T Credit and Loan (age 35):
'Katori-san was good at her job, but she had a stubborn streak. I don't think management trusted her, and she wasn't particularly popular with the rest of us either. I don't know what became of her after she quit.'

******

Masako Katori is reasonably well liked in her neighbourhood and at her current job, but most of her acquaintances seem to feel they can never be sure what she's thinking. There are no reports of extramarital affairs, and her home life appears to be stable. However, she has never been a member of any community group and has little to do with her neighbours.

There are also no reports of infidelity by her husband. He is not particularly popular at work, and colleagues report that he seems to have little real interest in his job, an opinion confirmed by the fact that his career has apparently stalled. The Katoris' son was expelled during his first year of high school. He currently works part-time as a plasterer. It is rumoured that he doesn't speak to them at home.

On a date subsequent to the incident, Yoshie Azuma and Akira Jumonji (alias Akira Yamada) of the Million Consumers Centre gathered at the Katori home. Jumonji arrived in a dark-blue sedan and carried a large object into the house. Three hours later, he emerged with eight parcels and loaded them in the car. I was not able to determine what the boxes contained or where he took them (though I was able to identify Jumonji himself from the licence-plate number).

REPORT ON AKIRA JUMONJI (ALIAS AKIRA YAMADA)

Former employee at Million Consumers Centre (age 25): 'The boss was always bragging that he used to be in that gang from Adachi, the Silk Buddhas or something, and that his buddy had gone on to head the Toyosumi mob. At the drop of a hat, he'd bring up his gang connections, and I have to admit we were all a bit nervous of him. I'd even thought of quitting because of it. Everybody knew we were a loan-sharking outfit, but he didn't have to go around announcing that we had the mob peering over our shoulder.'

Employee at a local game centre (age 26): 'He had a thing about younger women - the Lolita type - so he was always in here trying to pick up high-school girls. We used to kid him about it, but with his kind of looks, he didn't do too badly. You'd often see him with some cute little chick on his arm. He was always saying how well his business was doing, but something told me it wasn't all that great. A strange guy, too vain for his own good.'

Manager of a local bar (about 30): 'He came in here just the other night, laying it on about some money he'd come into. He said something about making a big score, but I knew he was in the loan business, so I had my doubts. He's a good customer, but can be a bit of a pain sometimes.'

*

The mound of reports painted a clear picture of what Masako and her little gang had done. But lately it seemed she'd hooked up with this Jumonji character and started a little business on the side. Satake smiled to himself, admiring her resourcefulness.

Tired of reading, he pushed the papers off to one side. The loudspeaker was still blaring somewhere outside. He parted the curtains slightly and let the last rays of the winter sun into the room, setting the dust in the air dancing. He stared at the narrow threads of light, impatient for the sun to set. Still several hours until seven, when he would head for work.

The buzzer on the intercom sounded and Satake jumped up to answer it, stuffing the reports in a paper bag and shoving it under the bed as he went. Kuniko's affected voice came blaring from the speaker over the whistling of the wind.

'Sato-san? It's Kuniko Jonouchi.' He had her! Satake smiled broadly and cleared his throat.

'Hold on just a second,' he said. 'I'll be right there.' He pulled back the curtains and opened the balcony door to let in some fresh air. While he was straightening the bedding, he checked to make sure the reports were out of sight. 'Sorry that took so long,' he said as he opened the front door, allowing a gust of cold air to blow a whiff of Kuniko's cloying perfume inside with it: 'Coco' from Chanel, he recognised. Anna had been given a bottle by a customer, but he'd told her to stop wearing it at the club. Strong perfumes follow men home and cause unnecessary trouble.

'I'm sorry to barge in like this,' Kuniko said, straightening her hair and smoothing her skirt.

'Not at all,' he said. 'Come in out of the cold.'

'Just for a minute,' she said, wedging her large frame into the cramped entranceway. She wore a black suit, new boots and a heavy gold necklace, as though she were going out somewhere. By force of habit, Satake immediately appraised her outfit and accessories: all cheap copies of expensive designer labels. While she stood in the hall waiting to be asked in, she peered curiously into the apartment. 'Quite neat and tidy,' she commented.

'My wife took everything with her, I'm afraid. That's all she left,' he said, pointing at the bed by the window. Kuniko stared for a moment and then looked away in mock embarrassment. There was something suggestive in the way she responded, but if she'd known what he was planning for her on that bed, she would have run screaming out of there.

'Did I wake you up?' she asked. 'I was wondering whether you were all right . . . since you weren't at work last night.'

'It was my night off.'

'Oh? I didn't realise. . . . To tell the truth, I just wanted to say goodbye.'

'Goodbye?' he said, startled. Was she thinking of running for it – just when he'd got hold of her?

'I quit my job,' she explained.

'That's a shame,' he said in a disappointed voice. The sound of it pleased Kuniko no end.

'But I'm staying here in the building,' she told him cheerfully. 'And I know we'll see each other around.'

'I hope so,' he said. 'I'd like that. . . . It's not very cosy, but would you like to come in for a minute?' Kuniko immediately reached down to tug at the zipper where her boot was biting into her calf. 'I'm afraid you'll have to sit on the bed,' he added.

Without a word, she walked toward it. Watching from behind, he ran through his plans. It was all happening sooner than he'd intended, but he couldn't ask for a better chance than this. Now there was no need to come up with a pretext to get her in here; and since she'd quit her job, no one would miss her when she didn't show up for work.

'She didn't even leave me a table,' he told her.

'I kind of like it,' she said, sitting down on the bed. 'My place is so stuffed with things.' She looked around doubtfully at the empty room. 'It's like an office, isn't it? Where do you keep your clothes?'

'I don't really have anything else,' he said, gesturing at the jacket and pants he was wearing, wrinkled now from his nap. Her eyes lingered for a moment on his body.

'Men are lucky,' she said. 'They can get along with almost nothing.' She fished a cigarette out of her fake Chanel bag. Satake produced a spotless ashtray and put it next to her. 'There's a decent bar not far away,' she said, lighting up. 'Would you like to go?'

'I'm afraid I don't drink,' he said. Kuniko seemed disappointed by this information, but she quickly rallied.

'Then let's go get something to eat,' she said.

'All right. Just give me a minute.' Disappearing into the bathroom, he washed his face and brushed his teeth. A glance in the mirror confirmed that his normally close-cropped hair had grown out and he needed a shave. The Kabuki-cho dandy had vanished, and a rumpled, middle-aged security guard stared back at him. Still, in his eyes there were signs that the beast that had lain dormant inside him for so long was coming back to life. He rubbed a towel across his face and opened the door. Kuniko sat on the bed in the empty room, staring idly around her. 'What would you say to ordering something to eat here?' he said.

'What did you have in mind?' she giggled.

'How about some sushi?'

'That sounds wonderful,' she said, smiling happily. Satake, of course, had no intention of ordering anything, or letting anyone know that she'd ever come to apartment 412.

'Would you like a cup of coffee first?' he asked. He filled the kettle with water and put it on the stove. The coffee, too, was a lie: the shelves were as empty as the rest of the apartment. But he opened a door and stood there for a moment, as if considering the contents. Sensing something behind him, he turned to find Kuniko peering over his shoulder.

'It's empty,' she murmured.

'What is?' he said abruptly, in a frigid voice. She froze, as if she'd just run across a snake in the road.

'I just thought I could help. . . ,' she stammered, backing away. She turned and moved toward the bed, but he slipped his arm around her neck and moved his hand to cover her mouth. Her thick lipstick smeared across his palm as he lifted the heavy body into the air. Though she struggled for a while, her own weight pulled her neck down on his arm and she soon lost consciousness. After he'd managed to lay her out on the bed, he went to turn off the stove.

He then rolled her limp body over and began carefully removing her clothes. When she was naked, he tied her wrists and ankles to the bed, just as he'd imagined doing that morning. It was a perfect dress rehearsal for what he planned for Masako; but when he saw Kuniko's large, bovine body stretched out before him, his desire withered, taking with it the elaborate plan it had given rise to. Suddenly fed up with the whole project, he crumpled the underpants he'd stripped off her and shoved them in her gaping mouth. At that, she woke up and her eyes shot wide open. She stared wildly around the room, trying to understand what was happening to her.

'Now you won't start screaming, will you?' The voice was low and menacing. She shook her head frantically, and a moment later he pulled the underpants from her mouth, leaving a thread of spittle hanging in the air.

'Please!' she gasped. 'Don't hurt me. I'll do anything you ask.' Satake ignored her. He was busy spreading plastic bags under her hips – just in case she soiled the bed. 'What are you doing?' she whispered, tossing and turning as he worked.

'Nothing. Just hold still.'

'Please,' she begged. 'Don't hurt me.' There were tears in her beady eyes.

'Tell me,' he said, 'did Yayoi Yamamoto kill her husband?'

'Yes, yes,' she said, nodding wildly.

'And Masako and you, and Yoshie, the older one, you cut up the body?'

'Yes.'

'Masako was the ringleader?'

'Of course!'

'And how much did Yayoi pay you?'

'Five hundred thousand apiece.' Satake laughed, struck by the irony of a bunch of housewives working for peanuts – and in the process bringing down his precious empire.

'Masako, too?' he asked.

'No, she didn't take anything.'

'And why was that?'

'She's got a stick up her ass,' Kuniko said, blurting out the first words that came into her head. Stick up her ass? Satake laughed again.

'And how did Masako meet Jumonji?'

She hesitated, clearly shocked that he knew this much about them. 'I think they knew each other from before,' she said eventually.

'Which is why he lent you money?'

'No, that was just a coincidence.'

'It's all a little too neat,' he jeered as she began to cry again. 'And it's a little late for tears.'

'Don't hurt me. I'm begging you.'

'Wait a second,' he said. 'How did Jumonji find out about this?'

'I told him.'

'Did you tell anyone else?'

'No.'

'And did you know that the rest of them have set up a nice

little business doing what you all did to Yayoi's husband?' As he spoke, Satake slipped the thick leather belt out of the loops on his pants. Kuniko's eyes, white with terror, watched him as her head shook violently back and forth. 'Did you?' he insisted.

'No!' she screamed.

'In other words,' he said, 'they don't trust you. They no longer need you.' As he wrapped the belt around her neck, her wail faded to a frantic gasp. Realising he might still need the gag, Satake reached down for the discarded underpants and forced them deep into her throat. As her eyes rolled back in her head from lack of air, he tightened the belt with a firm tug. He found this murder, the second he had ever committed, utterly uninteresting.

He untied the body and pushed it off the bed. Wrapping it tightly in a blanket, he rolled it on to the balcony, propping it carefully in a corner so that it couldn't be seen from the other apartments. When he looked up, the sun was just setting behind the mountains he had seen that morning, though now they were black and almost invisible in the fading light.

Closing the balcony door, he examined the contents of Kuniko's purse. He removed a small stack of ¥10,000 bills from her wallet and took two keys, one for the Golf and the other apparently for her apartment. Then he stuffed her clothes and underwear and shoes into a bag. Taking his own key and his wallet, he left the apartment with the bag. It was dark now, and though the wind had died down, it was cold. He climbed the emergency stairs at the end of the building to the next floor and looked down the passageway. Fortunately, there was no one in sight. Skirting the tricycles and potted plants that lined the wall, he made his way to Kuniko's door and opened it with the key he'd retrieved from her purse.

The apartment was strewn with new clothes and wads of torn wrapping paper and shopping bags. He emptied the bag of clothes he'd brought into the jumble and backed out the door. Checking again to make sure there was no one in the passageway, he locked the door and headed toward the elevator. He ditched Kuniko's key in the trash bin on the first floor and then went to find his bike in the parking area behind the building. A minute later, an ordinary security guard pedalled off to his job at a factory.

6

Jumonji was in heaven. Standing next to him was a beautiful girl in the uniform of a well-known high school. Her dyed-brown hair hung loose across the smooth white skin of her cheeks, and her pink lips were slightly parted. The arch of her narrow eyebrows set off her lovely eyes, and her miniskirt barely overlapped a pair of long, slender legs. She was so good-looking she might easily have been a model – and here she was, talking to him. It was all he could do to stay cool.

'What do you want to do?' he said, his voice low and urgent.

'I don't care,' she whispered, sweet and raspy. 'Whatever you want to.' Her whole body seemed to exude a perfume he couldn't quite place. Her accessories were all by the top designers. She was, in a word, perfect. But where could this miracle have come from? The high-school girls he was used to seemed to be a whole different species, girls who spent their time in dingy fast-food places, their hair reeking of cheap conditioner. But thanks to the money he'd realised on his little scheme, he could afford to take a girl like this to a real hotel, without so much as blinking at the ¥100,000 she wanted up front.

'What would you say to getting a room somewhere?' he said.

'That sounds fine,' she said.

'It does? You mean you'll . . . ?' The girl nodded shyly, and he began racking his brain for the name of a hotel they could reach before she changed her mind. But just then, the cell phone in his hip pocket began to ring. 'Excuse me a second,' he said. He had left everything at Million Consumers to a female assistant so he could relax and enjoy himself. She'd been with him for ever, so she ought to have been able to handle whatever it was – and she ought to have known better than to call him at a time like this.

'Yes. Jumonji,' he said, barely disguising his irritation.

'Akira? Where are you?' said a toneless but unmistakable voice.

'Soga-san? It's good to hear from you, and I want to thank you again for your help the other day.' The girl watched him grovel into the phone for a moment, then turned her back, pissed at the sudden change in his manner. Noticing her begin to slip away, Jumonji grabbed her elbow.

'Don't mention it,' Soga said. 'Are you in Shibuya or something?' he asked, puzzled by the background noise. Jumonji wanted to howl at the bad timing.

'Something like that,' he said.

'Shibuya? Really? You're amazing. I bet you're all dolled up like a teenager.' Jumonji scratched his head. He still had the girl by the elbow, but she was looking around for a way to escape. There were any number of men like Jumonji waiting here on Shibuya's main drag, hoping to meet a girl like her. In fact, a ring of them was beginning to tighten around her now. Seeing their hungry eyes, Jumonji began to panic. 'You still got the fuzzy dice on the rear-view mirror?' Soga went on, obviously enjoying the chance to tease him.

'Was there something you needed?' Jumonji said.

'You're with a girl, aren't you? Robbing the cradle again, you dope?'

'Guilty as charged,' Jumonji said. 'But I wonder if we could talk about this later?'

'Sorry, no can do.' Soga's voice was serious now. 'We've got ourselves a job.'

'What?' said Jumonji, releasing the girl's arm.

'Bye,' she said, wandering off with several Jumonji look-alikes in tow. Shit! He watched longingly as she disappeared into the crowd, saying a reluctant farewell to the short skirt, the cute little ass it covered. . . . But business was business, and he could afford ten girls like her with the money from another job. Pulling himself together, he apologised to Soga.

'Sorry, I was a bit distracted.'

'She get away from you? Well, you need to have a clear head for this anyway. You screw up and we're all dead!' Jumonji began to concentrate, imagining the look in Soga's eyes as he said this.

'I know,' he told him.

'Anyway, it seems that word got out that your first job was a success. . . .' The phone connection began to break up, so Jumonji moved under an awning, away from the crowd. 'Just make sure you do the same thing this time. They'll have it for you by tonight.'

'Tonight?' Jumonji repeated, wondering whether he'd be able to get in touch with Masako at such short notice. Glancing at his watch, he saw that it was barely 8.00. He should still be able to catch her at home.

'It's fresh, apparently, so we have to act fast.'

'Understood,' said Jumonji.

'It'll be at the rear entrance to Koganei Park, at 4.00 a.m.'

'I'll be there,' Jumonji said.

'So will I,' said Soga, his voice more subdued than usual. 'This one turned up by a slightly different route, and I just want to make sure everything goes as planned.'

'Different how?' Jumonji asked. The people pushing past him on the street eyed him curiously, apparently unused to seeing someone talking seriously on a cell phone.

'I have a supplier I'm sure I can trust – the old guy the other day came from him. But this one just showed up, you might say.'

'Showed up? Not from somebody in the business?'

'That's what I don't know,' Soga said. 'The guy just said he'd heard about the service and wanted us to do it. He wouldn't take "no" for an answer. Even when I told him it'd cost ten million, he didn't bat an eye.' Jumonji's heart leapt at the news.

'That means an extra million for you,' he said.

'And an extra million for you,' said Soga, enjoying the role of generous patron. By now Jumonji had forgotten all about the girl. If he kept this windfall a secret from Masako, he would clear three million this time.

'Soga-san, you're a prince.'

'Yeah, yeah. But I think we have to watch it with this one. I'll be bringing some muscle with me, and you might think about fishing your bulletproof underwear out of the closet.'

Jumonji laughed, then closed the cell phone. It occurred to him that perhaps Soga wasn't joking, but he was too excited by the prospect of the money to care. And he needed to get in touch with Masako right away. He began looking for her number in his book; if he couldn't catch her now, he would have to drive around all day with another of those spooky things in his trunk. Masako answered almost immediately. From the sound of her voice, she had a cold.

'We've got another job,' he told her. 'Can you manage it?'

'It's awfully soon,' Masako said, her voice louder than usual.

'Word gets around when you're good,' he said. Masako was silent, ignoring his enthusiasm. He could sense her uneasiness, but he had to get her to agree. 'Can I count on you?' he said.

'Why don't we pass on this one?'

'Why?'

'I just don't feel right about it.'

'Our second job, and you don't feel right? I'm not sure I follow you.' He was pressing now. 'I'll have egg on my face if we turn this down.'

'Better that than something worse,' she said enigmatically.

'What do you mean by that?'

'I don't know, I just don't feel good about this.'

'You've got a cold; you don't feel good. But that's got nothing to do with the job.' He was getting desperate. 'I have to go all the way to Kyushu to dump it. You're not the only one taking a risk here, you know that.'

'I know,' she murmured. Jumonji was upset now.

'If you pull out, I'll get the Skipper to do it, or Kuniko. That cow would do anything if the price was right.'

'You can't do that,' Masako said. 'If she messes up, she'll put us all in danger.'

'Of course she will!' he moaned. 'So you've got to do it. Just this once.'

'All right,' she said, giving in. 'Can you get some goggles?' As soon as she'd made up her mind, she was all business. Jumonji breathed a sigh of relief.

'I'll bring the ones I wear on my bike. They should be okay.'

'Then call me if anything changes.'

Satisfied that the negotiation had gone so well, Jumonji snapped the phone shut again and glanced at his watch. There was plenty of time before he had to be at Koganei Park – time enough to find another girl like the one who got away. With all that money coming in, he could pay whatever she asked. He looked out across the crowded street, resuming the hunt. He didn't have time now to wonder why Masako had seemed so hesitant.

Four a.m. As arranged, Jumonji parked his car at the back entrance to Koganei Park. A dense wall of vegetation loomed over the guard rail that lined one side of the street. On the other side, a row of houses lay sleeping behind tightly closed shutters. There were no streetlights in the area, and the neighbourhood was dark and lifeless. Jumonji turned his back to the line of black trees in the park, trying to ignore the eerie rustling of the wind in the branches. He suddenly remembered that Kuniko had left her share of a dead body somewhere near here, and he found the coincidence slightly unnerving.

It was cold. Sniffling a bit, he moved his hands toward the buttons of his coat only to discover they'd all been torn off. For that he could thank the girl he'd been with just a while ago, whom he'd taken for a teenager until he found out she was actually twenty-one. He had caught her searching his coat when he came out of the bath, and the buttons had come off when he'd grabbed it from her. Crummy luck – the words popped into his head – but he was quick to drive them out again. What was crummy about an unexpected bonus of three million? But just as he'd managed to steer his thoughts in this direction, he heard a car coming from the right, and a pair of headlights lit up the area.

Soga stepped out of the black sedan and raised his hand in greeting. Despite the time of night, he was wearing a camel-coloured cashmere coat over a black suit. The kid with the dyed-blond hair was driving, and another fellow had climbed out of the car behind his boss. Soga nodded to Jumonji with a sleepy look.

'Sorry to get you out so early,' Jumonji said.

'I wanted to see this character for myself,' Soga said, turning up his collar and shoving his hands in his pockets.

'And his little problem,' Jumonji added.

'If he's willing to pay ten million to get it fixed, it might not be so little.'

'You may be right.'

'You going to cart it away in that?' Soga said, pointing at Jumonji's car.

'What else?'

Soga pulled a face. For the first job, the driver and the other guy had brought the body and the cash to Jumonji; Soga had merely arranged things by phone. Jumonji had felt a bit resentful that he was making two million for a few calls.

'All part of the job,' he added.

'Well, you're a better man than I am,' Soga said, patting him on the shoulder sympathetically. At that moment, a van appeared from the opposite end of the street and rolled toward them with its high beams blazing, like the eyes of a wild animal.

'It's him,' Soga said. He ground out his cigarette on the guard rail and handed the butt to his deputy.

'What do I do with this?' the man asked, holding it in his outstretched palm.

'We can't leave any evidence in the area, asshole,' Soga said. 'Eat it.'

'Eat it? Really?'

'No, you idiot. Just take care of it.' The guy quickly shoved the butt in his pocket. Jumonji swallowed. He no longer felt cold. The van stopped in front of them, but the lights were still on high, obscuring their view of it. The door on the driver's side opened and a man stepped out. He was tall and solidly built, dressed unobtrusively in a jacket and work pants. His cap partially hid his face, but the sight of him made Jumonji shiver, though he wasn't sure why.

'Soga, from the Toyosumi organisation,' Soga said.

'Bit of a crowd, isn't it?' the man murmured.

'Sorry. It's just that we haven't dealt with you before. I wanted to ask how you heard about our service.'

'Does it matter?'

'I'm afraid it does.'

'Nosy, aren't you?' the man said, taking a paper bag from his pocket and tossing it toward them. Soga caught it and checked the contents. Peering over his shoulder, Jumonji could see bundles of ¥10,000 bills. Satisfied, Soga nodded toward the van.

'Okay,' he said. 'Let's get it.' The man pulled open the door.

Inside, they could see a human form wrapped in blankets. It was short and thick – a woman, Jumonji thought, frozen to the spot. It had never occurred to him they might be getting a woman's body.

'What's the matter?' the man sneered at him. 'This scare you?' He reached in and dragged the body out of the van. Soga's men came running over to help, but before they could get there, the man had dropped the body on the asphalt and slammed the door. Without another word, he got behind the wheel and backed down the road the way he'd come. The high whine of the engine in reverse filled the silence for a bit and then died away in the darkness. The whole transaction was over in a moment.

'That's one scary guy,' Jumonji said.

'What do you expect from a killer?' Soga laughed. Had he really killed her, Jumonji wondered, staring at the squat figure wrapped from head to toe in blankets and bound tight with rope.

'Why did he back away?'

'To keep us from seeing the licence plate and to make sure we didn't follow him,' Soga said. Jumonji began to tremble, finally realising that he might be in over his head. He should have known from the way he felt when he first saw the van.

Opening the paper bag, Soga extracted three of the bundles and shoved the rest at Jumonji.

'It's all yours,' he said, nodding toward the blond and the bodyguard who were struggling to fit the awkward bundle in Jumonji's trunk. Soga watched them at it for a moment, his face twisted in distaste.

'It looks like a woman,' Jumonji said.

'I was just thinking the same thing,' Soga said, turning to look at him. 'A high-school girl, maybe.' He wasn't smiling.

'Don't say that,' Jumonji murmured, feeling a chill come over him that was only partly due to the dawn air. The trunk closed with a bang, and the two men backed away, rubbing their hands and sniffing at them, as if what they'd just touched was unclean.

'We're off, then,' Soga said, patting Jumonji again on the shoulder. 'Good luck.'

Jumonji glanced at him with a panicked look. Soga's tongue flicked nervously over his lips.

'You're not chickening out, are you?' he said.

'No. . . ,' Jumonji whispered.

'Listen, Akira,' he said. 'This is serious business. Don't blow it.' The bodyguard had opened the door and was standing waiting. Soga signalled to him, and a few seconds later their car was speeding away, as if fleeing the scene of a crime. Jumonji was left alone in the dark. Resisting the urge to simply turn and run, he climbed into his own car and switched on the engine. As he crept down the street, he realised almost immediately that he'd never been quite so frightened in his life, but it took him several minutes more to understand that it wasn't the body in the trunk that scared him so much as the man who had left it.

7

Masako was finally getting over her cold. For the first time in a week, she was feeling good. The face that stared back at her from the mirror looked a bit drawn, but the cheeks were tight and the eyes were rested and less swollen – not bad for someone about to do the job she had coming up.

Fortunately, Yoshiki had left for the office on schedule, and Nobuki had an early start. Since their exchange that night, Yoshiki seemed even more set on hiding himself away in his room; probably strengthening his defences, to keep from getting hurt now that he knew she might be leaving. It was like being separated while still living under the same roof, and it made Masako sad despite her best efforts to forget the whole situation. On the other hand, Nobuki had started to say a few words from time to time, and even if it was only to ask about dinner, it was encouraging.

She had removed the soap and shampoo bottles from the bathroom and spread the vinyl sheet over the tiles. She opened the window to release the damp air from last night's bath. The day promised to be an unseasonably warm one, but even her restored health and the good weather weren't enough to mask the anxiety she was feeling. How could she explain her worries to Jumonji and Yoshie, especially when they seemed so eager for the work? A mysterious stranger, lurking in the shadows? They'd laugh at her. In fact, she now had a shrewd idea of his identity. It had come to her as she lay in bed with her cold. But there was no proof, of course.

Closing and locking the window, she wandered out to the entrance hall. She felt impatient, but it wasn't expectation, it was fear that made her like this. And it wasn't the body itself but the next development, the next act in the play, she was dreading. She felt as though she were out of control, hurtling along with no idea where she was going, and it made her nervous – and scared.

Slipping into her son's huge beach sandals, she stepped down into the entrance. She couldn't go back and wait in the house, and she couldn't go out to meet Jumonji, so here she stood, stuck in between. She stood with her arms folded across her chest, trying to keep uneasiness at bay.

'Shit,' she hissed, hoping that swearing would help. It all seemed wrong. More than anything else, she hated being pushed along by circumstances before she had time to prepare herself – which was probably exactly what this hidden opponent of theirs intended.

She knew that Jumonji's flashy car would be conspicuous parked in front of the house again, even for a few minutes, and she'd meant to use her Corolla this time. But there had been no time for that. They had been lucky before, but that didn't mean their luck would hold. It made her mad to think that she'd got herself involved in something so misguided; and she found she couldn't shake the nagging feeling that they'd overlooked something, made some terrible mistake. As she hesitated in the doorway, her uneasiness began to swell like a balloon, threatening to explode at any moment. Finally, unable to keep still, she opened the door and went out.

The day was warm. The neighbourhood was quiet as always. A single strand of smoke rose lazily from a pile of leaves burning in the field across the way. The sound of a propeller could be heard in the distance, and nearby the soft clatter of someone washing dishes. An ordinary morning in the suburbs. Masako stared at the red earth of the vacant lot across the street. The woman who'd made such a fuss about wanting to buy it had disappeared. Everything was exactly as it always was – then why did it seem so ominous? Her thoughts were interrupted by the sound of bicycle brakes.

'Morning,' Yoshie called. She had thrown on an old black windbreaker, probably one of Miki's, over her usual grey sweatsuit. Her eyes, red from lack of sleep, squinted in the morning light – just as Masako's did when she'd been at work.

'Good morning, Skipper,' she said. 'Are you ready for this?'

'I think so,' Yoshie said, her expression more determined than usual. 'I'm the one who bugged you about it.'

'Let's get inside,' Masako said as Yoshie was parking her bike. She slipped in through the door and pulled off her shoes.

'How's your cold?' Yoshie said with a solicitous glance in her direction. She had been sick ever since the night she'd gone to Yoshie's house in the rain, and hadn't been to work.

'Much better,' said Masako.

'I'm glad. But this can't be the best thing for it, not with all that cold water.' They had realised last time that it was better to leave the water running while they cut up the body.

'Is everything okay at the factory?' Masako asked.

'I'd been meaning to tell you,' she said, her voice sinking to a whisper. 'Kuniko quit.'

'She did?'

'All of a sudden, three days ago. The boss tried to get her to change her mind, but you know how she is. She hasn't shown up since.' Yoshie stripped off her jacket and folded it into a neat bundle. Masako stared idly at the white flannel lining that was worn thin in places. 'And Yayoi doesn't come any more either. I've been all by myself since you came down with a cold. It gets a bit lonely there, so I've been jacking up the speed on the line to eighteen. You should see them scramble – and hear them gripe. Bunch of babies.'

'Sounds like fun,' Masako said.

'And that Brazilian guy asked about you last night.'

'Brazilian guy?'

'The young one; Miyamori – I forget the other name.'

'What did he say?'

'He asked if you'd quit. I think he's got a thing for you.' Ignoring the teasing tone, Masako recalled the forlorn look on Kazuo's face as he stood staring after her that summer. It all seemed so long ago. Yoshie waited a moment for her to say something but then went on. 'I couldn't believe how much his Japanese has improved. I suppose you can do that when you're young.' Yoshie was unusually chatty this morning, presumably from nervous energy before the job. Masako let the words wash over her, like a sudden rain shower, waiting for a break in the flow to bring up her own worries. But just then they heard a car pull up outside.

'He's here!' Yoshie squealed, hopping up.

'Wait a second,' Masako said, putting her eye to the peephole and looking outside. Jumonji's car was backing up to the house, right on time. She opened the door a bit and peered out. He had already come around to the back of the car, his face wan and oily from a sleepless night.

'Katori-san,' he whispered through the door, 'I'm afraid you're not going to like this one.'

'Why?' she said.

'It's a woman,' he murmured. Masako flinched. The job was horrible enough, but it seemed even more gruesome to work on a woman's body. Jumonji glanced around and then quickly unlocked the trunk and lifted the lid. At the sight of the cocoon-like bundle, Masako backed away. The old man had been small, too, but he was thin, almost fleshless. This time the body was hefty, with a generous swelling at the chest.

'What's wrong?' Yoshie said. Peeking around her, she let out a little gasp. Kenji and the other body had also come wrapped in blankets, but there was something more sinister about the careful way this one had been tied around and around with rope.

'Let's get it inside,' Jumonji said, averting his eyes as he reached into the trunk. Masako went to help, grabbing one end of the limp, heavy form, and together they managed to get it back to the bathroom. 'This one really bothers me,' Jumonji said. 'The guy who brought it scared me to death.'

'Why?' Masako said.

'You could just tell he killed her.'

'How could you?' Yoshie said, holding her hand over her heart to stop the pounding. 'He was probably just delivering it.'

'I know it sounds weird, but you could just tell!' His eyes were bloodshot and he was half shouting. Masako said nothing, but it struck her that he was probably right. It had been the same with Yayoi that night: something about her made it obvious what she'd done.

'You're the man,' Yoshie said, holding out a pair of scissors. 'You unwrap it.'

'Me?' Jumonji said.

'I don't see any other men around,' she said, throwing the word 'men' at him like an insult. 'Show some initiative!' Gingerly picking up the scissors, he bent over and cut away the ropes. Then he gripped the edge of the blanket and pulled on it. Two thick white legs flopped out, with traces of purple bruising on the back of them. Yoshie screamed and hid behind Masako. Next came a fleshy torso, apparently unmarked, with one heavy breast falling away to either side. The woman was fat, but still in the prime of life. The naked body lay exposed before them, but the head was still shrouded in the blanket, as if reluctant to give up its secret. As Masako reached down to help Jumonji finish the job, her hand suddenly froze. The head was covered with a black plastic bag that had been secured around the neck with another rope. 'This is awful,' Yoshie muttered, backing into the dressing area. Jumonji looked as though he might be sick.

'You don't think they've cut off the face?' he said. 'I couldn't take that.'

'Wait a minute,' Masako said, struck by a sudden premonition. She took the scissors from him and cut away the bag with a few quick snips. 'I thought so,' she said. 'It's Kuniko.'

There she lay, her eyes half open, her tongue hanging out stupidly, and her shifty eyes and greedy mouth gone slack. The bathroom, which had simply been a convenient place to cut up unknown bodies, seemed suddenly transformed into a funeral hall now that it was filled with this familiar shape. Jumonji stood frozen over it as Yoshie sobbed in the background.

'What did that man look like?' Masako said, her voice urgent. 'Who was he?'

'I didn't get a good look at him,' Jumonji said, sounding exhausted. 'He was tall and he looked pretty tough. He had a deep voice. . . .'

'Like half the men in the city,' Masako said, her exasperation showing.

'How should I know what he looked like?' he whined, turning away. Yoshie had sunk down in the dressing area and was crying quietly. Masako could hear her mumbling to herself.

'It's our punishment,' she was saying. 'We should never have done this.'

'Shut up!' Masako yelled, lurching through the door and grabbing Yoshie by the collar. 'Don't you understand? They're after us!' Yoshie looked at her blankly, as though she were speaking a foreign language.

'What do you mean?'

'Isn't it obvious? They sent us Kuniko!'

'I'm sure it's just a coincidence,' she whispered.

'How can you say that?!' Masako could hear her voice rising to a shrill wail, but she couldn't stop herself. She shoved her finger in her mouth and bit it.

'I had a bad feeling about this,' Jumonji interrupted. 'They told me to pick up the body at the back of Koganei Park.'

'Koganei Park?' said Masako, feeling a chill run through her. So they knew everything. They knew how to get to Kuniko and how to send her as a warning. But why? She turned to look at the body sprawled out behind her. 'You fool!' she screamed at it. 'Tell us what's going on!'

Jumonji took her arm. 'Katori-san, are you all right?'

'Masako?' Yoshie said.

'Maybe now you'll believe me,' she said, spinning around to face them.

'Believe what?'

'That somebody's after us. They got to Yayoi and found out what we did; and they've been watching me, too. Now they've killed Kuniko and figured out how to get her body here.'

'But what do they want?' asked Yoshie, still sobbing. 'Even if they did kill Kuniko, why would they send her here? It's got to be a coincidence.'

'Don't be ridiculous,' Masako said. 'They wanted us to know that they've figured out the whole thing.'

'But why?'

'They want revenge,' said Masako, and as soon as the word had left her mouth the puzzle seemed to solve itself. Of course, that was it. He wanted revenge, an elaborate, expensive revenge. She'd been wrong in thinking it was about the insurance money. If it was money he wanted, would he have spent millions of yen to get Kuniko's body here to scare them? But that made the whole thing even more terrifying. She fought the urge to break down in tears.

'But who is it?' Jumonji said, frowning.

'I'm not sure, but I'd guess it's the casino owner. He's the only one that fits.' Yoshie and Jumonji looked at each other.

'Who is he?' he said. Masako was sorting through old newspaper articles in her mind.

'Mitsuyoshi Satake,' she said at last, remembering. 'He's forty-three years old. They released him for lack of evidence, and after that he disappeared.'

'Does the age match the man you saw?' Yoshie asked.

'I don't know. It was dark and he was wearing a cap. But the voice would be about right. So I guess I'm the only one who's seen him – and I hope I never have to again.' He grimaced at the memory.

'What are we going to do?' Yoshie said, beginning to cry again. 'What should I do?' Masako was still gnawing at her finger.

'Take the money and run,' she said.

'But I can't leave,' Yoshie sobbed.

'Then you'll just have to be as careful as you can,' she told her, turning back to the body. First they had to figure out what to do with Kuniko. Should they cut her up? But there was no need to go to all that trouble now. Their client wasn't interested in having her disappear; she was meant as a threat. Still, it was too risky to just dump her.

'What are we going to do with her?' she said.

'Let's go to the police,' said Yoshie, squatting by the washing machine. 'I don't want to sit around waiting to end up like her.'

'Then we'll all go to jail. Is that what you want?'

'No,' she stammered. 'Then what do we do?'

'We get rid of her,' Jumonji said, staring at Kuniko's heavy breasts.

'But where?'

'Anywhere, it doesn't matter. And then we lie low for a while.'

'I agree,' Masako said. 'But I think we need to make sure this murder gets pinned on Satake.'

'And how are we going to do that?' Jumonji asked, looking sceptical.

'I don't know. But I want him to know we aren't just running scared.'

'Are you crazy?' Yoshie groaned. 'Why do we care what he thinks?'

'We've got to hit back. If we don't, he'll come after the rest of us, one at a time.'

'But what have you got in mind?' Jumonji said, rubbing the stubble on his chin.

'You don't suppose we could send her back to him?'

'We don't know where he is,' Yoshie said.

'No, I guess we don't.'

'Okay,' said Jumonji, holding up his hands between them. 'Let's try to think this through slowly and carefully. We can't afford any more mistakes.'

Masako suddenly noticed the wad of black cloth protruding from Kuniko's mouth. Slipping on a pair of gloves, she pulled it out. Fancy panties, with lace trim. She remembered the cheap underwear Kuniko had always worn to the factory. Knowing Kuniko, she'd put these on hoping someone would be taking them off.

'He must have used them as a gag when he strangled her,' Jumonji said, examining the thick rope marks on the neck.

Still holding the panties, Masako asked him, 'Did he strike you as good-looking?'

'I told you, I didn't get a good look at his face, but he was well built.' He must have come on to her, Masako thought, trying to remember whether Kuniko had mentioned anyone who might fit the description. But they hadn't talked much lately, and it was unlikely she would have told her.

'I guess we have to cut her up,' she said eventually, abandoning the effort to solve the puzzle. 'We don't have much choice.'

'No, I don't want to,' Yoshie murmured. 'Not Kuniko.'

'Then you don't need the money?' Masako said. 'You can forget about the million I promised you, and I'll keep your share for this, too.'

'Wait a minute,' said Yoshie, hopping up. 'I still have to move.'

'That's what I thought. You can't stay in that fire trap.' Masako then turned to Jumonji, who was standing there, watching them argue. 'Why don't you go get the boxes? We'll stick with the original plan: you can take care of them in Kyushu.'

'So we're going through with it?' he said.

'What else can we do?' Masako tried to swallow, but the saliva stuck in her throat as if her body were loath to accept it. In the same way her mind refused to accept what was facing them.

Jumonji seemed only too glad of the chance to get out of there. Noticing how eager he was to go, Masako gave him a hard stare.

'You can start running as soon as we're finished,' she said. 'Not before. Okay?'

'I know,' he said.

'We've still got a job to do,' she added. He nodded glumly, like a child who'd been scolded. 'And what about you?' Masako said, turning to Yoshie who sat gazing at Kuniko's body.

'. . . I'm in,' she said. 'I can start thinking about moving as soon as we're through.'

'You do what you have to do,' Masako said.

'Where will you go?'

'Nowhere, for the time being.'

'Why?' Yoshie cried. But Masako didn't seem to hear her; she was busy thinking about something Jumonji had said – that he was the only one who had seen him. She wondered if this was true, if she hadn't seen Satake somewhere herself. The thought stuck in her head.

'I'll be right back,' Jumonji said, before disappearing down the corridor. Masako started tying on her apron.

'Skipper, set the line to eighteen,' she said.

8

The metal stairs creaked under him as Kazuo made his way up to his room in the two-storey, prefab building that served as a dormitory for the Brazilian employees. Couples had a room to themselves, but single men like Kazuo were forced to share with a room-mate. The living quarters were tiny – one small room with a miniature kitchen and a bathroom – but they had one good point: they were two minutes from the factory.

Kazuo stopped at the top of the stairs and looked around. The laundry left out by the farmhouse across the way fluttered in the cold wind. A row of dry, brown chrysanthemums was visible under the pale streetlights along the narrow road. Even for early winter, it all seemed so desolate. In São Paolo, it would soon be summer. The smell of *shoro* and *fejioda* cooking, the scent of flowers; pretty girls in light summer dresses, children playing in the alleys; the cheers from the Santos fans in the stadium. What was he doing here, so far from all that?

Could this really be his father's homeland? He looked out over the landscape again, but the quickly gathering darkness had hidden everything except the lights in a few neighbourhood windows and, further off, the blue fluorescent glow of the factory. Could he ever call this 'home'? Resting his elbows on the metal rail, he buried his face in his hands. Alberto was probably watching TV in their room, so the only place Kazuo could be alone was out here in the passageway.

He had set himself two tasks – or three, to be more exact. The first was to work in the factory for two years and save enough money to buy a car; the second was to get Masako's complete forgiveness; and the third was to learn enough Japanese to be able to do so. By this time, it looked as though the only one he would accomplish was the third. He had made a good deal of progress with the language, but the person he was learning it for had refused to talk to him since that morning. It seemed he wasn't even going to get a chance to try to convince her.

But then again, there was probably no such thing as complete forgiveness – at least not the kind he was looking for, the kind that would allow Masako to fall in love with him. And once this had sunk in, his resolve for the first task began to waver as well. In the end, his trials with Masako had been the hardest ones . . . but they weren't really trials or tasks or tests at all: they were just facts that he could do nothing about. And that in itself was probably the real test: his ability to accept something that was completely beyond his control. It made him want to cry.

It was time to leave, he suddenly decided. He'd had enough; by Christmas, he would be back in São Paolo. He didn't care if he couldn't get the car. There was nothing for him here but slopping together boxed lunches he couldn't stomach. If he wanted to learn about computers, he could do it in Brazil, but it was too painful to stay here any longer.

The moment he made the decision, he felt lighter, like clouds clearing after a storm. His various tests suddenly seemed irrelevant; he was simply a man who had lost his battle with himself. He stared off toward the factory again, a sullen look in his eyes. But then he heard a woman's voice calling quietly from the street.

'Miyamori-san?' He looked down, thinking he must be hearing things, but there was Masako standing in the street. She was wearing jeans and an old down jacket with patches of tape covering the holes. He stared at her, disoriented by the sudden appearance of the very person he'd been thinking about. 'Miyamori-san,' she called again, this time more clearly.

'Yes,' he called back, bounding down the wobbly stairs. Masako retreated into the shadows, away from the streetlight, as if looking for a spot where she would be hidden from the first-floor windows. Kazuo hesitated for a moment, wondering if he should follow, but then took a few steps toward her. Why had she come? To hurt him again? But her sudden arrival had already rekindled his interest in completing his task, as though someone had thrown a bundle of sticks on a smouldering fire. He stopped, confused by the rush of emotion.

'I've got a favour to ask,' she said, looking him in the eye. That was so like her, always so direct. Up close like this, her face looked taut, like a tightly knotted ball of thread that refuses to unravel. But still beautiful. It had been a long time since he'd stood there in front of her, and he found himself hanging on every word. 'Would you mind keeping this in your locker for me?' She took a paper bag out of her old black purse. It looked heavy. Kazuo stared at it for a moment without moving.

'Why do you want me to keep it?' he asked.

'You're the only one I know who has a locker.' His heart sank. It wasn't the answer he was hoping for.

'How long do you want me to keep it?'

'Until I need it,' she said. 'Do you understand?'

'I think so,' he said, but now his curiosity had been aroused. Why couldn't she keep it herself? Wouldn't it be safer at her house? Or if she wanted a locker, there were plenty at the train station.

'You're wondering why I'm asking you to do this,' she said, her look softening a bit. 'It's something I can't leave at my place, and I don't want to risk leaving it in my car or somewhere at work.' Kazuo took the bag from her. It was heavy, just as he'd imagined.

'What's in it?' he asked. 'I need to know, if I'm responsible for it.'

'Money and my passport,' she said, taking a cigarette from the pocket of her jacket and lighting it. Money? Then it must be a lot. Why would she be trusting him with it?

'How much is it?' he asked.

'Seven million yen,' she said, saying the figure crisply and clearly, the way she announced the number of lunches in the work order as she passed it down the line.

'Why not put it in the bank?' he said, with a quaver in his voice.

'I can't.'

'Why not, if you don't mind my asking?'

'I just can't,' she said flatly, blowing out a cloud of smoke. Kazuo stood thinking for a moment.

'What happens if I'm not here when you need it?' he said at last.

'I'll wait until I can get in touch with you.'

'How will you contact me?'

'I'll come here,' she said.

'All right,' he said. 'I'm in number 201. I'll leave it in my locker and we can always go get it there.'

'Thanks,' she said. He wondered whether he should tell her that he'd decided to go home by Christmas, but he decided against it. He was more worried about the trouble she seemed to be in.

'You haven't been at work,' he said.

'I had a cold.'

'I thought you quit.'

'I'm not going to quit,' she said, turning to look down the dark street. If you followed this road, you came out past the abandoned factory. There was an anxious look in her eyes he hadn't seen before, and Kazuo was sure that something bad had happened. Something that had to do with the key she'd thrown down that hole. He had always been sensitive this way; sometimes it caused problems, but it could also work to his advantage. He was determined to make it work for him now.

'Are you in trouble?' he asked. She turned to look at him.

'You can tell, can't you?'

'Yes,' he said, his eyes reflecting her anxiety.

'I've got a problem, but I don't need any help . . . just keep that bag for me.'

'What kind of problem?' he asked, but she pressed her lips together and said nothing more. He was suddenly afraid that he'd been too forward. 'I'm sorry,' he murmured, blushing in the darkness.

'No,' she said. 'I'm the one who should be sorry.'

'No,' he echoed, slipping the bag into the breast pocket of his jacket and pulling up the zipper. Masako fished a key ring from her pocket and turned to go. She must have parked somewhere nearby.

'Thanks,' she said.

'Masako-san?' he said.

'Yes?'

'Can you forgive me?'

'Of course,' she said.

'For everything?'

'Yes,' she said, looking down at the ground. The task he'd thought would be so difficult was accomplished as simply as that;

in fact, all too simply. He stood staring at her, realising it had been so easy because it wasn't the sort of forgiveness he wanted: he hadn't won her heart. Without that, it meant nothing really. He pressed his hand to his chest. As he felt for the key next to his skin, his hand brushed against the thick package.

'But you have to tell me. . . ,' he whispered. She waited, not looking up. 'Why would you leave something so important with me?' He needed to know. She dropped what was left of her cigarette and crushed it under her sneaker.

'I'm not sure myself,' she said, looking up at him. 'I guess I don't have anyone else I can ask.' He stared at the fine lines around her mouth, realising for the first time how alone she must be. Why else would she entrust all this to a foreigner she hardly knew, instead of to her family or friends? She looked away, as if to escape his eyes, and kicked at the gravel, sending a shower of little pebbles into the darkness. He swallowed.

'No one?' he said.

'No,' she said, shaking her head. 'No one to ask and no safe place to keep it.'

'Because there's no one you can trust?'

'That's right,' she said, looking him in the eye again.

'But you trust me?' he said. He looked at her, holding his breath.

'Yes,' she said. She met his stare for a moment longer and then turned and walked off toward the factory.

'. . . Thank you,' he murmured, his hand pressed not to the money but to his heart.

Exit

1

Yayoi stared at the wedding ring on her finger as if she'd never seen it before. It was a plain platinum ring. She and Kenji had gone to a department store to pick it out one warm Sunday in early spring. He'd taken one look at the showcase and then asked for the most expensive one they had; after all, it was a once-in-a-lifetime purchase. She could still remember how flustered and happy she'd felt that day. Where had those feelings gone? What had happened to that happy couple? She had killed Kenji. The cry of pain that she'd refused to utter burst from her now as the enormity of her act sank in at last.

She jumped up from the living-room chair and ran into the bedroom. Standing in front of the mirror, she pulled up her sweater and examined her bare torso, looking for the dark bruise on her stomach that had been the visible sign of her loathing for Kenji and the stimulus for killing him; but it had slowly faded, until now there was no trace left. That faded mark was why he'd died – a man who wanted her to have the best because it was meant to last for ever – and she wasn't even accepting the blame for what she'd done. Was she really so callous? She sank down on to the floor.

When she looked up a little later, she saw the photo of Kenji on the family altar staring out at her. By now the picture itself was steeped in the incense the boys were always burning at the altar. But as she gazed at the smiling face in the photo – a souvenir of a summer camping trip in happier times – she found herself getting angry all over again. Why had he changed toward her, become so mean? Why did he take such pleasure in hurting her? Why had he been so unwilling to help with the boys? The old feelings swelled up in her like a tidal wave, sweeping away any stirrings of regret.

It may have been wrong to kill him, but she still couldn't bring herself to forgive him. She repeated the formula to herself again and again: I still don't forgive you. I killed you, but I don't forgive you. I'll never forgive you. It's your fault for being unfaithful. I didn't change, you did. You killed the happy couple that picked out this ring.

She went back into the living room and dragged open the door leading to the garden. The narrow yard, ending at a discoloured cinderblock wall, was littered with tricycles and a tiny swing set. Standing there, Yayoi tugged the ring off her finger and flung it as hard as she could toward the neighbour's yard, though it bounced off the wall and landed somewhere in the garden. The gesture left her feeling both uncomfortable at being responsible for getting rid of the thing, and glad to have made a final break with it all.

She stared at the stark white area on her finger in the November sunlight. There was something pathetic about this band of pale skin, the mark from a ring that hadn't been removed in eight years. It was the mark of loss. But it was also the mark of liberation, a sign that everything was finally over.

Just as this thought was flitting through her head, the buzzer on the intercom rang. Had someone seen what she'd just done? She stepped down into the garden and craned her neck to see over the fence. A tall man in a suit was standing calmly at the front door. Fortunately, he didn't seem to notice her peering at him from the garden. She hurried back into the house and picked up the receiver, ignoring the spots of dark earth clinging to her stockings.

'Who is it?' she said.

'My name is Sato,' said a man's voice. 'I knew your husband in

Shinjuku. I was in the area and I was wondering whether I could pay my respects.'

'I see,' she said. Though it was rather a nuisance, she couldn't turn away people who came to offer their condolences. With a housekeeper's eye, she gave the living room and the bedroom, where the family altar was, a quick inspection. Deciding they would do, she headed for the entrance hall. A well-built man with short hair made a deep bow as soon as she opened the door.

'I'm sorry to show up suddenly like this,' he said, his voice smooth and low. 'I just wanted to tell you how sorry I was for your loss.' Yayoi returned the bow automatically, but some part of her was sceptical about such a late visit. And yet, though Kenji had died at the end of July, more than four months ago, she was still getting calls from shocked friends who said they had just heard what had happened.

'It's kind of you to come all the way out here,' she said. Sato was standing in the doorway, taking a close look at her – her face, her eyes, her mouth. There was nothing unpleasant in his manner, but she had the uncomfortable feeling that he knew something about her beforehand and was measuring her against his expectations. She took another look at him as well, and found herself wondering what connection he could have had with Kenji. He seemed completely different from the other people in her husband's life, the other men at his office. They were all so casual and easygoing, so uncomplicated, while this man struck her as hard to get a handle on, his expression unreadable. Nevertheless, the cheap grey suit and the boring tie seemed to suggest he was another office drudge.

'If it's not too much trouble, I'd like to pay my respects,' he said again, his voice even smoother than before, as though he sensed her reservations.

'Come in,' she said. Feeling slightly put upon, she led him down the passage to the living room, already regretting having let a stranger into the house, and vaguely ill at ease with him following right behind her. 'It's in there,' she said, gesturing toward the altar in the bedroom. Sato knelt down and pressed his hands together in front of the picture of Kenji while Yayoi went to make tea in the kitchen. Glancing toward the bedroom from time to time, she wondered why someone would show up like this without bringing the customary condolence gift. It wasn't that she cared about the gift, but it was just common courtesy, when you were coming all this way, to bring a present or a card or something.

'I appreciate it,' she told him when she was sure he'd finished. 'Will you have some tea?' She placed a cup on the table in the living room. Sato sat down in front of it and looked directly at her. It bothered her that there was no trace of sadness or sympathy or even curiosity in his eyes. He thanked her but left the tea untouched. She set out an ashtray, but he sat perfectly still, his hands clasped on his knees – almost as if he wanted to leave no evidence of his visit. She felt uneasy. Masako had told her to be careful, but she was just beginning to understand the urgency in her warning. 'Where did you say you met my husband?' she asked, trying to make the question sound casual.

'In Shinjuku,' he said.

'Where in Shinjuku?'

'In Kabuki-cho,' he said. She looked up, startled by his answer. Seeing her uneasiness, he smiled reassuringly. But she realised that the smile was confined to his thick lips; his eyes remained completely expressionless.

'Kabuki-cho?' she said.

'Let's stop pretending, shall we?' A look of horror came over her face as she remembered Kinugasa's call telling her that the casino owner had disappeared. But part of her still refused to believe it could be him.

'What do you mean?' she said.

'I had a little run-in with your husband . . . that night,' Sato said, pausing as if to gauge her reaction. She held her breath. 'You know better than I do what happened after that, but you may not know how much trouble you've caused me. I've lost my clubs, my whole business. I've lost more than a woman like you could ever imagine, living out here in the middle of nowhere, fussing over your kids.'

'What are you talking about?' Yayoi said, starting to get up. 'I think you'd better leave!'

'Sit down!' Sato said, his voice low and menacing. Yayoi froze.

'I'll call the police,' she said.

'Go ahead. I think they'll be more interested in you than me.'

'Why?' she said, dropping back on to her chair. 'What are you trying to say?' She was already numb with panic and her mind had shut down. All she wanted was to get this horrible man out of her house as soon as possible.

'I know all about it,' Sato said. 'I know you killed your husband.'

'That's a lie!' she cried, beginning to lose control. 'How dare you say that!'

'They'll hear you outside,' he warned her. 'The houses here are close together. And you do sound guilty, screaming like that.'

'But . . . I really *don't* know what you're talking about.' She pressed her hands to her temples, but the trembling in her arms made her whole head shake. Then, letting her arms drop back to her lap, she sat quietly, aware of the truth in what he said. She had spent the last four months worrying about the neighbours' reactions to Kenji's death. She knew it was paranoia, but she still had the feeling that everyone around was whispering about her.

'You're probably wondering how much I know,' he laughed. This time there was real mirth in his voice. 'It's simple: I know everything.'

'Know about what?' she said. 'I still don't understand what

you're getting at.' Yayoi was now petrified. She looked across the table at him. She knew very little about the world, but she could tell this man was dangerous, that he'd probably had experiences good and bad she couldn't even imagine, and that he was free now to do whatever he wanted. She had probably never passed anyone like him on the street. Their worlds were so completely different that it seemed strange they should even speak the same language. Part of her was even slightly impressed that Kenji could have had the guts to take on a man like this.

'Does all this come as a shock?' Sato laughed, seeing her dazed expression.

'I still don't know what you're talking about,' she repeated. Sato ran his hand over his jaw, as if considering how to proceed. Yayoi noticed his long, sensitive fingers.

'That night, your husband and I had a fight. He came home and you strangled him out there in the hallway. When your kids asked if he'd come back, you badgered them into keeping quiet. The older one . . . what's his name? Takashi, yes, that's it.'

'How do you know about him?!' she burst out.

'You really are as cute as they said,' he murmured, studying her again. 'A bit old maybe, but if we cleaned you up a bit, we could still find you a spot at a club.'

'Stop it!' she wailed, unable to keep her voice from sounding shrill. It felt as though a pair of filthy hands were stroking her. But then she suddenly remembered: it was in this man's club that Kenji had fallen for another woman, and the thought brought an angry flush to her face.

Sato noticed the change in her expression. 'What's up? Remembered something?'

'Yes. My husband got beat up at your place.'

'Yeah, well . . . ,' he murmured. 'You have no idea what your husband did when he was out by himself. Did you ever stop to think what other people saw in him? Did you ever once feel you had a responsibility to find out what he was up to? It must be nice being a know-nothing little housewife.'

'Stop it!' Yayoi cried, covering her ears against the stream of poisonous accusations. They were ugly beyond anything she'd ever experienced.

'I've said it before, but the neighbours will hear you. Seems they've been quite curious about your little drama, anyway. And you do have the kids to think about.'

'How did you know about Takashi?' she asked, lowering her voice at the mention of her children. His slow-acting poison had begun to take effect.

'You still don't understand?' he said, with a pitying look.

'Morisaki-san?' She stared at him, her eyes beginning to fill with tears. 'How could she have done this to me?'

'It's quite simple, really,' he explained. 'That was her job.' Job? Then the whole thing was an act? She remembered how Masako had warned her about Yoko from the start. How could she have been so gullible? Tears of self-pity began to roll down her cheeks. 'But it's a bit late for tears,' he told her, and his voice now had a vicious edge to it. 'I also know that you asked your friends to cut up the body.' She glanced down at her hand. What an idiot she'd been to think that it had all ended when she threw away the ring. This was the real ending, and it would destroy them all. 'A shame the way things worked out,' he sneered. 'I'm sure you were rooting for me to get the death penalty.'

Recklessly, she said: 'I'm going to call the police and tell them everything.'

'You're sweet, you really are,' he said again. 'Just a bit self-centred, maybe.' His hands moved quickly to his throat to loosen the knot of his tie. The dull grey silk, shot through with a fine brown stripe, looked like a lizard's skin. Would she dribble from the mouth the way Kenji did, she wondered, when he strangled her? She closed her eyes, shaking all over.

'Yamamoto-san,' he said, getting up and coming around the table to stand behind her. Yayoi shrank away from him, unable to answer. 'Yamamoto-san,' he said again.

'What?' she asked, looking around at him, her eyes filled with terror.

He was checking his watch. 'If we don't hurry, the banks will close.'

'What do you mean?' She turned to face him as his plan began to dawn on her. 'You mean . . . the money I got?'

'That's right.'

'No! We need that money. It's all we have to live on.'

'It's all you have to pay me with,' he said.

'I can't!'

'What do you mean, you can't?' he murmured, slipping his fingers around her neck. 'You want me to do this?' His fingers pressed into her throat, clutching her like a kitten caught by the scruff of its neck.

'Stop! Please!' she rasped out.

'Which will it be? The money or your neck?'

Her whole body was rigid, but her head bobbed up and down submissively. She felt herself lose control of her bladder.

'Phone the bank and tell them your father died suddenly and you have to take all the money in your account back there with you. Tell them you'll be coming with your brother to get it.'

'All right,' she whispered.

Sato kept his fingers around her neck the whole time she was phoning.

'Good,' he said, releasing her as she hung up. 'Now get changed.'

'Changed?'

He gave her scruffy sweater and shapeless skirt a dirty look. 'You think the bank's going to believe that story if you show up dressed like that? They'll think you've come for a loan.' Grabbing her by the arm, he dragged her up from the chair.

'What do you want me to do?' she murmured, still trembling uncontrollably. She knew there must be a patch on her skirt where she'd wet herself, but she didn't care any more. Her self-respect had disappeared, and she no longer even felt afraid. She moved almost mechanically, obeying his instructions. He took her into the bedroom.

'Open the closet,' he said. She pulled open the doors of the flimsy cupboard. 'Now find something to wear.'

'But what?'

'A suit or a dress. Something formal.'

'I'm sorry,' she said, starting to cry again. 'I don't have anything like that, nothing nice.' Not only had this cruel bastard invaded her house, but she was forced to apologise to him for not having any clothes.

'Sad,' Sato said, running his eye over what seemed mainly to be Kenji's suits and coats. 'What did you wear to his funeral?'

'You want me in mourning?' She pulled out a dry cleaner's bag that held the thin black summer suit she'd worn for Kenji's wake. Her mother had bought it for her when she realised she had nothing suitable. She'd worn a rented kimono to the funeral itself.

'That's perfect,' he said. 'If you're in black they'll have to be sympathetic and shouldn't make any trouble.'

'But it's a summer suit,' she said.

'Who cares?'

Half an hour later, Yayoi and Sato were shown into a private room at a bank across from Tachikawa Station.

'Did you really intend to withdraw the entire fifty million yen?' The branch manager himself had come to see them, obviously hoping to find a way to change her mind. Yayoi said nothing, just stared at the carpet and nodded her head as Sato had told her to do.

'Our father died quite suddenly, and we're in something of a hurry,' he explained. He'd introduced himself as Yayoi's brother and seemed to be enjoying the role. The bank could hardly refuse the request of bereaved siblings. Still, the manager was looking for a way of stalling the withdrawal.

'It's dangerous to carry such a large sum around,' he said. 'Why don't you let us transfer it to another bank for you?'

'That's why I've come with her,' Sato told him.

'I see.' With a sympathetic glance at Yayoi, slumped in the heavy chair, the manager decided not to press the matter. A short time later, a man arrived with the money and deposited it on the table in front of them. Sato shoved the stacks of bills into a bag the bank had provided and then put that in a black nylon bag he'd brought with him.

'We appreciate this,' he said, taking Yayoi's arm and standing up. She rose with him, but her body was limp and she began to fall forward. Catching her from behind, he held her up. 'Yayoi,' he said. 'You've got to get a grip on yourself. We've got the wake ahead of us.'

It was a convincing performance. Yayoi allowed herself to be led out of the room and through the bank. When they were finally alone on the street, he pushed her away and she staggered a few steps before clutching a guardrail. Ignoring her, he hailed a taxi. As he was climbing in, he looked back at her for a moment.

'You understand?' he said.

She nodded. She watched blankly as the door shut and the car drove away – taking her fifty million with it, her unexpected present from Kenji. It had just been a fleeting dream, and it was gone in an instant.

The shock of losing the money had been amplified by the horror of coming in contact with a man like Sato. But there was another part of her that was relieved just to have survived the encounter. She'd been sure she was going to die the whole time he had his hands around her neck. In the end, she'd underestimated them – men in general. Were they all like this? So cruel?

She stood staring vacantly at the clock in front of the station, feeling drained, exhausted. It was 2.30 p.m. She'd come out without a coat and she was cold. As she stood hugging herself through the thin summer dress, she decided not to tell Masako what had happened; she couldn't bear the accusing look in her eyes, not after their last argument. Still, she did feel rather abandoned. The money was gone, she'd quit her job, and she'd quarrelled with her friends at work. She had no idea what to do or where to go. For the moment, she could only wander aimlessly around the plaza in front of the station.

As she shuffled along, it occurred to her that, for better or worse, it was Kenji who had provided her life with a direction: Kenji's moods, Kenji's health, Kenji's job, Kenji's salary. She found herself wanting to laugh. After all, she was the one who had tossed the rudder overboard.

That evening, Takashi came in from the yard where he'd been playing. Finding his mother looking miserable, he held out his hand to her.

'Mama, look. You must have dropped this.'

'Oh dear . . .' Yayoi said when she saw her wedding ring there in his hand. It was a bit scuffed but otherwise unharmed.

'It's important, isn't it? It's a good thing I found it.'

'Thank you,' Yayoi said, slipping the ring back on her finger. Masako's comment came back to her: I don't see how it will ever be over for you. She was right, it wasn't over yet, and probably never would be. Her eyes filled with tears. At the sight of his mother crying, a look of delight came over Takashi's face.

'I'm glad I found it,' he said. 'Aren't you happy, Mama?'

2

Masako was shocked to the core, unable to think clearly, though physically she functioned normally as she guided the Corolla into the parking lot, pulled up at an angle behind her usual space, and backed the car in. In fact, she performed this little manoeuvre rather better than usual, but as the car came to a halt and she pulled on the parking brake, she sat there looking down, trying to control her breathing, refusing to let herself look at the slot next to hers. Kuniko's green Golf was parked in it.

Yoshie and she were the only ones in the factory who knew Kuniko was dead. Yet here was her car, parked and waiting in the usual spot, just as if she'd come to work. The space had been empty for the past few days, which could only mean that Satake or someone else involved with her murder had brought it back. And there could only be one reason: since the Skipper came by bike and never used the parking lot, it must have been left here to frighten her.

Satake must be somewhere nearby. She considered just turning tail right then and there. Filled with anxiety and irritation, she stayed inside a while longer, reluctant to trade the safety of the car for the dark parking lot. But she wasn't the only one there this evening. Two of the large white trucks that delivered the lunches to convenience stores in the area were parked near the entrance, and the drivers, indistinguishable from the other employees in their sanitary white uniforms, were smoking and chatting with the guard in front of his hut. From time to time, she could hear them laugh, even here in the car.

Plucking up her courage, she opened the door, climbed out and walked slowly around Kuniko's car. It was parked carelessly, exactly the way she always left it, slanting slightly to the right with the front tyres turned in, creating the illusion that Kuniko was still alive and waiting for her in the lounge. But hadn't she cut off Kuniko's head with her own hands? She stared at her palms for a moment, trying to convince herself, but then looked up, knowing how absurd this was.

So he had studied every detail of Kuniko's movements. In which case, he was probably also watching her. That morbid tenacity and attention to detail made her blood run cold. Now it wasn't just her mind but her body as well that threatened to shut down, and she stood immobile, her legs refusing to budge, distressed at her own reaction. But just then the guard stopped talking to the drivers and turned to give her a cheerful salute. Since she'd refused his help rather abruptly the other night, the gesture could have been taken ironically, but even so she was grateful.

'Good evening,' he called. The words seemed to function like lubricating oil, freeing her legs, and she walked over to join them.

'You didn't see who was driving that car, did you?' she asked.

'Which one?' the guard said.

'The green Golf,' she said, her voice cracking.

'Let me check,' he said, going into the guardhouse for his ledger. 'It says it belongs to Kuniko Jonouchi,' he reported, shining his flashlight on the page. 'She's on the night shift, so . . .' Masako interrupted him, irritated at being told what she already knew.

'Does it say anything about her quitting?'

'Now that you mention it, it does. Six days ago. That's odd,' he said, squinting at the page. 'Something must have come up suddenly,' he added, looking over at the car.

'Do you know what time she showed up?'

'Not exactly.' The guard looked at the truck drivers. 'I didn't really notice. My shift starts at 7.00.'

'I think it was there last night,' one of the drivers said. He had pulled a cotton face mask down over his chin in order to smoke.

'I doubt it,' Masako snapped.

'No?' He sounded annoyed at being contradicted. 'Then I guess it wasn't.'

'Sorry,' she said. It was less than three days since they'd cut up Kuniko's body, and her nerves were still raw, like her chapped red hands which hurt in the cold night air. She was struggling to control the distress she felt and to accept this new development. But the appearance of the car was just too unnerving, and she found it difficult to distinguish between imagination and reality.

Noticing that she'd gone silent, the other driver spoke up. 'Why are you so interested in the car?' he said.

Masako looked up at him. 'The woman who owns it quit. Did anyone see who was driving it?'

'No,' said the guard, flipping through the ledger again. 'We didn't actually see it come in.'

'Thanks anyway.' She left them, and started walking toward the factory, but after only a few paces she felt a warm, heavy hand on her shoulder.

'Do you need an escort tonight?' She turned to find the guard standing behind her. The badge on his uniform said his name was Sato. 'You look a bit under the weather,' he added. Masako hesitated, unsure how to answer. Part of her wanted his company while another part wanted the chance to think quietly during the few minutes she had before work. The guard laughed. 'I know you said you didn't want me to come along the other night,' he said. 'I don't mean to bother you.'

'That's okay,' she said. 'I'd be happy for the company, at least part way.'

Removing the flashlight that was dangling from his uniform, he switched it on and set off down the road. Masako took one last look at Kuniko's car before starting after him. He was walking quickly and was already well ahead.

'You going to be all right?' he said. 'You still don't look too good.' They had passed the houses on the right side of the road and reached the darkest part of the walk. The few buildings seemed to melt into the blackness around them. The only other light came from two stars shining dimly overhead. The guard stopped, his heavy black boots illuminated in the circle of yellow light at his feet. Masako stopped as well. She tried to get a look at his face, but the cap pulled down around his ears made it impossible. 'Is the lady in the Golf a friend of yours?' he asked.

'Yes.'

'Why did she quit?' His voice was soft and low. Masako slipped past him without answering. She didn't want to talk about Kuniko. But even in the dark, she could tell he was watching her as she went by. It was as though a magnetic field had risen between them. Her pulse quickened and she found it hard to breathe.

'I'll be fine from here,' she forced herself to say as she began to jog away. The guard stood watching her. Sato and Satake – not all that different. The hand on her shoulder had been a little too insistent; and why had he asked about Kuniko? She felt dazed, unable to gauge the depth of the darkness around her. She didn't know what to believe. Unable to bring her blurred suspicions into focus, she dropped them for the moment and started running.

When she reached the factory, she went straight to the changing room to look for Yoshie. She wasn't there, though. She hadn't shown up at work since the delivery of Kuniko's body, and Masako suspected she had used the money from that day to move out of her house. Or had something happened to her as well?

She sat at the long table shoving loose strands of hair under her work cap as she tried to think through recent events. As she lit a cigarette, it occurred to her that Satake might have found some way to get into the factory. She looked out at the groups of men in the lounge, but didn't see any new faces. She was jittery and restless, unlike herself. Taking a card from her wallet, she went out to the pay phone in the lounge and dialled the number of Jumonji's cell phone.

'Katori-san?' He sounded relieved.

'What's wrong?'

'Nothing. It's just that I've been getting these strange calls and I'd just about decided to stop answering.' She could hear the apprehension in his voice.

'What kind of calls?'

'They must be from him. When I answer, a man says, "You're next". I know who it is, but it still gives me the creeps, especially since I've actually seen him.'

'How did he get your number?'

'It probably wasn't that hard; I'm always giving out business cards.'

'Can you tell where he's calling from?'

'No, it's a cell phone – it could be anywhere. It's got me spooked. I feel like I'm being watched twenty-four hours a day. Anyway, I've decided I have to get out of here. So take care of yourself, Katori-san.'

'Wait a minute!' Masako said, determined to keep him from hanging up. 'I've got a favour to ask.'

'What is it?'

'Kuniko's Golf showed up at the parking lot.'

'What?!' he groaned. 'How?'

'I'm pretty sure Kuniko didn't drive it there herself, so it must have been Satake,' she said, almost whispering now.

'Then he's closing in. I think you should get out of there.'

'I plan to,' she said. 'But I'd appreciate it if you could watch the parking lot for the next few hours and let me know who gets in that car.'

'It's got to be him.'

'But I want to know where he goes.'

'I'm sorry, I can't.' She could tell he was already halfway out the door, thinking only of his own skin. She talked to him for a few minutes more, calming him down sufficiently to agree to meet her at a nearby Denny's after she got off from work.

The call had made her late. She ran to punch her time card and then hurried downstairs. The hundred or so part-timers on the night shift were lined up, waiting for the doors to open. Masako fell in at the end of the line. It seemed ages ago now that the four of them had jostled for a place at the front, competing with other groups for the better jobs.

The doors opened and the women filed in, lining up at the hand-washing stations. Masako waited for her turn. When it came, she pushed up to the sink and elbowed the handle on the faucet. As she began to scrub her hands, she felt that all the troubles of the past few days were clinging to her like a sick obsession, just as Kuniko's yellow fat had clung to her hands, stuck to her fingers, caked under her nails. No matter how hard she scrubbed, they refused to come off. She worked at her hands with the brush until they were red and raw.

'If you draw blood, you'll be off the shift.' The health inspector had come up behind her and was watching her grind away at her skin. Masako looked down at her scarlet hands and arms.

'I know,' she said.

'What's wrong with you today?'

'Nothing, sorry.' Masako plunged her hands into the basin of disinfectant and dried them with sterilised gauze. Then she started wiping down her apron, but the job reminded her how hard it had been to scrub off Kuniko's dark, sticky blood. She shook her head to drive the image from her brain.

'Masako-san,' said a voice. Kazuo was standing next to her, his cart already loaded with rice. 'Are you okay?'

'Yes,' she said. Pretending to be deciding which line to join, she stood with him a moment.

'I put it in my locker,' he said.

'Thanks.'

Realising that no one had noticed them yet, Kazuo whispered to her again, 'You seem overwrought tonight.' Overwrought? Where had he learned that? She glanced at him. He looked calmer than before, more sure of himself. The desperate puppy was gone, grown into a dependable young man. She realised how much she needed him, needed his calm, strong presence, if only for tonight.

Nakayama, the foreman, had spotted them and came running over.

'What do you think you're doing? Get on a line!' Masako quietly fell into place with this reminder that there was little to distinguish the factory from a prison. Private conversation, even a quick chat, was discouraged, and your bodily functions were monitored. You were expected to shut up and do your job. Nothing else.

'Don't let it get to you.' Kazuo's parting words seemed to cover her back like a warm, protective blanket. Still, Yayoi and Yoshie had stopped coming to work, and Jumonji was on the verge of skipping out. Kuniko was dead. That left Masako to take on Satake alone. She had a feeling that was exactly what he'd wanted all along. Everything seemed to suggest that he was after her and no one else. As she worked, she brooded about what it was he wanted from her.

At 5.30, when the shift ended, she quickly changed out of her work clothes and left the factory. It was still dark outside. That was the worst thing about the night shift in winter: it was pitch black when you started, and the same when you finished.

She hurried along the road to the parking lot. The Golf was gone. But who had driven it away, and when? She stood for a moment in the dark lot, imagining how Satake must have circled her Corolla, touched the doors, peered inside. How he must have smiled to himself, able to smell her fear. The thought made her bristle. She couldn't let him get the better of her. She wasn't going to end up like Kuniko.

She forced herself to swallow her fear, like a bitter medicine you choke down without tasting. It all stuck in her throat – the reality of Kuniko's death, of Satake – but she made herself take it. Then she opened the door, climbed into the cold car, and switched on the engine. There was a faint trace of light in the eastern sky.

Masako stared with red-rimmed eyes at the grounds in the bottom of her coffee cup. She had nothing else to do. She'd been smoking too much, and she'd had too much coffee. The waitress had stopped coming over to the table, realising that she wasn't going to order anything else.

She was waiting for Jumonji at Denny's, but it was past 7.00 and the place was crowded with people having breakfast on the way to work. The room was filled with the smell of ham and eggs and pancakes, and the busy hum of morning. He was already an hour late, but just as Masako had begun to think he'd left town, he abruptly sat down across from her.

'Sorry I'm late,' he said. He was wearing a soiled suede jacket over a black sweater. The worn look of the jacket seemed to mirror his mental state.

'I thought you weren't coming.'

'I couldn't get to sleep and then I ended up missing the alarm.' Masako scanned his haggard face, realising that she must look much the same herself.

'You didn't check out the parking lot at the factory?'

'No, sorry. I just couldn't do it.' As he offered his apology, he dug a cigarette out of his pocket and lit it. He was clearly frightened.

'I'm scared too,' Masako whispered, but he didn't seem to hear. They were silent for a moment, looking out through the large window at the peaceful winter morning. A stand of thin white birch trees shimmered in the sunlight.

'I'm afraid I'm not much use,' Jumonji said, apologising again. Almost overnight his young, handsome face had gone grey with tension.

'It doesn't matter. What's going to happen will happen.'

'That doesn't mean I have to like the idea of somebody coming to murder me,' he said, taking out his cell phone and putting it on the table as if he hated the sight of it. 'Even though I know who it is, it still scares the shit out of me when it rings, and it makes it worse that I've actually seen him.'

'That's why he's calling,' Masako said. 'He just wants to scare you.'

'I suppose so.'

'I wish I knew what he looked like,' she said, as though talking to herself. If only she could see the image retained somewhere on Jumonji's retina, or on Kuniko's the moment before she died.

'He's hard to describe,' Jumonji said, looking around as if he were afraid Satake might be somewhere in the area. The restaurant was full of businessmen reading the morning paper. Masako wanted to ask him to come to the factory to see if he could recognise a face, but she knew he wouldn't dare. 'At any rate, Kuniko's taken care of,' he said, slumping wearily in his seat. The waitress had brought him an enormous menu, which he left lying on the table. 'But I have to say, it wasn't easy.' He stretched his shoulders, as if remembering the weight. 'I bet she was twice as heavy as the old man.'

They had needed thirteen boxes to hold her, and it must have been a struggle to get them shipped on time, unloaded at the other end, and taken to the dump. Instead of answering, Masako made a casual check of the restaurant parking lot. She found herself constantly on the lookout for a green Golf.

To get her attention, Jumonji asked her, 'Will you be getting out of here? Or do you plan to stay on at the factory?'

'I'm not quite ready to run,' she said.

'You should think about it,' he said, sounding surprised. 'You must have seven or eight million put away. Isn't that enough? I know it's none of my business, but you wouldn't earn that in five years there.' Masako took a sip of water but said nothing. She knew that Satake would follow her no matter where she ran. 'I'm leaving today,' he added.

The waitress came over and he ordered a hamburger.

'Where will you go?' Masako asked.

'I'm hoping Soga-san can figure out some place for me. He's pretty scary himself.' Masako hadn't heard this name before. 'I'd like to be somewhere close, like Shibuya, where there's a bit of action. Anyway, I figure the whole thing'll blow over for me in a year or so. After all, I didn't have anything to do with that Yamamoto guy.'

So that was what he was thinking. His faith that things would get back to normal struck her as naïve. She had already burned too many bridges ever to return to a 'normal' life herself.

'I guess I'll be going then,' she said. 'But what were you planning to do with this?' She pointed at the orphaned cell phone.

'I'm done with it,' he said. 'I don't even want to get a new number for it.'

'Then you don't mind if I take it?'

'Help yourself,' he said. 'But the contract runs out soon.'

'That's okay. I just want to hear his voice.'

'Be my guest,' he said, sliding it across the table.

'See you then,' she said, shoving the phone in her bag.

'Take care of yourself.'

'Thanks, you too.'

'It was a pleasure doing business with you,' he said. 'If we both get out of this alive, maybe we can set up shop again some time.'

He smiled and lifted his glass of water in a toast, but the smile only lasted a moment.

The house was already empty when she got home. Yoshiki's cup was still on the table, half full of coffee. Masako dumped it in the sink and picked up a brush to scrub it out. A little later she realised she was still scrubbing, hard enough to scratch the porcelain. Could she really go on living here now? She turned off the water and tried to loosen up her shoulders. Just when she'd found a way out, her own private exit, this man Satake seemed determined to drag her with him down to hell.

She remembered what Yoshie had said to her that morning after the typhoon when she'd asked for her help with the body. After a moment's hesitation, she'd said she was willing to follow her into hell. Was that where she was headed after all? She sat down on the sofa feeling utterly exhausted, not so much from the night's work as from a sense that all her labours had been for nothing. Suddenly, Jumonji's phone began to ring. Masako hesitated for a second, staring at it, but finally picked it up and pressed the button to answer. There was silence at the other end. She waited quietly.

'You're next,' a voice said at last.

'Hello?' said Masako, her voice muffled. Silence. She had apparently surprised him. 'Satake?' she said.

'Masako Katori?' The voice was quiet, with a slight tremor that suggested pleasure. As if he had been waiting for this meeting.

'Speaking,' she said.

'What did it feel like to cut up those bodies?' he said.

'Why are you after us?'

'I'm after you.'

'Why?'

'Because you're a smart-ass. I'm going to teach you about the big, bad world.'

'Thanks, but no thanks,' she said. Satake laughed.

'I was wrong,' he said. 'You're next. Tell Jumonji you've moved up the line.' The voice was familiar. While she searched her memory trying to identify it, the phone went dead.

3

The voice was still there in her head. She'd heard it somewhere else quite recently. Jumping up from the couch, she grabbed her jacket and bag and headed out the door. The Corolla's engine was still warm. She was sure now: she'd met him several times. But she still needed confirmation, and that was what she was going to get, while he was still sleeping.

If the guard named Sato *was* actually Satake, it all made sense. He could have met Kuniko in the parking lot and struck up a conversation with her on the walk to the factory; and it would have given him a chance to keep an eye on Masako as well. She remembered how his flashlight had lingered on her face when they'd first met, the anger in his eyes when she'd turned to face him on the road, and the pressure of his hand on her shoulder last night. Little things that had seemed just slightly odd.

She was certain now. But she knew that confidence could turn to panic in an instant, and she might be forced to run. She couldn't settle for that. She wanted to see him dead, before she left. But was she really capable of murder? Probably not. Still, she wasn't willing to end up like Kuniko. Her body tensed and her foot touched the accelerator, sending her car jerking forward almost into the truck in front.

Yes, Sato the guard was Satake the casino owner. The memory of his dark eyes brought back the dream she'd had several weeks ago, one where she'd felt sexually aroused as someone was strangling her from behind. It had been a premonition, she realised now, and she had the strange feeling that if he ever did get his hands on her, she might actually give in. Last night, there on that ill-lit road, some sort of current had passed between the two of them, for just a moment. Even then she'd known on some level that Sato was Satake.

As she crawled along through the morning rush-hour traffic, she let her thoughts range over the past few months and on into the future. Was she the hunter or the hunted? Would she kill or be killed? 'Because you're a smart-ass,' he'd said. She couldn't let him get away with that. No, it was clearer to her than ever now: she and Satake were at war.

She headed back along the familiar route to the factory. When she got there, the parking lot was almost full for the morning shift. She checked the clock in the car; it was 8.30 and the shift started at 9.00, so there would be more cars coming. She pulled off to the side of the road that led to the abandoned factory, and walked back to the guardhouse. Satake had been relieved by an older man in glasses. As she came up, he was reading the morning paper, holding the tightly folded sheets close to his face.

'Good morning,' she said. He looked up at her over his reading glasses, at her bloodshot eyes and pale face. 'I work on the night shift, and I was wondering if you could tell me the address of the guard who's on duty then – Sato, I think his name is.'

'Sato? I've heard the name, but I don't get on till 6.00, so we haven't actually met up. You could try asking at the office.'

'The employment agency or just the main office?'

'No, not at the factory – the company we work for. Try calling this number,' he said, handing her a business card with the name 'Yamato Security' written on it.

'Thanks.' Masako tucked the card into the pocket of her jeans.

'Why do you need his address?' he asked, smirking.

'I want to ask him out on a date,' she said with a straight face. The man gave a snort and stared at her. She knew how grim and determined her face must look, how far from anything romantic, but the old man apparently saw something else.

'It must be nice to be young,' he said. Young? She smiled ironically.

'Do you think they'll give it to me?'

'Just tell them what you told me,' the man said, looking down at his paper. Back in the car, Masako called the number on Jumonji's cell phone.

'Yamato Security?' an older voice said.

'My name's Kuniko Jonouchi, and I work at the Miyoshi Foods factory. The guard on the night shift, Sato-san, found something I lost, and I wanted to send him a little thank-you present.'

'Is that right?' the man said.

'Would you mind telling me his full name and address?'

'His address here at the office or at home?'

'The home one, if you don't mind.'

'Hold on a second.' Masako was amazed how casual they seemed to be, as if the whole place were run by pensioners. It was a far cry from the security companies that used to transport the cash in the old days at the credit union. 'His name is Yoshio Sato,' the man told her after a moment. 'And he lives at the Tama Municipal Apartment Complex in Kodaira, apartment 412.'

'Thanks very much,' she said, closing the phone and turning up the heater in the car. She'd suddenly felt chilly. It had never occurred to her that Satake might be living in the same building as Kuniko. He must have been laying his trap for some time, planning it all with great care. Once again, his attention to detail amazed and horrified her. They were like so many fish being driven into nets he had set long ago. Kuniko had been first, but now it was her turn. The blast of hot air from the heater had brought out a light sweat on her forehead, but when she reached up to wipe it off, it felt oddly cold.

On an impulse, she thought of calling Yayoi. They hadn't

talked since they'd quarrelled some weeks earlier, and she wondered whether something might have happened that she wasn't telling her about. She dialled her number.

'The Yamamotos',' she heard Yayoi say in a slightly affected way.

'It's me.'

'Masako? It's good to hear from you.'

'Is everything okay?'

'Yes, fine. The boys are at day-care. It's been nice and quiet.' Her reaction to Masako's usual intensity seemed almost relaxed, for once. 'Why do you ask?'

'No reason. I'm glad things are going well.'

'Actually, we're going home to live with my parents soon.'

'That sounds like a good idea.'

'How are you doing? How's the Skipper?'

'She hasn't been at work lately.'

'Really? That's a change. How's Kuniko?'

'She's dead,' said Masako. Yayoi let out a little shriek but said nothing for a few seconds. Masako waited.

'Was she murdered?' Yayoi said finally.

'Why would you think that?'

'I don't know, I just had a feeling.' Masako was sure now that she was hiding something.

'Anyway, she's dead,' she said.

'When?'

'I don't know.'

'How did she die?'

'I don't know that either. I just saw the body.' She decided not to mention that it had rope marks around the neck.

'You saw the body?' Yayoi said in a bleak voice.

'I saw it.'

'Masako-san,' she said, sounding panicky now. 'What's going on? Why did this happen?'

'I guess you'd have to say we woke up a monster.'

'. . . You mean, he murdered her?' She'd said 'murder' again, and she seemed to know immediately that 'monster' meant Satake. She must have met up with him.

'Do you know who he is then?' Masako said. Yayoi was silent. There was the sound of talk-show chatter in the background. 'If something's happened, you need to tell me. Our lives could depend on it. Do you understand that?' The urgency in her voice vibrated in the tight space of the car. She looked frantically at the overflowing ashtray as she waited for an answer.

'No,' Yayoi said at last. 'Nothing's happened.'

'I'm glad to hear it,' she snapped. 'You're on your own then. . . .'

'Masako,' she said, as if to cut her off. 'Do you think it's my fault?'

'No, I don't.'

'Really?'

'Really.' And on this note, she broke the connection. She had never blamed Yayoi. If anything, it was her own fault. Still, she had no intention of apologising to anyone, no regrets about the way she'd handled things. The only thing that concerned her now was that someone was blocking her exit, and how she was going to get out. Even if she told the others what she was planning, she knew none of them would come with her; and she wasn't looking for company anyway.

Masako stared down at her bony hands, her only source of comfort now. Bringing them slowly to her face, she reminded herself that she was the only person she could trust. No one else. She remembered how lonely she'd felt when she first realised this, that summer day in the woods, when she went to check the spot where she had buried Kenji's head.

The air in the car had grown warm and heavy, and she suddenly felt sleepy. She closed her eyes with the engine running.

When she woke up half an hour later, she was still sitting there, parked by the quiet road leading to the factory. The grass along the verge was brown from the nightly frost. From where she sat, she could see the concrete cover that Kazuo had pulled off the culvert, still propped up like an open tomb. In ten hours or so, Satake would pass this way in his uniform, looking ordinary, anonymous.

The area in front of Higashi Yamato Station was empty, as usual. Dust swirled up from a vacant lot along the tracks, and a crowd of elementary-school children, brightly dressed for an outing, stood in front of the skating rink. Masako parked behind the station, pushed her way through the children, and hurried across the street, before ducking into an alley lined with tightly shuttered bars. The wind was cold and smelt vaguely of garbage. Worried she'd be too late, she quickened her pace.

She came to a small sushi shop with a 'Closed' sign in the window and ran up the flimsy stairs next to it, heading for the Million Consumers Centre. She listened at the plywood door at the end of the passage. For a moment she heard nothing, but eventually she made out the sound of somebody quietly moving about inside.

'Jumonji-san,' she called. 'Open up. It's Masako.' He opened the door a moment later, looking much as he had earlier. He was sweating now, though, perhaps from the hurry to finish his preparations. The drawers of the desks and the filing cabinet stood open. Knowing Jumonji, he was looking for anything valuable he could take with him, and his staff were in for a nasty shock when they showed up later.

'So it's you,' he said.

'Sorry. Did I frighten you?' she asked. He laughed awkwardly but said nothing. It seemed odd that no one else was in the office. 'Have your people quit?' she said.

'There's someone coming in this afternoon. She'll be a bit surprised, I guess.' He smiled again as he showed her into the office. 'What's up? I wasn't sure I'd be seeing you again.'

'I'm glad I caught you. I was hoping you could give me some information on Kuniko's loan. Did you fill out a credit history on her before you lent her the money?'

'Of course,' he said. 'But why does it matter?' She looked at him for a moment, realising he had reached his limit.

'I found out who Satake is,' she said.

His eyes went wide. 'Who?'

'A security guard named Sato who works at our parking lot.'

'Shit!' he said, amazed perhaps that Satake should have gone to such lengths, or that Masako had been able to ferret him out. 'Are you sure?'

'And not only that, he's been living in Kuniko's apartment building.'

'I knew some scary characters in my biker days in Adachi, but I never met anyone like this guy. He's on a whole different level,' he whispered, remembering the man he'd seen the night he collected Kuniko's body. He rubbed the corners of his mouth, as if rubbing something sticky off. Masako glanced around at the nearly empty office.

'Looks as though business has been slow,' she said.

'Slowing to a halt, you might say. At any rate, Kuniko's file should be over there. You're welcome to it, but I still don't see what use it could be.' Masako found the 'J' section in the drawer. She pulled Kuniko's papers and scanned the loan questionnaire, filled out in Jumonji's messy scrawl, searching for potentially overdue loans. 'What d'you have in mind?' he asked, slipping off his jacket. It seemed his curiosity had been aroused.

'I'm looking for something I can use.'

'Use how?'

'To give Satake a bad time,' she said.

'Don't even think about it,' he murmured. 'Let's just get out of here.' Masako examined the photocopy of Kuniko's licence. She was heavily made up for the picture and her face looked flat and sallow.

'Jumonji-san?'

'What?'

'How do you declare bankruptcy?'

'It's pretty easy,' he said. 'You just have to appear in civil court a bunch of times.'

'I don't suppose we could find somebody to play Kuniko,' she said, flicking her finger at the license photo. Yayoi, even if they got her to go along with the scheme, could never pass for her. Besides, there wasn't time.

'What are you planning?' Jumonji asked, staring at her.

'I was wondering whether we could have Kuniko file for bankruptcy and list Satake as co-signatory on her loans.'

'Clever,' he said, laughing nervously. 'Even if we can't fake the bankruptcy, we can still make him co-signatory and then tell the creditors she's skipped town. Everything's done over the phone nowadays, so all I'd have to do is make a few calls to some "colleagues" in the business. These guys'll take on anything as long as they think there's money to be made.'

'You can just tell people Satake co-signed her loans?'

'It's that simple. You don't even have to have a contract. The downside is, he's not really responsible for making payments, but they'll still bug the shit out of him until somebody does.'

'That's all I want,' Masako said. 'Then, can you put out the word that Kuniko's gone missing?'

'Consider it done.'

'Let's fill out some loan papers and stamp in his name. You must have some ready-made seals around here.' Jumonji went over to his desk and took a cookie tin out of the drawer. He had a mischievous look as he pried off the top and showed her the array of bogus seals inside.

'Serves him right for picking a common name like Sato,' he said, quickly producing three seals with the name.

'You can get out of here as soon as you're done.'

'I'll be finished by noon,' he said. The colour had returned to his cheeks.

'At least we can smoke him out of his hole,' she said, a little smile coming to her face as she imagined Satake sleeping unawares in his apartment.

4

Only scaring her was boring.

Satake was in the roof garden of a supermarket across from the station. The place was nearly empty, perhaps due to the cold, cloudy weather, or because the store was losing customers to the huge supermarkets being built further out in the suburbs. A few parents with small children were milling around the little playground, and a boy and girl of high-school age were necking off in a corner. Otherwise, it was empty.

For some time, he had been standing looking at the makeshift pet shop next to the game arcade. The five dirty cages out in front were occupied by drowsy puppies and kittens, common breeds that had been around the shop too long and seemed a bit large for their cages. As he peered in at them, cigarette in hand, they shrank away. He remembered how Anna had accused him of treating her like a lapdog. For just a moment, he missed the smooth skin and perfect features of the woman he'd turned into the top girl at Mika. The top pet in the shop.

Anna herself had known that once she'd realised this, she would never be able to keep that position, however hard she tried. That was just the way things worked. She'd been so popular precisely because she hadn't known she was a pet. But it was all over the minute it dawned on her, and there would always be a shadow of self-awareness from then on. It was a quality that was essential in a woman for a man to fall in love with her; but men who were only interested in buying a woman's body hated it with a vengeance. They wanted good looks untouched by any self-knowledge; not a cat but a kitten. This was why he'd been willing to spoil and flatter Anna, hoping to keep her in the dark – and why it was so ironic that falling in love with him had been her downfall. Anna seemed to be doing fine at the bar she was now working in, but that would only last another six months at most. He felt sorry for her, but the feeling was much the same as the pity he felt for the cats and dogs in these cages. He poked a long finger in between the bars, but the puppy backed away trembling.

'Don't be afraid,' he told it. It was boring when they sucked up to you, cringing and crawling all over you. On the other hand, if they were too trusting, they were just stupid. That was the thing about pets: they were either fawning or stupid. Suddenly fed up, he walked away from the shop. He poked his head into the empty, gaudily lit arcade next door, then walked through the small roof garden. The grey, seedy city stretched away toward the Tama Hills. A dump, Satake thought, spitting on the artificial turf. The lovers in the corner and the parents by the playground looked at him in dismay.

Masako Katori hadn't shown up at the factory for the past four days, not since he left Kuniko's Golf in the parking lot for her. Maybe she'd quit. But that would be deeply disappointing. He'd been so excited to find a woman he thought had nerves of steel, but if a little trick like that sent her running, she was useless to him. In the end, would she be just as scared of him as everybody else? Had he been fooling himself that night on the way to the factory, thinking she'd felt something – an affinity?

He turned back toward the pet shop. The dogs and cats

followed him with their pathetic eyes. He had a feeling that something was beginning to wither inside him, and he took the stairs down from the roof in a hurry. As he ran, his pulse quickened, his body remembering the excitement of that summer evening when he'd chased the other woman through Shinjuku. The look on her face had thrilled him beyond anything he'd ever known. But with Masako he felt disappointed, angry. He wanted to hurt her, not just snuff her out the way he had the fat one. Was it a mistake to think that he'd been fated to meet her? The hands in his pockets clenched into fists.

At a pachinko parlour by the station, Satake hit the jackpot three times with the same machine, which was the maximum allowed by the rules. Before leaving, he kicked the thing hard, and an attendant came running after him to complain.

'Sir!' the man called.

'What?' he said, turning to face him. The menace in his look made the man stop short. Satake took three ¥10,000 bills out of his pocket and threw them down on the sidewalk, then watched, scowling, as he picked them up. There was enough of Yayoi's money to allow this sort of gesture. He wasn't playing pachinko for the money anyway.

A head of violence was building in him. It seemed strange that you could kill someone and then become more violent still, but in the past few days he had been so full of impatient rage he felt it was about to spill out of him. At the same time, there was another part of him that was coolly observing his own progress toward eruption.

He walked through a deserted shopping arcade, his shoulders hunched, his mood sullen. The new storefronts were flimsy and artificial, while the older ones seemed dark and depressing. He was hungry, but he didn't feel like eating. Tonight, again, he had nothing to do but leave the Golf in the lot and wait for Masako.

He went back to the supermarket and found the car. Opening the door, he looked in at the jumble of cassette tapes and shoes; he had left Kuniko's mess just as he'd found it. A ruined pair of shoes discarded on the floor on the passenger side reminded him particularly of her, and he stared at them with loathing. The ashtray bore the only evidence that the car had a new driver: the butts were Satake's brand now, and he emptied them out regularly.

If he drove around these neighbourhoods long enough, he was bound to run into Masako sooner or later. He would like to see her face when he did. If she'd really quit the factory, he had little choice but to trawl for her like this, though it was a dangerous, obsessive business. He remembered how she'd looked when she pulled into the parking lot and found Kuniko's car there. For just a moment, her face had frozen, and then gone blank, as if nothing had happened, but the tightened lips betrayed her. He'd seen the reaction, even from the guardhouse. When she got out of the car and walked around the Golf, she'd been even more shocked to see the way it was parked, just as Kuniko used to leave it. He knew because she hadn't been able to hide the tremor in her voice when she'd come to ask him about the car. Just the right note of fear. He laughed quietly, remembering. But fear alone wasn't enough. Or, rather, fear was fine as long as it didn't lead to cringing and pleading. He thought of the dogs at the pet shop, and the ugly way Kuniko had begged for her life. Suddenly repelled, he threw her shoes out of the car, sending them bouncing off the stained concrete.

He pulled into Kuniko's parking space at the apartment building and was just locking the door when a young woman, who had apparently been waiting for him, came trotting over. He didn't recognise her, but from the apron and sandals he could tell she must be one of the housewives there. She had no make-up on her face, but her hair was pushed up and damp with mousse, like a wig put on in a hurry. Satake thought she looked awful.

'Do you know the lady who owns this car?' she said. 'Jonouchi-san?'

'Of course I know her. I'm borrowing her car, aren't I?' He knew that the longer he used the Golf, the more likely he was to get questions like this.

'I'm sorry, I didn't mean to suggest . . .' She blushed, having apparently drawn her own conclusions about his relationship with Kuniko already. 'It's just that I haven't seen her around lately.'

'I'm not sure where she's gone myself,' he said.

'But you're using her car?' the woman said, looking at him curiously.

'I got a job as a guard at the factory where she worked. When we realised we were living in the same building, she asked me to look after the car while she was away. It's not like I asked her.' He dangled the keys in her face, making sure she could see the initial K on the key holder.

'I see,' the woman said. 'But I wonder where she's gone.'

'I suppose she's just off on a little trip. I doubt it's anything to worry about.'

'But she hasn't been home in days, and I couldn't get in touch with her about her turn cleaning up the garbage cans. Her answering machine is on all the time, and no one's seen her husband either.'

'She quit at the factory,' Satake said. 'Maybe she went home to her family.'

'And you're using her car while she's gone?' the woman said, a note of suspicion again in the question.

'I'm paying her for it,' he said.

'Oh, I see,' she said, stiffening slightly at the mention of money. Satake found this amusing. She lived off her husband's salary, but she didn't like anything as tacky as money coming up in the conversation.

'Sorry,' he said, pushing past her. 'I'm in a hurry.' He decided that from now on he would have to stop using the car except when he was going to work. As he came toward the building, he noticed a middle-aged man in a new raincoat standing next to the mailboxes. His first thought was that he might be a cop, but after studying him out of the corner of his eye as he walked by, he decided he didn't have a cop's eyes. A salesman, he guessed, as he watched him checking the names on the mailboxes; but when he saw him stop at the box for number 412, Satake stepped into the elevator.

After he got out, he checked to make sure the elevator didn't go back to the first floor, then walked slowly along the passageway, ducking his head into a cold north wind. But as he approached the apartment and was taking out his key, he looked up to see a young man standing in front of his door. The man was dressed in a short white down jacket and purple pants, and his hair was dyed orange-brown. Satake saw him shoving something into his pocket – a cell phone, probably. He didn't like the look of this one bit.

'Are you Sato?' the man said, apparently sure of the answer to his own question. This obviously was not a cop. There was no mistaking the look of a yakuza. Satake ignored the question and moved forward to open the door, wondering how this one was connected to the guy downstairs. But as he reached for the doorknob, he found that it was covered by some kind of black fabric. The man watched in silence, suppressing a laugh.

'What the fuck?' Satake muttered.

'Take a good look,' his visitor said. The blood rushed to Satake's head when he realised the black material was Kuniko's panties, the ones he'd used as a gag on her.

'Did you do this?' he said, grabbing him by the collar of his jacket. But the man seemed unimpressed, and just chuckled softly, his hands still in his pockets.

'Not me. They were there when I got here.'

Then it had to be Masako. Releasing him, he pulled the thing off the doorknob and stuffed it in his pocket. The fabric was cold from hanging in the wind.

'It wasn't me,' the guy repeated, prodding Satake in the side. 'And where d'you get off shoving me around?'

'What do you want?' Satake said, pushing him back.

'To show you this.' He pulled a piece of paper from his pocket and stuck it in his face. It was a promissory note from a place called Midori Credit for a loan of two million yen to Kuniko Jonouchi.

'What's this got to do with me?'

'You're down as co-signatory, and this Jonouchi woman skipped town.'

'I don't know anything about it,' he lied – but he knew he'd been outmanoeuvred. There was no way that a loan shark would lend that much to Kuniko, so the whole thing must have been cooked up to get back at him. These punks would now be on his case, prowling around the building, drawing attention to him.

In a suddenly much louder voice, the man said, 'What d'you mean, you don't know anything about it?' A door opened just down the passage and a woman poked her head out. She watched them nervously, which was obviously the effect his visitor had wanted. 'Then what's this?' he said, holding out the paper again and pointing at the space for co-signatories. 'Yoshio Sato' was neatly stamped in it. Satake smiled.

'That's not me.'

'Then who is it?'

'How should I know?' Just then, the elevator opened at the end of the passage and the man who'd been standing by the mailboxes moved toward them. Obviously, he and the punk were working together.

'My name's Miyata,' he said when he reached them. 'I'm with East Credit. Our client Jonouchi-san is a bit behind on her car payments, and we heard she's disappeared.'

'Am I guaranteeing that, too?' Satake said.

'I'm afraid so,' he told him. Satake cursed, wondering how many more guys like this would be coming around. He was probably co-signatory now on a whole stack of loans. Masako, most likely with help from Jumonji, must have faked the papers and handed them over to their pals in the credit racket; then put out the word that Kuniko had disappeared, setting the dogs loose on him.

'Okay,' he said. 'I guess I don't have much choice. If you could just leave the paperwork, I'll see what I can do.' Apparently reassured by this sudden change in attitude, they both held out copies of their contracts.

'But when do we get the money?' the younger one said.

'I'll make the payments in a week at most.'

'If you don't, I'll be back with some friends and next time we won't be so sociable. You can count on it.' They weren't usually so heavy-handed on the first visit, Satake thought. Jumonji must have got hold of the toughest outfit he could think of.

'I get you,' he said. As they'd been talking, several more neighbours had come out and were watching from a safe distance. The two men seemed satisfied that they'd managed to put him on the spot this way. With a nod to Miyata, Satake opened the door and slipped inside. The younger man tried to peer in, but he shut it firmly behind him before turning on the light. When he looked through the peephole, they were gone.

'Shit,' he muttered, throwing Kuniko's underpants on the floor and kicking them away.

In the meantime they'd be watching him, pinning him down. Worse still, the other people in the building would start watching him, too. The woman in the parking lot had probably been talking to one of the men, and that had made her nosy. He could afford a few million yen to pay off the loans, but he couldn't afford to stay in this apartment now that the neighbours were on the alert; and Masako would have known that the credit companies would follow him to the factory if he didn't pay up, putting an end to his little game there.

Opening the closet, he pulled out the black nylon bag he'd brought with him from Shinjuku. He filled it with the bundles of money and the reports from the detective agency, and then, as an afterthought, picked up Kuniko's panties and shoved them in as well. His eyes swept over the empty apartment, settling on the bed next to the window. He'd dreamed of tying Masako there and torturing her . . . but it wasn't to be. Even so, he had a faint smile on his face. The pleasure he'd felt at finding her was returning; but stronger now, stronger even than what he'd felt the day he spotted the other woman on the streets of Shinjuku. He wanted to kill Masako even more than he'd wanted to kill the other one. And there was pleasure in that desire.

Leaving the light on, he took the bag and left the apartment. After making sure there was no one in the passage outside, he went down the back stairs. When he reached the first floor, he spotted the young guy in the down jacket standing a short way off, shivering in the cold as he stared up at Satake's window. Apparently reassured that the light was still on, the man dropped his scrutiny to watch a young woman just getting back from work. Satake, seeing his chance, ran behind the garbage shed, along a line of bushes, and out into the street. For the time being, he would have to find a hotel somewhere. He wasn't sure how long it would take them to figure out he'd given them the slip and come looking for him at the factory.

That night, he drove to work in a rented car. He was certain Masako would show up. By now she would have heard that her plan had been a success, and she'd come to see the results of her handiwork. He knew *he* would – and she was so much like him. He smoked a cigarette in the guardhouse, waiting for her Corolla to appear and wondering how she would look.

She arrived a little before 11.30, right on time. As he looked up, he caught a glimpse of her in the reflection from the headlights. Her face was expressionless as she drove past the guardhouse, and she made a point of not turning to look at him. Stuck-up bitch. She's probably thinking about all the trouble she caused me. His blood boiled with pure hatred and a perverse admiration for the way she'd managed to make him hate her. It made him feel dizzy.

He heard the car door slam and the sound of her footsteps on the gravel as she walked toward him. He left the shed and planted himself directly in her path.

'Good evening,' he said.

'Good evening,' she echoed, looking right at him. Her loose hair fell as far as the shoulders of a patched down jacket. There was a hint of a smile on her thin face. Solving the riddle of his identity and driving him out of his apartment had given her confidence. He forced himself to keep calm.

'Shall I walk you to the factory?' he asked, sounding almost respectful.

'No thank you.'

'It can be dangerous in the dark.'

Masako hesitated a second. 'You're the danger,' she said, taunting him.

'I'm not sure what you mean.'

'The game's over, Satake,' she said.

When he had hunted down that woman in Shinjuku, he'd felt an uncontrollable excitement; but this was different. This time he managed to contain his agitation, even though he felt it coursing through him, looking for a way out. The pleasure, deferred like this, was all the more acute.

'You're a tough bitch,' he said. Masako ignored him and set off toward the factory. Would she really risk walking all that way by herself? He followed a short distance behind, feeling as though he could almost hear her heart pounding, feel the tension in her shoulders. But she walked on in the darkness, refusing to show any sign of fear. He switched on his flashlight and lit up the ground a few steps ahead of her.

'I said I didn't want any company,' she said, rounding on him. 'I don't want to be strangled in a place like this.' He felt another rush of pleasure. How he hated her! And the feeling was so much stronger than anything he'd ever felt for beautiful Anna. Longing and hatred, linked somehow by the danger of self-destruction. What if he just grabbed her right now, knocked her out, and then killed her in the old factory? He toyed with the idea for a moment, but in the end it seemed a bit ordinary.

'This isn't quite the right setting, is it?' she said, as if guessing his thoughts. 'You want to make me suffer first. Why are you . . .?' The squeal of bicycle brakes interrupted her, and they spun around to see Yoshie pulling up behind them.

'Good morning,' she said. She glanced at the guard and then fell in step with Masako.

'Skipper!' said Masako. 'What are you doing here?'

'I wanted to see you. It's lucky I caught you.' Satake aimed the flashlight at her face for a second. She scowled in the sudden glare and glanced at Masako, who seemed to be grinning just outside the circle of light.

5

She was safe. Masako drew a deep breath when she saw Yoshie's face. Her breathing had almost stopped when she realised he might kill her, and she was sure he would have if she'd shown the slightest sign of weakness. It reminded her of her childhood, of the time she'd been chased by a wild dog after making the mistake of looking it in the eye. It had been a close call, she told herself, trying to breathe normally again.

She knew now that his hatred was on the verge of erupting, and that he seemed to be enjoying the game of pushing it toward the brink. She had seen the amusement in his eyes, seen how much pleasure it gave him to play cat and mouse with her. But she'd also seen that something in him was unhinged and impelling him towards an explosion. That same thing was inside her, too. It was the part of her that had secretly thought she might be willing to die as long as he were the one to kill her.

She stared at the dark, abandoned factory looming up ahead. The emptiness of the building seemed to match the void inside herself. Was it a symbol somehow of her own damaged life? Had she lived forty-three years just to discover this? She couldn't take her eyes off it.

'Who was that?' Yoshie said, looking back uneasily toward the parking lot. She was wheeling the heavy bike along the uneven road.

'The guard,' Masako said. The guardhouse stood like a beacon in the dark, with Satake beside it, watching them. He would wait for her to come back.

'He gives me the creeps,' Yoshie said.

'Why?'

'I don't know,' she said, but she didn't continue, apparently unwilling to take the trouble to explain. The headlight on her bike cast a faint glow on the road ahead.

'What have you been up to?' Masako asked. She hadn't seen her since they'd dealt with Kuniko a week ago.

Yoshie sighed wearily. 'I'm sorry, I just had a lot of things to take care of.' She was wearing the windbreaker she always used in winter, and Masako remembered how thin and frayed the flannel lining had become. She wondered whether Yoshie herself might simply wear out one day.

'What kind of things?' she said. She assumed Satake had not gone after Yoshie. It was clear that he was only interested in her now.

'Miki ran away from home,' Yoshie said. 'I haven't seen her since. I knew her sister was a bad example, but I never thought *she'd* go off like that. It's lonely around there now. I'm not sure I can stand it.' Masako listened quietly, wondering if Yoshie had any way out. 'It's all so stupid. She left before I could tell her I had some more money. As far as she knew, she couldn't go to college since the other money was gone. Everything seems to be going to hell.'

'I'm sure she'll be back.'

'No, she won't. She's just like her sister. She'll end up with some useless man, and there's nothing I can do about it. My kids are fools, and I can't do a thing about it.' As they walked along, Yoshie repeated this hopeless refrain. Her tone was almost apologetic, but it wasn't clear what she was sorry for. They passed the empty factory, the old bowling alley, and a line of houses, and came out in the wide street bordered by the long wall of the automobile plant. A left turn here and they were almost at the factory. 'This is it for me,' Yoshie said, stretching her back. Her stooped shoulders made her look old.

'You're quitting?'

'I can't work here any more,' she said. Masako didn't tell her that this was her last night as well. She'd come to give in her notice and collect the money and passport that Kazuo was keeping for her. If she could survive the night, she might be able to escape from Satake altogether. 'I wanted the chance to talk for a few minutes,' Yoshie said. 'That's why I came this way.'

Couldn't they talk in the lounge after work? Wondering what Yoshie was getting at, Masako waited by the stairs while she went to park her bike. There were no stars in the sky and a thick layer of clouds seemed to hang over them, but even the clouds were invisible. Feeling oppressed, as though a heavy weight were bearing down on her, Masako looked up at the factory. Just then, the door at the top of the stairs opened.

'Katori-san,' a voice called. It was Komada.

'Yes?'

'Do you know if Yoshie Azuma is coming tonight?'

'She just went to park her bike.' Komada came running down the stairs, her roller still in her hand. Yoshie appeared just as she reached the bottom.

'Azuma-san!' she cried. 'You need to go home right away.'

'Why?' Yoshie said.

'They just called to say there's been a fire at your house.'

'There has?' Her face was white. Komada looked at her sympathetically.

'Get going,' she told her.

In a flat voice, Yoshie said, 'It's probably too late to do anything.'

'I'm sure that's not true. Now hurry up!' Yoshie turned slowly back toward the bike racks. Several more women were arriving for work and Komada started up the stairs to meet them.

'Did they say anything about her mother-in-law?' Masako called up to her.

'No, but they said the house burned to the ground.' She looked back over her shoulder, aware that it was awful news to have to pass on, before going inside. Masako waited alone for Yoshie. It was several more minutes before she appeared with the bike, as if she'd been bracing herself for the ordeal. Masako looked at her tired face.

'I'm sorry, but I can't go with you,' she said.

'I know,' Yoshie said. 'I didn't think you would. That's why I came to say goodbye here.'

'Did you have insurance?'

'A little.'

'Take care of yourself,' said Masako.

'You, too. And thanks for everything.' She bowed and then headed back the way they'd come. Masako watched as her light grew dimmer and died as she turned toward the car factory. A faint, pinkish glow rose from the city in the distance, and much nearer, a pillar of sparks from the old wooden house. Yoshie had found a way out after all. Once her daughter was gone, she must have lost all hope, and with it her last reason for hesitating. Masako wondered whether she had been the one to push her over the edge. She'd told her about the danger from Satake, and that must have planted the idea in her head. She stood for a moment longer, unable to look away. When she did turn and climb the stairs, Komada seemed surprised to see her.

'You didn't go with her?'

'No,' said Masako. Komada ran the roller roughly across her back, as if blaming her for deserting a friend.

It was almost time for the shift to start. Masako hurried into the lounge and looked around for Kazuo. He wasn't with the other Brazilians or in the changing area, and when she checked his time card, she discovered that it was his night off. Komada tried to stop her, but she slipped into her shoes and ran out the door.

Everything had changed in a moment. This was the night. She set out on foot toward Kazuo's dormitory. Further down the road, Satake was waiting for her. She turned left, keeping a wary eye on the parking lot, peering at things imagined in the dark. The open fields around her were dotted with farmhouses, and beyond them was the dormitory. The only light in the building was in Kazuo's window on the second floor. She climbed the metal stairs, trying not to make any noise, and knocked at the door. There was an answer in Portuguese and the door opened. Kazuo, in a T-shirt and jeans, stood looking out at her, obviously surprised. The light from the TV was flickering in the background.

'Masako-san,' he said.

'Are you alone?'

'Yes,' he said, stepping aside to let her in. The air was filled with the smell of a foreign spice she couldn't identify. There was a bunk bed next to the window, and the futon cupboard stood open. They were using it as a closet. The tatami room held a small, square low table. Kazuo had apparently been watching a soccer match, but he switched it off and turned to face her.

'Do you want the money?'

'I'm sorry, I didn't realise you were off tonight. Would you mind going in to get it?'

'No, not at all,' he said, searching her face with a worried look. She took out a cigarette and glanced around for an ashtray, trying to avoid his eyes. Kazuo lit one himself and put a tin Coca Cola ashtray on the table. 'You wait here,' he said. 'I'll be right back.'

'Thanks,' she said. Looking around her, she had a sense that this tiny apartment was the one safe place to be right now. Kazuo's room-mate must have gone to work; the bottom bunk was neatly made.

'Can you tell me what's happened?' Kazuo said. He was lingering, wanting to talk, apparently afraid she would leave too soon.

'I'm running away from a man,' she said, speaking slowly, as if the warmth of the room were gradually thawing her out. 'I can't tell you why he's after me, but I'm going to use the money to get away, to leave the country.' Kazuo stared at the floor and thought for a moment. He blew out a cloud of smoke and looked up at her.

'Where will you go? It's not easy anywhere.'

'Maybe so,' she said, 'but I don't really care, just as long as I get out of here.' He put his hand to his forehead. He seemed to know without being told that her situation was a matter of life and death.

'What about your family?'

'My husband wants to be alone. He's withdrawn from life – that's just the way he is. And my son's grown up now.' Why was she telling him this? She hadn't told anyone. Maybe it was easier because he didn't really speak her language; maybe that made her relax. But as soon as she'd put her situation in words, tears welled up as if out of nowhere. She wiped them away with the back of her hand.

'You're alone,' Kazuo said.

'I am,' she admitted. 'We were happy once, a long time ago, but somewhere along the line, things fell apart. I guess it's probably my fault.'

'Why's that?'

'Because I want to be alone. Because I want to be free.' There were tears in his eyes now, too. They rolled down his cheeks on to the tatami.

'When you're alone, will you be free?' he asked.

'It seems that way to me, for now at least.' Escape. Escape from what? To what? She had no idea.

'It's very sad,' he whispered. 'I'm sorry for you.'

'No, don't be,' she said, shaking her head and clutching her knees. 'I wanted to get out, so this is just how it is.'

'. . . Really?'

'I've lost hope,' she said. 'And I don't care whether I live or die.' Kazuo looked troubled.

'Lost hope in what?'

'In life,' she said. He began to cry again, and Masako sat watching him for a while, moved that a young foreigner should be crying for her. His sobs showed no sign of subsiding. 'Why are you crying?' she said at last.

'Because you told me what was in your heart. You seemed so far away until now.' Masako smiled. Kazuo brushed the tears away with his arm. She looked at the green and yellow Brazilian flag that hung in the window.

'Where should I go?' she said. 'I've never been abroad.' He looked up, his big eyes red with tears.

'Why don't you go to Brazil?' he said. 'It's summer there now.'

'What's it like?' He thought for a moment, then smiled shyly.

'I'm not sure I can explain, but it's wonderful there. Wonderful.'

Summer. Masako closed her eyes as though trying to imagine it. The summer had changed everything. The smell of gardenias, the grass growing thick around the parking lot, the glint of dark water in the culvert. When she opened her eyes again, Kazuo was getting ready to go out. He pulled on a black jacket over his T-shirt and tugged his cap on to his head.

'I'll be right back,' he said.

'Miyamori-san. Can I stay until three?' He nodded. Three more hours. Satake would be gone by then. She propped her elbows on the table and closed her eyes, grateful for a little rest.

She woke up when he came back. He had apparently taken his time, since it was already 2.00 a.m. As he unzipped his jacket and pulled out the envelope, she caught a cold breath of the outdoors.

'Here it is,' he said.

'Thanks.' She could feel the warmth of his body in the envelope as he handed it to her. She opened it and peered in: a new passport and seven bundles of bills, a million each – the means of flight. She took out one of the bundles and set it on the table. 'This is for keeping it for me,' she said. 'Please take it.' Kazuo blushed.

'I don't need it. I'm just glad I could help you.'

'But you've got another year at the factory,' she said. She saw him biting his lips as he slipped off his jacket.

'I'm going home before Christmas,' he told her.

'You are?'

'Yes. There's no point in staying any longer.' He sat down at the table and gazed around the room. Masako felt a touch of envy at the nostalgic look in his eyes when he looked at the flag. 'I was hoping I could help you. Does it have something to do with this?' he asked, pulling the key out from under his shirt.

'Yes, it does.'

'Do you need it back?'

'No,' she said. He smiled with relief. The key to Kenji's house. She stared at it as it lay in his hand, realising that everything had started with the key. But that wasn't true: it had started with something in her. Her hopelessness and a longing for freedom – those had brought her to this point. She put the envelope in her shoulder bag and stood up. Kazuo picked up the money on the table and tried to give it back. 'Please keep it,' she said. 'It's my way of thanking you.'

'But it's too much,' he said, trying to force it into her bag.

'Keep it,' she repeated. 'You could call it "blood money".' His hand stopped and he frowned. Did it go against his conscience? 'You deserve it,' she said, 'after slaving away at that factory. Anyway, there's no such thing as clean money.' He gave a deep sigh and put the bills back on the table, perhaps afraid of offending her. 'I'm going now,' she said. 'Thanks again.'

He held her gently. It was the first time she'd been in a man's arms since he had attacked her that night by the old factory, but the feeling was one she hadn't known in years. The warmth seemed to melt her, open her bit by bit. She lay against him for a moment, and the tears came back into her eyes.

'I've got to go,' she told him. Releasing her, he reached into his pocket and brought out a slip of paper. 'What's this?' she said.

'My address in São Paolo.'

'Thank you.' She folded it neatly and put it in the pocket of her jeans.

'Come to see me,' he said. 'Come for Christmas. I'll be waiting. Promise you'll come.'

'I promise,' Masako said, slipping into her beat-up sneakers. A cold wind blew in as she opened the door. Kazuo stood biting his lips and staring at the floor. 'Goodbye.'

'Goodbye,' he said, as if it were the saddest word in the world.

She went down the stairs as quietly as she'd come up. The shutters on the nearby houses were closed and the neighbourhood was asleep. The only light came from the widely spaced streetlamps. Zipping up her jacket, she set off for the parking lot. Except for the sound of her shoes on the pavement, the night was silent and lonely. When she reached the spot where Kazuo had pulled the cover off the culvert, she stopped. She hesitated for a moment, but then took the paper with his address out of her pocket, ripped it to pieces, and dropped them down the hole.

She was still hoping to escape, but she had resigned herself to the fact that she might not live that long. Kazuo's kindness had been a brief comfort, but there was a crueller world waiting for her on the other side of the door she had opened.

She was nearing the parking lot. The lights were out in the guardhouse, which between 3.00 and 6.00 a.m. was empty. Even if Satake had wanted to wait until she got off work, he knew there would be more people here in the morning. He wouldn't take that risk. She looked around before stepping out into the lot, but it appeared to be deserted. Reassured, she started across the open space, kicking up the gravel that was scattered over the hard earth. As she approached her car, she realised something was hanging from the side mirror. She reached out to touch it and screamed. It was Kuniko's panties. She had left them on his doorknob, and now he was returning the favour. Feeling outraged, she threw them on the ground; but as she did so, a long arm wrapped around her from behind. She had no time to cry out. She struggled, but the arm held her fast. Warm fingers closed over her jaw, and the arm, in a guard's uniform, pressed up under her neck. She couldn't breathe, yet she wasn't really afraid. She didn't feel what she'd felt in the dream, but she did have a strange sense of recognition, as if she'd come to a place she'd been to before.

6

He wanted to merge into the night. He sat in the car with the windows rolled down, letting the air wash over him. This was the only way he could relax, and it was the one thing he had missed in prison, the feel of the air on him. His arms and legs were numb from the cold, and his whole body had begun to shiver. In the summer, his blood would have been thick with the heat, but now his mind was clear. Wrapped in the darkness, his hand could feel a density in the air that wasn't there in daylight. He stretched his long arm through the window and felt the cold breeze.

Still dressed in his uniform, he was waiting here for Masako. He had parked across from her space, in the dark at the back of the lot, and had settled in to wait until six. He wondered how she would react when she came back exhausted from the shift and found Kuniko's underwear on her car. He wanted to be there to see her face, her straggly hair, the dark circles under her eyes.

Just as he was about to light a cigarette, he heard the sound of footsteps on the gravel. A woman's light step. He stuffed the cigarette in his pocket and held his breath. Masako had come back. She looked around for a moment; then, apparently satisfied that he wasn't there, she headed for the Corolla, no longer bothering to be cautious. Without making a sound, Satake opened the door and slipped out of his car. She gave a muffled scream as she discovered his little present. Realising he would never get a better chance, he crept up and grabbed her from behind. As his arm went around her neck, her fear ran through him like a current, and he realised how much she attracted him.

'Don't move,' he said, but she began to struggle frantically. Pressing one arm into her thin neck, he wrapped the other around her body. Her fingernails dug into his forearm through the fabric of his uniform, and she kneed him between the legs. It took all his strength to subdue her, but eventually she lost consciousness.

At last he had her. Shouldering her limp body, he went back to his car for rope and bags. Where could he take her now that he'd been driven out of his apartment? With no place to go and no time to look for somewhere else, he set off toward the abandoned factory. When he reached the drainage ditch, he realised that the cover had been pulled up in one or two places, so he switched on his flashlight to see where he was going. The black water glittered beneath his feet, and the concrete cover shifted ominously under their combined weight, but he finally managed to cross the ditch. He threw her body down on a patch of dry grass and checked the rusty shutters. He could move them by pushing with all his might, but the grating noise made Masako stir and frown uncomfortably. Working quickly, he raised the shutters high enough to duck under and pushed her inside.

The building was cold and dark. It felt damp and smelt of mould. He let the flashlight play over the space, thinking how much it resembled an enormous, concrete coffin. But high in the ceiling he could see a row of windows that would let in light when the sun came up. The factory had apparently made boxed lunches before it closed down. The metal rack of an old conveyor belt and a counter for deliveries had been left behind. He smiled, realising the rack would be perfect for tying Masako on to – nice and cold.

She was still unconscious. He picked her up and laid her on the long ramp. Defenceless, with her mouth hanging slightly open, she looked like a patient anaesthetised for an operation. He slipped the jacket from her shoulders and tore off her sweatshirt. Then he took off her shoes and socks and dropped them on the floor. As he was pulling off her jeans, she began to regain consciousness from the shock of the cold metal on her skin. But she seemed disoriented, unsure where she was or what was happening to her. She lay on her back, staring around with a muddled look.

Shining the flashlight in her face, he called her name. She turned her eyes away from the light and seemed to search for him in the darkness.

'You bastard!'

'No, you should say, "Fucking bastard! What a lousy trick!"' She was still moving sluggishly. He pinned her arms to the rack and she stopped struggling.

'Why?' she said, looking puzzled.

'Just say it.' He had dropped his guard for a moment and her foot shot up, catching him in the groin. As he groaned with pain, she twisted away and jumped down. She was still nimble for a middle-aged woman, and she managed to slip through his arms and disappear into the darkness. 'Don't think you can get away!' he called. He searched for her with the flashlight, but it was too weak for the cavernous space; instead, he stationed himself in front of the shutters and waited. If he guarded the exit, he would get her eventually. Besides, there was something about the situation that amused him – the more she resisted, the more it excited him. She was so stubborn, and it made him feel loathing and elation in equal measures. 'You might as well give up,' he called, his voice echoing through the building. Her answer came a moment later, apparently from a distant corner.

'I won't give up,' she called. 'But I want to know why you're after me.'

'Because of what you did to me.'

'Then you've got the wrong person. It's Yayoi Yamamoto you want.'

'I'm done with her.'

'Done how?' she said. Her voice was trembling now, with fear or from the cold. She must be cold; her feet were bare and she had nothing on but a T-shirt and underwear. Moving quietly over to the ramp, he bundled up her clothes and tossed them in a corner to make sure she didn't get them back. Just then, she spoke again from the darkness. 'You took her insurance money, didn't you? Then why isn't that enough? Why've you got it in for me?'

'I'm not sure myself,' he murmured in her direction.

'Because you lost your business?'

'That's part of it,' he said. But it's also because you're the only one who knows the real Satake, the one who tore off the scab that had formed over all that time.

'But not the whole story,' Masako said, her voice calmer now. 'You also like me, don't you?' This time he didn't answer, but he edged toward her through the dark. 'It seems a bit weird, doesn't it? I'm forty-three, past the age when men notice you; and I was never that kind of woman. You must have some other reason.' His heavy boot clattered against a can and Masako fell silent. He listened, trying to tell where she'd gone.

There was a faint noise behind him, and he spun around and began hunting her in the other direction. She was trying to force open the shutter at the delivery bay and slip out. Lunging through the dark, he caught her just as she'd managed to get her upper body through the opening. He grabbed her legs and dragged her back in, then slapped her hard across the face. As she collapsed on the dirty concrete floor, he shone his flashlight on her, wanting to see her face. She shook back her hair and glared at him. It was the same – the same look as before. He grabbed her by the hair and forced her to keep looking at him.

'You *are* a fucking bastard!' she said, spitting the words at him.

'Yes, I am.' He peered into her angry eyes. 'But I've been waiting for you.'

'You're dreaming,' she said in a steady voice.

'No, I'm not,' he said, studying her face for a moment. The other woman's features had been as sharp as a knife, not really like this one's at all. This was Masako Katori staring at him now, her eyes loaded with hostility. Their faces were different; Masako's lips were thinner, more severe. But the eyes were identical. His heart filled with joy and anticipation, like a rising tide. How high could she take him? Would the pleasure he'd kept locked away for seventeen years return again? Would she be able to show him what that other experience had meant?

He ripped off her T-shirt, leaving her in nothing but her plain white bra and panties, but she continued staring at him.

'Stop,' she said. 'Kill me now.' Ignoring her, he stripped off her underwear. At this, she began to struggle again, but he held her arms and, lifting her up, carried her to the rack. He lay on top of her to stop her thrashing. She gasped under his weight and then went limp. He found the rope he'd brought with him, tied one end to each wrist, and then pulled her arms over her head to fasten them to the rack. 'It's cold!' she yelled, her body writhing on the icy metal. He watched her for a moment in the beam of the flashlight. Her body was thin, almost desiccated, and her breasts were small. He slowly began undressing.

'Go ahead and scream,' he told her. 'No one'll hear you.'

'You may not know it, but they're tearing down the building next door,' she said.

'And you're full of shit,' he said, slapping her again. He'd meant to hold back this time, but her head snapped to one side from the blow. He didn't want to overdo it, to have her die before he was ready; and it would be boring if she were unconscious. He was worried for a moment, but then her head turned and she fixed him with her cold eyes again. Blood was trickling from her lips.

'Kill me quickly,' she said. The other woman had been just as insistent, screaming at him to kill her while he was beating her. His excitement built as his mind raced back and forth between the two women, between reality and dreams, as if it were riding a high-speed elevator. He bent over her and bit her bloody lips. Then, with her cursing through clenched teeth, he forced himself between her legs.

'Dry as a bone,' he muttered.

'Bastard!' She thrashed about, trying desperately to fight him off, to keep her legs closed, but he forced her open and entered her. It felt amazingly hot, but she screamed with pain, perhaps because she was too dry. When he saw the look in her eyes, he realised she must have less experience than he would have thought. He began to move, ever so slowly. He hadn't been with a real, flesh-and-blood woman since that day in Shinjuku, since that dark dream. The thing deep in his soul began to writhe, rise up and become real, promising to take him with it wherever it was going. To hell, and heaven. It was only in the final moments of sex with her that the gap between them could be bridged. This was what he'd been born for, and this was what he would die for.

But then, suddenly and too soon, the first time was over.

'Pervert!' she called him, spitting bloody saliva at him. He wiped the spittle off his face and rubbed it back in hers. Then he bit her breast to punish her. She tried to scream, but the sound died in her throat behind her chattering teeth. The first light of dawn was shining through the windows above them.

As the sun rose higher in the sky, light came streaming into the factory, and their surroundings slowly became visible. The panelling had fallen from the walls, exposing the bare concrete underneath. The partitions that had separated the kitchen and bathrooms had come down, leaving only the bare faucets and toilets. Oil cans and plastic buckets littered the floor, and a mound of empty soft-drink bottles lay near the entrance. But even in the light, it was still a bleak, cement coffin.

Hearing a noise behind him, Satake turned. A stray cat had wandered into the factory, but when it caught sight of him it ran off. There must be rats. He sat down on the floor, crossed his legs, and lit a cigarette. Then he watched Masako struggling on the rack, her whole body shivering in the cold. In a while, the light would reach them; and when it did, he would rape her again, only this time he'd be able to see her face as he did it. He would wait until then.

'Cold?' he said.

'Of course I'm cold.'

'Sorry, you'll just have to wait.'

'Wait for what?'

'For the sun.'

'I can't! I'm freezing!' she said. There was rage in her voice, but her words were slurred now from the beating. Her cheeks were swollen and the lower lip was puffy. Even from a distance, he could see that her body was covered with goose bumps, and he remembered that he'd thought of using a knife to scrape them off. But it was still too early for that. That was for the very end.

He pictured the thin, sharp blade sliding into her. Would it give him the same deep thrill it had all those years ago? It was that thrill alone which had defined him ever since, and he longed to feel it once again. He pulled a black leather sheath from his bag and put it quietly on the floor.

The sunlight had at last reached Masako's body. As it crept over her, she seemed to relax, and her pale, bluish skin began to take on colour, as though it were thawing out. Satake stood up and came closer.

'Did you make all those lunches on something like this?' he said. Masako just stared at him. 'Did you?' he said, grabbing her jaw.

'Why do you care?' She was too cold to speak clearly, but her anger was unmistakable.

'I bet you never thought you'd be tied up on one.' She twisted away. 'Tell me,' he said. 'How do you cut up a body? Like this?' He held her neck and ran his finger down her front, pretending to cut from her throat to her pubic bone. The pressure of his hand left a pale purple line on her skin. 'How did you come up with the idea of chopping him up? What did it feel like when you were doing it?'

'What does it matter?'

'Because you're just like me. You've gone too far to go back.' She looked into his eyes.

'What happened to you?' she said.

'Spread your legs,' he ordered, ignoring the question.

'No.' She pressed her legs together, and when he bent over, trying to work his way in, she kneed him in the face. He tried again, delighted that she still had some fight left in her. The winter sun played on her face, and as he lay there on her, he saw that her teeth were clenched and her eyelids tightly shut.

'Look at me,' he said, trying to force them open with his fingers.

'No.'

'I'll poke them out,' he said, pressing his thumbs into her eyes.

'Then I won't have to look at you.' When he took his hands away, her lids opened a crack. Wild black eyes showed underneath.

'That's right. Hate me more.'

'Why?' she asked, sounding as if she might actually want to know.

'You hate me, don't you? Just like I hate you.'

'But why?'

'Because you're a woman.'

'Then kill me!' she yelled. She doesn't understand yet, he

thought. The other one did, but not her. He slapped her again, this time out of irritation. 'There's something wrong with you,' she said, 'something broken inside.'

'Of course there is,' he said, stroking her hair. 'Just like there's something broken in you. I knew it the first time I saw you.' Masako said nothing, but her eyes were wide open, with real hatred showing in them. He kissed her for the first time, tasting the salty blood on her lips. Blood had begun to ooze from where the ropes were cutting into her wrists – just as it had that other time.

He reached down and picked up the knife. Flicking off the sheath, he put it on the rack. She flinched at the cold, dangerous thing lying next to her head.

'Frightened?' he said. She shut her eyes, her body still shaking. Satake peeled the lids open again, searching behind them for fear, or the hatred that overcame fear. He entered her, searching inside her now. But searching for what? The other woman? Masako? Or was he looking for himself? Was it illusion or reality? Little by little, though he had no sense of time, her body seemed to be melting into his, her pleasure becoming his pleasure, and his hers. If they went on to the end, he felt he would vanish, disappear from this world, and he'd have no regrets if he did. He had never been at home here anyway.

He felt a desperate need to join her, to merge together. As he sucked at her lips, he realised with a twinge of sadness that she was looking at him with the same hungry stare.

'Does it feel good?' he said, his voice almost tender. She gasped but didn't answer. They were doing it together now, partners in it. Sensing that she was close to climax, he reached for the knife. He must get further into her. He could feel something stirring inside himself, feel the warmth spreading through his body. Together, they were heaven-bound.

'Please,' she whispered.

'What?'

'Cut the ropes.'

'I can't.'

'If you don't, I can't come. I want to come with you,' she pleaded, her voice low and raspy. He was ready now, so why need the ropes? He reached up and sliced through them. She wrapped her freed arms around his back and clung tightly to him. He reached behind her and cradled her head in his hands. He had never done it like this. Her fingernails dug into his back as their bodies moved together. When he was nearing the end, he cried out, feeling at last he'd overcome it, the hatred in him. But just as he was fumbling for the knife again, out of the corner of his eye he caught a glint of light. At some stage Masako had picked it up, and was on the point of using it. He grabbed her arm, knocking the knife to the floor, then punched her in the face.

She lay on her side for some time, her hands pressed to her cheeks. He climbed off and bawled at her, gasping with fury.

'You stupid bitch! Now we've got to start from the beginning!' It wasn't so much that she'd tried to stab him but that she'd spoilt the sensation he had worked so hard to bring back. But more than anger, he felt grief, that she hadn't shared his feelings.

She had lost consciousness. He touched her face where he'd hit her. If he began to pity her he wouldn't be able to kill her, and that deep need would never be fulfilled. She was right, there was something broken in him. He wrapped his arms around his head.

She woke up a short time later. 'Let me go to the bathroom,' she said. She was trembling violently and her head was still flopped to one side. He had hit her too hard. If he used her up like this, she might die before he could get what he wanted.

'Go on, then,' he said.

'It's cold,' she said. She sat up unsteadily and slid her legs to the floor. Reaching down slowly, she picked up her jacket and slipped it over her bare shoulders. Satake followed her as she made her way to the toilets in the corner. There were no posts or walls, just three seats that seemed to have sprouted from the floor. They were grey and grimy and there was no way of knowing whether the plumbing still worked, but Masako lowered herself on to the nearest one as if she had no more energy to waste. Ignoring Satake, she began to piss.

'Hurry up,' he said. She rose slowly and started back across the floor, but her legs were wobbly and she stumbled over an oil can, planting her hands on the ground to keep from falling flat. Satake ran over and grabbed her collar, dragging her to her feet. She shoved her hands in her pockets and stood for a moment, apparently dazed.

'Come *on*,' he said, raising his hand to hit her again. But before he could do it, he felt something cold brush across his cheek. It was like being stroked by an icy finger. The other woman's finger? Feeling as though he'd been touched by a ghost, he glanced around the empty plant, then touched his cheek with his hand. Blood was pumping from a deep gash.

7

Long before, when it had all begun, Masako had just lain there, motionless, feeling the cold seep into her. Her body seemed to be functioning, but her mind felt heavy, as though she were still caught between sleep and waking. Forcing her eyelids open, she stared into a black void that seemed to stretch far overhead. Somehow, she had found her way into a cold, dark hole. There was a faint light far above – the night sky, barely visible through a row of small windows. She remembered looking up at the starless sky a few hours earlier. Her sense of smell was returning, and with it familiar odours: cold, damp concrete and mould. A moment later she realised she was inside the abandoned factory.

But why were her legs bare? She ran her hands down her body and found she was wearing nothing but her T-shirt and underwear. Her skin was as dry and icy as a stone, as if it no longer belonged to her, and she was chilled to the bone. Then, suddenly, she was staring into a bright light. Squinting, she raised her hand to shade her eyes.

Satake's voice called her name. So he had her. She let out a groan, remembering how his arms had grabbed her in the parking lot. He would toy with her for a while now and then kill her. She was trapped here in this nightmare world, just when her exit was in plain sight.

Furious at her own carelessness, she stared into the light and yelled, 'You bastard!'

Almost immediately he answered with an odd command: 'No, you should say, "Fucking bastard! What a lousy trick!"' And for the first time she realised that she'd been caught up in some fantasy of his, that he was trying to relive something that had happened to him in the past. The full horror of the situation began to dawn on her: Satake's vendetta had more to do with this unknown past than with Kenji. She'd been right when she told Yayoi that they had woken up a monster.

Moments later, she managed to kick him in the groin and, slipping past him, ran off into the dark. Her head was filled with one desire as she ran: just to vanish into thin air, to hide and never be found again. Satake frightened her in a primitive way, the way nightfall frightens a child afraid of the dark. But it was more than him that she was fleeing; it was something in her own darkness that this man seemed to have aroused.

The debris on the floor hurt her bare feet and caught around her ankles – chunks of cement, scraps of metal, plastic bags and other, unidentifiable things that squashed unnervingly underfoot. But she couldn't worry about that now. She ran here and there in the dark, avoiding the beam of the flashlight and searching for an exit.

'You might as well give up,' he called from somewhere near the entrance. She told him that she wouldn't. He seemed reluctant to tell her what he wanted, but she was sure now that it wasn't simply revenge. She would have liked to know what was driving him. As his voice rang through the damp air, she imagined the expression on his face.

Something told her he was on the move now, using the sound of her voice to track her down. She crept toward the delivery bay as quietly as she could. There was another rusted shutter there, and she might be able to pry it open. In the meantime, Satake was playing the flashlight over the interior, as though in a game of hide-and-seek. She reached the delivery bay, worked her way on to the waist-high concrete counter, and pushed up the small metal shutter, not caring now about the noise. Freedom was just a step away, if she could get out in time. Squirming her head and shoulders through the opening, she smelt the air outside, fragrant with the odours of the ditch.

When he dragged her back inside and beat her, she felt no real pain, only huge disappointment at getting that far, with freedom within reach, and then probably losing it for good. And she still had no idea why it was her, and not the others, that Satake had singled out.

Now she was tied to the old conveyor belt. Even after her skin warmed the metal a bit, she could feel the cold creeping in from the edges, stealing her body heat. She had never felt cold like this, but she still wasn't ready to give up. As long as she was alive, she would will her body to resist the freezing metal underneath her. She began to twist back and forth, hoping that movement would warm her. If she didn't, she was afraid her back would stick fast to the rack.

He hit her in the face again. As she groaned with pain, she searched his eyes for signs of madness. If she could be sure he was mad, then she might resign herself to what was happening. But he wasn't. Nor was this just some sick amusement. He was beating her to see how much he could make her hate him. For some reason, he needed her to despise him, and when he'd brought this hatred to a peak, he would kill her.

When he entered her, she was filled with a sense of humiliation – that her first sex in years should be rape, that a woman of her age could be used by a man this way. Just a short time ago, another man had held her, and it had been a comfort; but it caused only loathing now. She had learned that sex could be a source of deep hatred. At that instant, she hated him as a man just as much as he despised her as a woman.

While he was doing it to her, she knew that he was living in a dream, an endless nightmare that only he could understand, and that she was just a living prop for his fantasy. For a moment she wondered how one went about escaping from someone else's dream; but then realised the more immediate challenge was just to understand him, to figure out what was coming next. If she couldn't, then she was suffering pointlessly. She needed to know what it was that had happened to him in the past. As he bore down on her, she stared at the void above them – her freedom was just there, beyond his back.

When he was finished, she called him a pervert, out of utter disgust. But she knew that wasn't right. He wasn't a pervert or a madman; he was a lost soul in desperate search of something, and if he thought he could find it in her, then she might be able to play along with him . . . and go on living.

She waited impatiently for the sun to make its way into the factory and warm her up a little. The cold was unbearable, painful in a way she never knew it could be. For a while, she had tried to keep moving to warm herself, but now her body was shivering uncontrollably, as if she were having convulsions. But the frigid air in the factory probably wouldn't get any warmer until the sun was high in the sky, and she doubted she would be able to hold out until then. She didn't want to give up, but she'd begun to realise that she would probably freeze to death here.

To distract her from the spasms that were shaking her body, she gazed around. The shell of the factory was like an enormous coffin. It occurred to her that she had spent nearly every night for the last two years working in a place like this, and she couldn't help thinking that she was destined to die in one, too – that this was the cruel end that was waiting for her on the other side of that door she had been so determined to open. Help me, she whispered to herself. But the help she wanted wasn't from anyone like Kazuo or her husband; it was from Satake, the man who had brought her here.

She turned to look at him. He was sitting cross-legged on the floor a short distance away. He was watching her trembling body, but not as though he enjoyed seeing her suffer; rather, he seemed to be waiting for something. But what? She studied his face in the half-light. From time to time he glanced up at the windows, as if he were waiting for dawn. He was shaking as well, but he sat naked on the floor, apparently oblivious to the cold.

He looked up at her, perhaps sensing that she was watching him, and their eyes met in the dim light. He flicked his lighter at her, as if in irritation, then lit a cigarette. Abruptly, she realised that he *was* waiting for the light, to be able to see whatever he needed to see. And when he found what he was looking for, he would kill her. She closed her eyes.

A little later, she felt the air stir, and opened her eyes to see Satake standing up and taking something out of his bag. It was a black sheath, presumably holding the knife he was going to use on her. The sight of it made the piercing cold even sharper. She began to shake more violently, but she managed to turn her head away, determined to make Satake think it was only the cold.

At last the sun came streaming through the windows, and she could feel the tightly closed pores of her skin opening, beginning to breathe again. If she could warm up even a bit, she might be able get some sleep. But then she remembered the knife and laughed at herself. What was the point, with that in store for her?

Most days she would just be getting home from the factory now, ready to put breakfast on the table and get a load of laundry started. Then, when the sun got to a certain point in the sky, she wouldn't be able to put off sleep any longer. What would Yoshiki and Nobuki think if she disappeared without a trace? It didn't matter whether she died here or somehow managed to escape, she was already beyond their reach. Hadn't Yoshiki admitted that he wouldn't come looking for her? There was something about this thought she found almost comforting, that made her realise how far she had already come.

When it was light enough, Satake came over to stand by her.

'Did you make all those lunches on something like this?' he said, apparently amused at his little joke. She lay on the rack, like a meal about to be rolled down the line, and tried not to show her fear. He was right: who would ever have thought she'd end up on the belt herself? Yoshie, who controlled the speed of the line, had found a way out; but not her. 'How do you cut up a body?' he asked, running a delicate finger across her neck and then down from her throat to her crotch, as though he were dissecting her. She cried out at the pain of it on her already raw skin. 'How did you come up with the idea of chopping him up? What did it feel like when you were doing it?' She realised that he was trying to whip up her hate for him. 'You're just like me,' he said. 'You've gone too far to go back.'

Again, he was right: there was no way back. She had heard the doors slamming behind her one by one. The first had closed the day they had cut up Kenji. But what had happened to Satake to make him feel this way? She asked him, but he didn't answer. She stared into his eyes – at the swamp concealed in there – or was it just a void?

She screamed as he suddenly forced his cold finger between her legs. But when he entered her for the second time, her body was surprised by his warmth. It seemed to rejoice at a source of heat so much more potent than the pale sunlight. The warm, hard thing inside her began to thaw her from the belly out. This link between them was the warmest object in that empty cavern; but it troubled her that her body could almost innocently take pleasure in it, and she was determined not to let Satake know it had accepted him. She closed her eyes again, and he seemed to believe she was rejecting him.

'Open your eyes,' he said, pressing his thumbs into them. Let him blind me, she thought, if it would keep him from finding out that I responded to him. She hated him with her whole being, and it horrified her to think that her eyes wouldn't show him that fact if he looked in them now. He told her he hated her because she was a woman. Then why didn't he stop forcing himself on her and just finish her off? He slapped her again to stir up her hatred, but somehow she found herself pitying a man who needed to be despised in order to feel pleasure. His past was beginning to take shape out of the fog.

'There's something wrong with you,' she told him, 'something broken inside.'

'Of course there is,' he said. 'Just like there's something broken in you. I knew it the first time I saw you.' For her, knowing it was the damaged part of her that had first drawn him to her only made her hate the man moving inside her all the more. He pressed his lips to hers, and she realised how desperately he wanted her. Then he reached over for the knife, shook it free from the sheath, and put it by her head. Her eyes closed instinctively from fear of the cold blade next to her, but Satake forced them open and peered at her. She stared back at him, knowing that given the chance she'd use the blade on him as readily as he'd penetrated her.

The factory was awash in sunlight now, but there was another kind of light shining in his eyes, the first sign that she was becoming real to him, that she moved him. But it wasn't a feeling that would ever grow or mature. Just as she had once thought she wouldn't mind dying by his hand, he was longing for the same end himself. Suddenly, she realised she understood him.

She felt the dream in which he'd been trapped begin to dissolve, felt him move closer to the living world. Their bodies came together and their eyes met. Seeing nothing reflected there but her own image, she felt a wave of pure pleasure rise and break over her. She could die like this. But the glint of the blade in the corner of her eye pulled her back to earth.

He beat her until she lost consciousness, but a nauseating pain in her jaw revived her a short time later. He was staring at her, enraged. She had spoilt things for him just as he was getting near a place he'd longed to reach.

She told him she needed to go to the bathroom. When he said she could, she let her legs slide to the floor and stood up. How long had she been tied up there? She could feel the blood coming back to her legs, feel the numbness becoming pain. It made her cry out loud. Reaching down for her jacket, she pulled it around her shoulders and closed her eyes, letting her raw skin adjust to the cold fabric. Satake watched her in silence.

She headed toward the toilets in the corner of the factory, but her legs were stiff and it was difficult to walk. Something sharp cut into the bottom of her foot, drawing blood, but she felt nothing. Lowering herself on to the grimy toilet, she relieved herself, ignoring Satake's watching eyes. She let the piss run over her fingers, which sent shooting pains through her hands as the hot liquid touched the numb, frozen skin. Stifling a moan, she stood up, thrust her hands in her pockets, and made her way back toward him.

'Hurry up,' he said. She stumbled against an oil can and fell. When she had trouble getting to her feet, he ran over and, grabbing the collar of her jacket the way a cat grabs a kitten by the scruff of the neck, he dragged her up, impatient to continue. Her hands, still deep in her pockets, were starting to warm up, her fingers beginning to tremble. 'Come *on,*' he said.

She closed her palm over something, and when he raised his hand again to hit her for moving too slowly, she reached out and cut his face with the scalpel she'd found in her pocket. He looked up for a moment, as if he didn't know what had happened, then felt his cheek. She held her breath and watched as the blood began to gush from his face, pouring over his outstretched hand. The scalpel had made a deep incision from the corner of his astonished eye to the base of his chin.

8

Satake fell backward, sitting down hard on the floor. His hand was clutched to his face, but the blood poured through his fingers. Masako cried out in shock. A sense of sudden, permanent loss had squeezed the sound from her.

'You got me,' he whispered, spitting out the blood that was quickly filling his mouth.

'You were going to kill me,' she said. He lowered his hand and stared at his bloody palm. 'I was aiming for your throat but my hand was numb,' she told him; her mind was reeling and her mouth seemed to run on without her. Realising she was still holding the scalpel, she threw it on the floor, where it bounced away with a hollow clatter. She'd pressed the blade into a wine cork and put it in her pocket before she left the house.

Though air was seeping into his mouth from the wound and he

had trouble speaking, he managed to say, 'You're special . . . I should've let you kill me before . . . would've been so good.'

'Did you want to kill me?'

He shook his head and looked up at the ceiling. 'I don't know. . .' The sunlight from the high windows was now blinding. Pillars of brilliantly lit dust linked the windows to the concrete floor, like the spotlights in a theatre. Her eyes followed his to the windows. She was shaking again, but not from the cold; it was from knowing that with her own hands she had cut off this life. The sky was pale blue beyond the windows and a quiet winter day was beginning, as though nothing had changed, as though last night's horrors had never happened. Satake stared at the pool of blood collecting on the floor before answering her. 'Not kill you,' he said, 'but watch you die.'

'Why?'

'Thought I'd be able to love you when you were dying.'

'Only then?' He looked at her for a moment.

'I guess so.'

'. . . Don't die,' she murmured. There was a hint of surprise in his eyes. By now, the blood flowing from his face had stained his body red, and he'd begun to moan with pain.

'I killed Kuniko. . . ,' he said. 'And another woman before that – looked just like you. . . . I think I died once, when I killed her. Then I saw you and thought – I wouldn't mind dying one more time . . .'

She took off her jacket so that she could hold him closer. Her face was swollen and heavy from the beatings, and she knew she must look hideous. 'I'm alive,' she said. 'And I don't want you to die.'

'Looks like I'm going to,' he said, with what sounded almost like relief. His whole body had begun to quiver. She brought her face close to his and examined the wound. It was deep and gaping, but she pressed the skin together and kept her fingers there. 'It's no use,' he said. 'Must be an artery.' But Masako refused to give up, continuing to hold his face as the life seeped out of him. She looked around the factory again. They had met here in this vast coffin, had come to understand one another here, and now would leave each other here.

'I need a cigarette,' he mumbled. Masako roused herself and went to find the pants he'd taken off. Getting a cigarette out of the pocket, she lit it and put it between his lips. In the space of a few seconds it was soaked in blood, but Satake still managed to blow a thin line of smoke from his mouth. She knelt in front of him and looked into his eyes.

'Let me take you to the hospital.'

'Hospital. . .' he murmured, with the ghost of a smile. A tendon had probably been cut, and all the smile amounted to was a slackening on the side of his face not bathed in blood. 'Woman I killed said the same thing. . . . Must be fate . . . my dying the way she did. . . .' The cigarette fell from his lips, sputtering out in the pool of blood that lay around him. He seemed to be giving up, and had closed his eyes.

'Still, we ought to go.'

'. . . Both end up in jail.' He was right – laws would still apply if they emerged from the factory now. She pulled him closer. As their heads touched, she realised that he was already colder. His blood continued to flow over them.

'I don't care,' she said. 'I want you to survive.'

'Why?. . .' His voice was barely audible. 'After what I did.'

'It would be like dying myself. I couldn't go on.'

'*I* did,' he said, closing his eyes again.

She began to get frantic, struggling to hold his wound together, to slow the bleeding, but he seemed to be slipping away. He opened his eyes again, this time barely a crack, and looked at her.

'Why me?'

'Because I understand you now,' she said. 'I see that we're the same, and I want us both to live.' His lips were covered in blood when she bent to kiss him, but his eyes were peaceful.

Haltingly, as though hope were unfamiliar to him, he mumbled, 'I've never . . . didn't think it could happen. . . . But who knows? – with fifty million . . . we might get out.'

'It's nice in Brazil,' she said.

'Take me with you?'

'Yes,' she said. 'I can't go back.'

'. . . go back . . . or go on.' He was right. She stared at her bloodstained hands. In a whisper, he added, 'We'll . . . be free.'

'Yes, free.' He reached out and brushed his hand against her cheek, but his fingers were quite cold. 'The bleeding's nearly stopped,' she said, but he just nodded, perhaps knowing it was a lie.

9

Masako was walking along a passageway in Shinjuku Station, though she barely knew what she was doing. She seemed to move automatically, planting one leg in front of the other. She let herself be drawn into the flow of the crowd, and eventually found herself heading out of the station. Once she had passed the ticket gate, she made her way down into the underground arcades. She caught sight of her reflection in a shoe-store mirror. The sunglasses hid most of the swelling, but she watched the woman in the mirror pull her jacket tightly about her, trying to hide the pain inside. She stopped there for a moment and took off the glasses to look at her face. The puffiness in her cheeks where Satake had beaten her wasn't so bad any more, but her eyes were swollen from crying. She put on the glasses again and looked up to find that she was standing in front of the elevator for the shopping floors upstairs. A moment later she had pushed the button for the top floor and was riding up. She had nowhere to go, nowhere she had to be.

When the doors opened, she was facing a line of restaurants. All she wanted was somewhere she could rest for a while, away from prying eyes. She lowered herself on to a bench by the window and put the black nylon bag between her knees. It held Satake's fifty million and six more of her own. Lighting a cigarette, she remembered how he had asked to smoke at the end. Her eyes swam behind the sunglasses. She dropped the cigarette into the grey steel ashtray. It sputtered softly as it hit the water inside, like the sound his cigarette had made in the pool of blood.

Wanting suddenly to get away, she stood and picked up the bag. All of Shinjuku was visible from the large windows. Beyond Yasukuni Avenue lay Kabuki-cho. She put her hand against the window and stared out at the unlit neon signs and gaudy, faded billboards, pale in the weak afternoon sunlight. The streets were quiet, like a sleeping beast that only hunts at night. This was Satake's town, a chaotic and seamily hedonistic place. The door she had opened when she went to work on the night shift had led here, to a place she'd never known before – his place.

She decided to take a look at the building where his casino had been; but the decision brought the other emotions to the surface again. For the past two days she had lain in a hotel bed, miserable and empty. Those feelings came back to her now, and with them the memory of how his body had felt. She gave a small moan – she couldn't help it – wishing she could see him one more time. She would go to Kabuki-cho to breathe the air he'd breathed, see the things he'd seen. Maybe she would find another man like him, and pursue his dream? The hope that she had lost was beginning to stir in her again.

Masako turned away from the view and hurried off, but the soles of her tennis shoes on the polished tiles sent a loud squeak echoing down the corridor. She stopped after only a few paces, startled by the noise, and turned back to the window. For a moment, the world outside seemed filled with the darkness of the abandoned factory.

No, she wouldn't go. She couldn't live her life as someone's prisoner the way he had lived his, caught up in a dream of the past, with no way forward and no way back, forced to dig down inside oneself.

But she'd come this far; where could she go now? She stared at her fingernails, kept short for the past two years for the factory. Her hands were chapped from the constant soaking in disinfectants. She thought about her twenty years at the credit union, about giving birth to a son and making a home for her family. What had it all meant? In the end, she was no more or less than the reality of all those years, with all the marks they'd left on her. And, unlike Satake, she had faced everything reality had brought her way. His idea of freedom had been different from hers.

She punched the elevator button. She would go and buy an airplane ticket. The freedom she was seeking was her own, not Satake's, or Yayoi's, or Yoshie's, and she was sure it must be out there somewhere. If one more door had closed behind her, she had no choice but to find a new one to open. The elevator moaned like the wind as it came to meet her.